TO SEDUCE A FAE

WINTER'S THORN

MILA YOUNG

For all of us who never want to grow up...

CONTENTS

TO SEDUCE A FAE

Luther is the most beautiful of my captors. Still I hate him more than the others. I hate him so much that the darkness inside me comes alive.

When I started university and moved out of my foster parents' home, I hoped everything would change. That the nightmares, the visions, the voices would stop, but they got worse.

Then three of the most dangerously stunning fae crashed into my life.
Intoxicating eyes.
Devilish lips.
Dangerous intentions.

They insist I belong with them in the Wandering

Realm. A place where love is lost, where war is brewing between two realms, and where the once powerful royals are being hunted down and slaughtered.

I'm their savior they say, but there are no saviors amid monsters. These princes who are tasked to keep me safe are keeping secrets of their own. Secrets that will kill me.

So, how am I meant to rid the realm of evil when I feel the dark spreading through my veins?

Scorching hot first book in the brand new 'WINTER'S THORN' Trilogy.

PART 1

Long ago, darkness and light came together and created beauty... a beauty that will destroy this world.

PROLOGUE

There was nothing right about the woods today.

I slipped backward a few steps, my heart thumping loudly as a figure watched me from behind a gnarled tree.

Shadows swallowed his presence, holding no shape and fading against the spreading darkness, but I felt his eyes—always on me. And the unease made me sick to my stomach.

Warped branches spiked into the stormy clouds, swinging back and forth in the wind like claws reaching out for me. Terror roared inside me, yelling at me to run, and my flesh pricked with electricity.

He'd kill me if I stayed. I knew it, felt it in my bones.

I swung away and darted down the strip of naked land, summoning the energy to push myself faster than before. His breath grazed my neck, his footsteps thumping the ground.

Panic tore through me at the idea that this time he'd catch me.

Thorny bushes and broken trees filled the land. Flashes of freedom lay behind the forsaken forest, snippets of a grand kingdom that reflected the golden rays of the sun. The kingdom stood so far away, reachable only by stairs made of twisted stone, and by crossing an arched bridge that spanned two mountains. I'd never get there in time. I might as well be trying to reach the moon.

The breaking of leaves and twigs came at me, and I jerked around, fear coiling over me like a heavy winter coat, smothering me.

Utter blackness closed in, the wind shrieking in my ears.

A cry fell past my lips. My palms tingled with power, its scorching pain spreading over me.

He slammed into me.

I screamed, my feet tangling beneath me. Pivoting back around, I jutted my hands out, embracing the power, and shoved it into the shadow.

Then I fell. My world became a pit of blackness, taking me, dragging me under.

And I let myself go. Like I always did.

CHAPTER 1

"Are you awake, Guen?" Debbie's voice broke through the silence, startling me back to the present. Reminding me that I sat in her office... Not that I hadn't known that, but sometimes I forgot things.

My foster mom nudged me in the arm, then shifted in her seat, huffing. "She's always daydreaming, this one. I swear she lives in her head more than the real world."

I slouched in my seat, meeting Ms. Williams' deep brown eyes. She sat across her desk from us, and she looked young except for the threads of white amid the brown curls. I'd guess she was in her mid-forties.

She studied me, probably making mental notes about how I'd changed since our last catch up. Her work desk was impeccable, like the rest of her sterile office, and she had her name and title on a plaque sitting on the edge of her desk.

Debbie Williams, M.D.

Clinical Psychiatrist

Like anyone coming here could forget they were seeing a psychiatrist who specialized in mental disorders.

"How have you been sleeping?" she asked.

"Not well." Never well. The dreams always came and when I woke, I'd be exhausted.

"Have you tried the new medication I prescribed?"

I nodded, as did my foster mom, who pushed the loose strands of chestnut hair out of her face. She made sure I took the meds. They knocked me out, but the dreams still came, no matter what I did.

Schizophrenia. I'd read the word in the doctor's notes a few weeks ago when she hadn't been looking. Even if she hadn't given me a diagnosis, at least now I had a name to what was wrong with me. I'd read up on it, tried to self-diagnose myself on Google, and found four types of Schizophrenia. I wasn't sure I fit a specific disorder; it was more like I had some symptoms of each of them.

But maybe Ms. Williams suspected something else was wrong, which was why she hadn't given me a final prognosis. Could there be something worse than Schizophrenia?

My stomach churned when I thought about it, and

for some reason, the room was too bright today, despite the lights being off. The sun's reflection on the white walls stung my eyes.

Ms. Williams stood from her chair, straightened her A-line blue skirt, and crossed the room to lower the blinds, stealing some of the glare. I liked her, even if she watched my every move, my every reaction, and made an analysis of my behavior. I'd been seeing therapists like her for as long as I'd been in foster homes… my whole life.

"Are you still having unusual dreams?" she asked.

I nodded, lowering my gaze, remembering the shadow who always came for me. "Sometimes. But I'm feeling better."

I raised my head as she jotted something in her notebook. I just forgot things sometimes, dreamed of a kingdom that didn't exist, and felt like I didn't belong… in my skin. No, in this *world*.

I glanced at the clock on the wall. Half an hour was almost up.

"Well, we might end our session there." Debbie handed my foster mom a new script. "Jen, if you have a moment?"

Up on my feet, I collected the bag from under my seat and headed to the door. "Thank you," I threw over my shoulder as I reached for the handle, hating these sessions that made me question everything about myself. The two of them often had a private talk. What secrets did they hold about me that I should know? But I'd learned long ago that reacting angrily only got me more medication prescribed because I was unstable. Crazy. Unreliable.

You're so much more than insane, little wolf. The low rumble of his voice wrapped around my mind, deep and smooth, reverberating through my bones. He who had no name, who refused to give me his name, who was always in my head. Something I never told a single soul; otherwise, I'd end up in an asylum.

"Wow, you're full of compliments today," I mumbled under my breath.

Outside, I marched through the waiting room, leaving my foster mom behind. Head low and pulling the jacket tighter around myself, I crossed the room, not wanting to exchange glances. We all lived with darkness in our heads, and I didn't want to see their insanity etched on their faces.

"Dad can't be bothered to come here and said I could collect the prescription on his behalf. I have a signed note," a guy growled at the nurse over the counter.

I glanced his way. His brow furrowed, ice-blue irises crowned by the longest eyelashes met mine. Short, black hair sat spiked on his head. I recognized him. He made every girl at school swoon with that sneer. His mouth twitched before he jerked his attention back to the nurse who lectured him, and I shoved through the front door and stepped outside, where I could breathe easier.

Seemed the most popular guy in school and me had something in common after all. Something crazy.

I rubbed my hands for warmth, staring out at the parking area for a bit before heading to the small convenience store nearby. There, I grabbed an energy drink from the fridge and scooped money out from my pocket before placing it in the hand of the old man at the counter.

"There you are," Jen bellowed from the door of the store, dressed in her tailored pants and white blouse that pulled taut across the buttons. She'd been on a diet forever and recently lost some weight, and she looked good. "Told you to always wait for me near the car. Between you and Oliver, you both drive me insane."

With the can in hand, I followed her out. "Just needed a pick-me-up before class. And Oliver is a pain in the ass to everyone." My foster brother was the devil incarnate.

She huffed. "He's only nine; he'll grow out of that stage. And I hate when you drink that stuff. It's not good for you."

"It keeps me awake." I pulled back the metal ring and the drink hissed. "So, what'd the shrink say after I left?"

"I like Debbie better than the last one. And she's just worried about you not getting enough sleep."

Swallowing the mouthful of cherry-flavored goodness, I waited for Jen to find her keys in her bag. A quick glance at my reflection in the car window showed my blonde hair fluttering in the breeze, light eyebrows I hated, and the blue eyes that did nothing to take away from the whole pale as snow look. I'd been contemplating dying my brows, a do-it-myself-job, but didn't want them looking like dark caterpillars across my brow.

Jen finally yanked open the passenger's door of her silver sedan.

"You gonna tell me what she said." I got inside, and she climbed into the driver's seat.

"What do you want me to say, Guen? She costs an arm and a leg, so she's got to know what she's doing." Jen looked over at me, her perfectly manicured eyebrows rising. She jammed the key into the ignition.

Pinning the can between my thighs, I strapped myself in. "The government pays for it," I reminded her over the groan of the engine. But she still complained about the cost at every fortnightly session like she somehow missed out on taking the cash herself.

She edged out of the parking and soon enough merged into the slow-moving morning traffic.

"So, you going to tell me?" I took several more mouthfuls.

"What difference will it make? You take your meds and you'll be fine." The corner of her eye twitched.

"I can tell when you're lying."

"Stop staring at me. Have you got your books for school?"

"Yes, I have them. Please, Jen, what did Debbie say to you for real?"

"I told you not to call me that."

I sighed heavily and shoved myself back into the seat, staring at the oversized buildings we passed, the storefronts, people darting amid the crawling traffic to cross the road.

"She said she worried you might be dangerous."

I stiffened.

Dangerous? I'd never harm anyone. Never had.

"Why did she think that?" Unease crawled over my chest. A small part of me died inside when I accidentally stepped on an ant. How could I be dangerous?

Her lips pursed when she looked over to me. "Because you don't need anyone and insist on being alone."

The words swam in my mind like flies on roadkill. So being a loner made me dangerous?

"Have you tried making friends?" she asked, like she hadn't seen me mingle with students at the last three schools I'd moved to because she kept relocating us to be near her newest boyfriend.

"I have a friend at Brax High."

"Don't say Antonio, or I'll—"

"Yes, Antonio is my friend."

Jen's grip tightened on the steering wheel. "And a bad influence. I told you I saw him once buying drugs at the corner store. Don't get involved with trouble."

I heaved and pressed my spine into the seat. "He's a nice guy, and he talks to me while others glare."

"Aren't there girls at your school you get along with?"

I gritted my jaw. "They hate me, so no, I don't get along with them."

I twisted away to stare at easing traffic we now passed. Other families laughing, talking about normal things, like what was on television that night.

"Maybe if you had more friends, you wouldn't always get in trouble."

When she kept going on, I leaned down and dug my hand into my backpack, finding my earphones. I stuffed them into my ears and jammed the connector into the base of the phone before blaring my music.

Let them hate you. His voice broke through the music. *As long as they fear you, little wolf, you will be fine.*

CHAPTER 2

"See you later." I slammed the door to Jen's car and turned toward the school as she drove away. Brax High was a long brick building with steps out the front, rusting racks, and, at the moment, locked front doors because class had already started.

Gray clouds spread over the sky while the wind howled, heralding an encroaching storm. A bitter cold crept over my skin despite my long-sleeved school shirt, and I rubbed the shivers out of my arms. My blue school pleated skirt danced over my thighs, doing nothing to keep the cold at bay.

I prefer it when it's just the two of us.

"It's always just the two of us." Which was sort of sad.

No, no, no. He laughed, the sound devious and, in a weird way, sexy.

I shouldn't think that about the voice in my head, but then again, I was talking to myself. If I was crazy, I might as well enjoy it, right?

When it's just us two, you respond, and I can make you feel things. Make you forget everything else.

"While that sounds tempting, I have school now," I mumbled. "Go back to wherever you came from."

Ouch. You want to know where I came from?

"Not this again. You came from the shadows, from the darkest of night, blah blah."

No response? Good.

With my bag in hand, I hurried up the front steps of the school and paused in front of the double doors before pressing the buzzer to be let in. I pulled the doctor's note out of my pocket. A whirring sound drew my attention to the camera overhead turning to check who was at the front door.

I can break you, he whispered.

I lowered my head from the camera to respond. "You can't break what's already broken."

I wasn't talking about your mind.

His words startled me. If he was just in my mind, how could he physically hurt me?

In the most delicious way, he said in a voice that could easily lead to sin.

Heat rose through me a bit too quickly.

The front door opened, and I flinched. Principal Johnson stood before me frowning, dressed in his tailored brown pants and matching vest over a black buttoned-up shirt. His gaze fell to my outstretched note and he clicked his tongue.

Without a word, he accepted the offering and scanned the note before waving me inside. "Classes just started. You shouldn't have missed much." His tone was harsh today. Someone had pissed him off.

"Thanks." I nudged the bag strap over my shoulder and swung down the quiet hallway fiercely lit by a line of fluorescent lights overhead, which cast the lockers in a yellowing hue.

I pushed open the door to history class, the hinges squealing like a banshee, and I stepped inside with every eye on me. Wonderful.

"Quickly, take a seat," Ms. Brown ordered in her black dress and heavy kohl eyeliner, making her look racoon-ish. "Who can tell me," she said, barely missing a beat, "why the church was upset with Galileo Galilei?"

Head low, I dragged my feet down the side aisle of seats, targeting the empty one at the back, watching every step I took on the linoleum floor.

"He was called a heretic by the Catholic Church," someone called out. "He believed that the Earth revolved around the sun."

"Yes, and what were the church's values that came under threat with Galilei's theory?"

Someone kicked me in the back of a knee, and in a

heartbeat, my legs buckled and gave out from under me.

I yelped as my feet teetered, losing their balance, my heartbeat pounding in my ears. I hit the ground with a thud, my knees and elbows taking the brunt. "Son of a…" I groaned.

An explosion of laughter flooded the room, students clapping.

I froze, my face burning up. Fury charged through my veins.

"Everyone sit down now!" Ms. Brown shouted.

Shoving myself off the floor, I glanced back as half the school stared at the loser—me—but my eyes locked on Sabrina. The beauty of the school with perfectly shiny hair, perfectly flawless skin, perfectly arched eyebrows. Five-foot seven, willowy, with blonde curls falling to her waist, I loathed her more in that moment than I thought possible.

I glanced down at my five-foot-three frame, not exactly thin, breasts too small, hips too big.

And I knew she tripped me… it was always her.

Anger glinted in her cruel, cold eyes, and all I could think was if she was going to take me down, I'd fight and drag her into hell with me.

I'd caught her smoking in the girls' bathroom a few weeks ago. She'd gotten busted, and ever since, I'd apparently been the one who must have ratted her out, but it wasn't me.

"Sit down this instant!" the teacher barked, but no one listened.

Students chatted and chortled at me.

Up on my feet, I bent over and swiped my bag off the floor, then swung it up and wide in the blink of an eye, side-swiping Sabrina across the face with it, wiping the grin right off her face.

She screamed, blood splattering across her lip where the zipper tore at her mouth.

I swallowed hard and rushed to my seat, not feeling guilty one ounce.

"She attacked me!" Sabrina cried, blood dripping down her chin.

"Enough," said Ms. Brown. "What I saw was you tripping Guen. Now hurry to the nurse's office and get that cut looked at, then go to the principal's office."

Sabrina's lips twitched. "But she just struck me. I'm bleeding."

A smile tingled at the edges of my mouth, but I lowered my head instead and slouched in my seat.

"Leave now!" Ms. Brown said, unmoved by Sabrina's pity-seeking.

I'd always liked Ms. Brown. She asked me how my day was while most teachers pretended I didn't exist.

Sabrina snatched her books and bag. "Why is a freak like her allowed in our class? I heard she takes medication so she doesn't lose control and kill us all.

Look what she did to me! Wait until my parents find out about this."

You should have pulled her tongue out for that.

I cringed on the inside, but I wasn't a fool. Everyone at school gossiped about me.

Laughter streamed through my head, the sound strangely soothing. *Let them fear you. It's better to be a wolf than the lamb.*

I kept silent, said nothing until the door slammed shut, and then raised my eyes. Sabrina's friend glared my way. In hindsight, maybe I shouldn't have hit Sabrina.

You should have hit her harder.

"All right, back to Galileo." The teacher clapped her hands to draw everyone's attention from me and to the front of the class.

I opened my textbook and drowned myself in words that blurred in my vision, letting the lesson swallow all my worries and dread over the can of worms I'd just ripped open. With pencil in hand, I sketched a tree in the corner of the page, limbs twisted and long, and I drew more of them to pass the time.

At lunch, I grabbed a quick sandwich, my head blurred with fog. I pinched the bridge of my nose to ease the pain behind my eyes, then shoved my backpack into my locker. Students crammed the hallway, their voices loud, blending into a cacophony of chaos. I pushed off the locker and went against the grain as everyone made their way to the cafeteria. Today I couldn't do crowds.

The way out stood just ahead, and I rushed past the swinging doors, gasping for air.

"Freak!" Someone nudged past, their shoulder knocking into mine.

Sabrina's friend glowered, hatred twisting her features. Black hair cut to a perfect bob-style without a strand out of place, she looked pale... too pale. Her school shirt tied across her stomach, showing flesh. All part of whatever look she was going for this week. The sad thing was that I didn't even know her name... didn't care to learn it either.

Hands deep in the pockets of my school jacket, I marched away from the main building and headed round the back to the outdoor basketball courts.

With concrete and metal everywhere, this school was older than my previous couple of schools, but they all merged into one in my mind. We'd moved here for Luke, Jen's newest boyfriend she'd met on Tinder. So far, they'd been dating for several months and had had no major arguments. Maybe I'd stay at Brax High longer than a year. That'd be a world record for me.

Dried grass crunched under my sneakers, and I hoped he waited for me, so I fluffed up my hair. The breeze picked up, and my school skirt fluttered over my thighs as I glanced out to the empty courts.

"Flashing your cute blue underwear?" a guy murmured.

Antonio! I felt his gaze on me before I turned around, and my heartbeat went into a frenzy.

He leaned against the rear of the school building. My pulse stopped in my veins at seeing him. Honey-blonde hair draped over his ears, complementing his tanned skin. He loved surfing, he'd told me, and when summer came back around, I planned to go watch him in action. Where he wore no shirt. Maybe I'd ask him to teach me how to surf.

With a wink that nearly melted me into a puddle, he took a drag from the joint pressed between his thumb and index finger, his cheeks growing gaunt as he inhaled.

From my first day when I'd met those brilliant blue eyes in the hallway, I'd lost myself to him. And like then, as he looked at me now, his eyes seemed to smile with a devilish glint in them.

He blew out lazy smoke rings that floated onto the air, stolen by the breeze, but not before the faint hints of pine mixed with a skunky smell filled my nostrils.

"Wanna taste?" He stuck the joint out for me.

I shook my head and moved to shelter beside the building, out of the wind. "My head's already feeling foggy."

"Might help with that." His voice was genuine and so dreamy.

So I reached over, our fingers grazing when I plucked the joint. My skin tingled from where we touched and my heart sprinted.

One inhale, and smoke rushed down my throat. My lungs seized, and I hacked a cough, cloudy smoke pouring from my mouth and nose.

Taking the joint back, he laughed. "Takes a bit of getting used to."

Catching my breath, I coughed again, my throat raw and chafed. Heat curled up my neck and cheeks as I choked. He'd know I had never smoked weed before.

Have another, he murmured in my head. *It'll calm you.*

"Think I've had my fill."

"How'd the session go this morning?" Antonio took another drag.

The meeting crossed my mind, along with the shrink's worry. "She thinks I'm dangerous," I blurted out, hating that I'd said that out loud. But Antonio was the only person I said such things to, even if I worried one day he'd stare at me like I was too weird.

"Dangerous to whom?" That smile returned, the one that calmed me, that promised me all the things I'd been dreaming about with Antonio.

"Exactly! If you have no friends, then it's loser city."

"Hey, you have me." He pointed to his chest while still gripping the joint, his brows pulling together in a cute way. "Don't listen to them. All docs are the same.

Need to make things up so they can justify having a job, to get money. Bet she offered you another script for meds?"

I chuckled and nodded.

He leaned back against the wall, his body slouched and still so freaking hot. His black pants hung low on his hips, the school shirt untucked, his collar sitting crooked. "God, I feel so high. This stuff's good. Been thinking of getting a tat."

"Oh yeah? What of?"

He shrugged. "Still thinking about it. But thinking of getting it here." He pushed the sleeve of his shirt up, and I traced over the line of his bicep, the muscle, the tanned skin. My fingers tingled.

A torn-up school poster with the words *Lighting It Up* tumbled past us and into the parking lot.

"Hey, so the school dance is coming up," I murmured. "You gonna go?"

He shrugged. "Haven't even thought about it. When is it?"

"Two weeks from Saturday." My stomach tingled with the notion of asking Antonio to go with me. I *should* ask him.

No, you shouldn't.

The question lingered in my mind, and I trembled with nerves at the idea of asking him. He was my only friend at school, so I didn't want things to be strange between us if he said *no*. He wouldn't say *no*, would he?

Then again, I'd seen the way he looked at me, like I was more than his friend.

Don't!

He took his final drag before pinching the smoke between his fingers and tucking the end into his pocket.

"Not sure if I'll go," he admitted. "But it could be a blast."

An explosion of joy burst through my chest at his *maybe* response. I sure as shit wasn't going alone if he said *no*. When I spent time with Antonio, he just got me. He spoke to me like I wasn't a freak, and somehow, I thought better of myself.

He doesn't know you like I know you. He can't...do things I can do to you.

I blew *him* off, tuning out my crazy mind.

Antonio was crazy hot, and if he went, maybe he'd say *yes* to going with me. He might even kiss me.

A rolling growl swept over my mind.

I really needed a mute button on *him*. I leaned back against the wall. "So, I was thinking." My face burned up, my palms sweating, and I wiped them down my black pleated skirt.

Antonio was busy staring out toward the basketball courts. "Think I can shoot perfect hoops if I played today?"

"Probably." I found my voice. "Anyway, I was gonna—"

The school bell rang like a church bell, deafening and persistent. I flinched, and Antonio shoved to his feet.

"Gotta go. I have P.E. Might see if Mr. Humphrey will let us play basketball." He threw one of his perfect smiles my way and took off. "Catch you later."

And just like that, I was alone.

"Yep, sure." I pushed off the wall. "Next time," I mumbled to myself.

You are meant for so much more than this.

"Shut up. I'm sick of you renting space in my head." I headed back toward the lockers to grab my books.

Before my ass hit the chair in algebra class, my name was called out.

"Guen, the principal's office," Mr. Carpenter called out across the class, eliciting *ooh*s and *ahh*s from everyone.

Just great.

CHAPTER 3

I sucked in a ragged breath as a chill worked its way along my spine. I'd busted ass to get my homework done on time and stayed up late studying to show Principal Johnson I could keep up with everyone else. To avoid ending up in his office regularly… And here I was again. I hated Sabrina.

You need to make her pay. Make her bleed.

I struggled to swallow past the boulder in my throat, shutting *him* out because I couldn't deal with this. Not now… Not when on my last visit to the principal's office, he threatened me with expulsion. Jen would go mental if that happened.

"Sit," he ordered, and I slid into the chair across the desk from him. He wore his tie printed with the Star Trek emblem again. He loved old geeky shows and if I ever got around to watching some, I might find myself with an upper hand for whenever I was called to his office.

His office reeked of sandalwood, his desk crammed with piles of folders and papers, two coffee cups, paperweights, a calculator, and pens. The miniature water fountain sitting on top of the filing cabinet emitted a faint trickle of water.

"Do you know why you're here?" he started, like he always did, his brown eyes fixed on me, his black short hair messed up like he'd been outside in the wind.

Panicked thoughts shoved through my mind that I'd be thrown out for hitting Sabrina.

Rain hit against the windowpane. *Tap. Tap. Tap.* Trees thrashed about in the front yard of the school.

I turned my attention to Principle Johnson and nodded. "I know it was wrong. It's just that they keep pushing and pushing me. I wanted it to stop."

His bushy brows pulled together in a confused frown. He plucked up a remote control from under the mess on his desk and turned to the TV on a stand in the corner. "Let's watch."

My heartbeat slammed in my chest, and I inched closer to the edge of the seat.

The TV screen flicked on, blurry at first, then it snapped to the image of the sidewall of the school, the CCTV scanning the grounds. God, he saw me taking a drag from Antonio's joint? I should have known, should have checked for cameras. But

Antonio had been smoking there for so long, never getting caught.

But that wasn't it. Dread punched me in the gut because I knew what I was looking at even before I stepped into view of the camera.

I couldn't breathe, couldn't move.

Standing in front of the wall, I pulled out two spray paint cans, one in each hand, and went to work on the brick wall. Something I'd done last month, weeks ago on a shithole of a day when my concentration had been shot, when everyone had seemed too loud, when I'd gotten shoved into the girls' bathroom and locked in there for three hours until someone had heard me screaming.

We'll get revenge on Sabrina, make her beg for mercy.

I ran a shaky hand down my face, mumbling, "Shut up."

Principal Johnson glanced my way with a raised brow, and I stiffened, refocused on the TV. On the screen, my attention was a million miles away, my eyes glazed over. Was that how I looked when I painted?

"I've seen enough," I murmured, lowering my gaze to my hands in my lap, well aware I couldn't deny my actions this time.

"I'll concede that the image you drew was spectacular," he started, drawing me to look at him, with hope in my chest. He handed me a photograph of the mural I'd spray-painted.

The path in the dark, twisted woods, the grand kingdom that reflected the golden rays in the far distance, the bridge arched between two mountains. And the shadow in the forest, lingering, always watching.

"But you vandalized school property." The principal's voice climbed. "And this isn't the first time. I can't overlook this anymore."

In the grip of silent panic, my mind lit up, my breaths coming too fast. My whole body felt like it had seized up. I didn't want to start another school when I had Antonio here, and I couldn't deal with Jen's fury.

"Please, sir. I'll do clean up duty for a year. I've really been trying." I wanted to crawl up inside myself and hide.

My little wolf, don't beg. I'll teach you to make them all fall to their knees at your feet.

"Have you?" Principal Johnson retorted. His annoyance was like fire on my flesh. "You got into a fight in history today, and from the moment you stepped into my office, I could smell what you've been smoking."

The room suddenly felt too small, too tight, the air heavy and wavering. He watched me, studied me just like the shrink had that morning.

I can tell you what to say to this man, what will make him keep you at this school.

My mouth couldn't open or respond, not while Principal Johnson glared at me.

I pushed my sleeves up nervously, my mind spiraling out of control.

Tell him Antonio made you smoke, convinced you it'd help, threatened if you didn't. That you'd listened to him for weeks, believing him, and his smoke made you paint on the wall.

My attention lifted to meet the principal's eyes, to see the disappointment on his hard weathered face, but I couldn't blame this on Antonio. Couldn't drag him into my shit, and he'd hate me if got him into trouble. I wouldn't do it. He deserved better.

"Please," I begged. "One more chance. I promise to change."

He shook his head. "Your foster mom is coming to collect you. A few days at home might do you well until I make a decision."

His words sunk through me like a boulder dragging me into the deepest pits of the ocean. I barely took a breath and slouched in my seat, trying to sort out my excuses to Jen. I wanted to fight and scream that he couldn't do this.

Trying my best to hide my fright, I said, "Okay. I hope you can give me one last chance."

Weak, so weak.

And I hated the voice in my head right then, loathed him.

Better to hate and not lose that fighting spirit.

"Go wait outside my office."

I jolted to my feet, bag in hand, and marched out, letting the door shut behind me. Slumped in a seat across from the front office desk, I closed my eyes and let a wave of dread wash over me, my body frozen. What I needed was a better-paying job than my weekend gig at the local cinema. Then I could save enough money to go off on my own, to not rely on anyone else. I knew it was crazy, but I'd had enough of constantly being reprimanded for shit.

Someone touched my arm. Startled, I looked up to find Jen there, her name badge over the pocket on her shirt from her job as a social worker. Her eyes glinted something dark, her mouth twisted. But she kept her composure, her voice sharp. "Just going to talk to your principal. I won't be long."

My knees bounced as I sat there, waiting as the receptionist offered me a curt smile, but she knew I was in shit. The whole school would find out soon enough.

Jen returned minutes later, her handbag clutched tightly under her arm. "Let's go," she barked.

The bell rang as we stepped outside into the hall-way. Students emerged from classrooms, heading down the hall to another.

Jen marched ahead of me down the hall toward the exit when I glanced up, seeing Antonio. My heart clenched, my eyes flicking from Jen, who was waiting at the door to get buzzed out, and back to him, wanting to tell him why I wouldn't be at school for a while. The guy didn't do texting, so I didn't want him to think I'd vanished.

I stepped closer toward him while Jen checked her phone. "Hey—" But my words dissolved when Sabrina emerged from around the corner, my pulse on fire over the fact that I'd been thrown out of school, but she remained.

"Sabrina," Antonio called out, and my stomach tightened. I'd never seen them talk before.

When she turned to face him, something gleamed in her eyes, her mouth pouty, her chest sticking out a bit too much.

The only similarity was our blonde hair, but mine sat straight to my shoulders, straggly, and nothing like hers. Nothing of me was like her. How could I compare to her?

Just seeing her stare at Antonio, share breathing space with him, left me shaking.

"Hey, what's going on?" she teased, smirking too widely. God, she was flirting with him.

I steeled myself for his response, holding my breath, hoping this was nothing more than him telling her she dropped something, or that someone was looking for her.

He ran a hand through his hair. "Heard the school dance is in two weeks. Wanna go?"

Her face lit up triumphantly while a sickening rage

tore across my stomach. It came through me like a hurricane, ripping me to shreds. I'd thought he... I choked on my breaths. I'd thought he liked *me*.

I just stared at them, my body numb, my heart on fire. I stumbled forward, part of me insisting I tell him how I feel. Maybe he'd never realized how much I wanted him.

"You coming?" Jen's voice made me flinch. Her hand was on my elbow and she wrenched me away, but on the inside I died. And I just stared at them still chatting, claws digging into my heart.

I staggered alongside Jen while an inferno swallowed me. He chose that bitch over me? When I saw her smile, the way she flicked her hair over her shoulder, I saw nothing but hate. Look at her. Those designer sneakers, the new phone, the expensive cordless headphones. She had it all, so why take Antonio from me?

Staring at him, all I felt now was the stab of a blade to my heart, pressing deeper, cutting me in two.

The rest of the world around me grew hazy. Tears blurred the darkness coming for me. Maybe she'd turn him down. Maybe then he'd choose me.

People lie, his actions don't. Told you, you don't need him.

Everything spun, my life, the school, the sky... me.

"Hey, you okay?" Jen asked, her fingers pressed into my arm.

My knees gave out, and suddenly I was shaking violently, my vision fuzzy. The last words someone screamed were, "She's having a fit!"

***

Someone poked my arm, over and over, and I grumbled under my breath, torn from my dream. The one that always came for me, the twisted forest, the fear, the promise of freedom if I escaped.

When I opened my eyes, Oliver's face was hovering over mine, smirking. I jumped in my skin at how close he stood. Those brown eyes, his nose smothered in freckles.

"What the hell are you doing?" I shoved my nine-year-old foster brother aside.

My gaze swept the pristine white walls, the window showing me only an overcast sky and rain hitting the glass. I inhaled the clinical smell of the hospital I lay in. The last thing I remembered was passing out at school.

"What am I doing here?"

I'll always be here for you. His voice softened my mind, caressed me into a lull, and the temptation to finally give in to him edged so close today.

Are you ready to fall?

"You're in so much shit." Oliver laughed the words, breaking me out of my haze.

"What?" The blue curtain lay half-closed around my bed, so I couldn't see the doorway. But voices I didn't recognize whispered from other beds behind the curtain. Other patients.

"Where's Jen?"

Just as I asked, she appeared from around the blue curtain with a tight smile. "How are you feeling?" She sat on the bed next to me, taking my hand in hers, and now terror choked through me.

"W-What's going on?" I stammered.

She glanced at me with compassion, with worry. She patted my hand. "The doctors think you may have had an epileptic fit, so they're running some tests. They say you might be able to go home tomorrow."

Epilepsy? I had enough crap to deal with. I didn't need this... didn't want it. Adrenaline pumped through me so fast, I tasted bile at the back of my throat like I might spew.

"It's not confirmed that's what happened. Personally, I think it was stress from everything that happened today." Her voice lowered. "Why did you let Antonio convince you to smoke weed? I bet that caused all of this."

Had it? Maybe... I had no clue. So much had happened too fast. "I'm sorry," was all I said.

Her phone rang, and she jostled to her feet before running out of the room.

Incessantly smirking Oliver sat in the visitor chair, watching me.

"Why aren't you in school?" I snapped.

He rolled his eyes. "Finished a couple of hours ago. God, you're stupid."

I shook my head, not having time for him.

"Mom's so pissed at you," he began. "You did drugs, she said. And she's had enough."

My stomach clenched at how out of control everything had gotten so fast.

"She said they're searching for a new foster family for you," he muttered.

I twisted my head in his direction, and he burst out laughing. "Oh my God, you should see your face."

Prick. There were times I hated my foster brother, like right now… that little shit lied through his teeth, yet his words scraped the insides of my head.

And now I couldn't escape the idea he'd planted in my head. Was Jen looking to find me a new foster home?

CHAPTER 4

The dream came again, always the same, a place I knew too well, a place I'd walked hundreds of times before. And the more times I visited, the more I couldn't help but feel this was where I belonged… in my head, not outside. Not standing here in front of the mirror wondering what to do for the day, not to mention my life. Not stuck in the real world with everything that entailed. Foster care, school sucking, and the part-time job that came with a few perks like free movies.

I dragged the orange tee over my head and down my stomach. The logo, *Cinemaximum*, ran across my chest. Then I combed my hair into a high ponytail and reached for the orange elastic band. Shadows still collected under my eyes, and I leaned closer to the mirror in my bedroom, pressing to find they weren't puffy anymore. My blue eyes looked pale like ice, too similar to my pale skin and white-blonde hair. I ruffled my bangs, looking half-decent, even if I resembled a bit of a ghost.

Wait till you show them the real you.

"I'd prefer that never happened," I murmured. "Not the girl who speaks to herself and has weird-ass dreams. Better they see the normal girl I am on the outside."

Normal is so overrated.

"Says the devil on my shoulder."

You haven't even seen my bad side.

I stilled, sometimes taken aback by the things that came from my head, things that seemed too real.

I'd definitely been cooped up at home too long for the past week, mostly in bed or on the couch watching reruns of *The Chilling Adventures of Sabrina*. It reminded me of Antonio asking Sabrina to the dance, and the scene replayed in my mind over and over. I shouldn't have tortured myself, but I couldn't stop. Maybe believing Antonio saw me as anything other than a friend had all been in my mind.

I'd spoken to my boss at the cinema the other day about going back to work this weekend since I'd missed last weekend's shifts. I hadn't experienced another fit for a week now despite the docs saying I could be suffering from epilepsy and they needed to carry out more tests. With all that shit on my mind, I had to get out and Saturdays were the busiest day at the movie theater.

If you head back to bed instead, I could make you forget.

"Whoa, where did that come from?"

Guess I'm in a playful kind of mood.

"Think I've fallen far enough by even talking to you."

Little wolf, you don't know the meaning of falling... not yet anyway. Like they say, the deeper you dig, the deeper you fall.

"Who said that?"

Someone.

"Ha. You just made that up."

Pretty poetic, hey?

"Actually, it's not bad. I'll give you that."

He laughed heavy and dark, coming from somewhere deep, eliciting a smile from me. *So, we're going back to bed to snuggle?*

"Very funny. I have work." I stepped into my black sneakers, noticing my bed lay undone, the blanket heaped in a mess. Then there was the worn easel near the window, along with dozens of my rough paintings in a messy pile on the floor, face down, knowing Jen would insist I clean up my room.

I can tease you endlessly and I do it very well.

"Well, showoff, I'm going to work, so feel free to take a cold shower."

Shooting sounds from *Fortnite* blared through the house. Oliver would spend the day gaming.

"What's for breakfast?" I asked as I entered the open living and kitchen area, where the sun drenched the space. He sat on the L-shaped couch, controller in hand, glued to the big screen. I turned to the side table against the wall. I stuck my hand into the bowl where we kept all keys, and every other knickknack like tiny screws, coins, hairbands, and miniature toy cars.

"I can whip up some waffles," Jen responded from the kitchen.

"Sounds good. Have you seen my car keys?" I scooped out the mess, searching for them.

I glanced over my shoulder to Jen, who poured premade batter onto the waffle maker, seeming to have not heard me.

"Oliver, turn that thing down," I yelled, but he simply stuck out his tongue and increased the volume on his game.

Luke, Jen's boyfriend, strolled into the room in his striped pajama pants and black tee. He was tall and thin, wore his brown shaggy hair loose, reminding me of a sheep, and he smiled all the time. Everything about him was kind and happiness. He was my favorite of all of Jen's past boyfriends, so I hoped it worked out for them.

"I need my car," I shouted over the gunfire.

"That old rustbucket was way past its retirement

date," Luke murmured as he passed me, his bare feet tapping the floorboards on his way into the kitchen. "Still, Collin's Car Yard gave us a good payout for it."

His words slammed in my head, and I jerked around. "Excuse me! Jen, what did you do? Did you freaking sell my car?"

She huffed and tossed her deadly stare at Luke.

His eyes widened and his cheeks blanched. "Didn't you already tell her?"

"No! I was waiting for the right time."

"*Right time*," I blurted out. I marched into the kitchen, keeping the island between us so I didn't throttle her. "Like the morning I was meant to go back to work. Why did you sell my car?" My voice climbed.

"Oliver!" Jen screamed and finally, he turned down the volume.

I shook from anger that she'd done that behind my back, hadn't even consulted me, had made the call on my behalf.

"Guen." She pulled down the waffle maker lid before turning to me, resting a hip into the counter like we were talking about the weather. "When I bought you that car, I didn't know it had so many problems. It's leaking oil among other things, and it'd cost too much to fix. Plus, the doctor recommended you don't drive in case you experience another seizure."

"You didn't have to sell my car! Or at least you could have spoken to me about it first."

Luke nodded, looking over at Jen. "She has a point."

"Oh, shut up, and you can finish the waffles now." She closed the distance between us, but I recoiled, unable to be in her company a second more. My life was spiraling out of control as it was. I couldn't cope with this on top of everything.

"Go get my car back!" I shouted.

"Sweetie, this is for the best. And we could use that money we got from the car yard."

"No, it's what's best for you, not for me. I can't believe you." I jerked around, grabbed my house keys and bag from the table, and rushed outside.

"Guen, your waffles," Luke called out as I slammed the door.

My back slumped against the door, tears flowing from my eyes. Everything in my mind was on fire, my body burning, but I wiped my cheeks dry. I hated how out of control I felt, how pissed I was at Jen for taking something I'd had for myself, for stealing the last thread of independence I'd held on to.

You will always have me.

"That doesn't make me feel better." I pushed off the door, wiping away the escaping tears, and swung down the sidewalk, past rundown townhouses, abandoned homes swallowed by weeds, and kids playing on the side of the road, drawing pictures on the asphalt. But I made up my mind right then that I'd find a way to claw myself back up, maybe save enough to get my car back, or another.

I pushed the earbuds into my ears, then let myself drown in the heavy beat, hurrying to work on foot.

She'd sold my car! I couldn't believe it...

Ten blocks away, I breathed heavily, and South-bridge city surrounded me, oversized and bright from the morning sun. My vision shimmered at the edges, and I couldn't tell if I was breathing right. I needed to get out and get more exercise.

People rushed in and out of stores and diners. Cars honked and filled the road. Everything blurred into one image and a sinking feeling of despair crashed through me, suddenly not recognizing the area, not knowing which direction to go.

I strolled near an alley and looked down a bright passage where the air quivered.

My vision cleared, the path darkening before my eyes, opening up to the twisted woods. Wind tore at the branches, shaking them viciously. Glimpses of the castle lay far in the distance, the bridge swaying, and the skies an ominous gray-black. Thunder roared, shaking the ground under my feet.

I stumbled backward, my heart racing.

"Watch out!" Someone shoved me in the back, and I swung around, my head whirring.

"Sorry," I muttered to the man in a business suit who marched down the sidewalk. Turning back to the alley, I saw only a dumpster and a pile of boxes. No sign of the kingdom I swore had been there seconds earlier, the same image as my mural on the school wall, on anything I sketched.

I rubbed my eyes and stared up at the Main Street sign.

Fear coiled around me too tightly, scraping my insides because, I didn't want to admit—*couldn't* admit—but maybe Debbie and Jen were right. Maybe I was losing grip on reality.

I ran the rest of the way to work. Didn't stop until I burst through the front doors of the movie theater, heaving for breath, shivers coating me. What was going on with me?

Instead of letting myself freak out, letting the panic rolling through me turn into an avalanche, I hurried into the back office to start my shift. A distraction was exactly what I needed.

"Never seen the cinema so packed," Lee, a woman only a few years older than me, said. She always wore her hair pulled into a ponytail and heavy Kohl eyeliner, bringing out her hazel eyes. "So glad you came in today." Her smile held promise and belief I wasn't a lost cause, and I liked her for not judging me, for not knowing anything about the real me.

We all carry a shadow with us, even her.

I glanced around the foyer to see several faces from school. My chest tightened at seeing them, but this was work, and I'd just put a smile on my face and ignore their stares.

Lee turned to the popcorn machine, refilling it while I approached a waiting customer, more pouring through the doors.

This menial task is below you, my little wolf.

I ignored the voice in my head and smiled at the customer as I handed her movie tickets.

I will teach you to be great, to take your place amongst the feared, and I'll show you pleasures you've never experienced.

"I'll be with you in a second," I said to the next customer with a smile, crouching down behind the counter and pretending to grab something from the drawer as I whispered, "Will you shut up and get out of my head?"

I only see the truth and you're refusing to open your eyes that you are so much greater than this, to make others who hurt you bleed, to remind them who lives amongst them.

"You're making me crazy."

I never said I was a good person. I heard the devious smirk in his voice, almost pictured his smile stretching from ear to ear.

Except this was all in my mind, in my twisted, broken mind.

"What do you want from me?" I mumbled.

"Guen, you all right?" Lee asked, and I freaked out.

I grabbed a handful of promotional flyers and jolted to my feet, forcing a smile. "Yep, just topping these up."

"Ah, good idea, but let's do that during downtime."

"Of course." I turned to find the customer frowning, so I stabbed his order in the register screen.

I want you to be mine. To tremble under my touch, to scream my name. To love my bad behavior.

I clenched my jaw, ignoring the words that made so little sense, the terror that somehow I could speak to myself this way, the fear that a part of me inside liked it more than I wanted to admit.

When the crowd finally dissolved, I turned to my boss. "I'll be back. Just need a quick bathroom break."

She nodded, and I locked my register before rushing to the empty toilets. There I threw myself against the sink and splashed cold water over my face with shaky hands.

"What's going on with me?" I asked out loud.

I lifted my head and stared into the mirror, at the dread etched on my face, the paleness of my lips.

"Please just stop. Stop saying shit about hurting people. That's not me. Just leave me alone."

Silence followed, and I embraced the peace, the absolute stillness. Wiping my face with a paper towel, I turned to the door.

I may be a monster, but you're naive.

CHAPTER 5

"Luke's daughter, Evelyn, is going to live with us for a short while. She'll take the spare room in the basement," Jen exclaimed as she pushed the bowl of mashed potatoes into my hands at the dinner table. She shared a hurried glance with Evelyn, who sat across from me.

Evelyn was the kind of girl I'd love to hate with her flawless red curls, the perfect bone structure, skin as smooth as silk. She was thin, and just overall radiated beauty.

"Why?" Oliver blurted out, his mouth full of potatoes, and I couldn't hide my smile to know he wasn't a little jerk to just me.

"My ex-wife is going through a rough patch," Luke explained, watching Evelyn with so much admiration it made me long to have a father who loved me that much.

If my parents hadn't abandoned me in the woods when I'd been only a few months old, would they look at me with that kind of love? Evelyn had someone who adored her, always would. Jen cared a lot in her own way, but it wasn't the same.

"I'd love to have her with us permanently," Luke added. "You know, Oliver, Evelyn works at the fair by the beach and runs the Ferris wheel. She might be able to give you a free ride if we all go down there one night."

"Yeah, I can do that," Evelyn mumbled, her voice strained.

How did one get a job to manage a Ferris wheel? What qualifications were needed to push a button?

But Evelyn wasn't smiling, rather, her brow furrowed into a dozen lines. "Mom's an alcoholic, Dad, just say it as it is. She passed out, then ended up in the hospital. That's what happened." Her voice cracked and she lowered her head, staring at the pork chop on her plate.

At first, she looked like the type of person who'd steal guys from other girls… but seeing the hurt on her face, the tears bubbling in her eyes when she thought no one was looking, my heart sank. She wasn't like Sabrina, not at all.

Life tossed shit her way as much as it did me, so I understood and sympathized with her.

"Evelyn's the same year as you," Jen continued. "You can go to school together tomorrow."

I cut her a hard stare. Was the woman going senile? "Did you forget I got suspended?"

Evelyn's eyes were on me. Maybe she saw another person in distress, someone who didn't have their crap together.

Maybe she's judging you?

"Guen." Jen finally looked my way, her mouth pulled into a tight smile like she was about to deliver good news. "Forgot to tell you, Principal Johnson rang up late Friday to say he's giving you one more chance, and you better not step a foot wrong this time or I'm sending you to a nunnery, I swear to God."

So many thoughts twisted in my mind, crushing my brain. "Why are you just telling me this now?"

"It slipped my mind." She shrugged and glanced over to Evelyn, then back to me. Was she trying to impress the new girl?

Everything was getting to me, and fire soared through my chest.

"Are you kidding me? First my car, now this. It's like I don't exist in this house." I shoved away from the table and marched out and straight to my room.

"You're on dishwasher duty tonight," Jen yelled out before I slammed the door shut.

A tiny bit over the top, but I like it. Show them who's boss.

I rubbed my eyes, exhausted from everything. Going back to school meant seeing Antonio, knowing he wanted Sabrina over me, and it tore me apart. Plus, I hated catching the school bus since Sabrina caught the same bus. But now I had no car. I wanted to scream.

I threw myself onto my bed and let myself drown. I didn't know how much time passed, but when the house finally fell silent, I returned to the kitchen to find everyone had gone to bed, the light still on and a pile of dishes waiting for me in the sink. *Gah.* So I got to washing them before Jen gave my room to Evelyn and made me sleep in the basement.

Ferris wheel? Is that some kind of weapon or sex toy?

I almost choked on my breath, the slimy plate slipping from my hands, but I caught it before it smashed to the floor.

"What are you talking about? It's just a ride at fairs," I whispered, looking toward the hallway momentarily.

There was no response for a while, so I went about washing the dishes, the only sound the clink of plates.

These rides are sold at fairs? Where do the rides take you?

I prodded my chin, thinking. "It takes you high up into the sky to see an amazing view, then back down. It's a huge circular ride made of metal and seats."

Do you like these rides?

I shrugged and pinched my lips. "Yeah, they're not bad. A Ferris wheel is where lots of couples go to kiss."

Is that what you wanted to do with Antonio?

My muscles tensed and a plate slid out of my hand and into the water. "Why are you bringing up that shit? If I were up there with him now, I'd shove him off the ride."

He laughed so beautifully evilly, I couldn't help but laugh with him. Glancing over, I expected someone to come and check on me, but no one did.

"Why do you think he doesn't like me?" I mumbled as I scrubbed the pot with mashed potato residue.

The question isn't why he doesn't like you, but why do you want him to?

"You're deep sometimes."

It's my curse. I am the prince of darkness, after all.

"Is that right, Your Highness?" I teased. "And why would someone so regal waste his time chatting with someone as mundane and broken as me?"

Because inside, you're a monster just like me. I'm here waiting for you to join me, to fall so deep, you'll finally find yourself.

"Yeah, you gotta know that sounds a helluva lot creepy."

I really shouldn't have been encouraging this or finding myself enjoying it to the point where talking to myself and responding was normal... exciting.

You can't run from your shadow.

"So is that who you are?" I wiped my hands on the kitchen towel and headed to bed, switching off all the lights on the way. "Who are you exactly? Someone I made up to keep me company? To deal with the crazy dreams and visions I have?"

Doesn't matter who I am. Who are you?

My brain cogs weren't working fast enough to make sense of his question because I had this feeling the answer was so much deeper.

"All right. How about you tell me who I am?"

Long ago, darkness and light came together and created beauty... a beauty that will destroy this world.

"Whoa, okay, wasn't expecting that. Where did you steal that from? The Bible?" Though I'd never read the Bible.

I stripped and climbed into my pajamas before getting into bed. I drew the blankets up to my chin and leaned over to switch the bedside lamp off.

You've been forgotten, little wolf. But I know exactly who you are. I just need to find you.

"Right! And you only speak in riddles when I ask you to elaborate? Whatever. I'm going to sleep."

The silvery moonlight from the large window fell over my bedroom, illuminating all the shadowy corners. That had been the exact reason I'd selected this room. I wasn't the biggest fan of the dark.

I turned over and shut my eyes.

***

I startled awake, coated in sweat, darkness clearing from the edges of my eyes. The shadow in the twisted woods always came for me—always. Night still cloaked the room. The clock on the bedside table showed 5:01 a.m. I fell back in bed, breathing heavily, still feeling like I remained in my dream.

I'll breathe so much easier when I feel your heartbeat, your weight against me.

Clearing my throat, I opened my eyes. "Very poetic for so early in the morning," I croaked.

Our conversations mean so much more than you'll ever know.

In all honesty, I didn't know how to feel, how to respond to the voice in my head saying that.

I thought about you while you slept, he teased, his voice sultry.

"Oh yeah?"

I crave to run my fingers over your body. Tell me... He breathed heavily. *Tell me how it feels?*

My eyes flipped wide open. I hadn't been expecting that in the slightest. "No! And if you're in my mind, you know."

I knew my little wolf was devious.

My cheeks shouldn't have heated up, but already a trickle of flames zipped through me, diving so deep, I tightened my thighs at the sensation.

"Stop talking crap." I pushed the blankets off me

and climbed out of bed, the floorboards cold under my feet.

These desires have delightful ends. Something about his voice left me trembling with an overpowering sensation that engulfed me fast and had my heart pounding so loud that I stumbled on my feet, barely able to catch my breath.

Let me show you.

"No! Just no." The notion terrified me that somehow I'd enjoy it so much, I'd lose myself even more than I already had.

I flicked on the lights and glanced over to my easel, deciding that painting was the perfect distraction from my mind seducing me. God, I was going insane.

With a fresh canvas set up, I prepped the paints and brushes before starting. I drew a long stroke, then another and more, the twisted tree coming to life. *He* no longer spoke and I let myself go.

"Guen, are you ready?" Jen called out from the hallway.

I snapped out of my concentration to find daylight flooded the room, and the clock flashed eight o'clock. "Oh, shit." Where had the time gone?

Setting the dirty brush in the water jar on the floor, I ran to the bathroom to get ready.

Once dressed, I took my meds and tossed my back-pack over my shoulder.

Jen handed me a brown paper bag. "Waffles and

sandwich. Now go. Luke's giving you both a lift this morning."

"Thanks." Rushed, I grasped the breakfast and headed outside to find Evelyn sitting in the front seat of the small hatchback. Fine by me. I jumped into the back, glad I wasn't catching the bus today.

Students crowded the school hall this morning, a few sending cutting stares my way, surprised I'd returned, no doubt. With Evelyn in the main office getting signed in, I stuffed my earbuds into my ears and shoved my way down the hall.

Before long, someone grabbed my arm, and I spun around to come face to face with Antonio.

My heart fluttered, my stomach dropping through me. I wasn't ready for this, couldn't find my words.

"I was calling out to you," he murmured.

I pulled out my earbuds, looking around for any sign of Sabrina and finding none. "What's up?"

"Heard you got kicked out. Great to see you're back." He had no right to smile that gorgeous grin and lure me into believing he liked me. I knew the truth now… It wasn't me he craved, but Sabrina. I was the freak girl he hung with, whom he probably laughed at behind my back about how I was more broken than him. Standing in front of him hurt, burned like acid in my throat.

All I could picture was him laughing with Sabrina.

"Yeah, thanks. I gotta go to class." I hurried away.

"Guen, you okay?" he called out, but I didn't turn around, didn't dare look back, or I'd crumble and give into him. I pushed the earbuds back in and hit max on the volume to tune out everything, even *him*.

Most of the classes passed in a blur, where I focused on lessons and nothing else. At lunch, I grabbed my meal and sat in the farthest corner, expecting to dine alone, but someone set their sandwich and juice near mine and sat.

Evelyn was grinning. "People are weird at this school."

"How so?" I took a bite of my waffles, staring at how viciously she ripped open her lunch, then tucked the red locks behind her ear.

"Like these girls were all chummy with me in biology, even shared their chocolate with me, then in the hallway, they tripped me and laughed."

"Rule number one: This school is infested by bitches. Rule number two: The guys here are the lowest scum on earth. Rule number three: Remember the first two rules."

She laughed and bit into her sandwich. A shadow fell over us.

"Hi, Evelyn."

I glanced up to see Noah with his black, spiked hair and those blue, dreamy eyes every girl in school swooned over. Did he remember me from the psychiatrist's waiting room? Probably not, considering his gaze wasn't on me.

"Hi," she responded, but she said nothing more and ate her meal.

"So, you want to go to the school dance with me this weekend?" The words just poured so easily off his tongue, as they had from Antonio's. In the background, half a dozen girls watched Noah, hypnotized by him. Were their hearts shattering to see him talk to the new red-haired beauty at school?

"Thanks," Evelyn responded. "But gonna say *no*. I'm probably just gonna go with Guen and have a girls' night out." She glanced over, smirking.

I liked Evelyn right then more than I'd thought possible. I grinned wildly, especially when Noah's mouth dropped open in shock. Without another word, he licked his lips, stuffed his hands into his pockets, and headed out of the cafeteria. I had nothing against the guy, but a sense of satisfaction filled me.

"He's not my type," she said. "He's been following me around all morning, talking non-stop about himself, how all the girls at school want him, but he only has eyes for me." She fake-gagged. "Who says that?"

"A desperate loser." I chuckled.

"Can you believe he tried to bribe me by saying his dad owned the biggest car yard in town, and he'd get me an amazing deal if I wanted a car?"

I half-snorted, but then reality punched me in the throat.

Wait! Collin's Car Yard. Noah's surname was Collin.

His dad had bought my car! The craziest idea crossed my mind, banging inside my head like a drum.

I shoved up out of my seat. "I'll be back."

Then I ran out of the cafeteria.

CHAPTER 6

"Get in," Noah ordered from the driver's seat of his red sports car parked under a broken streetlight.

I scanned the dark street I'd just run down, the wind shaking the trees along the sidewalk. No sign of Jen. I prayed she hadn't heard me crawl out the bedroom window and followed me. I dove into Noah's car, heaving for breath, and strapped myself in.

"You ready to do this?" he asked, his voice calm, his mouth curling into a smirk.

I nodded and turned his way. "God, you must really hate your dad! You don't look nervous at all." I was sweating like a beast.

He snorted a laugh. "My dad is a dick on a good day, and he deserves so much worse than losing one car."

His words surprised me, but like *he* said, everyone had shadows.

Good girl.

I shifted in my seat, staring out at the road. "You got all the papers signed and—?"

"Relax, you're making me jumpy. Got it all sorted. No one will bust you for stealing a car. I've got it signed back to you." He revved up the car, the motor purring, slamming the glass-knob gearshift into position, then he hit the gas, sending me back into the seat, and my stomach lurched to my throat. We raced down the quiet road. It was close to midnight.

"Bet your girlfriends love it when you woo them in this car?"

"Yeah, I guess." He glanced at me, the shadows dancing across his expression, his gaze all over me. "You spoke to her?"

"Yes, Evelyn will go to the dance with you. A deal's a deal."

Don't make deals, little wolf.

But I'd made up my mind. I'd tell Jen I used my savings to get my car back.

"So where am I picking up my car from?"

"The Car Yard."

My insides tightened. "You said you had it all ready." My voice strained and my knees bounced. "Don't tell me we have to break it out of the yard? Hasn't your dad got security cameras?"

"Just be cool. I said I got this, didn't I?" He shook his head and took the next turn a bit too fast, his back wheels skidding.

I grasped the door handle, convinced I'd made a terrible mistake thinking I could trust him. I didn't need Jen finding out since I wouldn't put it past her to actually send me to a nunnery.

Leave now then.

I raised a brow at his stupid suggestion. At the speed Noah was driving, I'd die if I tried to do a sudden roll out of the car.

Soon houses were replaced by the industrial district, and Noah pulled over in the shadows, far from the nearest streetlamp.

I squinted my eyes, staring into the dark. "Where are we?"

He fiddled with something in the middle console, his movements producing the jangle of keys, and excitement rose through me. I'd get my car back, gain some control of my life. Evelyn was easy to convince as long as I hung around with them during the night. I happily obliged.

You're not thinking straight, little wolf.

I reached for the door, whispering under my breath, "You're wrong."

"You're real cute, you know."

Frozen in my seat, I twisted my head around,

convinced I'd misheard. "Don't say shit like that. I don't need your flattery or whatever you're doing."

"Who have you been listening to that you can't take a compliment?"

"Okay, this isn't a conversation I expected to have with you—ever." Heat rushed up my neck and over my cheeks. "You've never really spoken to me before, so, well, you get the gist."

He shifted in his seat to face me, his hand in his dark hair, raking it back. "That was my mistake." He paused. "You look cute in that sweater, by the way."

I looked down at the black outfit I'd pulled out of my closet for one purpose: looking like a ninja to sneak out of the house.

"Why are you doing this?" I asked.

"Doing what?" He smiled so perfectly, his full lips delicious. There was something alluring, almost taboo, about him. Something I hadn't noticed before, but with the way he looked at me, my stomach unleashed butterflies.

"Being nice to me," I explained.

Little wolf, he growled a warning.

"Because you deserve it."

Noah reached over and his fingers pushed a few strands of hair off my face, his touch delicate... oh-so delicate. My heart's tempo rose and rose, and when I met his ice-blue eyes, I let myself believe his words. Let his hand cradle the side of my face. And for those few moments, it was Antonio I shared the car with, who touched me, who leaned closer. I needed him against me. To make me feel like it was me he chose. Me he wanted.

No, little wolf.

Lips clamped down on my mouth so fast, so chaotic—it all happened too quickly. His tongue drove against my lips, hands raking over my shoulders, down my arms, pulling at the fabric of my sweater.

Heavy breaths beat against me, and I could barely fill my lungs as he pressed closer, his arms pinning me to my seat.

Run!

A horrible feeling surged through my belly, and panic came with it, thick and fast. I shoved my hands into his chest, but he was a brick wall, unmovable.

His tongue licked at my neck, fingers curled in my hair. Something behind his eyes shifted, darkened with power. His hands grew forceful, more demanding.

The air was like molasses, heavy to breathe, and dread strangled me at the thought that he wanted more than a kiss, so much more.

"Stop, Noah, please!" I pushed against him.

Tell him... Tell him you want him to take you to a different place. To the backseat. His voice grew, furious. *Then run.*

My fear spiked as Noah's hand swooped under my

shirt, finding flesh. He moaned, and my heart thundered with terror. I thrashed against him. "Get off me!"

"Quiet down," he growled.

Tell him!

Noah kissed me again, harder this time, his hand pushing under the band of my jeans and underwear, his fingers gliding over the small bundle of hair and deeper.

I cried out. My body writhed, shoving against him, adrenaline beating into my veins. His mouth pressed fiercely on mine, and he half-climbed over the middle console like a monster mounting me.

Heavy, raging breaths swept over my mind like a thundering storm about to erupt. *Do it! he* bellowed. *Now!*

"B-Backs-seat." I reached for the handle, scrambling, straining to push the door open. My fingers curled over the metal, and I yanked, but it didn't budge. The bastard had locked us in.

"L-Let's go in the backseat."

Noah snarled against my mouth, his hand ripping at the buttons of my jeans. "I'm fine here."

"Don't!" I drove my fists into him, my world darkening the more I slammed my balled hands at his head, his shoulders. His teeth ripped at my lip with fierceness, blood coating my tongue, while his hand jerked at my underwear, the rip of fabric piercing the night.

"Be a good girl and shut the hell up."

Numbness took over me. My brain couldn't focus as I searched for a way out.

But the darkness feathered at the edges of my teary eyes while Noah's disgusting mouth pinned against mine, his grubby hands all over me.

The sports car gave a shudder under me, and Noah didn't notice that or the sudden creak.

He'll pay, little wolf. He'll pay with his life for ever touching you.

An invisible grip fastened around my neck, and I shuddered when another wave came at me, faster than the first, my world blurring, bile hitting the back of my throat.

In a heartbeat, my body burst into a fit on the front seat, fear sliding into my heart.

The car shook violently, the windows quivering. Metal groaned, sounding like a great beast roaring. Suddenly, the car hood flipped upward, the metal buckling right before my eyes.

Noah flew back into his seat, his eyes wide with fear, staring out the front window. "What the hell?"

In a blinding flash, everything was ripped out from under me, and I fell into a pit of darkness, the world stolen from me. My screams pounded in my head. I jerked my arms out, grabbing for something, for anything.

I tumbled so fast, seeing nothing.

With a thump, I hit something bouncy and soft that

caught my fall as a cry slipped from my lips. I swept my gaze around me to the large window, the chest of drawers, the mirror, the easel. And beneath me was my bed... I was back in my room, clutching the glass gearshift from Noah's sports car.

"W-What's g-going on?" I tossed the gear stick to the end of the bed as if it were some vile part of him.

Confusion pummeled into me, and I couldn't make sense of anything. My flesh crawled, my mind drowned over what had happened with Noah, how I'd gotten back here in an instant. How had the metal of his hood twisted on its own?

I kept glancing around the room, blinking hard, expecting this to be a vision, a dream—anything but reality. Expecting myself to wake up to clear the blurriness in my head because these things didn't happen in real life. They couldn't.

I hiccupped a breath and scrambled under my blankets, wanting to hide from the world, convinced this was somehow a horrible dream. As I curled in on myself, the tears refused to stop, and I couldn't stop the dirty feeling slithering over my flesh. I shut my eyes, praying I'd just fall asleep and never wake up again.

And I'll be here to catch you, little wolf.

CHAPTER 7

"**A**re you awake yet?!"

Jen's voice shook me awake, my eyes wide open. Sweat dripped down my back as threads of the twisted woods lingered like cobwebs, pulling me back into my dream.

I stared up at the white ceiling, my insides not feeling right, somehow tangled like part of me remained in the dream. The part that couldn't quite remember what day it was, what I'd done last. An in-between world where I floated freely.

Stormy clouds cast shadows through the window, reflecting the trees outside like broken and gnarled branches. Something about them looked familiar, and not because I'd seen them in my dreams or in my room before. Similar shadows I'd seen elsewhere, all warped and bent and tapping on my window, while I remained cradled and bundled in my blankets. I remembered a dim room that smelled of the sweetest clementine and someone's panicked whispers in my ears.

Not much of my early years stuck in my head, but this rushed forward, sitting on my mind like a rock, like it wanted me to remember.

"Are you getting up anytime soon?" Jen yelled from outside my room, shattering my concentration.

With a groan, I pushed myself upright before she barged in, but my attention fell on the glass gearshift at the end of my bed.

All the events of last night steamrolled through me, ripping the peace from my mind. Bile surged into the back of my throat.

Noah.

Forcing his hand down my pants.

Me falling out of his car and landing on my bed.

I wanted to crawl out of my skin and float away. Nothing made sense but the sickness sliding through my gut that Noah had forced himself onto me.

His tongue will be a trophy on my wall.

"Then make it happen already! Do something worthwhile! Be a hero... Something. *Anything!*" I growled under my breath, shaking over the fact of what Noah had done to me, that he'd deceived me into lowering my guard. Did he even have my car, or had that been a lie too?

I'm no hero.

"Then what are you?" I blurted out.

I'm the wolf who will take revenge. The monster behind you who bathes in your misery. The only one who will put you back together.

"Stop talking in riddles," I cried, fresh tears burning my eyes as I stormed out of my room, crossed the hall, and flung open the bathroom door before shutting myself in.

"You keep telling me you're here for me. That if I fall, you'll catch me." I trembled, my spine pressed against the tiled wall as I slid to my ass. "I'm ready now. Take me from this place. I've fallen far enough." Tears marked tracks down my cheeks, and I hugged my knees, torn by the hurt and disgust I felt inside.

Oh, little wolf... His voice cracked, then faded.

"Yeah, that's what I thought."

You have no idea how far I'll go for you.

I drowned in my sorrow and wanted nothing more than to be left alone. To be invisible. To forget all the memories, all the bad, all the hate. I recalled a memory that stuck with me from another foster home. An older girl had once told me that if I wanted to be forgotten, I had to ignore myself, a comment that took me years to fully understand, hating her all the while over the fact that she'd say that to me. But she knew better than me. To survive, I had to ignore my feelings, no matter how much they shredded and scarred me. No one saw my insides and all that ugliness but me.

Maybe all these occurrences were only in my head, and Jen needed to know, to help me. I considered what the shrink had written in her notebook. *Schizophrenia.* Was this what it felt like?

A bang came at the door, and I jumped in my skin. "Don't think you're getting out of school today," Jen bellowed.

I wiped my eyes and climbed to my feet. "Give me five and I'll be ready." Shoving all the pain and agony aside, I got into the shower and embraced the emptiness.

I could do this, and so I did.

The day flew by.

Hours.

Classes.

I kept to myself, didn't say a word, and skipped lunch to avoid talking to anyone... mostly Noah and Antonio and Sabrina.

When the last bell of the day rang, I joined the masses in the hall and let them carry me out. Someone grasped my arm and wrenched me out of the sea with such strength, I tripped over my feet. Lifting my head, my gaze met Noah's.

"Get away from me." I burned on the inside at seeing him, hatred bubbling like acid in my gut that he thought he had he any right to touch me again.

His mouth warped, making me sick, ready to vomit at what his lips had done to me last night.

His whispered words spat in my face. "What did you do to my car, freak? You went psycho and my car is all twisted and a complete wreck. I don't know how you did it, but you owe me for that car. You're not running away this time, you bitch." Hatred enveloped his expression, darkening his eyes. "And I want my gearshift back."

But all I saw was red. I didn't remember moving, but my fist swung and smashed him on the jaw so hard, my knuckles screamed with agony. I hit him again and again, seeing nothing but sheer rage. "You fucking asshole!"

He never struck back, but cowered, covering his face, recoiling. His gaze swung to the gathering crowd and back to me.

Adrenaline pushed and pushed me, my fists striking him until he turned and ran, shoving students aside like a piece of shit.

Heaving for breath, I didn't look up, ignoring the voices, the words I loathed. *Weirdo. Sick. Mental problems. Unstable.*

My breaths rushed in and out of my lungs, my adrenaline rampant. I grabbed the bag I'd dropped and ran down the corridor, past everyone, out of the school, and all the way home.

Emptiness gathered in my chest, and fear swept through me. How could I ever face anyone at school again?

I gasped for air, wiping away the constant tears. My legs cramped, but I didn't care or stop until I reached home. I slouched against the door and flicked on the camera on my phone to check my face. The tears had dried, but redness rimmed my eyes. Blonde hair sat flat against my head like I hadn't washed it. I stared at my knuckles, the skin bruised and scored when I extended my fingers completely.

So proud of you, little wolf.

"He deserved so much worse."

And it will happen.

I reached for the door handle, toying with the idea of telling Jen everything, getting it off my chest, having her help me decipher what had happened last night.

She won't understand. None of them will. They'll give you meds that will take you from me.

I nodded, but what if something was seriously wrong with me? Maybe Noah was right and I had run home last night, but my mind had blocked it out? Then how had I ended up with his gearshift?

They don't want you like I do.

My mouth opened with a response, but I stopped short. I'd been shoved from family to family my whole life because no one wanted me... Did *he* have a point?

I shoved open the door, dumped my bag near the shoe rack, and headed down the hall to my room. Without thought, I automatically picked up my paints and brushes with a new canvas I stored in the back of my closet.

Here I lost myself, forgot everything, and didn't have to be anyone but myself. My thoughts swirled with my dilemma. Tell Jen or keep pretending I was fine?

I couldn't tell how much time had passed before I took a bathroom break, but when I returned, Jen stood in front of my canvas tapping a fingertip on her chin like a critic.

My stomach dropped. "What are you doing in here?" I rushed toward her.

"Guen, you drew this? It's unbelievable." She stretched a hand toward the painting. "Especially—"

"Don't touch it. Don't look at it." I stepped between her and the image, something I'd never shown a soul. The snarled woods was my place, something only I knew about, not Jen or the shrink or anyone.

Except me.

She stared at the canvas. "That is incredible. How did you come up with something so beautiful?"

I'd never tell, ever. The place was my kingdom, the one in my head, the one no one could rip away and destroy.

Jen stepped back, and I hurried to grab one of my shirts from the floor and draped it over the painting.

"They're all of the same forest and castle. You've

painted the image over and over. Where did the idea come from?"

I turned and Jen was bent at the waist, flicking through my other paintings propped up against the wall. They were all two-foot square canvases because they were the cheapest sizes at the local discount store.

"Just leave them alone." I grabbed the bundle and moved them away from her reach.

"Sweetie, you're being rude. You're so talented. Don't hide them."

I shook my head. I didn't want anyone to see them because once they did, they'd find a way to rip that place away from me. To somehow turn the one thing I enjoyed into an explanation for my sickness. Or some other shit excuse to turn it into something ugly.

"Just leave them alone," I said. "They're not for anyone but me."

She nodded, her mouth pulling downward at the corners. "Okay, okay. Just open the window in here. It's stuffy."

When she left, I set the paintings back down against the wall and collapsed onto my bed, shaking, feeling like someone had just ransacked my room. This was why I made it clear that no one was allowed in my room.

Little wolf—

"Not now. Please, just leave me alone." I turned onto

my side and stared at the bruise forming over my knuckles, wanting only quiet.

Two more days passed. School. Home. Sleep. A simple routine, but it worked and I was left alone. As I stepped out from the school entrance on a sunny day, I rushed down the front steps and swung left, like I did every day to catch the bus home.

"Guen," a woman called me, and I turned around to find Jen poking her head out the driver's window of her car, waving at me to join her.

Hell yeah, I'd accept a lift home. I ran toward her, darting around students. In my rush, I bumped into Antonio, who grabbed my wrist in my attempt to flee.

"Hey. Haven't seen much of you," he murmured in that smooth, velvet voice.

But all I could focus on was his hand on me, my chest beaming with excitement… except when I looked at him, I only saw Sabrina. And on cue, the devil bitch sidled up to him. She must have felt her horns burning. Her eyes fell heavy on me as she curled an arm around his, possessively claiming her territory.

"Hey, babe. What are you doing?" she purred with the voice of a backstabbing cow, while her eyes narrowed, hurling hatred my way.

I ripped my hand free from his grip.

Kick him in the balls.

I ought to, but instead I didn't waste my breath on him before running to the car, hating how hot my neck and face burned from his presence. Hating that seeing him with her still sliced my insides. They deserved each other.

In the car, I buckled in and stared straight ahead, too shaken to look elsewhere.

Jen, to my surprise, didn't ask a question, but she would have seen me talking to Antonio, seen him with Sabrina. She just pulled away from the curb and drove away. Once we passed the swarming traffic around the school, I eased into my seat.

"Thanks for the lift," I said, looking over at Jen, who offered me a huge smile. I shouldn't have been suspicious, but my *shits-about-to-hit-the-fan* radar was blaring in my head. "What's the special occasion?"

"I wanted to show you something. And I need you to have an open mind."

I shifted in my seat, and there it came. "What did you do?" Part of me didn't want to know, but I wasn't getting a choice in the matter.

"I'm so proud of you, Guen, and I want you to see how incredible you are. The last couple of weeks, a lot has happened, and you handled it better than I thought. With everything from the sale of your car to that jerk Antonio having another girlfriend, you now need some good news."

I swallowed hard. If only she knew half of the shit I'd been going through.

"I've got a small surprise for you."

In general, I didn't do surprises well, but I nodded and smiled back. "Can't wait."

Twenty minutes later, we parked along the main road in the heart of our small city and climbed out. I scanned the surrounding stores. A pizzeria, café, clothing store. If this was the surprise, I'd take it.

But when Jen curled around the front of the car, she strolled past all three establishments, so I guessed we weren't going into any of them.

I rushed after her. "Where are we going?"

"You'll see." In a heartbeat, she grasped my hand in hers and whirled me in through an open door into a huge white room. The walls were covered in paintings, and my stomach dropped at the idea that she intended on taking me on some kind of art gallery tour.

A dome-shaped haystack sculpture made of thousands upon thousands of sharp sewing needles sat in the middle of the room. An old-fashioned spinning wheel sat on top, also made of silver. The sun pouring in from the floor-to-ceiling windows glinted off the structure like a star, and all I could picture was someone tripping and falling into the contraption. Death by a million pins.

Jen dragged me to the rear of the room, and dread rose through me like a storm.

On the back wall of the room hung my painting with a tiny plaque underneath with my name.

Guen's Fantasy

"What do you think?" Jen prodded my arm, but numbness spread through me. My private piece was tacked to a wall for all to gawk and critique. I felt sick to my stomach.

"You had no right," I muttered, keeping my voice low so the other couple in the room didn't hear us.

"Guen, honey. The moment I showed the artist running this exhibition your piece, she loved it and insisted she add it to her gallery. She had no hesitation and her only condition was that she could meet the artist. You have a real talent here. This could take you so far and be your thing."

"My thing?" I didn't even know what that meant, but I figured it had something to do with finding my path in life, to ensure I didn't end up a homeless loser.

"You should have—"

"Hello," a woman's faint voice came from behind us.

We both turned to face the most beautiful woman I'd ever laid eyes on. Tall, almost glowing with the sun at her back, porcelain skin seeming to glisten, and hair black as the night. The skirt of her golden dress billowed around her knees from the breeze rushing through the open door. Her pale gray eyes scanned me from head to toe, her smile widening as if she approved of what she saw. "Guen?"

"This is Guen," Jen responded for me, practically gushing. "She's talented, isn't she?"

"Absolutely." The tall, angelic woman took my hand in hers, her skin silky soft like she soaked her hands in a tub of moisturizer every night.

"My name is Áine."

"That's a beautiful name," I said.

"It's an Irish name, meaning 'radiance.'" Her smile beamed, perfectly matching her name.

"Are you Irish?"

She half-laughed. "No, dear." Then she turned me around to face my painting. "Your mom wasn't sure what you wanted to call this piece, so I'll have it amended right away. What do you call it?"

My head was spinning to think straight. "I-I'd never given it any thought."

"Don't think too hard," said Áine, all sweetness. "What's the first thing that came to mind when you painted this image?"

"You can do this, sweetie," Jen added.

I shrugged. "I don't know. Maybe *Twisted Dreams.*" The moment the words left my mouth, I wanted them back. I'd said too much, not wanting Jen to know this came from my dreams, but already I felt her stare on me, the wheel behind her eyes ticking away.

"That's perfect," Áine said before yelling over her shoulder. "Jean-Claude, a new tag for this piece, please. *Twisted Dreams.*"

I cringed on the inside.

Áine returned to my side in moments, her arm threaded through mine, pressing close, and all I could smell was her strong floral perfume with hints of citrus. Maybe she was French or from some other European country where being touchy-feely with strangers was the norm.

"I'd love to hear about your inspiration for this piece," she said.

Jen interrupted. "Oh, she's a closed book and won't tell anyone." I appreciated her saving me.

"Nonsense, every artist has a muse." Holding on to my arm, she swept me around the gallery. "All these works of art came from somewhere deep and personal to the artist, so where is yours from?"

Something about her pushiness was rubbing at my nerves. "What does it matter?" I glanced over my shoulder to find Jen chatting with a tall, man with gelled hair and black eyeliner busy replacing the tag under my painting.

Áine's grip on me tightened, and she was stronger than I'd expected. When I looked up at her, a glint of silver crossed her gray eyes, her beauty darkening, and for those few seconds, the room seemed to freeze over. Even my breath misted in front of my face.

"Let me tell you something." Her words sliced the air like a blade, her fingernails digging into my wrist. A greedy hunger tightened her features, her expression changing to someone who'd just found a dragon's treasure.

"Ow, you're hurting me." I pulled against her, her nails cutting into my flesh, her nose wrinkling, and she almost looked like a different person. "Let me go."

With the speed of a striking viper, her breath was on my ear. "Guendolyn, we finally found you."

CHAPTER 8

"Guen!" Jen called from across the gallery.

I jerked around, blinking fast to clear the fuzziness in my vision. Why in the world did it feel like I'd been run over by a truck?

Jen rushed forward, fear tightening her expression. Once at my side, she grasped my hand. "Are you going to be sick? What happened to your hand?" Her panicked voice was strained.

When I looked down at the inside of my wrist, blood bubbled and rolled over the sides of my arm from three small cuts the size of fingernails. Red dots hit the perfect white floor, like blood drops in snow. My heart was racing as I tried to make sense of what Áine had just done… had said.

Jen pulled a tissue from her handbag and pressed it to my wounds. "How did you cut yourself?"

Glancing over my shoulder, I found that Áine was nowhere to be seen. Had she run out of the store? "Where is she?"

"Focus," Jen insisted.

My head felt like someone had blown a puff of smoke right inside my skull. "Her fingernails," I murmured. "They were so sharp. Her face—"

"She did this to you?" Jen hissed, drawing the attention of the couple nearby in the main exhibition.

But I couldn't think straight and just nodded.

Guendolyn, we finally found you, she'd whispered.

The voice in my head had said something similar. *I just need to find you.*

They couldn't be related… no. How could it be? He was in my mind, my delusional mind, part of suffering schizophrenia… I guessed.

I read somewhere that coincidences meant you were on the right path. Except nothing felt right here, and only heaviness worried through my gut.

"Sweetie." Jen's tender voice lulled me out of my thoughts. "Stay here for a second. Don't touch anything."

As if I would. My sights swung to an enormous structure made of actual pins still attached to their metal heads. I stepped closer to the wall, terrified I'd have a fit and fall straight onto that thing.

Jen stormed to the back of the gallery, her arms swinging by her side, and shoved Jean-Claude aside.

She pulled my painting off the wall, then tucked it under her arm and marched right back to me before taking my hand and hauling me out of the establishment.

She turned back for a brief moment. "Don't buy anything from here. Áine is an abuser. She attacked my girl and made her bleed."

Without a further word, she guided me to her sedan. I adored Jen more at that moment than I'd ever thought possible. Despite all the shit I'd caused, she only wanted the best for me. She believed in me after all of my crazy drama.

Once we climbed into the car, she reached over and checked my cuts, wiping the blood clean with the stained tissue. "I'm so sorry. I never should have brought your painting here. I should have listened to you."

"You didn't know she was crazy and would attack me."

Her lips pinched, and her brow furrowed. "I'm supposed to protect you, do my best for you, and I should have known better." She met my drowning eyes. "Did she hurt you anywhere else? What did she say to you?"

"Not much, just gibberish about paintings."

"Tomorrow I'll put a complaint in with her landlord to ensure she loses her rental privileges at the gallery."

"How do you know she doesn't own it?"

Jen started the engine and merged into the traffic. "I know the person who owns the whole complex. He's a cousin of a friend at work." Her hands strangled the steering wheel. She shook her head, and every now and then, she glanced over with a sympathetic smile.

I kept repeating the incident over and over in my head, unsure what had happened, but I was left with more questions than answers. Why did Áine behave so weirdly... So aggressively?

What if she knew more about me than I did? My past was a black hole. No biological parents, no history —nothing but a single name. Was it even mine?

"Is Guen my real name?"

Jen studied me with a raised brow. "What do you mean?"

I shrugged. "They said I was found in the woods as a baby abandoned with nothing but a ribbon tied to my ankle with my name on it. So could Guen be short for something else?"

Her lips pinched to the side, thinking about my question for a long time. "Let me check the archives at work tomorrow, okay?" She patted my thigh.

"Thank you for everything. I know I don't say it often, but I appreciate it."

Her smile was so much more than words could express, and despite the outcome to the whole gallery shitstorm, I wouldn't change a thing, as it had made me realize something. Made me see that Jen was so much more than a foster mom. She was my guardian angel. My fairy godmother, if such things existed.

I wiped away the blood on my arm and stared at the half-moon-shaped wounds, blood already clotting at the edges. Áine had been so angry, so adamant to tell me she'd found me. None of it made sense, but maybe she was just another person whose head wasn't screwed on right.

"How does pizza sound for dinner?" Jen suggested.

"Luigi's? Pepperoni?"

"You bet."

"Perfect." I lounged in my seat, holding the tissue tightly to my cuts, and figured a night of stuffing my face with pizza to forget everything was exactly what the doctor ordered.

***

There was something unusual about the woods today.

Twisted branches stood still—too still, the breeze absent—and shadows crowded the woods like never before. They darkened the place I knew too well, stealing the breath out of the forest.

A chill slithered down my spine, and I turned toward the castle, the kingdom that promised freedom beyond the dark forest of teeth and thorns. A place to escape if I reached its sanctuary in time.

I swung away from the gloom swallowing the

forest, like I always did, my sights set on the place just out of reach, the place I felt I belonged.

A hum of whispers rose around me.

Not one person, but so many watched me today, their eyes heavy on my back. My skin crawled from the sharpness cutting into my forearm. I looked down and the blood ran free from the three wounds. The drops hit the dirt. Where once broken things grew, my blood turned anything it touched black.

My heart raced too fast, strangling me, and I ran to the only place I felt safe. The kingdom.

Movement darted through the woods alongside me, suddenly sliding across my passage.

I stopped dead in my tracks, my breaths ragged and harsh.

They'd catch me today—I sensed it deep in my bones. They had my scent now, the delicate spice of my blood on their tongues. Today was the end.

A figure emerged from within the darkness. A masculine man, tall and powerful. He stood in the distance. Dressed in a military-style coat that reached his knees, with silver buttons and a high collar, he was spectacular.

He carried power... Oh, so much of it dominated the land... and me. Dark leather pants hugged strong legs and a shirt the color of midnight, in what looked like silk or some kind of fabric that I'd never seen before. It looked wicked expensive. Pricier than anything I could ever dream about buying, that was certain. The shirt sat open around his throat.

This man couldn't be more than a few years older than me, but he carried enough confidence for both of us. Long hair fell to his shoulders, black as the night, skin lightly tanned like he barely spent time in the sun.

Sweat drenched my skin, and I glanced around for an escape, but thorny bushes and trees blocked my way. Except I knew this path; I'd traveled it hundreds of times before. I shouldn't have been afraid. This was my place… even if today the shadow that always just watched me emerged from his hiding spot.

"Who are you?" I called out, finding my bravery.

"Doesn't matter who I am. Who are you?" his masculine, seductive voice replied.

My mouth clamped shut in a heartbeat when my mind fixated directly on who stood in the distance, and I recognized him at once.

Him. He. The man with no name. The voice who made me laugh and fear him, who left me trembling. Who promised me things.

He stepped into the dim light, a breeze blowing around us now, rousing the trees from their sleep, greeting us with rustling songs.

I couldn't help myself, and my gaze roamed over his face, finding the most beautiful eyes I'd ever seen. Bright like fire dancing on water if such a thing were possible, but on him, they burned, crowned by dark eyebrows. Curiosity had me staring at the sharpness of his cheekbones, the rugged defined jaw, full lips with a slight curve in them, like he might break into a smile. What did he find so amusing?

He strolled closer, moving with the grace of a man used to being in the public eye—shoulders broad, chin raised, but those eyes... intense and powerful and dangerous. He saw everything, missing nothing, so why was he staring at *me* like that?

I stiffened. It didn't matter how drop-dead gorgeous he was; something about his presence left me uncomfortable. He moved closer, towering over me, and my feet shuffled backward.

Threads of fear coiled around my chest in his presence.

He smiled. Should I smile back or run?

At my hesitation, he raised an eyebrow, the corners of his mouth quirking. "Hello, little wolf."

The cogs in my brain still grinded to catch up, clouded further by the smoothness of his voice, the heat he ignited within me. "Sorry, what?"

His laugh boomed, just like the times I'd listen to him in my head. This was my dream... I knew, always knew, but this time was different. He was different and shouldn't have been here.

"What are you doing?" I asked, utterly mesmerized that my mind had conjured such a handsome man to go with that delicious voice.

"I told you I'd finally find you."

Heat crawled up my neck. "And *I* told *you* how creepy stalkerish that sounds."

His mouth pulled into the deadliest of smiles that left my knees shaking. When he looked at me with that grin, his gaze dipped over my face, boobs, legs. I felt utterly vulnerable, and extremely turned on. Except all of this was in my head, in my dream, right?

Yet part of me had this urge to run up to him and hug him like we were long-lost friends or something, but if I did that, I would be insane. Besides, he didn't seem the hugging kind, no matter how much I'd love to be in his arms. Point proven, I'd just gotten horny over the imaginary guy in my head.

So, I swallowed back the confusion and ignored the fire sparking in my gut. "Seeing as you've finally stopped hiding, want to show me around? Like maybe how to get to that kingdom over there?" I nudged my chin toward the palace in the distance. "And who the hell are you really? Do you have a name, or should I call you my shadow?"

A smirk slid over his gorgeous mouth, but he shook it off as quickly as it came, his gaze never leaving mine. "You still have a sword for a tongue, I see."

"And you still talk in riddles. What's new?"

"I have so many secrets to tell you," he began. "Things you've seen a thousand times, but never like this."

"What sort of secrets?"

"The kind that will show you the truth about your past."

"My past? Like my parents?"

Branches and leaves snapped in the woods around us. I turned when his hand grasped over my bloody wrist and hauled me against him so fast, my feet stumbled, and I slammed into a wall of muscles. My hand was trapped between our bodies, and panic had me clenching his shirt desperately. His woodsy masculine scent teased me and the earlier fire burned all the way through me.

"This place is no longer safe for you," he growled, then lifted my hand to his mouth and flicked a tongue over my wound.

"Eww, did you just taste my blood?" I tugged my arm from him, but he wasn't releasing me.

"It'll heal quicker."

My blood ran cold when the crunching of foliage came again. I jerked around, scanning the woods. Movement came from within the folds of darkness.

"Who's out there?"

"Monsters?"

I looked up at him, his eyes darkening. "You once told me you were the monster."

"How do you think one destroys them? By becoming one."

His words swirled in my head as fear clung to my

ribs, and I pushed myself away from him, but he held on tightly and spun around, then started walking away, hauling me behind him. My feet stumbled over the ground to keep up. I didn't relent and kept tugging against his grip, still half-baffled how broken my mind was to make up this shit. How I actually felt his grip on my skin. Dreams weren't this tactile.

My heart hammered in my chest, my skin pricked with shivers. "Let me go! I mean it."

"You need to leave," he chided, his words raw and savage, his grip so tight, he'd stopped the blood circulation to my hand. "Play nice."

"You aren't the voice from my head," I spat. "You can't be because he'd never hurt me. He promised to save me and to make those who hurt me pay." My voice quivered.

"And I said I was no hero. May the gods have mercy on those who wronged you because I won't." He paused and turned me so I was forced to face him. Shadows crawled under his eyes, and his smile terrified me.

"You're just words." I jerked from his hold, but it was useless. Disbelief raked through me over the fact that he'd changed so quickly.

"Those hiding in the dark will rip you apart, suck the marrow from your bones, wear your skin as decoration, but… my little wolf, most of all, you *should* be scared of the deadliest monster of them all. Me," he hissed. "You have no idea how far I'll go."

I swallowed the shudder consuming me, and he just sneered at the hitch of my breath.

I hated his words, his twisted face, him. My throat constricted. "You're a cold-hearted liar."

I hadn't realized until now that the man inside my head was the actual devil, and he glared at me with lustful hunger in his eyes.

He *tsked*, and deadly power rippled off him.

"Who are you?" I cried with terror in my voice as shock warped my insides.

"You'll find out soon enough." He shoved his hands into my shoulders, sending me reeling backward, my body going slack. A sob escaped from deep in my lungs. A spark flashed across my vision and my world faded fast.

Darkness took me, and even though I knew he'd still be there in my head, waiting for me, I screamed.

CHAPTER 9

"Guendolyn," I whispered, but she didn't stir. Shivers crawled down my back, but there was no time to waste.

This was a terrible idea, a shitty idea, yet here I stood in her bedroom, night draping over her but hiding nothing.

Somehow Guendolyn had opened the gateway to her whereabouts in the human realm, and about damn time, except her aura now revealed her to every damned soul-sucking deviant in the Wandering Realm.

Shadows already stretched and shifted across the land outside her window. I prowled across her chamber. Clothes and books lay on the floor, paintings and an easel near the window. I stepped past a book with the cover of a skinny, short-haired man in tight pants, his skin covered in markings, his ears pierced. Was this what females liked in this realm?

Looking around, I'd seen brothels cleaner than this.

Guendolyn laid in bed, the blanket pushed down to her waist, her top scrunched halfway up her stomach, exposing soft milky skin, and my fingers curled to reach down and run my hands over her, to taste her with my teeth.

If I were true to the Shadow Court, I'd walk away and let the wolves take her because the truth of who she was could destroy everything... including me. I should have done it long ago because looking down at her now, the tightness in my chest grew. I couldn't leave her, not like this.

Her heavy breaths filled the night, but her eyes flitted behind their lids. She was beautiful, a lot more so than I'd expected, even in the human rags she wore. A bit thin for my tastes, but her breasts were full. White-blonde hair draped over her pillow, and a light trail of freckles dotted her petite nose. When I'd first laid eyes on her in the woods, this damn iced heart of mine had thumped in my chest.

She shifted in bed and a moan escaped her red lips.

Captivating.

Intoxicating.

I had to have her.

Faint vibrations in the floorboards and walls alerted me. The wolves were almost here. Outside, the trees shook violently. The woman in front of me held the key to changing everything in the Wandering Realm.

But I was getting ahead of myself, dreaming of a darker world, a place now possible, but first Guendolyn needed to survive. Ice moved through me at the thought of her harmed.

And I'd take her away, protect her the only way I knew how.

The need to protect her roared through me with intensity. I bent over, sliding my arms under her back and knees, and pulled her against me, reveling in the soft curve of her breast pressed to my chest. She was light and so warm. Heat sparked across my skin. Her vanilla, sweet scent found me and my balls tightened. Those lips, so rosy, so lush. I wanted to taste them, mark them, feel her writhing beneath me.

My pulse pounding, I craved a taste of her.

Her eyes fluttered open… bright as the bluest ocean. Gorgeous. But there was fear behind them.

Innocent and so fragile.

Fear widened them, blanching her cheeks. She was even more beautiful when frightened.

"Sleep, little wolf," I cooed, power flooding me, floating on my breath, flickering and sparking over her face.

"Y-You," she mumbled.

She shouldn't have been able to resist me, but her eyes twitched, her body convulsing. She shook her head, fighting the enchantment sweeping over her. My voice carried power over those who didn't know better, who didn't recognize the strength of my words.

An explosion of growls came from outside, and I shot a glance to the darkness.

"Sleep." Panic strained my voice, my head spinning. *Your life will never be what it once was.*

Her eyes finally slid shut, and she fell limp in my arms.

Shadows strained in the corners of the room, and from them came the sound of something being dragged across the floor. A low guttural growl, a threat.

Fear choked me, not for my safety, but for my little wolf. How in the seven hells had they found her so fast?

I spun away, feeling their heavy presence, and my muscles tensed. "Open," I growled.

Thump. Thump. Footfalls hit the wooden floor, racing up behind me.

My hackles rose, desperation bursting through me.

The air in front of me shimmered. Not waiting for a second longer, I threw myself through the opening gap of the veil between our worlds, Guendolyn tight in my arms. "Close!" I barked.

Claws dug into the flesh of my back, slicing skin.

Arching, I grunted. I stumbled on my feet, swallowed by darkness, my back burning like flames.

I spun around, terror blinding my thoughts. The portal was gone. A severed clawed arm squirmed on the forest ground, blood soiling the dirt. "Lucky that's all you lost, you bastard."

Howls pierced the night, and sweat clung to my skin. *Fuck!*

I turned and ran through the woods, holding her tightly against me and praying I wasn't making the worst mistake of my life.

"Where is she?" Ahren's stiff words hung in the air between us, his shoulders growing rigid.

"She's safe here and nothing you need to worry about," I insisted as I shoved off the couch, my muscles tense from listening to my brother's ranting. I didn't for a moment think he'd let this go—I expected him not to—but hearing the disapproval in his voice was starting to wear on me.

A cold breeze swept into the room through the open window, carrying the chill of the encroaching winter.

Ahren pushed strands of his long hair out of his face, hair as white as snow, eyes ice blue. They matched the rest of the family's, well, except for me and Grandfather, the demented king. Many believed green eyes were signs of harnessing the power of second sight. The elders said spending too much time in others' minds drove him insane and killed him in the end. But I knew the truth. Grandfather's downfall had been because he'd entered my father's mind when he shouldn't have.

Deimos, my youngest brother, lounged on the sofa, smirking, watching us for pure entertainment. He still wore his leather hunting pants, mud splattered over them. Red blood streaked his neck and spotted his white hair that was pulled into a ponytail. He'd been hunting for fairies again, those blood-sucking vermin that had wiped out a nearby village loyal to our Court, leaving only decapitated bodies. They fed on brains and eyes. Filthy things.

"Don't feed me lies," Ahren barked, his face stern, the same look as Mother's when she was furious. Same high cheekbones and pale blue eyes. "And you know it's not her safety I'm worried about. You risked too much by going into the human realm. If Father finds out..." Disappointment crossed his face as he paced across the room, his heavy, black robe dragging behind him over the black stone floor. I looked away, tired of his theatrics.

I shook those memories away and marched to the window. "I don't expect anything less from you, brother."

The Shadow Court spread out below, palaces after

palaces of royals and aristocrats. Each building shone black beneath the midday sun with trims of varied colors around the roofs and windows. Down in the valley, the rest of the fae lived in small cottages. The higher anyone lived on the mountain, the more important their positioning. But I grew tired of the games, the backstabbing, the killings within the Shadow Court. Not to mention the endless battles with Ash Court. The Wandering Realms had been at war for as long as I'd been alive—twenty-five fae years.

Ahren's heavy breathing filled the room, and it irked me that he always had to oppose anything I suggested.

"You're not king yet," I announced. "You hold no power over me. And hell, you snort like a boar when you're pissed."

Deadly silence carved the space between us. Ahren's face twisted, his wry expression promising retribution. "Your childish remarks are not becoming of a prince."

"Fuck you. Is that preferable?"

"It might be entertaining to have a toy around the house," Deimos said, interrupting, his voice holding nothing but menace.

I turned on him, swallowing my anger. "Brother, you've killed every toy you were ever given. She isn't yours."

"And she's not yours, either," Ahren bit out, his mouth curling into a sneer.

My stomach warped in on itself, but fire soared through me. "I found her. She's mine," I snarled as a gust of icy air rushed into the room, pushing against my back, nudging me to step forward. I'd spent too long in her head to give her up so easily now.

"So, then, what's *your* plan?" Deimos reclined, one leg crossed over a knee, his arms stretched out on either side of the back of the couch.

"My plan is to save the girl. You know the stories of her past as well as I do. I finally tracked her down, so I took her before the wolves from Ash Court got a chance to slice her throat."

"Why? Her treachery isn't our business, and if that is her destiny—"

"Destiny," I bellowed. "Treachery? Have you forgotten what family you serve? That girl is the key to putting right what was wronged so long ago."

Ahren scoffed, forcing a laugh. "You're *not* my brother." He swung to Deimos. "Have you seen Luther? Because whoever this imposter is could never be my brother if he speaks of peace with the enemy Court."

I closed the distance to Ahren in two strides and grabbed him by the throat, my voice a growl. "You're going to be king one day. Do you intend to rule blindly or find a way to take control of both Courts under your command before every last standing fae is killed in battle? Otherwise, you may as well abdicate from the Shadow Court now."

Hate lashed his blue eyes. "Now, that's the Luther I know." With a hard shove against my hand, breaking my hold, he dragged me into a hug and pounded my shoulder with a flat hand. "We use the truth of who she really is to align the power to our side. Of course that might mean she must marry into our family so we can retain our power."

All I felt was anger boiling my blood, fury climbing over my body. Maybe I'd made a mistake telling them, but they'd have found out soon enough. We shared this palace… A location guarded and protected, enchantment instilled in the walls to make them impenetrable. This was the safest location for her, so I had to make them understand.

Ahren laughed, and a growl rolled through my chest, knowing exactly where he was going with his comment. When he said *marry into our family*, he meant *marry him*. I shoved against him, my vision blurred from the fury burning me. "She's not yours to take."

"Brother, since when are you averse to sharing?" Ahren's jaw clenched. "I haven't seen you this riled up since Father confiscated your pet eagle when you were six."

I arched a brow. "Confiscated doesn't come close to describe what he did."

"Told you not to go into Uncle's head," Deimos reminded me.

"Yeah, but we found out where he butchered that maiden girl," Ahren said.

"And yet I lost my pet." Because using my power of second sight on fae gave me away in a heartbeat, and Father forbade the use of such power in his kingdom.

"What's really going on, Luther?" Ahren asked, his voice softened for a change. "This isn't like you."

"They were going to kill her," I murmured, unwilling to share with them how I thought about her every day, how I longed to hear her voice in my mind, how I'd let myself fall so far that I'd risked everything to bring her to safety. "She holds power even if she doesn't know it yet."

"And yet you'll bring every wolf to our door because she might be special? She's been a rumor, a myth for so long… How can you be sure she is the one anyway?"

"You've both got it wrong." Deimos leaned forward on the couch, his arms pressed against his thighs. "If this girl is the rightful heir, if the stories are all correct, she's cursed. You both know the legend. If this is her, there's a reason she was sent away. Her return would cause both our enemies and even those in our family to wage war against us."

Ahren paused to consider the words, his posture still, a thumb running over the tips of his fingers as it always did when he was in deep thought.

"She won't be going near the Ash Court if I have anything to do with it."

Deimos and Ahren both stared at me with disbelief in their eyes. "Is that so?" Ahren said. "So you propose we keep her locked up forever? How will that benefit us?"

Deimos's mouth opened with a response, but the creak of the floorboards stole his words.

We stilled and swung our attention to the main door sitting slightly open.

A shadow slid behind the other side of the door, listening to us.

Something nudged my ribs.

I rolled over. "Stop it. I'll get up soon."

Another poke, and I grumbled. Swear to god, I just needed a few more minutes. Eyes opened, I croaked, "Jen, if—"

But it was a cat with eyes the color of topaz crystals staring at me. Another head bump from the black feline before she spun on her feet and leapt off the bed with a thump. "Hey, what was that about?" But when I looked around, my heart raced. Wait, this wasn't my room.

Black velvet curtains framed the windows in generous folds while lace curtains billowed in the refreshing breeze. This room was elaborate from the black granite walls to the carved mahogany headboard to the golden chair near the door with black cushion-ing, the arms chiseled to resemble bear paws.

Meow.

I leaned over the side of the bed, peering down at the little panther. "Where am I?"

She turned away, her head and tail high, and slinked across the room before hopping up on the chair. After turning in two circles, she curled up on the seat.

Right. Pushing my legs out of bed, I still wore my blue pajamas, the ones with the cute smiling moons. Dorky, but no one saw me in them.

At the window, I shoved the curtain aside to a bril-liant azure sky, free of clouds. A dark forest spread out as far as the eye could see, while mountains crowded in the distance like an army ready to strike.

Nothing seemed familiar, no sign of the castle or bridge. One minute I'd faced the man from my dreams —I rolled my eyes at how ridiculous I'd just sounded, even if he was the hottest man I'd ever seen—and the next, I'd woken up here. The rich room, the woods outside, me not at home. Yep, this was definitely a fantasy world inside my head.

I padded across the cold floorboards, unease curling in my gut. A quick scratch of the cat's head, and I stepped through the gap of the open door.

I encountered more elaborate furniture, where the black theme continued in a lounge room of sorts. I could get used to reclining in a pristine cushioned sofa with untouched silky cushions, overlooking the view. A huge stone fireplace swallowed the side wall. A thud came from behind me, and the small panther trailed at my feet.

"Decided to check up on me, I see?" I paused for her to catch up, then scratched behind her ears. She rubbed herself against my leg and led the way into a corridor with a garnet rug running the length of the hallway.

I should have been scared, but something about this place left me feeling calm. More than anything, I wanted to find out where I was because in the back of my mind, I suspected this might be the palace from my dreams. An explosion of warmth spread through my chest as I rushed along, staring at the dark walls, my bare feet tapping the cold stone floor. I ran a hand over black-and-white vases decorated in swirls and patterns that made no sense to me. Statues of lions and bears in attacking positions filled every nook. Walls barren of paintings and photos indicated a home devoid of memories.

Glass spheres hung from the ceilings on a chain, flames flickering inside them. They were mesmerizing and I had no clue how they burned.

Hiss...

I recoiled around so fast, my head spun. The little cat, her fur spiked, her tail bristled, stood on the tips of her paws inches from my leg. *Hssss.*

"What is it?" Dread skated down my spine. The

whole sixth sense animals had played on my mind. What in the world did the cat see? I retreated farther along the hall until my back hit something... or someone.

My heart in my throat, a small cry fell from my lips, and I jerked around to find an ornate vase wobbling back and forth.

My fear spiked, strangling my heart. My arms jutting outward, I steadied the damn thing that stood taller than me.

"Sweet freaking Jesus." I didn't need the vase smashing. Sure, it was a dream and all... I thought. But this place just felt real somehow. My dreams usually made my head feel fuzzy, but not now; this felt like a crisp new day. Regardless, I'd seen enough movies to know that making noise brought out the bad guys.

Hiss.

Behind me I found a dog sitting in the middle of the corridor, a cross between a German Shepherd and a Doberman, easily reaching my waist. Fluffy and golden in color, he stared at me with the biggest puppy eyes that melted me.

"Hey, where did you come from?" I asked in a singsong voice.

Little Panther backed away. I glanced around, and only the door I'd emerged from stood there. Moving closer to the dog, I reached out a hand. "Where were you hiding?"

A spark of electricity raced down my arms, and the air around the animal shimmered. Then his fur faded into thin air, vanishing, leaving behind a brown pelt, ears narrowing, stretching to sharp points, a long, thin tail whipping behind him with a barbed club on the end.

My mouth dropped open.

I couldn't breathe, couldn't comprehend what I'd just seen. My feet slipped backward. I had to leave. My heart thumped while somewhere behind me the cat hissed again. She knew better than me. This wasn't a cute dog, but a freaking hellhound.

His ears flattened, two rows of teeth bared.

A whimper fell from my lips.

Don't run from dogs, they say. They smell fear, they say.

To hell with sayings. I was about to die, so I catapulted myself away from the beast, a scream shoving forward. Heavy footfalls pounded the rug behind me. Heavy breaths, a snarl that promised my death.

My feet slammed the ground and a scream tore free past my throat. This felt too real to be a dream… God, I was going to die here and never wake up again. I'd heard that somewhere. Die in a dream and you're a goner.

Hissing buzzed right past my ear, and a black blur zipped in front of me. Panther had grown black bat wings, and she rushed ahead, beating them furiously.

Wait! Cat wings?

Nothing made sense right now, nothing but running for my life, knowing somehow that if the hound caught me, I'd be dog food.

Deep guttural threats thundered closer, and my skin rippled.

Panicked, I darted around the curve of the hallway, desperately searching for a way to escape.

Several doors lay ahead, and every muscle in my body clenched.

A sudden tug on the fabric of my pajama pants pulled them down.

I cried out, grappling to keep my pants on. "I swear to god if you eat me, I'll haunt you for eternity."

Panther hissed at the goddamn dog, and I grabbed the closest weapon: a golden statue of a rodent that weighed a ton, even though only the size of my head. I hurled it at the mutt.

Black eyes pierced my soul. He leapt out of the way inches from the statue slamming into his head and growled. The rodent hit the ground and cracked in two halves.

I threw myself at the nearest door, my hand scrambling with the handle, and fell through. The bat-cat swooshed inside just before I slammed it shut.

One hand tugging up my pants, the other shoved to the door, my heart pounding.

Thump.

The door shook, its hinges groaning. I flinched but stayed there, plastering a shoulder against the door, holding it, terrified the hound would chew his way in here. What dogs had two rows of teeth anyway?

Shaking like a leaf, I reached down to the back of my pants, finding a gaping hole. That shithead could have ripped my leg off. I could barely make sense of what that dog was, let alone what was going on in this weird building.

Meow.

Bat-cat fluttered to the ground, her little black wings folding and tucking against her body, blending into her fur.

"What exactly are you?" I crouched low and scratched her head, then slid my hand down her back as she arched, my fingers reaching over to her side, the thin bones of her wings sitting under her fur perfectly snug. They were real, all right. She curled against my hand, purring, and strolled deeper into a large room.

Several black couches sat in a U-shape, facing statues of beautiful women dressed in warrior Xena-like skirts, holding shields across their chests, carved into the sides and mantel of the fireplace.

Tapestries of lions and wolves caught in battle covered one wall, while an enormous butterfly display case hung from another. Wings of all colors... silver, mauves, coral, apple green, and so many more sat pinned to the white board. Butterflies? Couldn't be.

They were twenty times larger with a slightly transparent hue. Each was pinned to the board, on display. What flying insect carried such huge and beautiful wings?

A thump crashed into the door, the dog scratching to get in.

Adrenaline pulsed through my veins. With hurried steps, I rushed across the windowless room to another set of dark doors, far from the hellhound. The handle was icy to the touch, and I pushed it open, heading out just as the mutt growled furiously. Shutting the door to the room quickly, I retreated.

Except I hadn't stepped into a room, but some kind of indoor bridge. Wooden planks ran across the floor and an arched ceiling, tiled in the color of pearls overhead. Beautiful. But when I glanced to the waterfall cascading down a rockface to my right, my mouth fell open. I rushed over, and I hit a glass wall enclosing the beauty.

Sunlight poured in over the edge of the cliff. Was there a way out of this place? I'd never climb that sheer rockface safely, but maybe I'd find a way behind this glass.

Below, there was only darkness from my vantage point. Panther strolled past me, rubbing herself along the wall where glass globes sat on small pillars. Real fire flames flicked inside them.

Where was I?

I moved with fast steps along the wooden bridge that curved around the waterfall only to come upon another set of doors, one slightly ajar.

Faint voices floated from inside, and my stomach clenched. Definitely male. Quick steps took me closer, and I pressed an ear to the wood listening, while Panther looked up at me.

I pressed a finger to my mouth, praying she kept quiet.

"She won't be going anywhere near the Ash Court if I have anything to do with it," a masculine voice insisted, and I recognized him at once. The voice from my head, the man from the twisted woods who scared the hell out of me. And now I couldn't breathe and it felt like someone was choking me.

"Right?" another male responded, his voice deeper, more authoritative. "So you propose we keep her locked up forever? How will that benefit us?"

Were they talking about me? What in the world was Ash Court?

Panther shifted to head into the room, and I lunged after her, snatching her into my arms. The floorboards groaned under my step.

I clutched Bat-cat to my chest, not moving an inch. No one said a word from inside for a long moment.

"I know it's you, Guendolyn," *he* called out.

Hell!

CHAPTER 12

Shoulders back, I sucked in a breath and pushed into the room, my chin high. The first rule of intimidation was looking confident, even if I was crapping myself on the inside. And what was the worst that could happen? I'd wake up from this insane dream?

Panther purred in my arms as I stalked into the room.

I raised my head to find three men looking my way. My feet stopped working, as did my heart, because these guys... Sweet Jesus!

They were handsome... impossibly handsome. Pale skin. Red lips. Eyes full of sin.

I was helpless... and standing here in my pajamas left my cheeks burning up. But with their presence came a desire swirling inside me when I should have spun on my heels and marched the hell out of there, remembering the sexy man's words back in the twisted woods.

My attention lingered on him with his midnight hair draped over his shoulders. His presence left me covered in shivers.

When he smiled, his amber eyes lit up. He had something about him that made me swoon on my feet, left me staring, trying to work out what made him so perfect.

These three were unlike anyone I'd seen before. The tall guy stared at me with a crooked grin like I wasn't exactly what he'd expected. Long, white hair draped over his shoulders, adding a strange allure to him I couldn't quite work out.

The stranger on the couch wore his white hair loosely pulled into a ponytail. His shirt sat gaping open at the throat, splattered with a spray of blood. I should be afraid, well aware of how cruel guys could be.

"W-Where a-am I?" My voice shook in front of them. I wasn't the best around guys, even in my dreams apparently. Sucking at this was my specialty.

"You're home, little wolf. Well, not quite, but close enough." He bit his lower lip like he was nervous, and my heart clenched.

He strolled toward me in a deep green sleeveless robe over a shirt, tied together with a thick leather band around his waist, and dark pants. Already a smile played on his face, and he reminded me of Robin Hood. When he stretched his hand out to scratch the cat's head, my gaze raked over his strong forearms, corded muscles that could overpower me. Everything about him was dangerous… Yet all I could think about were the things we'd said to each other while he'd been a mere voice in my head. All the promises he made.

"You'll like it here."

His voice… melted me. It was the one attribute that belonged to the guy who comforted me after Noah had tried to rape me, who'd been there when I'd felt so alone in the world. But something about this dark-haired stranger stirred anxiety within me, a thick knot forming in my throat.

Panther leapt out of my arms, her wings extending in an instant, and she jumped onto his shoulder, sitting there like a parrot. With a shake, her wings tucked away and she rubbed her head against his.

"I see you've met Viper."

"Never seen a flying cat before, but cute name." Viper was the type of name I'd expect a guy to call his cat. "Sure beats Cujo in the hallway." I snorted a laugh and regretted it at once, my cheeks burning up. *Great job, Guen.*

"Cujo?" He arched a brow.

"The hell dog in that movie who attacks everyone?"

"Think she must be talking about Sir Wolf-A-Lot,"

the guy on the couch murmured. His voice was so deep, it cut through my heart.

"Fancy name for a hellhound who almost ate my pants," I blurted out, garnering no reaction aside from a cheeky grin from Amber Eyes scratching the cat on his shoulder.

Silence.

I felt their gazes on me, hungry eyes sliding over my moon pajamas, covering me in electric tingles. The tall guy was beyond good-looking and why was he wearing a cape? Everything about these three told me to run, but instead, my mind danced with other possibilities. Insane things like flirting and finding out who they were because anything was possible in a dream.

"So," I said, slicing through the awkwardness in the room, my voice deciding at that moment to break. "Is someone going to tell me what's going on? How I got here?"

Hunger burned in the tall one's eyes, blue as ice, and I lowered my gaze from his. I ought to be wary of him, I felt it in my bones.

"Yes, Luther," the stranger on the couch with the cutest, most devilish grin teased. "You going to tell her? Today might turn more amusing than I thought."

Luther? I stared at the man in front of me, the voice who I'd been talking to for years. Every day I'd expect to hear his voice, even if he annoyed me. I'd gotten used to having him there for me. But standing in front of him now, I kept losing my thoughts.

I rolled this name over in my mind, liking how it sounded. Luther. Dark and sexy. "Why didn't you tell me your name before when—?"

His hand took mine, his touch warm but firm, and he dragged me in a rushed walk across the room. Viper flew off in the opposite direction, while I stumbled after the man.

"Come, you must be starved."

We moved at a fast pace to another door at the other end of the room, the two others watching us with curiosity.

"I'm not hungry," I began, preferring to chat about who everyone was, but the moment Luther pulled open the enormous mahogany door, the waft of cake had my stomach rumbling. "Well, maybe a bite. I'm curious to see how food tastes here."

He looked down at me strangely. "You're suspicious?"

"Should I be?"

He guided me to a round table with seating for at least ten people. Designs of animals were carved into the molding of the high ceiling, vases flowing with white and yellow flowers filled the shelves, and statues of more animals adorned the corners.

"Fancy dining room," I said. "We usually just eat on the couch while watching TV."

"Take a seat." He shut the door behind us, closing the others out, and a chill hit my middle. Why was he shutting us in here alone?

He strolled across the room to a small side door, vanishing inside. I toyed with the idea of heading back the way I came. I wasn't sure who to trust here.

I looked out past the floor-to-ceiling windows to the ocean of trees, to the snowcapped mountains, the sun sitting high, meaning it had to be around noon.

The view was extraordinary and made the perfect postcard shot. Where was my phone when I needed it?

Footfalls sounded as Luther marched back into the room, carrying a bowl. He placed it in front of me on the table. "The kitchen is preparing more food for you."

Stew sat in the bowl with large pieces of carrots and potatoes and meat, the aroma overwhelming and delicious. Taking the spoon, I flopped in the seat and dug right in when an older man in black clothes and a white apron rushed out to bring me a plate of freshly cut bread and butter. His face remained stern, and I caught him sneaking a look up at me... curious to see who I was.

I smiled, but he lowered his gaze and marched back to the kitchen. Okay, strange.

I had no idea how hungry I was, but I grabbed a piece of bread, smeared it with butter, and ate like I'd been starved for days.

Luther sat one chair away, reclining. I pushed the bread plate to him and he helped himself.

"This is good, especially for a dream. I mean, technically, I can eat what I want without getting fat, right?" I pushed another spoonful into my mouth.

"You think this is a dream?"

I raised my gaze to him. "This is all in my head. Just like you."

"You think I'm just in your head?" He took a bite of the bread in his hand.

His question threw me. "When you say it like that, I don't know."

The servant returned with a silver dish piled high with slices of steaming roast, surrounded by vegetables, as well as a plate of various cheeses and fruit.

Everything smelled divine. "Thank you," I called out as the man rushed away.

"Eat up," Luther murmured, watching me with curiosity in his gaze.

"This is a lot." But I didn't stop and filled my plate. "So let's say this isn't a dream as you say. Why did you bring me here? What do you want?"

He just sat there, watching me eat. His lips twitched each time I opened mine to take another bite. He was enjoying himself, enjoying just staring.

"Enjoying the show?" I asked.

"It's a fascinating one."

Everything he said was deliberate and intended to

affect me. Just like the things he'd say in my mind. Before, his voice had been enough to leave me breathless, but now merely looking at his full lips undid me, the intensity of his eyes. I kept having thoughts I shouldn't have. Like how his lips might feel against mine, if someone like me even interested a man like him.

"Is it good?" he asked, continuing to stare at me.

"Delicious."

Sitting in such close proximity, all I could do was admire him, those perfect angles, the square jawline… Flawless.

"Why didn't you tell me your name whenever we spoke?"

"Names come with power and you never know who's listening," he said bluntly.

"Listening to our thoughts?" I huffed and dug back into my food. "As if."

His eyebrows arched, but he just ate his sliced bread, amusement behind his irises.

We'd spoken every day for years, his presence my only companion. He was the only one there for me when shit had gone sideways. It was always me who'd opened up, never him, but he'd listened… had always listened.

So how well did he know me? Because he wasn't what I'd expected.

"Am I what you expected?" I felt stupid asking the

question and lowered my attention to the food. "That's dumb. Forget it."

"Not at all. You are… like a storm that's burst into my home and nothing will ever be the same again."

I stared at him, lowering the bread from my mouth. "Wow, really? I'm that bad?"

"Why do you consider that bad?" His lips tensed, but he remained reclined in his seat, studying me.

I rolled my eyes. "Forgot. You answer everything with a riddle."

"They're not riddles. You're not listening."

With more food in my mouth, I answered, "Because I'm naive."

His lips curled into a smirk, and that right there was exactly how I'd pictured him every time he'd made such comments to me. He'd always clearly been dripping in arrogance, but I'd never expected to react to him so insatiably. To see chemistry behind his eyes, an invitation to get closer. My heart beat harder.

"Who are you really, Luther?" I bit into a piece of roast when the servant returned with gold decorated glasses filled with something reddish and a plate of purple cake.

I smiled at the older man, who nodded and left with haste. Chasing the food down with grape juice, I kept looking up at Luther, who watched every move I made, never missing a beat, not even when I picked a crumb off my pajama top. He looked at me as if he knew my desires, my wishes, my fears, leaving me trembling. When he was in my head, was it only my words he sensed, or everything?

"In the Wandering Realms, I'm the prince of darkness, a lord, a master." He spoke so smoothly, but beneath his words stirred power. "My older brother is the heir to the throne, while my younger brother and I will remain princes by his side."

"Throne? Who is your dad if he's king? What country are we in?" I wasn't sure my mind was this elaborate to make up such stuff.

"You still seem to think this is a dream."

I offered him a crooked smirk. "Well, isn't it?"

"You'd wager your life on that?" His mouth tightened. He climbed to his feet, but I stood with him, my pulse racing.

"Don't go. Tell me more. What is the Ash Court?" He'd make me wait when I had so many questions.

His eyes narrowed, his breathing quickened. "Spying is an offense punishable by death in the Shadow Court."

I studied his beautiful face, waiting for him to break into a smile, to laugh, something to indicate he was joking. Except his gaze darkened.

"How much did you hear?" he demanded to know.

"J-Just that part," I croaked, clearing my throat. We both stood there, not a word spoken. My mouth was parched and I wracked my brain for something to say.

What didn't he want me to have heard? That they were going to keep me locked up forever?

"Come," he said. "You'll wash and then I'll properly introduce you to my brothers."

"I'm perfectly fine." But my words went unheard as he stormed toward the kitchen like a charging bull.

"Hey, I said *no*," I called out, standing my ground.

He halted and looked at me over his shoulder, his brows pulling together. "You seem to have forgotten your place."

My jaw clamped together. He was a man used to getting his way, to others doing as he ordered. I knew this… had heard it in his voice so many times, but I kept my head raised, not hiding my defiance.

"I don't belong to you."

He licked his lips and the fire in his eyes ignited. "You were always mine, little wolf. You just never knew it."

"Don't touch me," I yelled, batting away the servants' hands.

Two women, older than me, tugged and pulled at my pajama pants and top. It was bad enough they'd dragged me through the kitchen, down a hallway, and into another room, but now I had to take a bath? They each wore a floor length black medieval-style dress with short, flared sleeves, and an elastic waist.

And Luther leaned a shoulder against the doorway, smirking, enjoying himself. Was he going to watch as they stripped me?

"I'm not going in there. My pajamas are staying on." I stumbled from their reach and eyed the freestanding metal tub with golden clawed feet, filled with water. At home, I'd jump at the chance, as we only had a shower, but I didn't do communal baths. I wanted to be sick.

"Mistress, you need a wash and to wear proper clothes. Not those…" The redhead flapped her hand toward my pajamas, scrunching up her nose. "Those are not fit for the princes' eyes. They'll be burned."

"No!" I squeaked. "They're from Jen. Don't you dare." I wrapped my arms around my middle, recoiling. Jen had gifted these to me on my last birthday, insisting I'd look cute in smiling moon PJs. I'd disagreed but had never had the heart to tell her, yet I wore them regardless.

The brunette with bouncy curls lunged from my left, and I darted in the opposite direction, swerving around a chair, my sight on the doorway. I'd bowl right through Luther if he didn't get out of the way.

I threw myself past him, but his hand lashed out across my stomach, and roughly swooped me off the ground, cradling me like I was a child in his strong arms.

I lost my breath from the sudden impact, being so close to him, from the solid hardness of his muscles, but it didn't stop me from driving a fist against his chest. "Put me down. I'm serious."

Not a word. He carried me across the room and dunked me straight into the tub, clothes and all. Lukewarm water swallowed me. I splashed and sat upright, water sloshing everywhere. I wiped my eyes, fury bubbling in my veins.

"Who do you think you are?" I yelled.

Luther stared down at me, his gaze laser-beaming to my chest. My nipples pushed against the wet pajama top, and my arms twitched to cover myself.

"This is my home and that means following my rules." He ripped his attention from me and marched out of the room, his boots hitting the tiled floor before shutting the door behind him with an echoing thunk.

"Asshole." My fingers gripped the edge of the metal tub.

The maids were on me in a second, both pulling the wet sleeves of my top, dragging the rest up and over my head.

"Hey! Don't take my pajamas."

One lathered my hair roughly, taking out her revenge on me refusing her orders. Water sloshed over my face, getting into my nose and mouth.

"You're either a very brave or stupid girl," the red-haired woman murmured.

"How do you figure?" I winced at their roughness, searching for my top outside the tub.

"You raised a hand to the prince. That's instant death." Shadows danced over her face from the sphere lights, but fear pulled at her expression.

"Is there anything you can do here that won't lead to *instant death*?"

The brunette grinned, her eyes laughing at my comment.

The red-haired woman heaved at my pants. "Take

them off," she barked, fierceness behind her gaze, her hands already pulling on the fabric. I shuffled out of them, sliding them down my hips, and yanked them off me. I sat in the water naked and curled my knees to my chest, feeling vulnerable, ashamed. She stared at my bare body with a smug grin. My hips were too big, my chest not big enough, and I had no waist. I pushed their hands off me. "Let me wash myself. I can do this. Just don't destroy my clothes," I pleaded, not meeting their judging eyes.

"Fine," the redhead huffed. "I'll get them washed." With a flick of the soap into the tub, she hurried out of the room, her steps heavy despite a slight limp. When the door shut, I raised my gaze to the brunette.

"She has a snake's tongue but is harmless. She can't let the princes down. None of us can." The rest of her words went unsaid…

The maid sat on the edge of the tub folding several towels, and in a way, she reminded me of Jen. There was an easiness about her, a caring nature, even if she wasn't the most tactful person in the world.

"So, he's really a prince? Or…"

"Absolutely, mistress."

"You don't need to call me that. Makes it sound like I'm having an affair." I found the soap in the water, rolling it over and over in my hands, suds building and spreading over my hands. "And his brothers, one is to be the king?"

She nodded. "Be wary of him most of all."

Dread cut across my gut. The heir's icy eyes had carried a savage hunger and my instincts screamed to not trust him.

Her cheeks paled, and she gasped with panic. "Forgive me. I never should have said that." Her attention sailed to the door and back, panic buckling her posture, her hands gripping the towel. What had the princes done to scare her so much?

I reached over, laying a wet hand on hers. "It's okay. I won't say anything. Promise." In truth, the more time I spent in this world, the more I questioned if this was a dream. And with that came a fear that squeezed the life out of me. Such places didn't exist, but I'd seen the kingdom my whole life through my dreams. Even once in an alley. It looked as real as the buildings back home. I wasn't sure of much lately, even my own identity.

"Do you know who I am?" I murmured, drawing back into the water, lathering myself.

She stared at me with her brows pulling together. "Should I? You're just another woman the princes bring to their palace. It isn't our place to question such things."

I splashed the soap from my arms, unsure what to make of her response. So they brought others here regularly... I wasn't a fool, knowing what she implied, but her words left me torn, my insides cold that Luther had had others here just like me.

The red-haired lady stepped back into the room, distracting me. Deep violet fabric draped over her arm, satin and spiderweb-like. Her bulging eyes locked on me. "You're not ready yet?" she snapped.

"Give her a few moments, Lys. She's just a child." She spoke almost like she pitied me, as if she knew my fate. I wasn't being sacrificed… was I?

I ran the soap over my legs before the woman with red hair and redder eyes manhandled me again. Out of the tub, I dried myself as they watched me, and then they drowned me with the dress.

My arms shoved in the air, the towel tumbled down from around my body. The women poked and pulled, shuffling the outfit down over my head and dragging it down my body. Soft satin brushed over my skin, tight across my chest, the skirt made of several layers that fell to my feet. Long sleeves sat off the shoulder, lacy and loose down to my knuckles.

Taking in a deep breath came with effort. "I think it's too small. I need the next size up."

I ran a hand over my chest, squished into the dress, the tops of my breasts sticking out like perfect half-balls. On the bright side, this made it look like I had bigger breasts than I did, and that was a bonus in my books any day. I shifted the material around my waist, but the red-haired woman slapped my hand.

"Do you wish to ruin the gown?"

"It's too tight. I need to breathe." The deep violet

gown shimmered like a night's sky. For the first time, I had a thin waist. Maybe sacrificing breathing was worth it to look like Barbie.

"Sit," the bossy woman ordered, and I did as she instructed, the taut material digging into me, making bending close to impossible. They combed my hair while I grimaced and gritted my teeth, convinced I'd have no hair left after they were finished. The brunette stood in front of me and placed a golden band around my head, settling it high on my brow. I reached up, fingers fumbling over the thin band made of lots of small joined stars.

She then pinched my cheeks hard.

"Ouch." I flinched away. "What're you doing?" My face still stung from her attack. "Why would you do that?"

"To bring color to your face, girl." She rolled her eyes like this was common practice.

"That's why blush was invented." Damn, my cheeks hurt like hell.

The red-haired woman kneeled in front of me and pushed my feet into pointy, black flat shoes that hugged a bit too tightly around my toes. She shook her head. "You say strange things. Now up. We need to go." On her feet, she grasped my hand and hauled me out into the hall, dragging me with haste.

Dark stone walls, fire spheres, and rugs. No paintings to decorate the hall. Even the statues were absent in this part of the mansion.

With each step, the fabric of the skirt split from ankle to mid-thigh across each leg, revealing too much leg.

"Wait. I'm not ready," I insisted, pulling against her, straining to make out in the dark where she dragged me.

"You're more than ready," she murmured while wrenching me by her death-grip. We passed so many doors in this palace, I couldn't remember how to get back to the bedroom if I tried.

I stumbled after her in our mad rush, where there wasn't even a mirror to view how I looked, but there was a bigger problem.

"Stop. I'm not ready," I said.

We paused in front of a door and the woman faced me, a sneer twisting her lips. "You won't last, none of them do, so just follow the rules and get this over with. Never say *no* to the princes. Never talk back. Never insult them."

I stilled, my mind reeling from her instructions. "I can't say *no* to anything?"

"No one says *no* to them. Do you understand?" Her voice grew stern.

The idea of them having such control of me was terrifying.

She glared at me before pushing the door open. I blinked into the brightly lit room.

"Smile and do as they say," she whispered, shoving a hand into my back.

I stumbled into the room on wobbly legs. She slammed the door, closing me in there alone. I rushed to grab the handle, trying it, but it was locked.

"Yeah, thanks for that," I mumbled.

A light breeze brushed through my wet hair, down my arms, and fluttering through the layers of fabric from my skirt, the touch like tender fingers running over my legs.

I glanced around the narrow room with a long, wooden table and a dozen chairs made of deep cherry wood.

A battle scene between bears was carved in the mantel over the fireplace. Flames crackled and spat embers, casting long shadows over the rug woven with intricate patterns. Tapestries hung off the rest of the walls, each depicting landscapes. Men on horses hunting in the woods. Castles glimmering beneath the moonlight. I stepped in front of one image… a bridge suspended between two mountains. Just like the one from my dreams. I'd always thought the kingdom had to have been a special place. Why else would one have to climb a mountain and cross such a long bridge to reach it?

Across the room, double doors suddenly opened,

sunlight pouring into the room. I flinched, my heart slamming into my ribcage.

Luther stood there, his expression full of surprise. Intrigue. A smile crept on his face, and the air in the room thickened.

Heat seared my cheeks. Any intention I had of demanding the truth and forcing the point until the princes relented dwindled.

Luther's gaze sharpened on me with that raw hunger I'd seen his brothers wear earlier. His stare was the kind I'd expect from a predator stalking me.

He rocked on his feet toward me, tall and so handsome. For those few moments, as he closed the distance between us, he'd captivated me. The power he carried. The breadth of his shoulders. The intensity of his stare, his gaze roaming over my body, his lips curling into a devilish grin.

Something about him drew me toward him like we were bound by an invisible string, drawing us closer and closer together.

"You look spectacular." Leaning in, a brush of his breath over my cheek left me quivering.

He smelled masculine and of musk, and my heart thumped so hard, its thunder beat in my ears.

"The fabric of your dress is feather-light, following every delicious curve. Looking like this..." He shuddered, his hands on my arms tightening, but he never finished his sentence. He was holding back, but why?

"What's wrong?" I whispered.

His eyes narrowed with intensity, as if whatever was on his mind was overwhelming, consuming. "What do you want to hear? That I can't get you out of my thoughts? How I want you pinned to the wall, beneath me?"

Fear should have pulsed through me, and I ought to have been scared, but arousal settled through me instead. With those few words, a tickle stroked my inner thighs, and I pictured myself beneath him, begging him to show me how to forget the world. I yearned to touch him, to see him fully. I'd never felt this way before, not to this intensity. I'd never had a guy speak to me in a way that left me too paralyzed to respond.

"You're not ready for me. I see that now." He gripped my hand and drew me toward the balcony, our connection electrifying, leaving me breathless, unable to think about anything except his fingers on me.

But his words hurt. He thought I wasn't ready to be with him? That I was too young, too naive, too… too what?

Except I was letting him get to me, allowing him to play with my mind.

Swallowing hard, I followed him onto the balcony, a red-tiled oversized ledge with a black metal fence around us, formed into roses and thorny stems.

An ocean of green and blues and whites burst

across the forest landscape beyond. "Wow, it's incredible from up here."

"Best view in the kingdom."

I glanced over to him, my heart still racing, my body tingling all over.

"Come. Take a seat."

Behind him, his two brothers reclined in grand golden chairs. Mesmerizing eyes. Lips parted. The whitest hair that seemed to gleam in the sunlight.

A rush of air and something nudged my hip. I turned to find no one, but when I glanced down, the blackest irises met mine. Pointy ears, short brown fur, and his pointy tail stilled. The hellhound!

My stomach dropped like a brick sinking to the bottom of the ocean. Instinct flexed through me. I flinched against Luther, my hands grappling for him, my fists holding on to his shirt while I shoved myself behind him. Not my finest moment, but I didn't need that beast ripping me apart.

The two princes laughed. Yep, they'd watch me get eaten without breaking a sweat to help, and I hated them for enjoying this moment.

"He won't hurt you," Luther insisted. I didn't believe him.

"Sir Wolf-A-Lot wouldn't hurt a fairy," Luther cooed and reached over, scratching the mutt's head.

"Is that meant to make me feel better?" I murmured, then remembered the maid's warning about dealing with the princes. But I didn't care, not when my heart pounded so hard, it might break through my ribcage.

The mischievous prince with his hair pulled in a ponytail reclined back more in his throne-like seat, watching me.

"It's true," he said. "That's why he's our pet dog now. He runs away from things he ought to hunt. Luther came up with the childish name, but now the animal won't answer to anything else. It's like he enjoys mocking us each time we call him."

The dog stared at me intently and not with loving eyes. Yep, he saw me as a meal.

Luther's hand was on mine. "You're safe. I give you my word."

I loathed that they saw me helpless, scared.

"Sit," the tallest prince commanded in a low tone, gesturing to the small stool in front of them.

I raised a brow, but with a push at my back from Luther, I moved to my designated seating, gritting my jaw.

In my perfect gown, I hunched low on the small wooden chair with only three legs, my knees tight and raised from the low seat. Gripping the fabric of my gown, I kept shifting around, annoyed I didn't get a fancy chair. Knowing my luck, this thing would break under me, and I'd flash them all gloriously.

Sir Wolf-A-Lot padded toward me and sat less than a foot from me, staring at me as if he might lunge at any moment and bite my head off. My hands shook while I clenched the fabric tighter.

Ignoring the sweat rolling down my back and the mutt who probably smelled my fear and was licking his lips, I stared up at the three princes on their regal seats.

"Why don't I get a proper chair?" I blurted out, not wanting to be at the same head height as Cujo.

"Why do you think?" Luther asked in a serious voice.

"So you can feel superior." I smirked at him.

The prince with a ponytail laughed. "She has a spine. Let's keep her."

Luther wore a grim expression. "I'll get her a different chair." He huffed and got to his feet, leaving the balcony.

I turned away, staring out at the landscape, still clueless as to where I was, and I hugged myself over the fact that I had to deal with this stupidity, these games. A test of obedience? Trying to see if I'd sit there like an idiot or stand up for myself?

Moments later, he returned with a chair and I slid into it once he set it down, crossing my legs and facing the three of them. Now I felt less of a peasant and more like someone at an interview.

"Guendolyn, let me introduce you to my two brothers," Luther began, and my mind pulsed at the name he'd called me like he knew more about me than I did.

He glanced over to the tallest man. "Ahren Lorcayn,

the eldest and heir to the Shadow Court. Next to him is Deimos Lorcayn, my younger brother and third prince of the throne."

They all stared at me as if waiting for me to introduce myself. "I'm Guen."

"It's Guendolyn," Luther corrected with a smirk, to which I furrowed my brow.

"It's Guen." My voice rose more than I'd anticipated, rousing Cujo into a low, gravelly growl.

"Never talk back," the maid had said.

"Guendolyn," Luther warned.

"The thing is…" Ahren leaned forward, his ice blue eyes invading my space, spearing through me. "Everyone knows who you are here, that your name is Guendolyn, what you represent… Everyone except you."

My defiance crushed down around me. To have him speak as if he knew me, of things they kept from me, left me feeling hollow, like someone had stolen everything I owned while I wasn't looking.

"I know of your dreams of our land. How it possesses you to paint what you see," Ahren declared.

"What do you know?" I whispered, terrified of what secrets had been kept from me.

"That you have fae blood in your veins, that Guendolyn is a name that has passed over the lips of most in the kingdom, that you're the lost girl taken from our world."

I blinked a few times at Ahren, waiting for my brain to catch up, for the wheels to make sense of what I'd heard. Breaths came too fast while the three of them watched me like somehow Ahren's words were real. Fae? Really? Taken from their world?

Yep, I'd finally broken down. My brain had snapped, and I'd watched way too many fantasy movies.

A nervous laugh fell from my lips. "Well, if I were a fae, I'd have found my wings long ago, my ears would be pointy, I'd… I don't know, what else do fae do?"

There was no crack in their stiff demeanors, and it felt surreal to speak so seriously about such things with three men who belonged on the covers of magazines, who left me swooning.

"Only fairies have wings." Deimos scoffed like I ought to have known that tidbit. "And you don't want to go anywhere near them. Now, as for pointy ears"— he shrugged—"some fae have them; others don't. It's more of a family line attribute."

My mouth gaped open, unsure how to take his response. Luther had implied earlier that this wasn't a dream, but if he'd spoken the truth, then what? I'd somehow come into a fantasy land of fae and fairies and kings?

Sir Wolf-A-Lot licked himself loudly. Oh, right, and freaking shape-shifting hellhounds.

The servant from earlier came in carrying a silver

platter and handed Ahren a drink in a jewel-studded crystal goblet, then the other two princes, then me. I accepted and drank two mouthfuls, quenching my dried throat. "So, I'm a lost person from this world, you say." I pressed the goblet to my lips, finishing the refreshing minty iced tea. The man refilled my drink from a golden pitcher.

"Something like that," Luther added.

I shifted in my seat. They might have been the most beautiful men in the world, but they lied through their teeth and kept secrets. It lay behind their gazes, their clipped responses.

"If I'm from this place, where are my parents?" I asked.

Something shifted behind Ahren's eyes but vanished as quickly as it had come. "There's no news on your parents. We've searched." The corner of his eye twitched.

Liar. Big, fat liar.

My breath came too fast, and I couldn't hold back the words. "If you don't intend to tell me the truth, don't mock me with lies," I retorted. "Speak honestly."

Never insult them.

Ahren bristled, his nostrils flaring as he glared at me with narrowing eyes. "Do not challenge me," he roared, his hands gripping the arms of his chair. "On your knees."

Fear strangled me, and I looked to Luther for help,

but he sat back with a curious expression, goddamn enjoying himself.

I shouldn't have said anything when I had absolutely nothing nice to say, but the response flew out. "Like I told your brother, I'm not yours to control. You hide so much behind that smile, but like someone once told me, we all have shadows. I'd rather we speak the truth."

Never say no *to the princes.*

Ahren shot to his feet, his expression twisted and warped, darkening, but his gaze never left me. He marched closer, and panic soared through me. I jolted to my feet, but he moved too fast. His hand shot out and seized me by the throat, squeezing.

I grasped for his hand, pulling at the fingers that blocked my breathing. And terror... real terror locked around me like a straitjacket. This was real and this madman would kill me. Tears sprung to my eyes.

"Little girl, you keep pushing me," he spat. "Next time, you'll learn how to fly off my balcony."

CHAPTER 14

A scream tore from somewhere in the distance behind the walls of the bedroom.

I shuddered. The terrible sound came every now and then for the last hour, drowning me in images of the princes torturing someone... picturing how it could be me next.

I paced from the locked door to the lush bed I'd woken in that morning. The servants had locked me in here at Ahren's furious command, terror etched on their faces for their own safety. Except I'd been warned, and I hadn't listened. Stupid.

Didn't make me hate him less. I hated all of them, and more than anything, I prayed I'd wake up from this horrible dream. I'd had enough of this pretend world.

Except the worrying ache in my stomach told me

otherwise. I shook my head, refusing to believe this was real. It couldn't be…

Images of Noah hurting me in his car burned across my mind, pushing and pushing. He'd thought he could take what he wanted from me.

Fingers pulling at my sweater.

Lips clamped on my mouth.

Stop, Noah!

But he never did… Never listened to me.

I hugged myself, trying to shake away the memories.

Memories that were scars on my mind, deep and painful, hateful things that reminded me how alone I felt in this world.

I'd begged Luther to take me from that life… just as he'd promised he would, but if this was the world he'd brought me to, was it any better?

For so long, I'd dreamed of a fantasy world and wondered what lay behind my dreams…needing an escape. But now, all I thought of was home. To hear Jen bossing me around, Oliver saying crappy stuff, and Luke being the voice of reason over dinner. I didn't miss school, especially not after my last encounter with Noah. Those jerks never let anything slide. My mind started to spiral down into that darkness, but I shoved it aside, marching back toward the tiny window.

I didn't miss Antonio and sure as hell never wanted to see Sabrina again.

I'd only been here a day, but it felt like a week.

I was the girl who wanted to fit in. To be normal. To be accepted.

I was the girl needing to understand who I was. Where I'd come from.

I was the girl dying to find my real parents.

The broken girl.

Ahren said they'd searched for my parents. I didn't believe him, but he'd revealed that indeed, I belonged here.

Hours passed.

Tired of pacing, I slept most of the day, and someone must have come into the room to leave my smiley moon pajamas, freshly washed and laid on my bed.

The sun had long ago dipped behind the mountains, and a single fiery globe flickered in the corner of the room, suspended from the ceiling, tossing shadows about. I padded toward the window, where the breeze rushed in, sending the lace curtain into a flurry and chilling my skin.

Outside, the drop from my window was a fifty feet drop into woodland, and my stomach lurched. I'd never get out. Forest spread outward on either side of the black stone building, revealing nothing else. Even if I tied all the bedsheets together, I'd never make it all the way down. An urgency pulsed through me that I'd die if I remained imprisoned in this room.

Are you hurt? Luther's voice startled me. I turned toward the room, expecting to find him there, my gut tight with anticipation… betraying me when I found myself alone and his voice lingering in my head.

Are you mad?

I instinctively touched my neck where his brother had choked me. "A bit."

A bit hurt or a bit mad?

"Both."

My brother has a temper, but he'd never endanger your life.

"Could have fooled me. He threatened to throw me over the balcony." My voice climbed, my breaths racing more than they should have.

You were very confrontational…

I bristled, my mouth gaping open at his comment, but I shut it back up because it wasn't like he was standing in the room with me. "Are you kidding me?"

This isn't like your realm, little wolf. Speaking out of place can get you killed here. There was almost a thread of concern behind his voice, like he feared the trouble I'd get into by not thinking things through.

"Well, I'm sick and tired of the secrets. Why won't you tell me who I am and where my parents are?"

Silence fell. At least he had the decency not to lie to me like Ahren, but was ignoring me any better?

There are two sides to every story.

"I get the feeling I'll be the sucker in both stories."

Why would you think that?

I shrugged to myself and flopped onto the hard mattress. "Because with my track record, things never go well."

I have a surprise for you.

"Yeah, what's that?"

You shall see soon.

"Like *tonight* soon?"

He laughed, the sound honeyed, breaking through my defenses, reminding me of the times we'd talk for hours about nothing and everything.

You miss me already?

Mischief curled over his words, and unlike previous times we'd talk, now I pictured the devilish grin, the amber eyes lighting up, the full lips I wanted to taste. Heat swept over me so fast, I collapsed onto my back, hugging a pillow.

I was a walking contradiction, but Luther had been part of me for so long. Without him... I wasn't sure what was left. Loneliness?

"I said nothing about missing you. I was just curious about this surprise."

Promise it will be worth your while.

"I'll hold you to that."

Silence.

"Why am I locked in my room?" And why hadn't he come to talk to me in person instead of speaking through my mind? The words played on my mind, but

I couldn't say them out loud, still torn between being pissed at him and wondering if this was a dream. Or was I simply having the biggest infatuation with a made-up guy in my head? The latter worried me... *terrified* me. To add to that, he had two douche brothers I wanted to punch in the face and kiss at the same time. I was completely and utterly broken.

For your safety, in case anyone outside the palace finds out you're here.

Almost too afraid to ask, the words came in a whisper. "Who wants to hurt me?"

It's complicated. I'll tell you soon, I promise. You need to trust me.

Trust was the kind of word that grew thorns and drew blood when you least expected it.

"It's funny, you know," I began. "Talking to you like this feels like just us in the world, and I can say anything. Hell, you've seen me at my worst."

But?

"But... When I see you in person?" I grimaced to find the right way to say this; some part of me worried I was headed down a dangerous road. Did I really know him despite talking to him for years, sharing all my fears and worries with him? "It doesn't feel like you," I breathed.

You think I'm a different person?

"No, not like that." I rolled over on my stomach, swinging my feet up and down on the bed. "More like I struggle to find my words. You…" Intimidated me. Looked so freaking hot that if I'd worn panties, they would have melted right off me. I'd fantasized about feeling his hands and lips on me.

He said nothing and my heart stopped.

"Can you hear my thoughts when I don't speak them?" I had a heady feeling at what he secretly knew about my innermost desires.

Would you like me to?

"Hell no!" My cheeks were on fire. "I don't even know how this is happening."

It's a bond I created. I can't tap into your thoughts unless you open a link and let me in.

"Yeah, it's better we keep it this way." My mouth felt dry and I licked my lips, convinced I'd die if he heard all my thoughts.

But I can feel bits of your emotions when we're connected. Like right now, I'm burning hot… I know you desire me, that you—

"Stop. Don't." Oh, my god, I wanted to fall into a pit and vanish. Keeping my words in check I could do, but my emotions… they were uncontrollable beasts.

I meant what I said earlier today.

His voice slid over my skin like tender fingers, and I didn't need to ask—I knew exactly what moment he spoke of. His words rolled over my mind: *"I want you pinned to the wall, your legs open."*

Those words tortured me, leaving me consumed by

so many thoughts. I never expected to feel such things, never expected him to react the same way to me.

Until now… until Luther breathed hope into me.

Or was it another cruel joke? I got the impression these three brothers loved to play games.

Did I embarrass you?

"No." I forced a laugh that had me cringing at how fake I sounded, but his question left me feeling more exposed than when he'd whispered those words. He saw right through me, all pretense aside, so how could I be anything but myself with someone who sensed every emotion I had?

I will let you sleep, little wolf.

"Goodnight."

I curled up in bed, clutching my pillow, and hated the tingles in my stomach, for believing Luther wouldn't harm me. I closed my eyes. *Please let me wake up at home. Please.*

***

"Guen!" Jen yelled from across the living room. "What were you thinking?"

I just stood there, back at home, staring at her, at Oliver playing a game on the TV, Luke cooking in the kitchen. And I knew this wasn't real. I always knew when I dreamed… I was there, but not really.

"Are you even listening?" she ranted, rage warping her features.

"What?" I mumbled, running a hand through my

hair. My fingers caught on the metal headband and I pulled it off my brow. Why was I still wearing this? I ran a thumb over the golden link of stars.

"We have to pay for all damages to Noah's car!"

Her words grabbed my attention and I jerked my head up. "I didn't damage his damn car."

She stormed across the room and yanked open a drawer in the kitchen, pulling out something, but I didn't feel right, like I was the intruder in this home... in this life. Like this whole time I'd been an imposter pretending to fit but never could, no matter how hard I tried.

"Then why was this under your bed?" She gripped the glass-looking gearstick from Noah's car.

My heart squeezed. "Were you searching my room?"

"It's not your room anymore," she snapped, her voice shaky. "You're moving to the basement. Evelyn will stay in your room now. And you will pay back every cent to Noah's dad with the money you earn from your part-time job."

"No, that'll take me forever. I did nothing to his car." Even in my dream, the guy was a douche.

"Guen." She kept shaking her head, her disapproval cutting through me.

Fury curled my hands into fists, the golden stars of the headband digging into my palms, breaking skin. I'd had enough of everyone blaming me, thinking I did everything wrong. The constant accusations stung, fueling the flames inside me.

Stop.

Breathe.

But my brain refused to pause.

"You wanna know the truth?" I shouted, my words quivering. "I tried to get my car back because Noah said he'd help, but instead he tried to rape me." Words and tears poured from me, the world shattering around me.

I blinked back the tears, but already the darkness came for me, and while I couldn't hear Jen's words, her terrified face cut into my heart. But I knew that had been a dream with Jen, it felt fuzzy in my head like the twisted woods dreams I'd had in the past. And in a heartbeat, my world fell into darkness.

***

My eyes flipped open to the perfect white ceiling, to elaborate moldings in the corners. I didn't move, didn't breathe, didn't do a damn thing.

I'd woken up back in the fae world, and my insides sank.

But my head remained at home... focused on the pain I'd seen in Jen's eyes. The sharpness in my chest deepened, and tears drenched my cheeks.

I shouldn't have told her. And I wouldn't tell her when I finally returned home from this place. I'd rather she believed I'd crashed the car than see the anguish on her face at knowing what Noah had done. She shouldn't hurt for me—I didn't want her to. I lifted my hand to find no cuts in my palm, and on the bedside table, sat the golden headband. Just a dream. A freaking stupid dream.

When I finally pushed my legs out of bed, a piece of paper tumbled out with me.

I snatched it off the floor and unfolded it, moving over to the window for better light.

Leave this place. Run before it's too late for you.

I stilled on the words before turning the note over, finding no other message. The longer I stared at the warning, the more chills crept down my spine.

Footfalls sounded in the other room, and I shuddered, my hands fumbling just as the wind snatched the paper from my hand. I reached for it, but it was gone, floating outside.

I trembled, unsure what to make of the message. Where would I run anyway? Were the woods safer than this palace?

Turning to the door, I pulled on the handle and it opened.

"Hello?" I peered into the adjacent room, only to find a dress draped off the back of the couch. A platter of food sat on the small table near the couch. Porridge and honey, bread, jams, and fruit. My mouth salivated.

I collected the burgundy-colored dress and headed back into my bedroom to change before they forced me into a bath again. A fitted bodice, with wrist-to-shoulder lace-up sleeves, and a straight skirt down to my ankles. Back in the bedroom, I stripped and slipped the dress over my head and down my body. It was a looser fit than the last gown, with only a single layer of material. There was no sign of underwear, and I sighed. But I did find black slip-on shoes near the door.

Footsteps sounded in the other room, and I rushed there, expecting Luther.

The brunette maid was setting a teapot and cup on the table. Viper bound into the room, too, heading for the windows and staring out at the falcons flying past.

"Morning, mistre—my lady." Her eyes lit up when she found me dressed. "That color suits your blonde hair. Come eat and I'll style it for you."

I wanted to ask her about the note, if she'd put it there, but the red-haired lady waltzed in as if on a mission. Her lips in a grim line, she marched into my room, presumably to tidy up. Had she left the message?

"What's your name?" I asked, feeling bad for never asking before now.

"Dana, my lady. Livy also helps me, even if she's grumpy often." The smile on her face told me the women were close.

"You can call me 'Guen.' So, what's on the agenda today?" I flopped onto the couch, my stomach growling for food, and I picked up the bowl of porridge and the spoon.

"Agenda?" she asked.

"What am I meant to do today?" I scooped a spoonful into my mouth, the creamy cinnamon-and-apple porridge melting on my tongue. It was to die for.

"The princes have left the court for a few days. Until then, we're instructed to keep you in your chamber."

I dropped my spoon into the porridge glob. "For a few days? I wanted to explore the palace." Find out more about my past, my parents—somehow come to terms with the fact that this could be real.

"Out of the question." Dana shuffled to stand behind the couch and collected my hair roughly into her hands before pulling it off my face. "We will bring you entertainment to keep you busy. This morning, you will learn the art of needlepoint and later the skill of using a harp."

I rolled my eyes and remembered Luther's words about someone wanting to hurt me if they discovered my whereabouts. Then why was someone warning me to leave the palace?

My feet tumbled across the forest floor, foliage crunching and getting caught on the hem of my dress.

"I missed you all day," Luther murmured, his voice silky and tempting.

In the dark of the night, I could barely discern his black clothes and hair while his amber eyes held a glint to them.

"Hey, wait up," I called out as he walked backward, smiling wickedly, his hand stretched out to me.

"Hurry, little wolf."

I stretched out an arm, my fingers grasping on to his. He held on and drew me closer.

"You need to move faster. No one can know we're out here," he whispered with a forbidden tone that drove me insane. This felt like we'd run away from our chaperones to steal a first kiss. If only.

I glanced over my shoulder at the lights of the palace through the trees: the enormity of the place, the fiery torches outlining the servants' door to the building we'd snuck out from.

"Why didn't you reach out through my thoughts while you were gone?" I pressed close to him as we stepped over a fallen log, his hand interlaced with mine. "I endured three utterly boredom-inducing-harp-and-needlepoint-days. God, I was at the point where I would either poke my eyes out with the pins or strangle myself on the harp strings."

He laughed. "We traveled with Father. Others in close vicinity can sometimes sense it when I use my power, and I couldn't risk it."

"Risk them finding me?" I tensed at being kept in the dark with what was going on.

He nodded. "Father's forbidden me from using my ability."

"So you're the rebel of the family," I teased.

He brought my hand up to his lips, kissing my knuckles quickly as we walked. "If you only knew, little wolf."

So many questions whirled on my mind, and I was left conflicted about my feelings for Luther. About being stuck in this world... or "realm" as he and his brothers called it. And with each passing day, the truth grew inside me that maybe this was where I belonged. That this was a real place and I'd got myself stuck here.

That only opened up new questions, like why had my parents abandoned me in the woods near a hospital? What was wrong with me? Was I really a fae? I had no idea what being fae really meant, but it might have explained the dreams, the episodes I had felt since arriving here... the reason I'd fallen out of Noah's car and right into my bed.

"Are you ready for your surprise?" he teased.

"What is it?" I squeaked.

Something looked different about him tonight. He smiled too much, his touch warmed my body, and why was he so excited? I longed to sit with him and just talk about us, learn more about him, but when he'd burst into my room excited, insisting we had to leave right away, his exhilaration was a fever enveloping me. Talking could wait, I'd guessed.

"You'll see," he said, his grin captivating, and we ran on through the woods. With him, I didn't feel scared. Maybe I should have, but not tonight.

When he finally came to a stop, we stood in front of a square wooden platform with a railing on three sides. It was big enough for two or three people inside.

"What is that?" I breathed heavily, while he barely broke a sweat.

He stepped inside and guided me to follow him. "Welcome to my Ferris wheel."

I eyed him suspiciously, but on the inside, I squirmed with joy that not only had he remembered what we'd talked about, but he'd made one? I looked nothing like the ones back home, since this was made of a simple platform that I assumed planned to take us upward. But he'd never seen one and based his creation on my description, so I was excited to see what he made. My stomach somersaulted at the notion that he made this for me.

"I'm at a loss for words." I stepped onto the platform. This was nothing like a Ferris wheel back home, but I was willing to try out his version.

"That'll be a first." His hand found my lower back, drawing me closer, and I sagged against him. "Now hold on."

He was so close now, I felt the hard muscles of his chest, smelled his breath. Honey and blueberries and all masculine. He tugged hard on a rope with one hand, and in a heartbeat, our platform lurched and catapulted upward. A whirring sound buzzed like rope running over a metal wheel.

My stomach pitched. I shuddered, clutching on to him, my hands bunching up his shirt, while I plastered myself to him.

He laughed as the wind brushed against us, his large hand holding me in place, his other gripping the wooden railing. We could be soaring through the skies with how fast we traveled, sliding up alongside lofty pine trees, their scent wafting on the breeze.

"Do you like my Ferris wheel?" he asked, his voice buffeted against the rush of air.

I held on to him for dear life, the heat of his body pouring over me. "It's fantastic."

Wind fluttered through my hair, pushing it into my face when we finally jerked to a stop.

I glanced around at the tops of pines spreading out in every direction. The waning moon hung high like a Viking horn, throwing silvery hues over the forest. "Wow, people would pay a fortune for this view."

"Turn around."

Grabbing on to the railing, I shifted on the spot, the platform giving a slight wobble, and my heart thumped.

But I forgot everything once I lifted my gaze. I was captivated.

A majestic castle stood atop the nearby mountain, as if conjured out of a fairy tale, and I gasped out loud, inciting an amused laugh from Luther.

"Holy crap on a stick, it's a real-life castle," I murmured. Steadfast stone walls, towers, moonlight shining on its proud turrets, dark windows like slits in the thick walls, flags fluttering in the breeze. Globe lights everywhere brought the spectacular fortress to life. Trees clustered close to the walls looked like an army ready to defend.

I glanced at the palace we'd come from, farther on my right. I'd thought that was the most elaborate thing I'd ever see, but I'd been so wrong. "That castle is insane."

"It's where my parents live." Luther leaned in behind me, his solid chest against my back, his arms grasping the railings on either side of me, and I lost all ability to think. Gone were the questions I'd promised myself to ask him.

All that remained was the heat pouring from his body, his quickened breaths grazing over my hair, and I knew what was coming, I craved it, *needed* it since the first time he'd entered my head and scared me half to death. But this was deeper. We were so much more than burning up with desire. After tonight, he'd hold more than just me as hostage. My heart would shatter. He'd have my heart, too. I wasn't foolish enough to forget the truth that even if I was from this world, he was a prince. Me... who knew? Except this moment had been in the making for years and I wouldn't ruin it. Couldn't.

"It's peaceful up here, away from everything and everyone," he whispered in my ear, sending sharp shudders of pleasure down my spine. His hand slid to my jaw, his fingers tender and so warm. He tilted my head back and looked down at me, the moonlight brightening his face.

How had I never noticed that the color of his eyes

with the outer ring of the iris a strong amber? I studied his defined cheekbones, his square jaw, his full lips that seemed slightly crooked from my angle.

"I have a gift for you," he said.

"Really?" I pressed my back to his chest and he wrapped his arms around my shoulders, holding me tightly.

"Remember when I promised you revenge for what Noah did to you?"

Worry dragged over my mind on what a gift and getting revenge had in common. "What did you do?"

"Not enough, but from this realm, it was the closest thing to making him regret touching you."

I blinked hard and twisted around in his arms to face him. "I'm scared to ask."

The corners of his mouth twitched, like he was holding back a grin. "I arranged a small glamor over his dreams. Whenever he sleeps, he dreams of being savagely murdered, experiencing every ache, every fear, every moment like it was real. Each night, a different girl whom he's hurt will visit him." His wicked smile split his lips. "It will slowly drive him insane."

Staring at him, I wasn't sure how to feel. I didn't hate the idea because that jerk-head deserved so much freaking worse, but it also showed me Luther reveled in his cruelty.

"You don't like it?" Worry pinched the bridge of his nose. "I could arrange for something worse."

"No. Actually, it's rather creative and clever."

"Exactly." The moonlight hit the side of his face. My back to the railing, I glanced up, and his hand cupped the side of my face.

"You deserve so much more than the life you've led. All those who hurt you had no clue who you were."

"Wish *I* knew who I was."

Slow and sweet, his thumb dragged over my lower lip. "You will as soon as my brothers and I work out a solution."

"Solution?" He made it sound like I was a problem.

He pressed the edge of his nail down on my lip, eliciting a sharp pain, but I didn't wince. Not when I struggled to tame my wandering emotions and the heat flaring between my legs.

I parted my lips, slipping my tongue out, flicking the tip of his thumb. The amber rim of his eyes lit up like fire, and I indulged him, leaning closer, sliding him into my mouth, inch by inch. Lips clamped over him, I closed my eyes and tasted his saltiness and traced my tongue over his thumb, enjoying the way his breath hitched.

"Look at me." His voice was raspy and fierce.

My eyelids flipped open and stared into his intoxicating eyes.

Arousal curled behind his intense gaze, and I

clenched my thighs. I adored that look, the idea that I held control over him.

Electricity sizzled over my flesh, and he pulled his thumb out of my mouth with a faint popping sound.

He leaned closer, burying his face in my hair, inhaling me. "Mine," he murmured.

His lips closed against mine, and lust flooded me. A desperate ache blazed through me, my brain firing off sparks. I opened my mouth and moaned as he slid his tongue inside, battling with mine.

I drove my hands into his long hair, tugging on the roots, breathing heavily.

His grip on my hips tightened.

I ran my hands down his strong shoulders, over the hard planes of his chest and stomach. My fingers slid under his shirt, finding fiery skin. He hissed a breath at my touch, pulling me against him roughly, kissing me with such savagery, I lost myself to him. It scared me how much I let myself go, how much I craved him.

I wanted him. Needed him. Plain and simple, I had to have this gorgeous man.

His kisses drifted over my cheek, across my brow, and to my ear, leaving me trembling. "There are so many secrets I plan to share with you, my little wolf. Secrets that will make you the most powerful fae in Wandering Realm."

I froze and looked up at him. Gone was the deadly edge of arousal he'd brought me to, replaced with curiosity. There was so much I didn't understand. "What are you talking about?"

His hands snaked down my back, curving over my ass, infusing me with heat, his gaze narrowing on me. "Why do you think everyone in the Realm knows you?"

"Maybe because—"

A piercing hoot sounded from somewhere down in the woods, and my heart shuddered.

Luther jerked away from me and glanced down over the railing. His face paled two shades when he met my gaze, and my breaths stopped for a moment.

"We need to go. Now!" he hissed.

He reached out with his hand to the rope, golden sparks erupting from his touch. The platform beneath us lurched and we dropped. My stomach hit the back of my throat, arms frantically grabbing for the railing, wind throwing my hair everywhere.

Luther's arms grasped around my waist, holding me tight. "I've got you. Once we land, we run. Whatever you do, don't look back, don't let go of my hand. Understand?"

I nodded, my heartbeat galloping. "You're scaring me."

"Good, then you'll follow my instructions." His words deepened.

Darkness reared up around us as we dove into the woods, fear churning in my veins.

I jostled on my feet as the platform hit the ground.

Luther snatched my arm and lunged into the forest, dragging me after him, and we ran. He moved with such swiftness. I felt like I flew through the air, my legs barely keeping up.

Panic lashed over my chest, squeezing my lungs. I pushed myself to keep up. Goosebumps shivered up the back of my legs like someone watched us. Ducking under branches, we never stopped, but kept moving. Adrenaline drove me faster and faster. Fear shoved against me like the cold wind.

Whatever you do, don't look back.

Desperation begged me to glance into the woods, see what scared Luther so much, what terrified someone who looked like he could wrestle a bear. But I never did… I couldn't bring myself to see the monsters hunting us down.

Darkness closed in, and only the fiery lights of the manor in the distance called to us.

Branches snapped behind us, and a guttural growl shot through the night.

Goosebumps raked over my flesh as Luther's grip tightened, drawing me forward quicker. My foot caught on a tree root, and I fell forward. My heart dropped.

I gasped out loud, reaching for Luther, the floor rushing up to me.

Luther pivoted, swinging his free arm and swooped it under my arm, steadying me. I stumbled to find my footing, and instinct had me turning around. I shouldn't have.

A hulking shadow on two legs charged forward from deeper in the woods, breaking branches, feet pounding the ground. White glinted in his eyes, a savageness in his curled posture. This wasn't a beast, but a lunatic chasing us.

A scream rushed past my lips.

With a grunt, Luther wrenched me after him. "Run, little wolf, run," he yelled.

The wind blasted into us, and we moved with speed.

We rushed out of the woods and darted to the shadowy edges of the mansion.

I glanced back as Luther fumbled to open the side door, the servants' entrance he'd told me.

The man chasing us emerged from the woods, eyes shining in the moonlight. Clothes ripped and ragged, he heaved for breath, his chest rising and falling, mouth gaping open with a terrifying growl no human should make. He burst after us, and I retreated just as Luther seized my arm and dragged me inside. He slammed the door shut and locked it with several bolts.

Night smothered the empty kitchen. No one else was around.

"Quick, you need to get back to your room. You'll be safe there." He grabbed my hand and we ran through the dark kitchen as something slammed into the door behind us.

I could barely catch my breath, and it had little to do with the endless running. But everything to do with whatever lingered outside.

CHAPTER 16

"Luther!" I mumbled, panic turning into something else… something with sharp teeth and aching pain. "Don't go." The darkness of my bedroom pressed around me, choking the breath out of my lungs.

He shook his head, dread darkening eyes that earlier had held intense desire. His hand slipped from mine, the cold already enveloping me, and he hurried to the doorway.

I staggered after him, fear burrowing through me. What was he running from? "Who was that in the woods? Why were they coming for us?"

"You're safe here. No matter what, never leave this room with anyone but me or the maids. Understand?"

"You're scaring me." Shivers crept down my spine, as I was unsure I could stop anyone if they found me.

Where could I hide in here? And what had he meant back in the woods about me being the most powerful fae? The whole being-a-fae thing still hadn't gelled.

The familiar sound of claws tapping the floorboards came from the hallway and Sir Wolf-A-Lot wandered into the room, right past me without a glance.

"I have to go." Luther retreated, his gaze over his shoulder, his brow furrowed. "I have to go."

"Don't leave Cujo in here with me!" I gasped, watching the furry little beast walk around like he owned the place.

Luther shut the door and left nothing behind but his faded steps.

The mutt leapt onto the couch and lay on his belly, making himself comfortable, like he somehow knew his tasked mission was to defend me. While I worried I'd wake up with him chewing on my leg, part of me liked having company. Someone other than just my thoughts.

Flames crackled and spat in the fireplace, tossing light across the living room.

I stood there for a few moments, drowning in too many emotions. The consuming heat Luther stirred in me, the dread that someone wanted to hurt me, the need to go home.

I pictured Jen panicking that I'd been gone for a few days, reporting me as a missing person, and guilt pressed down on my chest.

Only the crackling logs and the dog licking himself permeated the dimly lit room. I paced to the window and stared down at the forest drenched in night and the light of the silvery moon and tried to find the location Luther had taken me to in the woods. But my search proved fruitless, as it was too dark.

I smiled at how far from the real thing his Ferris wheel had been, but I'd adored it to bits. I still burned on the inside for him, still ached to kiss him all night, still wished he'd slept in here with me.

My heart pounded, and the taste of Luther lingered on my tongue, flowing into me. I inhaled his scent. Honeyed, masculine, and something dark. They poured through me, almost like he'd tried to leave his mark on me so I'd never forget him. But that was insane, right?

"Looks like it's just the two of us." I swiveled toward my companion for the night, but he already had his chin resting on his outstretched paws, his eyes closed.

I dragged myself into the other room and pulled out the chamber pot from under my bed, hating that this was my toilet. Then I'd go to sleep and maybe, just maybe, I'd wake up back home.

***

Something feathery brushed over my face. I shook my head, my nose itchy, and opened my sleepy eyes. At first glance, I could have sworn I was hugging a massive fur blanket, but when the reek of dog hit me, I startled and scrambled out of bed, my heart slamming into my ribcage.

Cujo remained on the mattress where I'd been snuggling him seconds earlier, and he strained to look over his shoulder at me with that look in his eyes, like sleep still clung to his brain.

I glared at him.

He made a whiny sound and flopped his head back on my pillow. "Wow, you're a bed hog, and for your information, if we're gonna share, stay on your side of the bed." He lay right down the middle.

The floorboard creaked in the next room, and my ears pricked. Cujo scrambled to his feet, kicking my pillow aside, and lunged out of bed before running into the living room.

"It's just me, Sir Wolf-A-Lot," Dana responded, and I dragged myself toward her to find she was placing my breakfast on the small table.

"Morning, my lady."

"Hey." I rubbed my eyes, yawning, still smelling like wet-dog Cujo. "Any chance of having a bath?" As much as I disliked taking a bath with maids watching me, I needed a wash badly.

She glanced at me, smirking. "Of course. I knew you'd enjoy them."

I liked her. She always greeted me with a smile and made me feel comfortable.

Dana bowed her head, a smile pulling on the

corners of her mouth. "Enjoy your meal and I'll come back to collect you shortly." She spun on her heels, holding on to the white apron over her navy blue dress as she rushed toward the door.

"Dana, have you seen Luther this morning?" I called out.

She shook her head and turned around. "Not yet. But could I be so bold as to speak my mind?"

"Of course. What is it?"

"My father, Goddess bless his soul, once told me that sometimes it is difficult to break one's path to embrace a new future. But to survive among monsters, one must adapt any way possible."

I stared at her, trying to wrap my brain around what she'd said, convinced most in this world spoke in riddles.

She wiped her hand on her apron, her mouth pinching. "You look confused, my lady."

"Just a weensy bit."

"I know this place must seem strange to you, but this is a deadly realm for someone so unfamiliar with the dangers. Just be cautious, but be quick to accept this realm as your own before it's too late."

"Too late?" As my own? This wasn't my home.

She bowed her head. "I've said too much and I'm out of line. I just don't want to see you…" She cleared her throat. "Hurt."

"Thank you."

Dana hurried out of the room, and now I was a thousand times more confused.

And I wanted to speak with Luther desperately. He'd left me with so many questions last night. Not to mention the memory of the most divine French kiss in the world. Some guys knew how to kiss, others were like dribbling fountains and sucked. Luther had left me breathless, like I couldn't live without kissing him again.

When I turned around, Cujo had his front paws up on the table, lapping up my porridge.

Gah.

***

Deimos circled me in slow, soundless steps. He was tall, six-two maybe. Gorgeous from the depths of his green crystal eyes to the rugged expression on his face. He'd let out his hair tonight, white strands cascading over broad shoulders and down his back, almost glinting with a bluish tinge in the flames of the fireplace. Predatory eyes swept over me, corded muscles moving under his skin. I shouldn't have felt a thing for him but hatred, not the shortening of my breath, and definitely not the bursting desire inside me to have this powerful guy stare at me like I was his meal.

Dangerous.

Vicious.

Gorgeous.

I watched him, my breaths quickening. His hand

was on my chin when he stopped in front of me. Like Luther, his touch warmed me in a heartbeat, and he forced my head up to face him.

"I expected more," he growled.

"More?" I strained my eyes to look over to the dinner table set up with plates of stew, roast pheasant, baked vegetables, and a number of other things I didn't recognize. "I'm sure the cook can whip up more food if it's not enough."

His eyes narrowed, and I offered him my cheekiest grin. The guy had cornered me the moment I entered the dining room. After a day on my own in my quarters, I'd hoped to finally find Luther, but instead it was Deimos who'd waited for me.

His hand slid over my cheek, his fingers combing through my hair, dropping to my shoulders. Greedy fingertips explored my neck, leaving a trail of shivers in their wake.

"More beauty, more elegance, more everything," he said softly.

I stiffened and flinched from his hold, but his hands were fast; they grabbed my arms and drew me against him. "I didn't say you could leave."

"You aren't too great yourself," I muttered, completely and utterly lying. He was perfection, indulgence, temptation standing before me.

"Watch that mouth of yours," he threatened with a smirk, enjoying his power play.

I swallowed hard and reminded myself whom I was dealing with… a prince used to getting his way. But gorgeous hunk or not, it wasn't okay for him to step into my personal space. I pulled back, but he stepped forward with me, my back pressed to the wall, his face in mine. He was so close I inhaled his scent… masculine and woodsy and the sweetest citrus combined in one. Something stirred in my gut, and my gaze fell to his mouthwatering lips, which sat in a crooked grimace.

"Luther will break you easily, then he'll get a replacement." He spoke so calmly, like he might be ordering a latte—which he'd never probably tasted in his life—but I didn't believe his threat. Not after the night I'd had with Luther. He wouldn't.

"I know what you're doing," I quipped, glaring at him.

He pushed closer and brushed his lips over mine, my whole body bursting with adrenaline. "Is that what you expected?"

I clenched my jaw, my skin burning over the fact that he dared—

"You'll be fun to keep. Might even take my turn breaking you."

"Is that your idea of sweeping a girl off her feet?"

His laughter sounded divine, which was wrong because he wasn't allowed to sound like the best thing I'd heard my entire life.

"I prefer girls with more, not less."

A shiver shook me, and I pushed my fists against his chest, but he stood there, trapping me, unmoving. His fingers slid into my hair, twining the strands.

"Maybe you should have put your hair up tonight," he said. "Would have looked prettier."

"Is that all you do—insult? Well, it's not working on me, so move out of my way."

His hand grasped my hair, and I winced. "You're adorable when you're angry. Think we'll have a lot of fun together."

"I'm not yours and I sure as hell ain't staying in this insane place." Despite my words, my body hummed from his closeness. My body betrayed me when it came to this jerk, my lips still tingling from his kiss.

His breath washed on my face, and as much as I wanted to say it reeked, I loved the way he smelled. Damn him… I hated him.

"You're not Luther's, either, and where will you go? It's no easy feat moving between realms without magic. You're stuck in our realm now."

"I'll find a way back."

He pressed his mouth to my ear. "So human of you."

I stiffened. "What's that supposed to mean?"

His green eyes flashed to mine, desire deepening within them. He lips met mine too fast for me to react, and he nipped my lower lip, his teeth nicking flesh.

"Ouch." I shoved my hands into his chest, but he

didn't move. He just stood there as hard as a boulder, licking the trickle of blood on his mouth.

I touched mine and my fingers came back bloody. "What are you doing?"

Fingers slipped over my shoulder, drowning me, clouding my thoughts, leaving me leaning into him while trying to recover any control of my wavering emotions.

He pressed his face to my neck, inhaling, tasting, and I shuddered under him, the softness leaving me shivering with a new kind of arousal. I should have stopped him, should have shoved him away, but I couldn't. Something brushed over my mind, feather soft and blurring my thoughts for a moment, before it pulled away.

Teeth were on my neck, a sharp prick fast and electrifying.

Mist blurred my mind, everything erased except Deimos and me. Focusing on steadying my breathing did nothing to calm my thundering heart. Arousal trembled down my spine, invisible fingers sliding over my back and lower still.

A sudden roar tore through the room, ripping me out of my lulled state.

"What the fuck are you doing?" Luther growled.

Deimos stumbled away from me, his laughter hypnotic. He wiped his bloody mouth with the back of his hand, his eyes devouring me, calling to me like nothing I'd ever felt.

"She's exquisite, brother. So much more than we could have anticipated. You were right to collect her for us."

"She isn't yours to touch or mark. Fuck, Deimos!"

The wall held me up as the fog in my head faded, my thoughts clearing, and there was a pinching ache at my neck. I clasped the wound where he'd bitten me.

"Bastard," I mumbled. Whatever he'd done had served as some sort of magnet, luring me to him.

The tension in the room exploded. Luther heaved like a beast, his arms trembling, and when Deimos's eyes fell on me, they felt like marks on my body.

"Why?" Deimos asked with a raised brow. "You think I don't know you already marked her too? I tasted it in her blood. Anyway, we both know Ahren will claim her in the end."

Luther moved in a flash and bulldozed into his brother, both of them slamming into the side of the table before tumbling to the ground with several chairs and the platter of roast veggies.

I flinched, trying to clear my thoughts.

Potatoes and carrots rolled around on the ground with the two brothers punching and kicking each other, their growls escalating.

A kitchen servant appeared at the commotion but

froze in fright in the doorway, his eyes enlarging at the sight before he swiftly retreated.

My stomach dropped at their battle. They were the worst kind of animals. Fighting over me... over marking me. What about what I wanted? Deimos's words lingered in my mind about Luther getting another girl after breaking me... was it a lie or me being too blindsided by their attention to see the truth?

I trembled.

Fear radiated through me and nothing would have prepared me for this. I inhaled sharply and burst into a run past the brawl and out into the hall. I didn't stop, never looked back, until I reached my bedroom and shut myself in there. My back to the door, I hugged myself and slid to my ass. "What the hell just happened?"

My hand shook as I pressed it to my neck, which stung, and I sucked on the cut across my lower lip.

How could I stay here with three princes who were more dangerous than I'd first thought? One dominant and terrifying. One cruel with his words. And one who'd unmistakably stolen my heart.

CHAPTER 17

"Wake up!" A female's voice grazed over my ear, her hand on my shoulder, shaking me.

It took me a few seconds for my thoughts to slide back into place. The palace, the princes, Luther... "Dana?" I groggily asked, rubbing my eyes.

Someone was standing over me in bed, the dark stealing her features, leaving the hair on my nape bristling.

"Get up, Guendolyn. Fast!" Terror pulsed behind her words.

"Wait, you're not Dana." Or Livy. Panic slammed into my chest like I'd been hit by a wrecking ball, tearing the sleep from my head.

"Who are you?" Had Luther left the door unlocked?

She straightened her posture, revealing a lithe body,

standing tall, six-foot or six-foot-one. A flash of silver glinted in her eyes, and something familiar came to me, but I just couldn't place who I was staring at.

With the click of her fingers, a flame ignited within a small globe sitting in the palm of her hand. Light burst outward, brightening her face, and I pushed myself upright in bed, squinting for a better look.

Gray eyes. Porcelain skin that glistened. Her hair blended into the night, and long, elf-like ears poked out from her hair.

"Pointy ears are more of a family attribute," Deimos had said.

"You're in danger, Guendolyn. We need to go, now."

"Wait, Áine?" It was the gallery owner who'd dug her nails into my arm, drawing blood, who'd vanished... She'd called me Guendolyn back at the gallery but hadn't had long ears then. "What are you doing here?" But even as the words left my lips, I knew the answer. Knew that she'd somehow come from this realm. The whole time, she had to have known more about me. My head spun.

I shuffled backward across the bed, farther from her reach, kicking the blankets aside as I got out of bed.

"You knew, didn't you? When you saw my painting, you knew that I came from here?" The words felt clunky and odd on my tongue because now I was admitting I'd been born in the Wandering Realm. Since arriving, I hadn't experienced a single psychotic episode. Maybe it had all been in my head, but my emotions and thoughts just felt too real.

Áine nodded and sighed. "I've been searching for you, and you couldn't have ended up in a worse location." She rounded the bed, and I backed away. "These are your enemies," she explained.

"Okay, you found me. Can you take me back home?" I swallowed hard. Maybe this was my chance to finally return.

She shook her head, and my hope shattered.

"I'm here to take you to your mother. Your real mother."

I stiffened and looked at her, trying to detect the lie on her face. "You know my mom?"

She nodded, her hair bouncing over her shoulders as she stepped closer. "Why do you think I had to meet you after viewing your painting?" She reached for my arm, and I pulled away.

My mouth was dry, and I couldn't move. Couldn't think straight. Everything from the past week was muddled inside my head, and all the conversations I'd had with Luther over the years were crowded over me.

"You dug your nails into my arm, breaking skin, and then vanished."

Her overexaggerated exhale sliced through the air. "I have so much to teach you about this realm. Unless you're gifted with the power of the tongue, like some fae, the only way to travel between realms is magic and blood. But I don't have time to explain the details... not yet."

I was shaking my head, trying to process everything, but it all kept coming back to my mom and how long I'd waited for such a moment. "But Luther—"

"Do you even know who the three princes really are?" She towered over me, the globe flame in her hand beaming under her chin, tossing shadows upward, disfiguring her face. For those few seconds, she looked different. Wider eyes, a longer nose, pinched lips.

My stomach clenched, and my back hit the cold wall.

"They're monsters who'll break you until there's nothing left. Thank the moon I found you before it's too late." Her hand reached for mine, her fingers coiling around my wrist. "They aren't even the real heirs to this court." Her words flew out fast and clipped.

"What do you mean?"

"When the King of Shadow Court remarried, his new queen brought with her three sons, who became the next in line since she was barren after having them with her first husband. But I can explain those things once we're safe. Someone wants to hurt you, they're coming for you, and I'm here to help."

"I want to speak with Luther first."

A whimpering sound came from somewhere in the hall, and she glanced over her shoulder, tugging me closer. "You'll have time, but first, come and see your mother. Find out the truth of what happened, how you ended up being the lost girl in the Wandering Realm."

For so long, I'd fantasized about the day Mom would finally come for me and explain how someone had stolen me. Or a dozen other scenarios I'd made up. Anything but Mom abandoning me. She'd never do that.

But now I felt torn in half, remembering Luther's warning, while a savage desperation ripped through me that I might finally find my mom, discover who I was… How I might no longer be the girl who had a mental disorder. I'd been searching for this my whole life, wanting… *needing* a way out.

A feather-soft touch brushed over my thoughts, stealing the anxiety, and I lowered my shoulders, the decision suddenly clearer.

When I looked up at Áine, her eyes seemed to glow, then she smiled. "Shall we go? We won't be long." She pushed the light into my hand, the globe fleshy in my hand, yet a tiny flame flickered and danced inside, curving and turning upright as I rolled the ball in my hand.

She drew me across the room, and I hurried with rushed footsteps behind her, excitement building in my chest that I'd see Mom, finally be able to ask her why I'd ended up abandoned in the woods.

"Your mother is so excited to meet you."

I nodded, my throat thickening, while I trembled with fear that I'd find out she'd decided to get rid of me because I hadn't been what she'd expected. Because something was wrong with me.

Out in the dark hallway, Áine drew me to the left. I glanced back down the corridor smothered in night, where something thick and dark lay on the floor near a bear statue. I lifted my hand with the globe, the light stretching outward, finding someone lying on the ground face down, red hair sprawled across the rug. Blood smeared the floor and the bear's leg.

Goosebumps raked over my flesh, and I rocked on my heels, pulling against Áine. "Livy?"

"She's the enemy," Áine growled in my ear. "She would have led those who wanted to harm you to your door."

"So you killed her?" Ice wrapped around my heart so hard, it almost stopped beating.

"We need to go before they come." She wrenched my hand, and I tripped over my feet, but I fought against her grip, only then noticing that part of the wall had opened up to a secret passage.

My pulse raced because nothing felt right. I should have followed my gut instinct. "Stop. I'm not going anywhere with you."

Áine spun toward me with such speed, I barely caught my breath. Her hand pressed to my brow, and the smell of bitter lavender flooded my senses.

"Sleep."

I shoved her hand away, and that feathery touch skimmed over my mind again, blurring thoughts, stealing them from me. My eyelids heavy, they fell, and darkness took me so fast, my world vanished.

*J*ostled about in a cold seat, my nose frozen, and forced my eyes open as fresh air rushed into my lungs.

My vision sharpened to reveal a small carriage around me, walls covered in lush, black fabric, silver studs peppering the frame of the windows and door. Áine sat across from me, one leg crossed over the other, studying me with a raised brow.

"Did you sleep well?" she asked, sounding calm, as if she hadn't just kidnapped me.

I frowned, gritting my teeth. "Of course I didn't." I looked outside the window to discover we were rushing through the forest with extraordinary speed. What was pulling this carriage, dragons?

"Where are we going? Take me back to the palace— now." I trembled so hard but refused to let her see. She didn't seem to be the kind of person who was swayed easily by emotions. And I didn't trust her at all, though my mind swung back and forth between attempting to escape and finding out if she actually knew my mom.

"Too late. We've already been traveling for most of the night." She shrugged, and heaviness dropped through me at the revelation that we were so far from the palace.

She was wrapped in a white coat with fur along the lapels, gloved hands in her lap. Dark hair pulled off her face, and she seemed so at ease, while pins and needles raced up my arm from lying on it. "I used winter cherry," she explained, like I should know what that meant. "And a little lavender powder to help you calm down. Seems it put you to sleep." She smirked, knowing that was exactly what would happen.

Wind whistled through the gaps in the carriage door, the draft reaching me with its icy fingers. I shivered and rubbed my hands together, finding myself wearing a long, black coat. I tugged it open to find I still wore my smiling moon pajamas underneath. Well, why the hell not meet everyone in my pajamas? Then I spotted the black boots on my feet and wriggled my toes inside them. Pretty decent fit, considering they weren't mine.

"We'll dress you accordingly before your greeting with your mother."

"Why would it matter what I wore?" Nothing about

this felt right, and being forced to go with Áine raised the hairs on the back of my neck. I insanely wanted to see my mom, but there was still so much I didn't understand about the games these fae played. Especially this fae.

"You still don't believe me?"

"Not after you killed Livy!" I snapped. Images of her dead body in the hallway clawed over my thoughts. "Why not tie her up or something? Her family is going to be devastated."

"She has no family. None of the servants do. It's part of working as a servant. No connections to the outside world."

Even though she'd been grumpy most of the time, Dana and I would still miss her and mourn. Poor Livy!

The carriage wheels hit something hard, and I was thrown back into the seat. Áine lurched forward, her arms jutting outward, her hands plastered to the windows of the small carriage on either side to catch herself.

"I don't show sympathy to my enemies." She straightened herself in her seat, pushing hair out of her face. "The royals in the Shadow Court are as cold as our winters. They've spilled enough blood in my kingdom to know they are the real monsters in this realm."

She sounded so bitter, but hatred did that to someone if they held on to it long enough.

The carriage jostled about and we swayed left and right, starting to feel sick, but I'd missed dinner after Luther and Deimos had broken into a brawl, so I wouldn't be vomiting anything up. I raised my hand to the side of my neck, a small scab already healed over where he'd torn skin, my spot still sore. I didn't understand his flirty aggression, or why my knees weakened in his presence. Did he have some kind of power over me?

Áine watched me, and I pulled the collar of my coat tighter, glancing outside as we rushed through the woods. My head felt queasy. What if she was right about my real mom? Would I stay here or return to Luther's palace? I couldn't wait for him to wake up already and find me missing so he could reach out to my thoughts.

"Why are we going so damn fast?" Dread curled in my throat that we were so far from the kingdom, I'd never find my way back.

"Bloodcursed," Áine stated, and I stared at her blankly.

"Am I supposed to know what that is?" I scrubbed a hand down my face, frustrated to hell and back over being taken like this. No one would know what had happened to me, and would I even see Luther again? My life was sailing away, and I was losing control of everything.

"Cursed race of blood suckers. When they haven't

eaten in a while, the blood frenzy hits, and they attack anything that moves."

"And you think they're out there now?" My voice almost squeaked as I searched the woods outside, squinting for any sign of movement. Fear tangled within me, tightening my chest.

"Perhaps. Hard to tell, but if we move fast, we might not catch their attention." Her smooth tone suggested we were talking about the weather, not beasts that could kill us.

I couldn't stop staring at the forest now. My knees bounced. "So what do they look like? Rabid wolves? Bears?"

"Fae."

I lurched forward from the bumpy road and thrust out my hands, clasping the sides of the carriage to stop myself from falling face-first into Áine. "They're fae?" I gasped.

"Once upon a time they were, until the curse infected them and changed them. Now they're sensitive to light, they hunt for blood, and they grow in numbers each time they kill."

My stomach roiled. I thought back to Luther when he'd taken me up in his Ferris wheel, the sound he'd heard. Had that been a bloodcursed? "So they're like vampires?"

"If that's what you want to call them."

My back pressed to the wooden seat, I couldn't stop

staring outside, imagining fae with red eyes and huge fangs. The fae already had the whole pale-thing going for them. "Can we go any faster?"

Áine gave a soft laugh.

"Tell me about my mom," I said. Anything to distract me from the monsters living in these woods. "Is Dad with her as well?"

She paused for a moment. "It's complicated with your parents. Your mother is beautiful, with the most magical smile. Her kindness is unlike anyone else's in the realm. She gains the eye of any man she favors, like you, I'm sure."

Her comment threw me off, but I just sighed and glanced away, still heartbroken over Livy, scared of these bloodcursed, terrified of where exactly she was taking me. I didn't know what to make of Áine and I couldn't decide if I could trust her motives.

I shivered again, and we fell silent. All I could think about was Jen, and how she'd not always been the perfect mom, but she'd looked out for me. What was she doing now? Crying after finding me missing? It hurt to think of her in distress, and I couldn't reach out to tell her I was alive.

I didn't remember how much time passed, but in the distance, the golden-blue glow of the rising sun had already emerged, and my back pressed into the back of my seat as we climbed the mountain. Better than Áine, who pressed a hand to the wall to keep herself from sliding forward.

A sudden thump slammed against the metal roof of the carriage, sending us into a small wobble.

I slunk low in my seat and glanced up, curling in on myself, then shot a stare at Áine.

Her lips thinned and fear slashed across her gaze. "Hellish bastards."

"Please tell me it's not the bloodcursed."

She bent forward in her seat and reached a hand under her seat. "Would that make you feel better?"

"Yes!" My heart was beating so hard, I swore it would explode.

She pulled out a long dagger, the silvery hue from the moon glinting against the steel.

Áine grasped the hilt with two hands, waiting.

I shuddered, hugging myself.

Áine smiled, enjoying this, while my breaths raced, heavy and raspy.

"So a sword kills them? Guessing it's to their heart?"

"Just the heart? They can die just as easily as you and I, but their real danger comes when they hunt in numbers. They're fast and unstoppable. Luckily, they're not always coordinated."

"Great." Now all I could picture were the zombie movies I'd watched, and how the worst looking zombies were running at you. They freaked me out the most.

Áine sat back in her seat. "Not long now." Just as she spoke, something slammed against the window and clung there like a spider, sending the carriage into a sway from side to side.

I flinched backward, ice punching through me. "Holy sweet Jesus, we're going to die."

Torn clothes hung off the creature, cuts and wounds slashing over his arms and neck, his skin pale and filthy. Eyes black as midnight sunk into his hollow face, and fangs pressed over his lower lip. The bloodsucker hissed, his hand ripping at the door.

Áine jostled with the dagger. She kicked open the door and shoved her blade right through the monster's throat.

His eyes bulged out before he tumbled backward.

A flurry of freezing winds rushed into the carriage, ripping at my hair and clothes.

I cowered in the corner as Áine lunged forward to shut the door, leaving the cold outside. She wiped the blood from the dagger on the sides of her pants and sat back down, holding the weapon.

"See, you never should have taken me from the palace," I said. "At least I was safe there."

"I highly doubt that." Her smugness irritated me.

Dread pounded through my mind at the thought of how I'd survive this. "The horses and driver!" I blurted out. "They could be attacked."

A blur zipped past my window, and I jumped in my seat.

"Calm down. There were none. This is an enchanted carriage that knows where it needs to take us and won't stop for anyone. I just need to keep pushing these filthy things away until we arrive."

"I am not calming down with those things out there. I'm going to die out here, aren't I? Then I'll come back as one of those soulless things, and the first thing I'm doing is coming for you."

She raised a thin eyebrow, then dropped her gaze to the sword in her hand and back at me. But I wasn't scared of that when monsters outside wanted to drink my freaking blood.

Thoughts collided into me, raging inside my skull. Something else blurred past outside, and I shuddered. "I hate this place. Everything wants to kill me, and why the hell does everything want blood? The zombies in the forest, the freaking prince, and next—"

"You let them taste your blood?"

I shut up and said nothing.

"Tell me the truth!" Her face hardened, her eyes filled with horror. Was that look of disgust over the fact that I'd let the princes get close to me, or something worse?

"Why are you asking me that?"

"Stupid, stupid girl." She shook her head. "An

ancient one is going to have to cleanse you. Maybe it's not too late to get it out of your system completely."

"Get what out?" She was scaring me.

She leaned over and snatched my arm, drawing me closer.

"Once a fae takes your blood, you belong to them. It's like what you humans call marriage."

I jolted backward, laughing hysterically even if I found nothing funny. Nothing in the slightest. "That's ridiculous."

"If we don't remove the mark quick enough, you'll forever be bound to serve them until they decide to release you. Which is never. Those bastards would kill you before letting *you* go," she spat, the cords in her neck flexing. "They'll hunt you down, and that mark they placed on you makes you a beacon to them."

Air rushed from my lungs, and all I could picture was Luther when he licked my bloodied wrist in my dream. Deimos biting my lip and neck, tasting my blood. *Motherf—*

Something slammed into the carriage so hard, it rocked sideways and flipped us up on two wheels.

I screamed, sliding down the seat, slamming into the wall. Áine groaned across from me, pushing herself toward the uplifted side of the carriage.

"Shit!" I was going to die out here—I knew it, knew it!

Everything happened so fast. We traveled for a split

second on two side wheels, and I held my breath, gripping hold of the seat. Then the whole thing flopped onto its side. I jostled and smacked my head on the ceiling, stars dancing in my vision, my arms and legs flailing about, tangling with Áine, her feet at my head.

She wrestled with the dagger in her hand, the weapon swinging toward me from the momentum.

My life flashed before my eyes.

Death was coming swiftly.

I'd never see my family, Luther, or anyone again. The monsters would drink my blood and I'd come back as one of them.

God no!

The tip of Áine's blade stopped inches from my face. I lay on my back, my legs in the air, practically upside down. Sweat drenched me. Breaths raced. I'd almost died. Almost died. Almost freaking died.

Áine stood over me gripping the dagger, frozen for a few seconds, all the blood drained from her face, before she rapidly drew the weapon back.

"You could have killed me!" I shouted.

Áine grumbled, her lip split and blood dripping over her chin, while my head felt like it'd cracked in two. I rubbed the back of my skull, my fingers coming back spotted with blood. *Crap.* Did I need stitches?

A savage growl roared outside, and I trembled, staring up at the door sitting above us. We were like sardines, waiting for those things to come in and tear us out. I scrambled to get up.

Áine reached down, grabbed my coat by the shoulder, and dragged me to my feet with ease. "I'll hold them off, and you run. Run like you've never run before and go through the golden gates at the top of the hill. The palace is protected. The bloodcursed can't cross. Don't look back, no matter what. Understand?"

I nodded but couldn't move, terrified to go out there.

"Can't we wait here until sunlight?" I hugged myself tightly, my back pressed to the wall.

She shoved open the door and waited for a moment, watching the forest. "The scent of our blood will draw them to us in no time. They'll tear apart this carriage to reach us."

She slid her dagger out past the door and set it on top of the carriage. One foot propped up on the seat, she heaved herself out. Kneeling, she scanned the area rapidly and stuck her arm back inside.

"Take my hand," she whispered. "We move fast."

I grabbed her arm, followed her lead, and pushed off the seat inside. She dragged me out toward her, and my stomach pressed against the door frame. Legs kicking, I wriggled myself out.

Áine swept her gaze over the landscape. The fiery sky over the horizon lit up the tops of the trees, but within the woods, it was so dark, I could barely see a thing.

One hand on the dagger, the other on mine, Áine drew me to the edge. Before I got a chance to catch my breath, she tugged me forward and we jumped off the carriage.

My stomach lurched and we landed with a thud on the hard soil.

My heart pounded against the inside of my ribs, my gaze swinging left and right.

"The sun's almost here, so they'll be retreating. Now go."

"Maybe we risk waiting in the carriage?" My words raced.

She glared and shoved me by my shoulder toward the path that climbed at least a hundred feet to the top of the hill. Lofty, enormous pines crowded either side. Night still clung to the path, and dread froze me on the spot. I had no weapon, nothing.

"Run!" Áine shoved a hand against my back and pushed.

I burst forward in an instant, racing up the hill, my boots punching the ground.

I couldn't help it—I looked back, just for a split second.

Áine ran up behind me, sword in hand, her gaze sweeping the grounds, protecting me.

I had no idea who this woman was… a guard of my

real mom? She resembled nothing of the gallery owner back home.

Twigs and foliage snapped in the woods on either side of me, and a scream pulsed in my throat.

From the shadows on my right, a figure darted toward us. Skin pale and blotchy with blood. Clothes hanging off his lithe frame.

"Run!" Áine screamed, and I drove myself up the hillside as she'd instructed, never stopping.

Growls and the horrific slurping sound of body parts being ripped apart erupted behind me. Terror smothered me. The crest of the hill came into view. I pushed one leg after another when another blood-cursed emerged from my left so fast, I didn't react quick enough.

He crashed into me, throwing me off my feet.

I screamed, kicking, punching.

Teeth gnashed so close to my face, he smelled like rotten garbage. I shoved my fists into his neck, yelling, my muscles straining to keep him from my face. His eyes black as hell, his fangs extended, his lips peeled and cracked.

Something slammed into the vampire and suddenly they rolled off me with such speed, I didn't see what happened. I shoved myself off the ground.

Then I sprinted up the hill.

A cacophony of snarls burst around me. I hesitated for a split second to glance back, to see a black wolf with enormous fangs facing off three vampires where a second ago, Áine had been. I knew somehow it was her… had to be. I turned to run, but the image of Livy's corpse lashed my thoughts. I wasn't like Áine. I couldn't run if there was a chance she might die.

"Fuck," I mumbled, spinning, racing back toward her, scooping a branch off the ground as a weapon.

Strong arms swooped around my waist, my back pressed to a rock-hard body. The branch I'd held fell to the ground from the impact. I screamed and bucked against my attacker.

"Quiet, little wolf." The hushed words grazed over my ear.

I startled and turned my head to find Luther behind me. Blood streaked his cheek, another gash over his shirt, the material torn. No gaping wound that I could see.

"Oh my god, where'd you come from?" I turned and hugged him, never wanting to leave his side. "Why didn't you reach out to me in my thoughts?"

He didn't answer at first, just snatched my hand and charged with me up the hill. "I couldn't reach you no matter what I did, but I could sense you, so I rushed to track you down."

Dread burned up my spine that Áine's sleeping powder had been responsible in blocking out Luther from my mind. Over my shoulder, she lunged at two bloodcursed, the third fallen to her feet. Even if she had killed Livy, she tried to protect me. I couldn't just leave her. "We need to help her!"

His hand tightened around mine. "She's an assassin and can look after herself," he hissed while running, tugging me alongside him.

Assassin? My head hurt to keep up with everything going on. If she intended to kill me, why protect me from the bloodcursed?

Luther charged with lightning speed, and my feet tripped over one another to keep up with him. As we crested the top of the mountain, an enormous castle rose into view. The same kingdom from my dreams. A strange déjà vu hit me like I'd been here before...

I shook with disbelief as the castle gleaming over the horizon. Five broad towers with pointed roofs dominated the heavens, all connected by fortress-strong walls made of white stone. Ornate windows peppered the upper walls far from the ground.

"The castle..." I began, but Luther wrenched me away from it and to the right. I stumbled after him, unable to stop staring at the enormous arched gates forged of gold sitting splayed open just feet from us. Fifteen-feet high, made of golden, twisted rods, the tips curled into spear heads. They led to a passage made of flat gold stones and the castle from my dreams. Stone walls spread out from either side of the gate, enclosing the castle.

I slammed into Luther, who'd stopped running.

Peering past him, half a dozen bloodcursed had tipped another carriage. It must have been his.

My brain short-circuited. I couldn't deal with this. I whimpered, pulling back, ripping my hand from Luther.

Several guards lay dead on the ground in pools of blood, and others were being devoured by the monsters. Throats ripped open, chest cavities slashed.

Bile hit my mouth and I tore my gaze away, terrified, my feet already retreating, a branch snapping under my foot.

A bloodcursed with the whitest eyes jerked his head up toward me, unleashing an ungodly screech. I winced and covered my ears.

The other creatures' heads popped up as well. My heart pounded and if there was ever a time I'd suffer a stroke, this was it.

The white-eyed bloodcursed hissed and nearly levitated off the ground as it leapt toward us.

Luther moved like the wind. Grasping two blades from his belt and in a blink, he crisscrossed his arms, then slashed them apart at the attacking monster. Its head lopped right off and hit the ground before the body followed like a sack of potatoes. Blood gushed over the ground, squirting disgustingly.

Footfalls pounded the ground behind us.

I turned around. A dozen or so bloodcursed rushed

forward, like starved beasts, mouths gaping, eyes ravaged.

I seized Luther's arm and hauled him with me. Fear clawed at my chest, and my sights fixed on the gate.

"They won't follow us in there, Luther. We need to go!"

He jerked backward with me, his gaze leaping to the gate, to me, and the oncoming monsters. Dread stole all the life from his face.

"No, I'll fight to save you. You can't go in there or you might as well be dead."

"Are you insane? There are too many. Luther, no," I pleaded, tears already sliding out. I held on to him like a lifeline. "You're not doing this. You're not, you're not." My pleas were a broken record, but I died on the inside.

At least a dozen bloodcursed raced toward us, the gate but ten feet away from us. Luther nudged me to stand behind him with an elbow. "Stay close, little wolf." But his words trembled, and it scared me to hear so much fear in his voice.

"You won't beat them." I ripped my hand from him and ran toward the gate, panic gripping me so tight, I thought of nothing but the need to escape.

"Guendolyn, no!"

Inches from the gate, he snatched the back of my coat, dragging me against him, his lips on my ear.

"You're cursed!" he yelled. "Always have been. You cross that threshold into Ash Court and you'll fall into an endless sleep and the blood of fae will spill for eternity."

I couldn't breathe; his words barely made sense. "Wait, what? Why am I cursed?"

A sudden hiss scraped my ear, and Luther's hand flew to the monster at my side, jamming a blade into its eye. The horrible squidgy sound it made disgusted me.

Grubby hands grabbed for me, ripping hair, tearing at my clothes.

"Luther!" I screeched.

He punched one and sliced his blade at the onslaught, but it was useless. We stood no chance. Couldn't he see this?

Every muscle clenched. I'd never been this close to the door to escape.

I wrenched free from their grip, seeing nothing but more monsters pouring out of the woods. I reached out after Luther, fisted the back of his shirt, and hauled him backward with me.

"Guendolyn!" he cried. There was such darkness in his voice, such desperation and fear.

His foot hit mine and he tripped. Momentum sent us reeling through the open gateway, both of us hitting the ground in a heap.

I scrambled backward, but the bloodcursed threw themselves toward us. They hit an invisible barrier that sparked with energy, zapping the creatures until they collapsed to the ground.

A heavy sense of drowning seemed to swallow me from the inside. Something felt wrong. Like I didn't quite fit together, my body twisted.

Luther scrambled over to me, cradling me in his arms, tears on his cheeks. "What did you do, little wolf? I'm not ready to lose you. I just found you."

"I don't understand." I held on to him, clutching his collar, but my insides were twisting and knotting. Shadows feathered my vision. My arms weakened.

"Don't let me go," I cried, and Luther held me tightly to his chest. His shaking was a blade to my heart.

My hands trembled, the sensation spreading over me so fast, I started falling into a familiar darkness.

"I'll find you again," Luther promised. "I'll tear down the world to find you."

And in a heartbeat, I was gone.

***

There was nothing right about me today.

I didn't know who the person staring back at me from the mirror was.

205

Eyes of every shade of the sky. Cheeks rosy like I'd been running. White, shining hair. And lips red as blood.

I wanted to scream, laugh—feel something. Except I couldn't remember my name, the black coat I wore wasn't right, and I didn't even know this room.

Not the bed with a smiling moon comforter, or the stack of schoolbooks, or the easel sitting near the window. Sunlight poured inside, and the room seemed nice, I guessed.

But it wasn't me.

The mirror shimmered and I rubbed my eyes, but the closer I looked, the more my features changed. My hair extended to my waist, my nose was stronger, my lips paler, my cheekbones sharpening. Within seconds, the image faded away and the most beautiful man I'd seen in my life smiled back at me from the mirror, like he knew something I didn't. His eyes were crystal blue, and everything about him was perfection, intoxication, danger. I couldn't look away if I tried.

"Who are you?" I asked, and he just kept smiling.

The mirror's surface suddenly started to ripple.

Without warning, he pushed out of the mirror, first his arms, then the top half of him following rapidly.

My breaths raced, turning ragged and harsh. "Get away." I recoiled, but hands clasped the side of my face, holding me. His mouth captured mine, kissing me so brutally, so forceful, I winced, driving my fists into his shoulders.

Our tongues fought hungrily. Persistently, he pushed and pushed, sending wild shivers down my spine, awakening sensations that felt so familiar, so devilishly tempting.

My heart raced, and my toes curled against the floorboards, leaving me breathless. That fire raced through my veins, my flesh electric, flooding me with memories.

Palaces.

Fae.

Three princes.

Guendolyn… That was me!

And everything came back with the force of a storm. Everything I'd gone through hammered into me.

A rush of euphoric rapture engulfed me. I inhaled his musky and citrus smell like it was our first time, his scent imprinting on my mind like a photograph. Relief beat into me, and I desperately pressed myself toward him, needing him like I needed oxygen. I kissed him back, kissed him deeper, my fingers spearing through his hair. I thought I'd lost him.

My hands at once fell through him, and I stumbled forward, fear ripped in my heart.

"Luther!"

His breath ghosted over my face, and I reached for

him, my fingers and head bumping into the hard surface of the mirror as he faded away. I gripped the edges tightly, my hands sore, burning, anything to hold on to him.

"Luther, no!" I cried. My voice broke. I thumped my fists into the mirror. "Take me with you. Don't leave me." Whimpers beat out of me, dragging me deeper.

He never came… Never returned.

I was alone.

Startled and teary-eyed.

Guen.

Guendolyn.

The lost girl from the Wandering Realm.

The girl misplaced in a world I didn't belong in.

I knew that now.

I wasn't asleep, and this wasn't a dream. Two worlds existed, and for years I lived in one, but dreamed in another. Until recently when I went into the realm with Luther. He woke me up from the curse, but left me behind.

I lifted my fingers and probed my lips, staring into the mirror. An ache flared from the pulsing, soft, reddened flesh, and I winced. As I stared, the redness darkened to a bruise from his fierce kiss.

The voice in my head, the prince who'd stolen my heart, had reached through the void to claim my lips with his hunger. A hunger I felt in the depths of my soul now shredded me into a thousand pieces.

My heart tumbled and ached.

This was no dream.

This was a nightmare.

"Luther!" I pounded my fists into the mirror once more, tears drenching my cheeks as my world crumbled. I smashed and smashed until the glass shattered under my fist, splintering outward like hundreds of tiny daggers. I suffocated on the pain, blood staining the mirror, but there was nothing left. Nothing left.

I fell to the ground, the sharp ache in my chest breaking me, and cried for the prince I lost.

PART 2

2 YEARS LATER

You're cursed. Always have been. You cross that threshold into Ash Court, and you'll fall into an endless sleep during which the blood of fae will spill for eternity.

"He's definitely watching your ass," Nickie whispers in my ear, glancing over her shoulder at the line of guys by the bar. "I bet he ends up being your date."

I exhale loudly. "Why did I let you talk me into a blind date? I suck at talking to strangers. My tongue does that thing where it swells to twice its size and I drool."

"Flimflam. You just need to find the right guy. There are guys who love droolers." She pokes her tongue out at me.

What sucks the most is that I think she's right. About finding the right guy part, not the drool-loving thing. Find the perfect match, and everything will come together, right? Except I'm not sure I believe in the whole fairytale ending, the prince coming for me, and me discovering I'm perfect just as I am. Maybe some people are just not meant to find their mates or live happily ever after.

Someone clears her voice from somewhere behind me. I turn to the organizer. She's in a short skirt and tank top, standing near the doorway to this small private room next to the bar. "Ladies, please take your seats. We'll begin in one minute." Her voice is stern, and I can tell this isn't her first rodeo.

Nickie nudges me in the back toward one of ten two-seater tables set up around the room. "It's show time."

"By the way, you sound like a granny saying *flim-flam*. Just letting you know as a friend." I smirk at her and poke my tongue out this time. I love my best friend, even when she's being super pushy. Except, she's radiating excitement from getting me on this blind date, and as much as I hate to admit it, the energy is contagious. What if I meet a decent guy? What if I find myself easily tossing out smiles that demand attention? I've watched guys fall prey to Nickie's flirting, so tonight might be a good time to try it out myself.

"I'm on a no-swearing diet," she admits, which is news to me since she was swearing like a sailor this morning. She pulls down on her tight red skirt that inches up her thighs, though she can wear a hessian sack and she'll still attract attention. She has a blue band around her wrist just like I do… this bar allows those under twenty-one to enter as long as we wear bright bands so no alcohol is sold to us.

Nickie has that girl-next-door beauty where she barely wears makeup, and yet, has unblemished skin, lips that are naturally pouty, and stunning red curls I might kill for. Me… I have to work to look half as good as her, but what I adore about her is that when we're together, she's down-to-earth and she doesn't judge me.

"Plus, Jack loves when I talk like this in the bedroom." She winks.

"Ew, I don't want to know. But for real, what the hell am I meant to say to my date? Talk about the weather? Ask what he does for a job? God, I'm already bored." And I'm talking too much, a sure sign of nerves, not to mention my hands are sweaty. I can't shake anyone's hand now. I rub them down my black dress. It's simple with spaghetti straps, and the best part, the shape gives me a cinched-in waist. Brings out my slightly curvy bust and hips that hide in most clothes.

"You look hot in that dress by the way, the black really makes your pale skin pop. Like one of those porcelain dolls."

"Is that a compliment?"

She scrunches her face and shakes her head at me. "Of course it is. Have you not seen the latest run show models? Tans are no longer in style." Her eyes dart around the room. "Now, when the lucky man arrives, just chat to him normally like you're at college."

"I can't even do that." I start to walk away because this isn't going to work, and I made a mistake agreeing to this in the first place.

Nickie tugs my arm and pivots me back to my seat, to the table with a big number seven painted on a piece of paper.

That's what I've been reduced to. Specimen seven for a random guy to come and try out, as if this were an ice cream sampling booth.

"It's just a blind date, and it's being done as a group so everyone feels more comfortable, so you don't need to be nervous. Sugar knows, with all those strange dreams about kingdoms and princes you keep having, you need to get laid by a real guy."

"I do get action!" I whisper a bit too loudly, gaining the attention of a cute redhead girl two tables away, who winks at me. But Nickie's words hurt because I confided in her about the dreams that have been plaguing me my whole life. Dreams that I swore were real two years ago... Dreams I can barely remember anymore.

"I've seen all my potential dates somewhere at the bar, and none—"

"Gah! Just sit your ass down and stop overthinking this." Nickie flips open her tiny silver purse and pulls out a small piece of folded paper. "I made you something to help if you get stuck, because I knew you'd freak out." She leans in close and presses the note into my hand. "I pray your date is that fine glass of whiskey in the pin-striped suit. Did you see the size of his feet? Always look at a man's feet for everything you need to know. His shoes tell you how wealthy he is, how much he takes care of those close to him by the state of his shoes, and how loud he'll make you scream in the bedroom."

"If this goes wrong, I'm blaming you."

"Have fun," she murmurs before strolling across the room toward the door that leads into the main bar area, while the desperate and lonely remain gathered in this room. Balloons decorate the corners, obscuring lights covered in a red fabric, tainting everything in a reddish hue.

I feel stupid and uncomfortable and—

"Let's begin." The organizer draws the glass door shut to our room, closing out the chatter from the bar, and all I see is Nickie pressing her face to the glass, pulling a face at me.

I flip her the finger, and she laughs before vanishing into the crowd in the other room.

And this is why no one ought to ever let their friends set them up on blind dates, or any dates for that matter. Though I'd be lying if I said I'm not a tiny bit excited to see whom I've been paired up with out of pure scientific curiosity, of course.

The man who joins my table offers me a gentle smile. He's tanned with beautifully inviting green eyes and short-cropped hair. He's cute, not panty-dropping hot, but easy on the eyes. Probably a couple of years older than me. Twenty-one or twenty-two.

"I'm Holt. Great to meet you." His expression is neutral. He looks at me and sticks his hand out as if this were a business transaction, and maybe that's how some see the whole blind-date gig. Punch your details into a machine, and then it matches you to the most compatible person. And apparently, Holt is the one for me based on whatever Nickie added into my profile.

"Hi, I'm Guen." I shake his hand, and he sits down quickly, his hand on his lap, and I don't miss the quick swipe of his palm over his jeans.

Why did I shake his hand?

My heart is beating a million miles an hour, and heat is crawling up my neck.

"You look a bit different to the profile photo you sent in," he says right off the bat, so that's not a good sign. "Didn't realize your hair was so blonde. Is it dyed? Not that it's bad, I just wasn't expecting it."

I stiffen. Who in the world raised him? Wild dogs? I'm trying my hardest to give Holt the benefit of the doubt, but the shit dropping from his mouth has me clenching my teeth. "Actually, funny story, my roomie submitted the photo on my behalf, and well, I had just gotten out of the shower. So, I wasn't wearing makeup, and I only had a towel wrapped around me before she snapped the pic. Crazy friends, right?" I reach for my complimentary glass of cool water and gulp down a large mouthful.

"I prefer the natural look on women. Fewer clothes, less makeup, hair down and not dyed. Why mess with what God gave us, right?" He juts out his chin and chest with smugness, and I hold back an eye roll.

"This *is* my natural hair color!" I'm gobsmacked and push back the blonde hair I spent all night trying to add small curls to. My hair has a terrible time holding curls.

He stills, then eyes me like I might be the monster from his dreams, and already alarm bells are going off in my head. There is no way in the world Holt can be my perfect match.

In reality, I thought I had met my real match two years ago in another place, another world...

Luther.

One of three princes from Shadow Court in Wandering Realm in another world to ours.

But with so much time passing, I've forgotten many things, including why I thought he was the one for me. I'm starting to question if it wasn't all in my mind as the clinical psychiatrist my doctor ordered me to see insists. It's the only reason I agreed to this blind date. As a way to move on with my life and forget the imaginary man in my heart. The man who promised to come back for me, which he didn't. Which further confirms my theory that fairy tales don't exist.

Holt fills my glass with the jug of water from the table, giving me a wonky smirk. "I didn't mean to offend you; sometimes I have a way of saying the wrong thing."

"It's okay." I nervously drink more of my water, already out of ideas for a conversation.

I remember Nickie's note and fumble with opening it in my lap.

"So, what do you like to do in your spare time?" Holt asks, not sounding nervous, while I'm drowning in sweat.

"Paint landscapes when I can." Landscapes of the world that used to come to me in my dreams of castles, and a deadly forest made of twisted trees and teeth and claws. "But most of the time I'm completing assignments. I'm studying art at the local university. And you?"

"Scaffolding on construction sites is my day job. My newest project is just down the road. Maybe later we can go for a drive, and I'll show you. My last couple of girlfriends live on the way."

I'm at a complete loss for words, unsure what he's implying, and now all I can picture are all his girlfriends tucked in a row for Holt to wave to as we drive past. But I won't be going anywhere with him tonight or ever. Over my dead body. "Oh, that's nice."

He breaks into more chatter about how many girls he's dated this year, because that's fantastic conversation on a first date.

In all honesty, this date is cringe-worthy as hell. Perhaps I should have stuck to my guns and said no to Nickie when she told me she arranged this for me. There ought to be an escape button.

The back of my neck prickles with a warning, like someone is watching me from behind.

I quickly glance around to see everyone is focusing on their date, and I look across to the glass door leading into the main bar. People are everywhere, but no one is staring my way. Still, my skin crawls.

I glance back down at my note from Nickie.

If you're reading this, you've hit the desperate stage.

If you like him, ask him about sports or gaming or (you fill in based on interest) and listen to him.

If he's a creepo, tell him you're into foot fetishes or something gross and plan to move to Japan in a month.

I scrunch up the paper and fidget. *Wow, great advice, Nickie.* Around us, women are giggling, flirting, one couple holding hands. I want to exchange my date. I've never had luck with guys. Back in high school, one guy I crushed on hard saw me as nothing but a friend and ended up dating my arch-nemesis, while another guy I didn't like thought I was good enough for a forced one-night stand. Maybe the universe is trying to tell me something. Though one day, I like to think I'll find someone who doesn't just jerk me around.

"My last girlfriend had a lot of bad experiences with guys mistreating her. As a man, I will admit so many of them suck."

"Yes, we can agree on that. Guys suck." I'll go further and say falling in love is tragic. I've seen Nickie so miserable after her last boyfriend dumped her. They dated for eleven months, and now, I really hope Jack will be different. She once compared finding love to Russian Roulette with the true man of her dreams being the one bullet, and the rest are the empty chambers. I tried explaining to her how her analogy was wrong. Finding the one bullet is the one thing you do not want in Russian Roulette. She brushed me off and insisted it made sense in her mind.

I glance around for the organizer to try to call her over to escape, because Holt is definitely like finding the bullet under my definition.

"Ugh, right?" he says. "Except me. You can ask my exes."

"Will you excuse me for a moment? Just need to use the ladies'." I'm on my feet before he can respond. "Won't be long."

I saunter out of the room, noticing Bigfoot had scored himself a petite little brunette with tight curls who is batting her eyes. Well, at least someone is going to be screaming with pleasure tonight. I push open the door and slip into the other room, where the chatter and music engulfs me, then I rush like a madwoman through the crowd.

My body goes rigid when a guy calls my name behind me. All I can picture is Holt following me. I turn around with a *fuck off* on my lips, except there's only a crowd of partygoers behind me. Weird. I shove myself through the masses until I finally track down Nickie, who's sitting in her boyfriend's lap near a small table, swinging back a drink.

I march up to her and shout over the music, "I can't do this!"

Nickie flinches, spilling some of her orange juice down the front of her chest. "Fuc... Furry fudge, Guen, you scared the hell out of me. What are you doing here?"

I'm shaking my head. "I got the whacko of the bunch, Nickie, and your tips sucked." With a flick of my hand, I toss the scrunched-up paper on the table in front of her. I flop into the empty leather couch nearby and cross my legs. "He was so creepy. Talking about his ex-girlfriends, and he likes girls *au naturel*. He's probably a nudist. Why did you send that photo of me in a towel?"

Her boyfriend, Jack, is kissing her collarbone, licking up the spilled drink. He's handsome with short blond hair, and a perfect match for Nickie. They both have quirky personalities and click.

She's laughing, then refocuses on me. "Just give him a chance. He's nervous. Look how nervous you were."

I dig my claws into the couch. "You'll have to drag me back in there before I return to creeper town."

But she doesn't hear me, as she's kissing Jack, and I just roll my eyes and check out the number of other men in the bar who might have made more suitable dates. Most are drinking while trying to pick up. Maybe Nickie is right, and I was too quick to judge Holt?

My gaze lingers over the crowd to a man with broad shoulders and a smoldering look amid the shadows. The chatter and music are deafening, but in those moments as I lay eyes on this stranger, I hear nothing but the steady rising of my heartbeat. Alongside everyone else, he stands out, like he doesn't belong here. And I can't look away from him, as if I'm lost in a trance. He's powerful, and he radiates a sheer aura of danger, sending my pulse into a frenzy.

I want to look away, do something other than blush like a fool.

He's tall. Six-two, maybe six-three, his shirt hugging those wide shoulders and width. Dark clothes and short black hair blend into the shadows like he's morphed from them. And that face—sharp angles and strong jawline, eyes crystal green, almost glowing amid the darkness surrounding him.

Sweet hell, he's scorching hot, and his presence is

arousing something from deep within me, something primal and fiery.

I get to my feet and gravitate to him in a lustful trance I can't seem to shake. Maybe this is my chance to find out who he is. The only other person who has ever made me feel this way was Luther, but that was two years ago, and apparently, in my imagination. Except it had felt so real, especially after he promised to come back for me... but never did.

Someone moves between the hunk and me, our eye contact broken. I'm swooning for this stranger, and when the crowd parts again, he's gone. Scanning the room, I can't see him anywhere.

Nickie says, "Get back in there and get him."

"Yeah, sure," I mumble before strolling across the room, staring where the sex god was seconds earlier.

I'm lost in my thoughts when the organizer from the blind date session suddenly steps in front of me, her expression filled with disappointment.

My stomach drops to my feet, and I wrack my brain for the perfect excuse as to why I can't return, except the opposite slides out. Saying the wrong thing is what I excel at. "Oh, I'm on my way back now." I mentally slap myself for giving in so fast. I've never been good at saying *no* to people. If I ever became a superhero, that will be my kryptonite.

I'm already walking with her and glancing over my shoulder for my mystery man.

"If you don't give people a chance, how will you ever meet your perfect match?" she reprimands me as we step into the dating room, and I lower my gaze cringing further on the inside.

"Sorry," I repeat, staring into her kind hazel eyes, deciding then I'll be honest with Holt and end this now.

"It's not too late," she says with hope in her voice, and I quickly turn around to take my seat to find it's not Holt sitting across from me.

"It's you." The words slip from my lips.

I twist in the seat when my skirt catches on the edge of the wooden chair, and I hear the first rip.

Sweet Jesus, no!

"Is everything all right?" his deep, raspy male voice asks… the complete opposite of Holt's.

He's the same man I spied back in the bar with those bejeweled green eyes that shone so brightly, they might be polished emeralds.

Up close, he's so much more handsome and divine, and did I mention *large*, like he might have eaten Holt to take his place? Short chestnut hair, longer at the top, a strong jawline and nose, full lips. But his eyes keep calling to me, like somehow they belong on a different face. I have no idea why I think that, but I'm lost for words.

That smoldering look of his assesses me as I'm scanning him, my mind racing ahead to figure out what to say. I feel the rising panic inside me, my face burning at being so close to him and likely making a fool of myself. He looks like he can pick and choose his girls, and doesn't need to work too hard for their attention.

"I may have sat at the wrong table." I go to leave as I feel my skin surging with embarrassment, but the rip in my skirt grows longer, and I'm about to scream, picturing myself with a huge hole over my ass.

"No, it's the right table. You're seven. The previous boy had to leave urgently."

Fisting the fabric of my skirt caught somehow on this hellish chair, I look up to the sex god staring at me, waiting for my response.

"Seven, yep, that must be me." I tug on the fabric to free myself, but it's jammed in there like Satan himself has sewn it to the chair to make me suffer.

"Oh, I'm Guen," I say, flushing so hard, I'm burning up. I take my glass and drink it down in one go.

"Dei—Doohickey," he says, seeming to struggle to remember his name.

I arch an eyebrow. "Doohickey? Really?" His lie makes me tug harder on my skirt in an effort to get out of here while smiling at the man my ovaries are preparing to marry. Then a louder rip sounds. I half-fall out of my seat, the chair coming with me.

My heart soars to my throat, and I'm picturing myself on the ground and my skirt up to my waist.

Strong hands catch me, and Doohickey—god, I feel stupid just thinking that name—is at my side incredibly fast, lifting me back upright. My heart is racing so hard now. If I was blushing before, now I'm a supernova, diving back into Earth's atmosphere at five hundred degrees.

He's kneeling near my seat, finding the cause of my small mishap.

"You seem to have your gown caught."

Gown? I shake my head and glance around to find others looking at me, and I'm mortified. "It's nothing, seriously. Don't worry," I insist, placing my hand over the gaping hole revealing my thigh to just below the line of my thong.

But he's fiddling with something under my chair, and having him kneeling, reaching me at head height, my whole body is tingling.

His fingers gently graze the side of my thigh. Just a simple touch, but it's enough to leave me losing my breath and get my nipples tightening. I imagine his hands all over my body, his mouth dragging over my skin, his head between my thighs.

What is wrong with me?

He takes hold of the fabric to release me from my torture, causing electrifying shivers to race through my body. My mind is speeding with wild thoughts of me leaning over and tasting this stranger's lips. But my head is waltzing with the commotion and embar-rassment.

The couple close by keep watching us, and I just smile and give them a small wave, then drop my hand, feeling dumb.

"It's stuck in there hard," Doohickey says.

Oh, god!

He wrenches the caught-up fabric so suddenly, my whole body shuddering from the move. A horrendous rip screeches, and I'm about to die.

I look down to see him holding half my skirt in his hand, and the rest partially covering my thong.

Kill me now.

I stare at him hard, and if I had the power, I'd shoot laser beams from my eyes. "Are you kidding me?"

His mouth curls into a smile. "That wasn't meant to happen."

"Really? *You think?* Oh my god," I mumble, reaching over to find half of my ass exposed, and this is my worst nightmare come to life. Finding myself naked in public. Maybe I'll wake up and find that this is another of my insane dreams. Please let it be that.

"God won't help you, but I will." Doohickey is unbuttoning his shirt, revealing a strong, broad chest with not much hair, but so many muscles.

My mouth drops open as I take in the sight of a half-naked, muscular built man with a mouth poised in a smirk. He knew exactly the effect he has on me. Panty-melting gorgeous… hell yes.

"What are you doing?" My eyes are twice their size. I reach out to pull his shirt back on before everyone sees and assumes we're about to do something, considering I'm missing most of my skirt. Thank god it's dimly lit in here.

"As much as I'd like to take this moment to admire your naked rear, I insist you take my shirt." He shakes the shirt off his log-sized arms and hands it over.

I waste no time to slide it over my arms, his manly scent invading my senses. Oh, why does he need to smell so divine? This is completely unfair. The black shirt swims over me, and as I finally stand, the fabric falls to my knees. No ass cheeks in sight.

"Thank you." I look over to Doohickey, who's on his feet, topless and the most incredible thing I've ever seen. Planes of muscles and ripped abs all taper into the perfect V, where his black tailored pants hang low on his hips. My fingers tingle with the temptation to reach over and see exactly how hard those muscles are. In all honesty, my head is still spinning at how fast everything went down, and I offer him a piece of advice as I'm still fuming. "Next time, use your real name on a date, and try not to rip a girl's skirt off her body."

"I just saved you." He stares at me with amusement in his eyes.

I raise a brow. "*Saved* in the very loosest sense."

"Think I'll call this my very lucky day," he muses with a twitch of his lips.

I want to punch him in the arm, though by the size of him, I doubt he'd feel it.

"It's not often I get to help a maiden who flashes me her beautiful round rear." He eyes me, lips curling upward.

"Round?" I was wrong about him being oblivious—he knew exactly what he was doing with my skirt. "Yeah, it was your lucky day," I say. "Hope you got an eyeful, because it'll be the last time you see any of my *rear*." Why is he talking so strange anyway?

Someone nearby gasps, and the redhead girl sitting near us has her mouth hanging open, drawing everyone's attention to us, stealing envious glances.

"Put it away," a guy hisses, and the organizer is rushing over, her eyes flickering between me and the gorgeous, partially naked guy.

"Is everything all right?" She gasps, her eyes lingering on Doohickey's bare chest.

My mouth opens with an explanation, but Doohickey butts in. "We've had a splendid night, and now I'm taking the lovely lady to her friends. Farewell." His hand is on my back, and he's ushering me to the door.

My head is all over the place, while my body is trembling with tingles from his large palm against my back, from each inhale of his sexiness smothering me.

True to his word, he guides me through the crowd, who cheer us on as if we've just had sex in the bathroom. The night is going from terrible to horrendous.

Before we reach Nickie, Doohickey's hands slide to my hips, his bare chest pressed against my back, warmth spreading over me like an inferno. We pause near a quiet spot along the wall. His breath is on my neck as he inhales deeply.

"Did you just smell me?" I murmur, but despite wanting to shove him off me, I find myself clenching my thighs from the sparks erupting deep in my stomach. Something about the darkness of the bar, the thumping music, and his closer proximity has me trembling with lust, blurring my thoughts.

His teeth are on my neck, dragging over my flesh, and there's something almost deliciously familiar about the way he does that.

"Don't stop." My whisper slips past my lips.

Hard breaths are on my neck, and a moan slips past my lips as a pressure is mounting inside me.

"What's your real name?" I manage to speak the words, unsure where they're coming from. I'm trying to swim my way out of the fog swallowing my ability to think.

He exhales loudly, filled with arousal and frustration. Then he breaks our connection in an instant and steps back from me. "I'll be seeing you around, Guendolyn." His words fade.

Everything inside me stills at hearing him call me by my real name.

The last person to call me that was… "Luther?"

I whip around to find him gone. With it comes the void in my heart that I thought I'd buried after two years, gaping awake like a giant black hole.

CHAPTER 20

DEIMOS

Guendolyn is as tempting and dangerous as the Seven Hells of Wandering Realm.

Following her energy to this tavern, I tracked her to that glass room and can't tear my gaze from her.

Captivating.

Alluring.

Sinful.

One look at her, and the world dissolves around me.

Her black dress falls mid-thigh, showing off toned legs, the bodice tight, maybe too tight as it pushes up her breasts, showing them off. Stunning, but I'm not impressed by the asshole in front of her leering. So when she excuses herself, I summon him to me with a little of the influencing magic the gods blessed me with, and I boot him out the door. Then I take his seat to talk to Guendolyn and discover how much she remembers about her past. I was warned that her memories would most likely be wiped of the events.

But I fail in my mission miserably tonight and gain no answers, what with her skirt incident, the image of her ass on my mind, and my thoughts not on returning home with her. That's not easy on any man. My stepfather, the King of Shadow Court, would lecture us that a man should never let his dick lead him. I was too young to understand how hypocritical those words were coming from him. Until I grew up to discover I lived in a kingdom of lies.

I shake those thoughts away and keep my attention on beautiful Guendolyn to make the best of the situation.

With what she is, I shouldn't be staring at her this way, thinking about the things I want to do to her, but I am.

Images flash of those legs around my hips, her head back and moaning as I drive into her.

I take in a sharp breath to steady myself. She's changed in the two years since we last met, her figure curvier, her beauty as brilliant as the rising sun. The girl who came to the realm then seemed younger, wary, still beautiful, but not like this. Not like this woman, whom I can't stop staring at. There's something about her beyond her hair falling perfectly over her bare shoulders, those hypnotizing blue eyes, and how much I want to rip those clothes off her body.

I can't stop remembering our first encounter alone two years ago in the Wandering Realm... our dance of words, her resisting me. One quick nip of her neck, and her blood flowed onto my tongue. Guendolyn now doesn't remember the night, but her taste has stayed with me. Indescribable sweetness like nectar and unlike any female fae I've tasted.

There's a power I sense beneath the surface in her presence. It's dark and deadly.

As Ahren, my eldest brother, once put it, *"Everyone knows who she is, that her name is Guendolyn, and what she represents... Everyone except her."* That's why I'm here to collect her. To take her back to the Wandering Realm and help us end the curse she unknowingly started two years ago.

Now, I watch her from within the shadows. My shirt covers enough of her, but it isn't like I can forget the creamy curves of her ass and what lies underneath the rest of her dress. Those long legs stretch out from the shirt, and in black heels, she fills me with filthy thoughts. She strips me of my focus and mission. Gods, she has the full package, and coupled with her blushing, my dick punches again in my pants, against the zipper.

She stole my second eldest brother's attention, but I

barely knew the girl two years ago… Now I see what Luther means by his soul shattering for her.

Hell, she's gorgeous.

Everything about her calls to me. She's perfection. And maybe Luther isn't wrong in insisting we come to collect her and use her power to save our Kingdom. Sure, his intentions are to claim her for himself, but now… I exhale deeply. Now, I need to remember my mission and nothing else.

I track her movements from the glass room where she's gone to search for me, and her action ignites a spark of fascination within me. Confusion stains her expression, and she is off again, searching for her friend and passing two men, who eye her head to toe and look at her as a girl they plan to fuck and be rid of. She shouldn't be in a place like this.

I don't like it.

I should have stayed with her, but in her presence my head blurs, and remaining close to her tonight will end with me hilt-deep in that tiny thing. A shiver shudders over me at the thought, and I groan as a pulse rages in my cock.

Focus evades me, but I need it to help her open the gateway between our worlds so we can return home, before the curse spreads into Shadow Court and kills everyone. The trick is going to be getting her to tap into her powers.

She doesn't know that yet, but I'm an expert at getting people to do what I want.

For tonight, she's my concern, and that means ensuring no one touches her.

By the time I'm in bed, I'm exhausted. Nickie and her boyfriend are already in her bedroom, and the thump of her headboard hitting the wall is an irritating rhythm. I reach over and grab my earphones, then push them into my ears before selecting a playlist—any playlist—just to shut them out. A pop song begins, and I crawl under the blanket with only the silvery hue of the moon from the huge bay window drenching the bedroom. Yet all I can think about are those green eyes.

I shouldn't drool over the first cute man to cross my path. I shouldn't daydream about him endlessly. I shouldn't picture him naked. But it's all happening. His words ring in my ears, while my skin tingles with the memory of his hands at my waist, his broad chest pressed flat against my back.

I'll see you around, Guendolyn.

Who in the world is he? He looks nothing like Luther or his brothers from my dreams, yet he knows my real name. Nickie swore on her life she had nothing to do with setting me up with him, so I'm at a loss.

It took my shrink two years to finally convince me the dreams *were* all in my head. Most of the memories from those hallucinations, as my doctor calls them, have faded now. They left after I no longer heard Luther's voice inside my head… words that are like a memory I can't quite grasp. Now all I'm left with are recollections of three princes, longing emotions, and an extravagant kingdom.

Maybe it's for the best… except after tonight, old anxiety threads through my veins.

I roll over in bed and hug the blanket tight against me, then close my eyes, urging sleep to sweep me away.

Still, all I see are green eyes as he kneels before me, staring at me with a look of utter lust.

His hands touch my knees and push them wider apart.

Of course, I resist, but he's too strong to fight, and when his touch slides along the inside of my thighs, I tremble, unable to make a sound. I'm terrified he'll uncover my shameful secret.

The tips of his fingers are gentle, so tender and electrifying against my skin. He grazes me ever so lightly over my bikini line. Nothing stops him. He edges closer to my heat, where he'll discover how wet I am for him.

I draw in a sharp breath, unable to move, waiting for his fingers to slide into me. But he never does, not even when I'm pulsing with desire. My nipples tighten, rubbing against the fabric of my dress.

"Please," I beg, my body thrumming with arousal.

He laughs, making a sound that covers me in shivers, and when he slides two digits under the elastic of my underwear, I melt under his touch. My legs widen for him, and he swallows me with his gaze.

"You've wanted me from the moment you saw me, haven't you?"

I want to respond, but I can't, not while his touch is sliding up and down over my slickness, then circling over my clit. I'm muffling the sounds of my moans, and an orgasm rips through me fast like an earthquake, shaking me at the core. My muscles tense as I quake with pleasure. My eyes shut, and all I can think of is him.

Sprawled across my bed, I'm smiling insanely. Drawing the blanket over my chest, I take a deep inhale and count slowly to ten to calm my raging heart. It's been a long time since any man has had such an effect on me, and no man has ever had me climaxing by thought alone.

And still, I have no clue who he is, or even his name.

Luther scrambles over to me, cradling me in his embrace, tears on his cheeks. "What did you do, little wolf? I'm not ready to lose you. I just found you."

"I don't understand." I hold on to him, clutching his collar, but my insides twist and knot. Shadows feather my vision. My arms weaken.

"Don't let me go," I cry, and Luther holds me tight to his chest. His shaking is a blade to my heart.

My hands tremble, the sensation spreading over me so fast, I start falling into a familiar darkness.

"I'll find you again," Luther promises. "I'll tear down the world to find you."

And in a heartbeat, I'm gone.

Have you heard from the mysterious hunk?

I stare at Nickie's message on my phone and consider the orgasm I had last night from thinking of him, so yeah, I remember him well. My recent dream with Luther also pushes to the forefront of my mind. It's been two years since I last dreamt of him, and the memory leaves a deep ache in my heart I can't explain. I can't seem to recall what came before that part of the dream, or after—just the heartache that sits on my chest, like I've lost something so precious to me that I might die if I don't find it again.

I blink hard to push those thoughts away, then I look down at Nickie's message. Right. She's waiting for a response.

You know I didn't give him my number. I go to slide the phone into my back pocket, then remember I'm at work and wearing my black skirt—knee-length, skintight, which makes walking close to impossible and offers no pockets.

Painting has been my passion since forever, plus I needed a part-time job, so when my foster mom sent me a job application for the local gallery in Hyde Park, not too far from my university, I applied and got it. I manage the front desk for most of the hours I spend here. I'll admit, answering calls isn't fun, but Johanz, the owner, has been kind, and he put one of my paintings up in the lobby for show. That brings a smile to my face every time I glance to it hanging over the waiting room couch.

Thorny bushes and broken trees fill the landscape. Snippets of a glorious kingdom that reflect the golden rays of the sun can be seen in the distance, reached only by stairs made of twisted stone, accessible by crossing an arched bridge that spans two mountains.

I meander over to the reception desk and flop into my leather chair when my phone beeps with a message.

Your Cinderella man may turn up and surprise you yet. He has a shirt to claim back, remember?

At the mention of his shirt, I catch a light whiff of that delicious manly, outdoorsy scent, as though he's right next to me. Heat ripples down to the deepest pits of my stomach, as it had last night. Except, I'm only deluding myself if I let myself crave this stranger, and tonight I decide I'll throw his shirt in the wash to rid my room of the smell.

I reply to Nickie, *If only fairy tales were real.*

The office door to my right opens with a swishing sound.

Panic throws me into motion, and I toss my phone under the unopened letters on the desk. With a smile, I raise my head to see Johanz emerging. He's a tall man who wears a navy, pin stripped Armani suit like a second skin. Johanz is a handsome man, a lot more on the thin size for my liking, and he wears his black hair slicked back with a dash of blue color that glints in the sunlight. Though made of money, he didn't grow up rich. He once confessed that he came from a poor family, which is why, in my opinion, he's so humble.

"Guen, I'm out for a couple of hours. You're okay on your own, right? There are no showings today." He smiles, and all I see are those glorious pearly white teeth, the tanned lines bracketing his mouth.

"Of course, Mr. Landstone. I've got this covered."

He nods, pushes past the glass door, and makes his

way to a black Mercedes parked right in front. One day, this will be me… owning a gallery, selling my own masterpieces, and driving the flashiest car around.

I reach for my phone, when the door suddenly jingles open.

"You forgot something?" I ask, tilting my head up, except it's not my boss but a man in jeans, sneakers, and a long-sleeved tee. Not the usual clientele, since the cheapest piece on sale is just over a thousand dollars.

The man with dark hair and a large, crooked nose shuts the door, then strolls past the reception area and through the arched passage into the gallery without a glance my way. We're open to the public, of course, but in all honesty, those who visit usually have a huge bank account. It isn't uncommon for people to wander in off the street, but most of the time, they leave very quickly once they see the price tags. The guard who normally sits at a little podium just inside the gallery is at lunch, and it doesn't occur to me until now that I should have locked the door until he returned, so I'm not alone.

Except, I'm sure this is just another wanderer about to walk out.

"Hello, how are you today?" I make my way toward the main showroom and find the man with short, messy hair staring at a painting of a train speeding through an old village on a rainy day. "That's an Ellaine

Gray piece. She's a local artist here in town." I've always loved the rawness of this piece. "See how the juxtaposition of the industrial train against the wooden huts of the small town reflects the progression of civilization and lets go of the past? I mean to me. Everyone sees different things in paintings." Which is why I love them so much.

When he doesn't say anything but continues to stare, I figure I was wrong about him and maybe he is a buyer. I try to shake off the eerie feeling he gives off and treat him like any other customer. "What do you like about the painting?"

"Do you know this location?" He points to the image, and I'm shaking my head, even if he isn't looking my way.

"Sorry, I don't, but the artist will be coming into the gallery next week, and I can ask her."

He nods and looks around at the other pieces, and there's an unsettling strangeness about him I can't quite put my finger on.

The door behind me opens as a second man with a thick neck, tanned skin, and short, blond hair enters. He reminds me of a bodybuilder. He's also dressed in casual attire.

"Hello," I offer, like I do to everyone who arrives at the gallery.

He nods at me and makes his way over to the other

man. He leans in close, exchanging heated whispers before they both look over at me.

The hairs on my neck rise, and I feel sick on the inside. I'm alone in the gallery, and concern has me glancing outside to see if Ted, our guard, has returned. I should call him to return. I swallow hard, and my feet slip backward as I turn toward my desk. My phone and bag are there, and I have pepper spray in the inside pocket.

"Um, excuse me, ma'am," one of the men asks, his voice raspy, like he's chain-smoked his entire life. Except the reek that normally comes with smokers doesn't linger in the air from his arrival. "Do you have any paintings with dragons?"

His question stops me in my tracks, and I turn to face him. He seems genuinely curious. I'm not sure how to respond at first, when the sign outside the building clearly states contemporary art.

"Unfortunately, no, but you'll find a gallery several blocks away specializing in fantasy, so they may have something you're looking for.

"What about that one?" His friend points into the reception, and I turn to see he's referring to my painting.

"Oh, there are no dragons in that image."

They both meander toward my piece, the blond guy striding so close to me, his arm brushes over mine.

I flinch backward from his unwanted touch, but he keeps walking to the painting as if bumping into me is meaningless. The nerve of that prick.

I rub my arm where he touched me. The skin is icy cold beneath my fingers. It's nothing, I'm sure, and I rub my arm to bring warmth to my flesh.

Both of them now stand in front of my work, staring at it, and I'd be lying if I didn't admit there's a moment of pride to have someone paying attention to my creation for a change. Even if it is two men who leave me uncomfortable. I move closer to my painting but keep a nice distance between us.

Blondie's nose flares at the image, and a tinge of sharpness pierces my chest at the thought that he might be mocking my piece, stealing my earlier joy.

"I'd recommend going to the other gallery for what you're looking for." My words come out harsher than I anticipate, but I don't care and march over to my desk, but footfalls follow me. Shivers zip up the back of my legs, and I move faster.

"That's your painting, isn't it?" one of them asks, and I'm too panicked to discern who's speaking.

I turn to face them and find they're both standing less than a foot away, towering over me, somehow looking taller than they were moments earlier. Something glints in their dark eyes, something almost fiery and red.

I stumble back, my hand reaching for anything on the table to use as a weapon. Pen. Stapler. Where in the world is my bag? All rational thoughts dissolve, and I struggle to unstick my feet from the floor. My heart is thundering harder when Blondie steps forward.

"You need to leave," I demand as my fingers graze the metal envelope opener on my desk, and I clutch it hard in my grasp. It's sharp enough to pierce flesh and do some real damage if they step any closer.

There's no surprise or shock crossing their faces. Blondie rolls his eyes, then checks his watch, as though he has another appointment with someone else to creep out.

"Is it time?" the dark-haired man with a crooked nose asks, and his friend's lips twist into uncertainty.

"Should have happened by now. I touched her, so it should have triggered the portal."

I grab my phone from under the envelopes on the desk and dial 911. "One tap and the cops will be here in a flash. Understand? Now get the fuck out of the gallery!" I have no idea what they're talking about, but they're freaking me out.

A heavy silence thickens the air between us, and I'm shaking.

The front door opens, and I'm about to cry with happiness when Ted, our guard, walks in, all broad shoulders and furious. He's in his black uniform and the best sight in the world. His gaze meets mine, and I try I give him my best panicked look before eyeing the two men near my desk.

"Can I help you two?" he growls, stepping closer, rather intimidating with his height.

The two pricks retreat, with Blondie taking the lead. "Not at all. We were just leaving."

"That's a very smart idea!" he booms.

They stroll out of the gallery, as if Ted doesn't look like a bear about to rip them apart. The bastards aren't afraid of him, and that realization punches me in the gut.

"You okay, Guen?" he asks me, his voice is gentle.

I'm nodding before he finishes talking. "Just freaked out."

"I'm going to check the back entry and lane. Stay here." He storms into the gallery to reach the rear door.

I'm frozen with shock, my brain screaming. I run for the door, slam it shut, and lock it with shaky hands just until Ted returns. Retreating, I keep scanning the sidewalk outside through the glass door and windows, expecting them to come back. The white walls of the gallery feel like they're closing in around me, and I'm choking for breath. Biting down on my lower lip brings a sharp sting. It tells me this just happened. It's real.

All I want is to go home and hide in my room. I start searching for my handbag near the desk to find it's fallen behind the chair.

A sudden pounding sound comes from the window behind me, and I flinch so hard, a small scream streams past my lips. I grab my pepper spray and swing around, ready to spray the hell out of the person's face if they break into the gallery.

CHAPTER 22

GUEN

Johanz frowns at me from outside of the gallery window, and it takes me a few moments to unstick my feet from behind the reception desk. I exhale with relief and hurry over to the door. My hands are still shaky as I unlock the bolt and let my boss inside.

"I'm so sorry I locked the door. These strange men came in and… Did you forget something?" My breaths came in shallow puffs, my mind whirring with memories of the incident.

"Just breathe, Guen," he says, worry threading his words, his gaze sweeping the gallery behind me. "Did they hurt you?" He's rubbing my back, and his eyes show the same genuine concern my foster mother had every time she took me to see the shrink. She never gave up on me when everything seemed to be against me. Not even when the doctor suggested that I might be suffering from schizophrenia.

"I'll bring you some water," my boss insists. "Lucky I came back. I just forgot my wallet."

"These men were standing really close, saying weird things." I feel stupid in this moment as I hear my words and what I'm freaking out about. But it's the eerie feeling that leaves my skin crawling.

"You did the right thing by locking the door."

I sit at my desk and feel like there was more I could have done. My boss quickly crosses the room and collects a bottle of water from his office before return-ing. After several mouthfuls of the cool water, I feel somewhat calmer.

Ted returns from the back room, his cheeks flushed, as though he's been running. My gaze falls to his hands, half-expecting to see blood on them from a fight, but aside from the rapid rise and fall of his chest, he's fine. "They're nowhere in sight."

"Come," my boss says to me. "I'm going to drive you home, and you can tell me what happened. Then you're taking some time off, all right?"

I'm shaking my head, my stomach suddenly hurting over the idea that he might not see me as fit enough to keep running the front of the gallery. "I'm fine, really." I tilt my head up and clear my throat, not wanting him to think that I'll freak out when any strange men enter the gallery. I love this job, and he pays so well. "I need the—"

He raises his chin, persistent enough to get his way, stealing my words. "I'm not taking no for an answer, and you'll be paid normally on those days off, I promise."

I nod and am already grabbing my bag and phone, struggling on the inside to accept that this is nothing more than a bit of time off. "Thank you."

"I'm sorry I left you alone. I should have made sure Ted was here. This is my fault."

My throat tightens at the heartfelt worry in his voice. "It's not your fault there are shitheads in this world."

He turns away, not seeming to listen, and walks toward the door. I grab my coat off the back of my seat and chase after him, braving the cold weather.

"Shit, Guen, you need to keep a baseball bat under your work desk," Nickie says while fluffing up her red curls in my bathroom mirror. "But on the bright side, you have some paid time off."

"Yeah, that's the part that worries me. The gallery has a huge showing this weekend. I might call Johanz in a couple of days and reassure him I'm doing fine." I lean a shoulder against the doorway to my bathroom, my gaze slipping to my friend applying ruby lipstick. "Do you think I overreacted in front of my boss?" She's wearing a body hugging dress in a metallic silver. She glints every time the light hits the fabric. It's hugs her from the bust to her butt, and the rest is flesh. On her, that dress makes her look like a goddess. On me, I'd be an embarrassment.

She whips around to face me, her eyes widening. "Why would you say that? Those two douches saw you alone and thought it was an opportunity. Sick fucks. Don't apologize for your reaction. Your boss should have ensured the guard was there." She lowers her lipstick to the counter and strides over to me, dragging me into her arms until I can't breathe. Despite her strength, her touch is warm, and she smells like a meadow of flowers. Kind of overpowering and sweet. I like it. "I'm always here for you, babe."

"Thanks. That means everything." When I can't take enough air into my lungs, I wriggle free from her anaconda-like grip. "Maybe I should stay home tonight? What if those jerks show up?"

"Babe, I bet they were just some dicks on the street and saw you alone in the gallery and thought you might be easy. Don't let them get into your head. But if you're really not up to it, we can hang out here and celebrate my birthday." She smiles widely, and I know she genuinely means it. Except, she's been talking about going to this club for her twenty-first for six months. The place is impossible to get into as it is.

Maybe she's right. I shouldn't let those asses get into my head. "Nah, let's go out. Some fun will help me forget the shitty day."

"Yes!" She jumps on the spot, then studies me up and down, her lips pinching tight. "So, you wearing that tonight?"

I stiffen and glance down at my blue skinny jeans that took me a legit fifteen minutes to climb into, so no way in hell are they coming off. I've also got on black combat boots and a button-up transparent black shirt with a black bra underneath. "I'm going for the casual, I-don't-give-a-fuck-but you-can't-glance-away look."

She makes that humming sound like she always does when she doesn't agree.

"You'll need the jaws of life to pry me out of these jeans, so they're staying," I say.

"At least put some heels on. I'm going to get you mine."

"No, it's—" I reach out to stop her, but she darts out of the bathroom too fast. There's no stopping her. I step closer to the mirror and run my finger under my eyes where the makeup is slightly smudging. The woman staring back at me looks so much more confident than how I feel inside. Blonde hair cascading over my shoulders gleams from the glitter I sprayed it with, the same rainbow of color lashing over my eyelids.

Kohl makeup lines my eyes, which look particularly blue tonight. Though, underneath, unease bubbles in my chest. There's a fog in my head, like I'm only half-living in this world. That sense of forgetting something is always with me… always has been, for as long as I can remember.

"Here you go." Nickie returns and places a pair of shiny black heels near my feet.

"You had to get the tallest ones, didn't you?"

She smirks with an evil glint in her tawny eyes, and I can tell she's loving this. She's been trying to dress me up in her clothes ever since we moved in together two years ago. "You look so sexy with heels, girl. Put them on, and let's get going," she orders with a laugh.

By the time I'm geared up in shiny black stilettos with open toes and straps around my ankles, we're rushing outside where an Uber awaits.

The city blurs past in bright lights and cars, and after a flash of the tickets Nickie bought months ago, we're in the club before I know it.

Strobe lights throb across the room, people crowd together on the circular dance floor, and the floorboards thump beneath my shoes from the thundering music. The whole place is a heartbeat coming through the speakers.

"This place is insane," I shout at Nickie, just to be heard over the noise.

"And it's just getting started. Wait until the dancers

in the cages come out." She snatches my wrist with an excited giggle, and we force our way closer to the bar, then she lets go of me. I'm caught up in the enormous pedestal in the middle of the dance floor with people up there dancing for everyone. A loud cheer explodes around us, and I lift my head to the four large bird-style cages lowering from the ceiling. They pause halfway down and inside each is a woman in a bright pink sparkling bikini, pole dancing with the bars.

People shove past us to join the crowd, and I've never seen a place this crazy. I love how my pulse dances in my veins. Everything about this club is made to invigorate you as soon as you walk inside.

Nickie slides a glass of something green into my hand, and it smells like Midori. "That was fast service," I say before I drink it easily, it being so sweet. Exactly what I need to forget the day and have a wild night.

"A guy at the bar bought them for us. How generous, right?" She's sipping hers, staring out into the crowd.

I blink hard. "Wait, you accepted a stranger's drink? He could have spiked it." Oh geez, I just drank mine as though it were candy water. If I make myself vomit, will I stave off any drugs in my system?

My chest tightens as I turn my head toward the bar. So many people are huddling close to the counter. "Where is he?" I ask.

"It's okay, babe," she reassures me by nudging her

arm up against mine. "I accepted it from the bartender directly, and the guy just paid. He insisted it was for both of us. He was a freaking hot beast."

"Really? Hot beast, you say?" I glance around.

As we finish our drinks, a tall man in his mid-twenties with short, sandy hair and tanned skin approaches Nickie. He's in a shiny blue shirt and black pants, hair parted down the middle. Not handsome in my books. Even with them standing so close, I can't hear the whispers over the noise in this place. Is he the hot beast? He's too much on the skinny side for my liking.

Next thing, Nickie grabs my arm and draws me toward the dance floor. Launching forward, I stumble on my heels, convinced I just murdered half a dozen toes on the way. I quickly slip my and Nickie's empty plastic cups onto a nearby table we pass.

Bodies sway around us. To be surrounded by so many people all dancing is electrifying, and I'm loving every moment of this. Somehow, we end up in the middle near the pedestal. I can't recall how long we've been dancing when someone catches my eye from across the masses. Familiar dark hair and a crooked nose. Next to him is Blondie, the other stalker from the gallery.

Air chokes out of my lungs, and I feel as though I'm suddenly drowning.

My feet are sliding backward. No, this can't be happening. That can't be them.

Panic lashes over my chest.

Run.

That's all I'm thinking.

Nickie. I find her in the crowd to my right. "Nickie," I call out over the music, but it's impossible to hear anything in here. I push myself through the masses to reach her, when a new song comes on and the whole crowd goes insane with excitement. Screaming and shoving as more people enter the dance floor.

Nudged and elbowed, I stumble about and lose sight of Nickie. The stalkers are gone too.

I press myself in the same direction Nickie was moments earlier as I scramble to pull my phone out from my back pocket. Bumping into others doesn't stop me.

"Watch it, bitch," someone snarls, and another person shoves me in the back.

My heart is pelting against my chest with the need to escape.

The phone is trembling in my hand as I frantically hit Nickie's number. Pressing it to my ear, I shove past the masses and glance around, unable to see the stalkers.

My chest constricts desperately with fear. All I want to do is scream for help, but I can barely hear my own thoughts.

"Hello," Nickie answers, her voice barely reaching me.

"Where the hell are you?" I stare out over the crowds, shouting at her so she hears me.

"If I haven't answered, it means I'm out having fun. Leave a message."

"Fuck," I mutter under my breath as I hang up and jam my cell into my back pocket.

At the edge of the floor is a huge guy in a black T-shirt. Out of instinct, I gravitate toward him. "Excuse me, are you a bouncer here?" I ask, but he doesn't seem to hear me and pushes right past me.

Rude much?

I retreat and move past him.

There are people everywhere, and my heart is hammering hard. I don't know where to look. Everyone is exploding with applause from the tune. I don't know the song, don't care. People are pushing past me, and I want to hide somewhere. My stomach in my throat—I should have stayed home, should have followed my instinct.

Someone grabs my arm, and I swing around, my skin pricking with dread.

Blondie's wry grin greets me. He says something, but I can't hear him.

I don't think but fight back, kicking him and trying to wrench my arm from his, but it's useless and he just laughs at me. With one swift pull, I'm stumbling on my feet after him toward the rear dark corner of the club.

"Help me," I choke out as I reach for people. I grab

their shirts, their arms, bags, anything, but they all shake me off, don't even bother to look at someone kidnapping me right in front of them.

Dread is choking me when the other one shows up. Dark hair. Crooked nose.

"Leave me alone!" I shout, but it's too loud in here.

They leer at me, and I feel violated before they even hurt me. Blackness pulses through every inch of me, emptying me of any possible hope. Blondie grabs my arms and slams my back to a wall, my skull hitting it hard. Stars explode behind my eyes, pain jolting over my head.

My blood runs cold as he pushes up against me, his face in mine, and all I can smell is putrid decay. A chill creeps up my spine.

I don't know these men, but I despise them. I hate the terror throbbing inside my chest. Hate how petrified I feel with every breath that I take. I want them to scream with pain.

I stare in the face of my nightmare and battle against him, punching and shouting at him. He moves so fast, I don't see the hand coming until it grips my neck, lifting me off the floor, and I'm on tippy-toes as he pins me to the wall.

The sounds around me seem to fade, the nightclub receding into the distance.

"Your fate is death, Guendolyn," he snarls. Big brown eyes and bushy eyebrows are all I can see.

I don't know how he knows my real name, but I loathe the sound of it on his lips. Loathe how he stares at me like I'm dirt.

His fingers squeeze harder, and I'm suffocating, my lungs strangling themselves for air. My heart punches into my chest, faster and faster, until darkness feathers the corners of my eyes.

Suddenly, he's flying backward, ripped from me.

My knees buckle, and I drop to the floor as the air buffets against me. I drag breaths into my starved lungs, trying my best to see through the tears and dimness of the club.

A large figure emerges out of the shadows and approaches me. But I'm too far gone.

Darkness swoops in and steals me from the terror.

CHAPTER 23

I open my eyes to a white ceiling and circular chandelier, dripping in crystals. It doesn't look familiar. This isn't the club or my apartment, and a sliver of fear creeps through me as I try to recall how I got here.

Buzz...buzz...buzz. My pocket is vibrating.

I push myself up from a black leather couch and grab my phone from my back pocket. Fog blurs my mind. I'm waiting for my brain cogs to restart. To remember where I am. There have been many times when I've woken up and couldn't remember my own bedroom, as if I didn't belong there, as if it weren't my room. It used to scare me to hell to feel so lost, to feel like my life was a maze I couldn't escape from. I wondered if one day I'd wake up and not remember who I was at all. I shake those thoughts aside, focusing on the now, on the thoughts pushing forward.

A luxurious open room surrounds me. White walls, paintings of beautiful landscapes and women in golden frames. An unlit fireplace sits in front of me, and a large dining area to my right has an enormous television on the wall. There's a hallway that leads to more rooms. I twist my head to see floor-to-ceiling windows behind me. I'm on my feet and staring outside at the bright lights at night time.

I swallow hard and turn back around fast. Someone brought me to a hotel. The club incident grows crystal clear. I slump my back against the window, heaving for breath.

Thoughts blur in my panicked mind, but I don't want to be one of those women who crumble and scream. I need to think this through and get the hell out of here. I start crossing the room to the door.

So many things aren't making sense, such as why I'm in such a fancy hotel. If those stalkers kidnapped me, why here and not a dingy basement? Someone would have seen me carried up here unconscious. Maybe it's not them who brought me here?

My phone trills again, and I look down at the ID splashing over the screen. *Nickie.* I answer the phone.

"Holy shit, where are you? I've been calling for hours. You had me freaking out. Where are you?" Her panic is contagious, and now I'm pacing faster toward the door.

"I-I don't know where I am." Dread climbs through me, heavy shattering dread that tells me I've been kidnapped. What other explanation is there? "I'm in a hotel room, maybe the penthouse, somewhere in the heart of the city."

"Fuck, why didn't you tell me you were leaving? We had a pact."

"Nickie, I've been kidnapped. Call the freaking cops."

"Son of a bitch. Run. Get out of there. No, wait. First, tell me where you are."

I'm frantic, my gaze swinging left and right, and I spot a phone near a hotel notepad. I launch for it just as the front door clicks and swings open.

My heart freezes in my chest, and I try to change direction to hide. But I'm too slow, and already, a man is striding inside.

I turn to run away, but when I catch a glimpse of his face, I'm utterly shocked. My feet tangle in the lush white rug under me, and I fall before I can stop myself.

Thump. I hit the rug with my hip, and I'm scrambling back to my feet as I mouth, "Doohickey?"

He stares at me as if confused, then realization washes over his face as he clearly remembers his made-up name. Dickhead.

"What the hell is going on?" I bark.

His eyes sweep over me appreciatively, and then he smirks.

"Guen, what's happening?" Nickie is yelling from the phone in my grip.

Doohickey shuts the door and stands there, huge and sexy as hell, wearing black jeans and a matching tee. He's carrying a plastic bag with three large cola bottles. Serial killers wear black, right, but what's with the soda? He steps past the fireplace and sets down the plastic bag.

I break out in a cold sweat and feel myself falling apart into hundreds of pieces as I consider the idea that this man has been stalking me for god-knows-how-long. And now he's got me where he wants me. Serial killers do that. Follow their prey, keep a wall of pinned photographs of their victim until they make their move. And his plan must include a penthouse for some reason I don't understand.

"I'm not going to hurt you, Guendolyn. I'm here to protect you." He walks closer. "Now, give me your phone."

"H-Help me?" I stammer. My breath catches in my lungs.

I run for the door, grasping the handle and rattling it, but it's not opening.

"Locked," he says.

With the phone to my ear, I'm breathing heavy now, and spy the notepad with the hotel name again.

A shadow falls over me.

He snatches my phone from my hand.

I lunge after him, but he drops the phone to the floorboards and stomps his heel onto it, smashing it.

I scream and punch him in the arm. "Why did you do that? I'm still paying it off."

He walks away nonchalantly and picks up his bag of soda before placing them on the table. I fall to my knees.

The front panel of my phone is completely shattered, his heel having crushed the entire life out of it. Nothing is salvageable. When I hit the power button, nothing happens. *Sonofabitch.*

"Fuck you! You're buying me a replacement," I growl, though on the inside I'm shaking. If he meant me no harm, why lock me in here and smash my phone?

He's at the table, opening one of the soda bottles. He then proceeds to gulp down most of it in one go. Is that part of my torture? Make me listen to him burp endlessly?

As if on cue, he unleashes a belch that rivals Godzilla's roar.

"That's disgusting, and why are you guzzling that shit?" I yell.

"We don't have such sweet, fizzy water at home." He reaches for the second bottle.

"That stuff will kill you," I remark.

He halts with the bottle pressing to his lips, then lowers it. "It's poisonous?"

"In a way. If you drink a lot of it."

He honestly looks confused and blinks hard as he studies the bottle. "Then why do you people drink this?" He sets it down and wipes his mouth with the back of his mouth.

I raise a brow as I climb to my feet. "*Us people?* Whatever! Let me out of here before I scream for the whole hotel to hear."

"Not happening, so get comfortable. I have a lot to tell you." He grabs the hotel food menu and tosses it to me. It hits me in the stomach and falls to the floor. "Order us a feast. I'm starved."

For a moment, I think he's going to stand over me to make sure I order him food, but he meanders over to the fireplace. While tempted to hurl the menu at the back of his head, I play along.

"Sure thing, asshole."

His lips break into a smile when he looks at me over his shoulder. His teeth are perfect. Everything about him is perfect. And if he can afford a penthouse, why kidnap me? Sweet talk me, and I'd probably come with him here on my own. Something isn't making sense about this whole scene. I can't help but feel as though I'm being pranked.

I pick up the phone on the small table near the window and hit the front desk button.

"Hello, how may I assist you?" a female asks.

"Yes, call the police. I've been kidnapped. He's locked me in the penthouse." My words are rushed, and I steal a glance at the dick who's lighting up the fireplace, chuckling to himself.

"Ma'am, I assure you that you are in safe hands. Mr. Lorcayn is highly regarded here, and he has informed us that you might call us. Guendolyn, if I may call you that, you are one lucky woman. I will arrange to send up champagne and strawberries for your honeymoon."

"No, wait… What?"

She hangs up, and I'm gritting my teeth.

I slam the phone down, and questions are reeling over my mind. Listening to my inner conscience, I pick up the receiver and dial 911.

The phone line goes dead in an instant, and I look up to see the asshole standing at the other end of the couch, the cut phone line in one hand and a *blade* gripped in the other.

Fear spreads its vicious wings, and the food I ate earlier in the day lurches in my stomach. Except I won't be a victim or show him I'm scared. I swallow the trepidation buckling through me and lift my chin.

"So is Lorcayn even your surname, or is that another lie?"

He doesn't respond right away, but I hear the sharp intake of breath. "Would have preferred if you'd ordered us food." He tucks his blade back into his boot and flops down into the single-seater couch.

"I don't want food. Who are you? Are you following me? And how do you and those creepy asses from the club know my real name? And why am I here?" Half a dozen more questions pepper my mind, but with the amused way he's staring at me, I'll be lucky if he answers one.

My life has sucked enough as it is. Growing up with hallucinations, dreams that felt real, voices of a prince in my mind, and now this. I'm already broken. After this shit, I'll need therapy for life.

Feigning courage, I fold my arms over my chest and press my hip against the side of the sofa. All I can see are those green eyes. He stares at me as if I ought to apologize for something. It might have to do with how my body reacts around him, how I'm picturing his hands on me and him naked. Thoughts that don't belong in my mind, since I'm his captive.

We stare each other down. I pray Nickie is smart enough to call the cops, and that the cavalry arrives soon.

Eyes the color of a stormy ocean, green with tinges of blue and gunmetal gray study me. He lounges in the seat, and the corded muscles in his neck twitch. His T-shirt sits a little too tight on him in the most delicious way. I can't tear my gaze from his full and expressive lips. The sincerity in his dark gaze confuses me.

"Are you just going to stare at me, or tell me what's going on?" I chastise, intending to keep him talking until help arrives.

His face is solemn as he speaks. "Deimos Lorcayn is my real name. I came to collect you to help save my family, except it seems first you need *my* help. And that might be partly my fault."

All I can remember is his name.

"Deimos?" I repeat. "Why does that sound familiar?"

"Because we've met when my brother, Luther, brought you into Wandering Realm two years ago." He blinks with those thick eyelashes most girls would kill for.

Disbelief crashes over me, and the more I stare at this man, the more I don't remember seeing him before. "Luther had two rude brothers, but…Wait. How do you…? If you know…" I'm rubbing my eyes, my brain stretched taut with confusion.

Something is very wrong here.

My dreams aren't real. My shrink said so.

Two years of no dreams.

Two years of no Luther in my head.

Two years of no memories.

"Please don't tell me you've been stalking me and found out about my past from the shrink's files? Seriously, that would freak me out beyond belief."

"Shrink? And I'm not rude. Just honest." A glimmer of amusement flashes in his eyes.

"You *are* rude," I correct him as he tries to get under my skin. "Why didn't you use your real name the other night if you're telling the truth?"

"I had to be sure it was you, and when I was… well…" He licks his lips. "There were distractions that caught me off guard. Like when you had your skirt ripped off you."

He seems to catch his breath.

"*You* ripped it off me, remember?" I snap, and at the memory, my cheeks flush.

He responds with a grin that tells me he regrets nothing.

"I don't believe you, by the way," I retort.

"Are you calling me a liar?"

"If the shoe fits."

His gaze lingers over me.

Something about the way he looks at me triggers a longing that sings in my heart, a feeling that haunts me, and yet, I have no recollection why.

"Guendolyn, you don't belong here. I've come to take you home, before it's too late. And maybe your memories about what happened two years ago will come back once we leave this place and enter our realm."

It takes a moment for his words to sink in. *Home.* I've never felt quite at home anywhere, but to think my home is in a different world feels odd. Two years ago, I believed in the other realm, the kingdoms, and the fae who lived there. A child's fantasy, my psychiatrist insisted. Now my brain fights against his words and their implication. Two years it took to finally feel semi-normal. Now my brain resists the possibility that I might have been right all along. This can't be.

"What happened to me?" The words fall from my lips.

There's sympathy in his eyes at my question, but I brace myself for the answer, to hear the truth I've missed my whole life. Is it that bad that he hesitates?

I blink slowly, trying to calm my accelerating heartbeat.

"It's complicated," he insists. "Half of what I've heard are from legends."

"Legends?" Okay, so the vagueness is a sure sign of him fabricating his stories. I won't deny a sting of hurt jabs me in the heart because for a few seconds there, I believed that maybe this might be real.

I glance over to my phone, smashed to smithereens on the ground, then back to Deimos. Seeing this man sit back and relaxed has me uneasy. This isn't how kidnappers are supposed to behave. Well, based on the knowledge I have from books and movies.

Bang. Bang. Bang.

I flinch and jerk my attention to the door.

A muscle twitches in Deimos' jaw.

Sweat beads my palms, and I'm backing up. The cavalry has arrived.

In the same heartbeat, the door bursts off its hinges. Blown apart, shards of wood fly in every direction.

A shuddering scream rips from my lips. I drop to the ground. Arms over my head, I crouch near the couch for protection.

My heart's pounding.

The police aren't messing around.

An explosion of sounds detonates around the room. Growls and shouts. I glance up just as the small couch is tossed across the room. It crashes into the table, breaking its fall. Bottles of cola explode like they'd been shaken. Fireworks of foamed soft drink pepper the air.

A flinch of terror pricks through me. I peek out from behind the couch, my stomach balled up tight.

Deimos hurls a fist into a man's face, sending him flying into the wall with unimaginable strength. The blond man doesn't even groan and peels himself out of the hole in the wall. He growls, his eyes as red as blood, and I know him.

Oh, fuck. He's the stalker from the gallery, from the nightclub. I'm too shaken to think straight or work out why he keeps following me. But it's clear he isn't working with Deimos.

His mouth stretches into a grin. Sharp fangs slip out, pressed over his lower lip. He throws himself at Deimos, both of them hitting the ground in a swarm of violent hits and punches.

It's too fast… too fucking much. Maybe I'm not seeing clearly, because this isn't right.

My gaze swings to the smashed door lying open, and I shove up off the floor and run. The fight rebounds behind me while the faint wail of a siren echoes in the distance.

"Guendolyn!" Deimos roars from somewhere behind me.

I don't look back as I bolt out of there.

Instinct drives me out into the small corridor leading to an elevator.

Footfalls pound the floor behind me.

I'm freaking out, my hand reaching for the elevator button.

A swoosh of air collides into my back, sending me reeling over my tripping feet.

Fierce hands snatch my hair and wrench me backward. My legs buckle under me. I'm screaming. My arms fumble out for anything to grab on to. A bowl of apples sits on a small table against the wall. My fingers grip the edges and I seize it. I swing the bowl and whack it against the stalker's head.

Crack!

He releases me, and I stumble away. I'm trembling, my whole body racked with terror. I press my spine against the metal elevator doors, and my hand frantically slaps the button. *Come on. Come on. Come on. Open already.*

I stare straight ahead at the hulking man with a crooked nose. Something's wrong with him. His back is curled forward, eyes a smear of red and black. Fangs slip out from under curling lips. He moves with shoulders curving forward, a snarl rolling through his heaving chest. He closes in.

This can't be real. It can't be real.

Through pasty lips he hisses, "Fucking abomination. Enough games. We will take you back tonight to face your judgement."

"Whoa, that's a bit much." I have no idea what he's talking about, but I can't stop shaking.

Deimos is flung out of the hotel door and smashes into a mirror hanging on the wall in the hallway. Shards of glass shatter over him. Hundreds of pieces fall down over his head. I jump in my skin at the sight of him slumping to the ground with a loud grunt.

But the monster in front of me flies at me.

I scream just as the elevator door dings and opens with a *whooshing* sound.

He slams into me.

We tumble inside, my head cracking against the floor. Pain spears over my skull. In the tussle, the fight for my life, darkness surrounds me from all sides, swallowing me.

Claws and teeth scrape my flesh. His body shoves onto mine, his weight like a mountain. Breath that reeks washes over me.

My panic flares. I buck against him, hands and legs shoving everything I have to get him off me. My breaths come raspy and hard. I lash out, scratching his face. But terror is beating into my body.

Waves of a chilling cold crash through me, faster and faster. The world around me blurs, in and out.

My whole body is convulsing. No, no, no. I haven't been sick like this for the past two years. Fear shackles my chest. I can't breathe, can barely move. A bitter scent of electricity floods the air.

I know what's coming. Death is coming for me. The word reverberates through my mind. *Death.*

The elevator shakes ferociously. A terrifying sound of metal buckling roars like a dragon.

With those dead fucking eyes piercing into me, darkness calls to me.

The world recedes in a flash… gone is the elevator. Trees and night engulf us. A bitter cold sweeps past, ripping its fangs into my flesh.

I scream and the strange world is ripped away. A fraction later, we're back in the elevator.

The fucker on top of me freezes, his eyes wild. "There you are… There you fucking are! I knew you would open up the portal for us. Now do it again!" he bellows. "The King of Ash Court has called for you."

His mouth gapes open, his fangs exposed.

Cries fall from my lips, and I only see the end coming.

CHAPTER 24

DEIMOS

I hit the floor like a sack, pebbled glass raining on my head and shoulders. Sharp edges cut into flesh. But I don't care. I don't give a fuck about me. I'm on my feet in a heartbeat, when the hairs on my body rise.

Magic.

It pricks over my skin, lapping at my insides like a cruel sea. Sharp and jagged, it spills into my chest and curls around my heart. Dark magic, the same kind that ripped the Wandering Realm in two.

Power ripples from within the elevator… I'm drawn to it. Guendolyn and that Bloodcursed vanish from existence before my eyes, then flash right back.

She opened the portal. She fucking opened it, but can't hold it long. Never mind. That time is all we need to enter our realm.

The sonofabitch throws himself on top of her, and my muscles tense, my nostrils flare.

I shove forward as dust falls from the shaking ceiling and walls. The elevator doors are closing, and fear squeezes my heart. I throw myself between them just as they jam against my shoulders, then bounce back open.

Adrenaline pulses through my veins with a thunderous beat.

She's screaming, and her gaze finds me from beneath the blood-sucker, cutting me like glass.

I snatch the back of his shirt and wrench him off her, then hurl him out of the elevator. But in the next second, the Bloodcursed lunges at me out of nowhere.

His fist connects with the side of my face. I reel backward as he launches at me. My back smacks into the elevator wall, and my head explodes with pain.

Fuck!

I throat-punch him, but the bastard barely reels.

Guendolyn huddles in the corner, hugging her knees, mumbling things I don't understand.

The damn Bloodcursed comes at me, all claws and teeth. I duck his attack in the small confines of the elevator, then pivot. I fist his hair and the back of his top, then toss him out as hard as I did his friend. He flies across the hall and crashes into the other fucker as he tries to get to his feet.

Stay down!

The doors of the elevator shut with a ding, and we're lurching. I turn to Guendolyn and reach for her arm. "Get up." I yank her to her feet. My heart is thundering. "Open the portal now!"

She's shoving a hand into my chest, wriggling out of my grasp. "Get the hell away from me!"

"I'm not going to hurt you, but you need to open the gateway before they return. They'll never stop coming for you, do you understand?" I growl.

But she's shaking her head, looking lost. Her eyes are huge. She's terrified. "What's going on?"

"You vanished a few moments ago with a Blood-cursed, then reappeared. Whatever you did then, do it again."

She hugs herself as she pushes herself into the corner like she might vanish. "I don't know how I did that."

My thoughts are too scattered, and I don't have time to train her to use her power in the little time we have and while she's scared.

The elevator dings, and I jerk around. My hand instinctively grabs hers, and I drag her behind me when I see the foyer of the hotel is clear of those blood-suckers. There's only one person at the counter and two staff. I wave at them while Guendolyn calls out for help.

All fae carry a power unique to them. My brother Luther has second-sight and can enter someone's mind, even if it's forbidden in our kingdom. Me, I have the power of persuasion via the sound of my voice. It's not foolproof, nor does it always work, but it got me a free hotel room and kept them from believing her when she called reception. She's very predictable.

The two women behind the counter smile at me, their eyes lustful like so many females in this world.

I rush outside with Guendolyn in tow.

She cries out, and we're drawing more attention.

My muscles tense. I can't persuade whole crowds.

"Let me go!" She batters her fist into my arm, and I have half a mind to toss her over my shoulder and run. Except they don't do such things here, Luther told me. Along with giving me lectures on everything human he could think of. I have the knowledge, I know many things, but experiencing this world is a very different thing.

"Quiet!" I bare my fangs out of pure frustration. "Believe me, I'm helping you."

Her cries cease, but now she's thrashing and kicking me in the leg. And I'm staring back toward the foyer through the glass doors, expecting those two Blood-cursed to spill out after us. Thankfully, they're nowhere in sight. Though I don't trust that to remain the same for long.

To my right, I spot the young valet man I spoke to when I first checked into the hotel. The tall and lanky guy is in an ill-fitted blue suit with his hair combed off his face.

"Hello, sir." His gaze falls to a wild Guendolyn. I draw her against my side tightly, my arm clasping against her side, pinning her arms down, and I pretend to push hair out of her face as I cover her mouth.

"Is she all right?" he asks, his brow quizzical.

"Yes, of course," I growl. "She hasn't had her beauty rest, so she gets grumpy. Now bring me your fastest carriage. Hurry."

"Carriage? You mean car? Can I see your ticket, please?"

I exhale loudly. Remaining calm is getting harder to do with Guendolyn thrashing and trying to bite my hand. I glare into the man's eyes. "Go get me the fastest car you have—now!" The brush of magic floats on my breath, and the young man stiffens suddenly.

"Right away, sir." He runs down the driveway.

Please let something go my way for a change.

Just go to Earth, Luther said. *It'll be easy. Find Guendolyn, and she'll open the portal for you.*

I'm seething because everything's gone wrong. Hell, two Bloodcursed snuck through the portal when I crossed over a few days ago, and now I can't use magic to return, and Guendolyn has no clue who she is or how to open a portal.

Looking down, I pull my hand from her mouth. She's gasping for air.

"Are you trying to kill me? What the hell is wrong with you?" Her words are venomous, and despite the shitty night, all I can stare at are those full lips and how cute she looks when angry.

I glance into the hotel foyer. Clear for now.

A roaring sound comes from behind, and I snap around with Guendolyn, still holding her tight against me.

Red is all I see. Glinting and shining in the lights. A car glides up in front of us, and the driver's door pulls open in an upward motion, reminding me of a butterfly's wing.

The valet climbs out of the car and runs over to me, leaving the motor running.

"Here, sir. You are ready to go."

"What is this?" I gape at the car with a golden bull symbol on the front grill. "Why is it so low to the ground? I wanted the fastest car, and one I can fit into."

"This is the fastest, sir." He simply stares at me, his eyes glazed over.

I roll my eyes. "Help me get her into the car."

He rushes to open the door.

"No you don't," I cry. That vixen slips from my grasp, and I lunge after her. Grabbing her around the waist, I lift her off her feet, even if she's screaming and kicking, then I shove her awkwardly into the passenger seat and quickly shut the door.

She's fiddling with the door but seems unable to open it. "Good. Stay in there."

I dart around the car when I spot the Bloodcursed tearing across the foyer. My stomach drops. I dive into the driver's seat and drag the door down.

"You're going to get arrested and shoved into prison for life. A pretty guy like you will be hot property in there." She's shouting at me, but I have no idea what she's talking about. I'm trying to remember all of Luther's instructions for driving a car.

Why does this one have so many gadgets?

I shove the gear into first, one foot pressing down on the clutch, something I remember from Luther. I push down on the handbrake in the middle of the console. Except it isn't going down, and I'm thumping my palm down on it. *Come on, you bastard, go down.*

"Geez!"

Then I see that the end of the handbrake is tipped with a button. How in the Seven Hells did I not see that? I click it and shove the whole thing down.

We're moving as I maneuver the dual pedals. The whole car jerks, the engine squealing. Fuck, what I wouldn't give for a horse and carriage right now.

Bang.

The door shakes and Guendolyn screams, deafening me.

I twist my head to see a Bloodcursed has thrown

himself at her window and is clawing at it in an attempt to get inside.

"Go! Hit the gas!" she yells.

I punch a button and blades wipe across the windshield. Another button and a clicking sound echoes around us.

"The gas, the gas, the long pedal on the right."

I slam my foot down on the thing, and we lurch forward. The tires screech around the next bend I take a bit too fast.

We take off like thirty galloping horses are pulling us. I'm thrown back in my seat. The motor is roaring, and that bastard flies off the car. This vehicle has speed.

"Where are we going?" she asks while staring behind us, back at the hotel.

"No idea, just getting as far from them as possible."

"Good, then tell me what's going on."

The car is making a groaning sound. "What now?"

"Change the gears," she instructs.

"Right." Luther told me about this part, but it slipped my mind.

I push the gearstick, and a horrid clunky sound comes from the motor.

"You're killing it," she hisses. "Do you even know how to drive a sports car?"

"Yes, of course I do." I'm lying. I've never driven anything like this. But I'm smart, and I catch on quickly. I shove the gear into place, which refuses to budge at first. I release the accelerator and hit the other pedal. This time, the gear shifts. And we're running smoothly again.

"Where to start?" I say as I curve onto a highway where there are hardly any cars, and that's good. No traffic.

There's a silence between us.

"Okay, where to start?" I repeat. "Those two coming after you are Bloodcursed. It's a long story, but in short, they're cursed fae who have been outcast from the kingdom and have an addiction to blood. Thing is that two years ago, they were as wild as animals, unable to think beyond the lust for blood. But now they're unlike the creatures back home. They're intelligent, so I don't know what's going on. But I do know they're tracking you down by your scent."

She just stares at me, and I can't work out if that's a sign things are sinking into her mind.

"My what?"

I cut a quick glance at the disbelief washing over her face. Her mouth purses. I expected more of a protest or something, but she doesn't say anything else. So I continue.

"It's a thing fae emit because of the magic we use. It makes us easy targets, which is why we use cloaking potions. Sometimes, it's just a touch that's needed to trigger the scent."

I wait for her to speak, but when she says nothing, I

continue. "You are highly sought after back in Wandering Realm, and it's about time you returned home so we can keep you safe."

"Why?"

That one word seems to apply to everything, and I know she means it that way.

"Because you're a fae like me. Because of the blood in your veins, and your magic. Because if they kill you, the curse can never be incinerated."

She fumbles with her hands in her lap. "So you're telling me I was born in this realm because I'm a fae, and somehow ended up living here with humans, and now you want me to go back there where there are freak vampires on the loose? Oh, and I can do magic? As in Harry Potter magic?"

I look at her, my eyes narrowing, unsure what she just asked me. "Not too sure what vampires or Harry Potter are, but yes." I give her a smile, but she doesn't seem to notice as she stares out at the straight road. The city and its neon lights fade behind us.

I feel her eyes on me, studying me, trying to make sense of everything. This would have been so much easier if she had her memories, if Luther had made it through the portal with me.

"Are you saying I'm a fairy?" She chokes on a fake laugh.

"Fairies are blood-sucking vermin. They feed on brains and eyes, so no, you're not a fairy."

She swallows hard, studying me like I might be lying.

Back in the Wandering Realm, my two brothers and I were ambushed in the forest while we used a potion to open the portal between our world and Earth. The Bloodcursed have risen against us in the thousands, killed so many, and spread their virus. I made it through to this realm, and when I looked back, an onslaught of Bloodcursed rushed for my brothers. Then the portal shut. I pray my two brothers survived. We risked everything to find Guendolyn, because the only person who can stop the curse on our land is the person who unleashed it. Her.

Coming to this world is our only chance of survival... Guendolyn is our last hope. She's so much more than she realizes.

I steal a glance at her in the passenger seat, and frustration twitches in the corners of her eyes. Feet tucked up on her seat, knees to her chest, she leans against the door to be as far from me as possible. She's small, and still, the power in her veins can undo so much right...and so much wrong too. It comes with cruel memories of the cost we all paid two years ago. An ache settles beneath my ribs. An ache that cuts so deep at the losses in our families, the death, and the curse unleashed on the Wandering Realm.

"There's so much more to tell you, but not tonight. Try to get some rest."

She doesn't respond. Just stares out into the night.

There's a reason I never planned to wed. Life, and mostly watching everyone else's mistakes, has taught me to avoid attachments or anything long-term. Because nothing is permanent. Such things make you weak… something my stepfather, King of the Shadow Court, would tell me constantly. Might explain why he rarely spent time with us; then again, our real father walked out on us to marry a fae princess young enough to be his daughter. That kind of shit makes you question the value of marriage.

CHAPTER 25

The wind rushes in through the open window of the Lamborghini, swirling in my hair, buffeting against my face. Night smothers everything in sight. Not that I can see much from the freeway. We've been driving for hours without a break, and I'm still processing everything Deimos told me... Deimos Lorcayn to be specific. My mind is still blurry from two years ago, but what I do recall is he's the youngest of three princes to the Shadow Court. Luther is the middle son, and Ahren is the eldest and heir to the throne.

No matter how much I wrack my brain, the other details don't come to me. I grit my teeth, frustrated with the memories I know are there. I can feel them, but just can't grasp them. The man driving this car looks nothing like the prince I met two years ago.

Anxiety pours through me at the realization that I can't remember everything, and how it could all be such a blur.

I turn in my seat and hit the button for the window to close, shutting out the ferocious wind. All I can smell is fine leather and his ridiculously sexy scent. Woodsy, earthy, and laced with a hint of a crisp meadow.

"Feeling better?" he asks, his voice almost unbearably tender.

I meet his gaze, determined to show him I'm grasping on to some semblance of sanity. I have no clue where we are and have no phone or wallet. Though if there's a silver lining, it's that I'm far from those two stalkers. Or whatever they were. I shiver, still feeling their claws raking down the elevator walls and the evil in their eyes that wasn't human. I push the bad thoughts aside and turn my attention to Deimos.

"Why don't I recognize you if we've met before?"

"Glamor," he answers, like that tells me everything I need to know. "An ability all fae have to modify their appearances."

My mind buzzes with half a dozen more questions, his intoxicating scent making me woozy, but they evaporate in an instant.

Before my eyes, Deimos is changing. His dark hair fades until it turns as white as snow and extends, growing past his shoulders. Cheekbones sharpen, his jawline becomes stronger and more pronounced.

Shoulders expand, as does his chest, now making him look huge in this sports car.

I'm frozen, my mouth hanging open.

His spectacular eyes, greener than I could have ever imagined, drill into me as my brain scrambles for an explanation. Except as he looks at me with a crooked smartass grin, I recognize him. I've definitely seen his face before, that much is clear. But all the other memories of our interaction and what he did—they aren't in my head. My hand instinctively goes to the side of my neck, a tenderness stirring there.

Goosebumps ripple down my arms and warmth seems to engulfs me, swallowing every inch of me in its wake. I can't look away from that gorgeous face as he rakes a hand through his hair.

God, if I thought he was spectacular before, now… now he is every woman's wet dream. I suddenly feel intimidated in his presence, like there is no way someone like him can see me as anything but plain.

He keeps glancing at me and back to the road, waiting for my reaction, for me to say something. "Do you like?"

I've forgotten how to breathe.

"Deimos!" My heart stutters. "I do remember you." Well, his face is familiar, which is a start to maybe more memories coming back to me. But now I know for certain that we met before… and just like that, Luther comes to mind. So either I've completely lost my mind and am hallucinating everything, or the fragments of memory I recall are real.

My world is spinning. I want to ask him questions… things that seem to be on the tip of my mind, but I can't grasp them. I blink hard, wracking my brain, chasing those thoughts. Except they evade me.

His thick eyebrows arch slightly. "We've already established that you remember me."

I punch in him the arm. Not that he'd feel it with all those muscles. I'm not someone to react in such a way or throw tantrums, but with his smugness and him only telling me this just now… What can I say? Something inside me lashed out.

"*Hey*." He groans.

"Why didn't you show me the real you earlier?"

"My appearance isn't exactly made for blending in amid humans."

I tell myself not to react, even if his smile makes me want to punch him in the face. Except, now I'm more confused than ever. The more I stare at the white-haired fae swerving the Lamborghini all over the empty road, the more I can't deny the truth. It's staring me in the face.

He's a fae.

He's come from another realm.

He's come to take me with him.

Monsters are freaking real!

"If I'm a fae, where are my wings, and my ears would be pointy, right?"

"You asked almost this exact question two years ago." He speaks with absolute conviction, and I can't help but believe him.

"Only fairies have wings, not fae. And pointy ears are a feature some family lines have and others don't."

We keep driving. His big hands grip the steering wheel as he concentrates on keeping us in one lane. I drop my gaze to my hands and try to think everything through. How my parents abandoned me at a refuge when I was only a few months old with nothing but a ribbon tied to my ankle with my name on it. *Guendolyn.*

It lends itself to me coming from this realm—their realm—but it's the whole fae-and-fantasy part that baffles me. Yet, I've seen things with my own eyes. Those stalkers had fangs. Deimos transforming in the car. And I know that back in the elevator I slipped into another world. I felt it in my bones. Something I'd done before... well, the shrink made me believe I'd dreamed it. But what if she was wrong about everything?

That reality is like a kick to the teeth. Bile rises to my throat. I open the window again for fresh air and stop myself from spewing all over this expensive car.

"Once we get some rest, I need you to remember how to use your magic to open the portal."

In truth, he might as well be asking me to lasso the moon. I swallow down the fuzziness in my head.

"Sleep will be good," I mumble. Anything to make it stop feeling like I'm sinking in a vortex.

I don't know how long we've been driving, but I drift to sleep, and it's the crunch of gravel under our tires sounds that wakes me.

There's a huge neon *Motel* sign in front of us. The bright blue light whips over Deimos' exhausted face.

He brings the car around the back of the long one-story building, slowing down.

"Where are we?" I shuffle upright.

He starts to talk but we're interrupted by the horrendous crunching sounds from the car as he tries to change gears. I'm cringing on the inside. We are bunny hopping down the driveway. I'm jostling and jumbling about. Then the car just dies.

"This spot will do," he announces.

I look out to see we are parked right in the middle of the parking area. "Yep, sure. Perfect." My voice is filled with edginess. Outside are forests and endless darkness behind the motel. "We're in the middle of nowhere."

"Exactly. It'll take those Bloodcursed longer to track you down. We sleep for a few hours, eat, then we leave before dawn."

"So do you have a destination in mind?"

"Nope. We keep driving until you work out how to tap into your power and get us home."

"This *is* my home," I explain quickly, gaining myself a side glance as if he's surprised by my comment.

"Not your true home."

A headache crawls up the back of my neck. My bladder is full, and I'm suddenly bursting to find a toilet. Once he switches off the engine, I reach for the door, but he grabs my wrist and forces me to face him.

"Don't think about running, understand? You do, and I'll tie you to me." There's a darkness to his eyes, and I don't for a second doubt he wouldn't enjoy binding us.

Heavy shadows dance over his face, and in the back of my mind, I remind myself that Nickie will call the cops when she doesn't find me at the hotel. They'll have a nationwide manhunt and are bound to track us down. Until my thoughts come back to me to be sure this isn't part of some strange... whatever it is, I need to remain cautious.

"I got it." I rip my hand free from his grip and climb out. The wind is cold tonight and just staring out into the pitch black of the woodland beyond the parking area leaves me trembling.

"Let's go," he says, his body shimmering back to his glamored self. He waits for me, and I join him, and when I stare up at him, I can't help but feel like he's the guy who kidnapped me, and in his blond form, he's the man who is brimming with mysteries I'm dying to discover.

Together we head to the front of the motel.

He's the lesser of the two evils, right? He hasn't tried to kill me.

As we draw closer, I note only a single light shines from a glass door with the word *reception* printed on the window.

Inside, it smells of smoke and the front desk is unattended. I can make out a shape through the doorway leading to the back room. A short man pops out, a cup to his lips and his eyes widening at the sight of Deimos. He's burly and powerful and intimidating, even dressed in casual jeans and shirt.

Spurting coffee everywhere, he places his cup on the counter in a hurry. "So sorry. Didn't hear you come in." He's plucking a tissue from the box on the counter and wipes his mouth and chin, staring up at Deimos.

I smirk to myself. Yep, when the police plaster details about Deimos on the television, Mr.—I glance around to see the man's name on the business cards in a small Perspex holder—Mr. Peppers will remember this moment.

"We'd like your finest room," Deimos starts, and already I see Mr. Peppers' expression shifts. From one of shock at seeing such a huge, glorious man who belongs on the front of a magazine to one of spellbinding charm. Deimos is entrancing the poor man somehow, just as he did that valet guy back at the hotel. "My wife and I will be staying here for one night. No disturbances. And we need food. Bring me one of everything you make."

"Motels don't do room service," I explain.

Except, Mr. Peppers just nods blindly. "There's a small town not far and they deliver food. I'll arrange it right away."

I roll my eyes at how much he's trying to impress Deimos. "And wife? Who do—?" I begin, but his hand lashes out and grasps the back of my neck, then wrenches me against him. Bastard shoves my face into his side, and all I can inhale is that hunky masculine scent with a hint of perspiration that makes me melt on the inside. I hate him for smelling so divine, how my gut explodes with butterflies at being so close to him. I shove my hands against his side, to rip myself away from him. I kick his leg, and he finally releases me.

I gasp for air and glare at him with the dirtiest stare I can manage. "Stop freaking doing that."

Mr. Peppers hands Deimos a key. "Number thirteen."

"Let's go." He growls, an edge of impatience in his tone. He grabs my arm again before whisking me out of the reception. I toss a look over my shoulder to see Mr. Peppers not paying attention, completely oblivious to what just happened.

"You hypnotized him, didn't you? Are you doing to that to me too?"

"Trust me, if I could, I would. It'd definitely be easier." He offers me a mocking grin, and I glare at him in response. His eyes darken, a serious expression washing over his face, and I can tell he means every word. Bastard.

All the rooms we pass have no lights on, like the motel is completely barren of guests. Then again, why would anyone stay out here?

We stop in front of a door. His vise grip on my elbow releases. I stare at the bronze number thirteen on the door. I'm pretty sure that's an omen of bad luck to come. Why doesn't that surprise me? Behind me, the night has claimed everything. Even the freeway out front is silent and barren of cars or street lights.

I step back from him, but he lashes out an arm and seizes me by the back of my top before shoving me inside.

He kicks the door shut, and my pulse skyrockets, then he switches on the light, illuminating the wonderland of brown dullness. Wooden walls and ceiling, faded carpet and bedspread, even the paintings…. You guessed it. Brown.

"Wow, they spent a lot of money on the decorating here." My shoes are sticking to the carpet, and I'm gagging at staying here.

Deimos locks the door.

I traipse across the room and push open the bathroom. Shower, bathtub, and toilet. I turn to face him toeing off his boots. At his own demise because no one ought to walk on this carpet barefooted ever. "You're sleeping on the..." I glance at the tiny two-seater couch that would have his legs hanging over the edge. "On the sofa."

Unconcerned, he blinks and shakes his head. "Not happening. We're both sharing the bed so I can keep an eye on you all night." He speaks without a hint of emotion, like this is an everyday occurrence, but I see his roaming gaze over my body as much as he pretends he isn't feeling the inferno between us.

His delusional assumption surprises me. As if he can watch me all night. The car keys are in his pocket, and I can stay up all night without a problem. Nighttime is when I do my best homework for college. I'm a pro at this.

He's studying me, leering at me with distrust, and I just grin. "I spread out when I sleep, so if I kick you a dozen times, don't be surprised. You're safer on the couch."

Not a single reaction, and he's reading me. Keep it cool. He can't read my mind... or can he? I stare back just as intently. *I want to lick him all over.*

Wait, why did I think that? Heat swims over me at the thought of him naked, me in charge of such a man, and discovering how big he really is. I shove the images out of my head. They can't belong to me, except my gaze has dipped to his groin and now my cheeks are ablaze.

Calm down.

He's still watching me, but he's not reacting to my thoughts, so I'm taking that as confirmation that he can't read my mind. There's a fierce fire in his eyes as a slow grin pulls on his lips, and his expression is confusing me.

My breaths are racing now. God, maybe he did hear my thoughts? "So… what's your superpower as a fae?" I burst out laughing, and if anyone ever sounded like a hyena, I just pulled it off royally.

His eyes narrow. "Power of voice. Have you not noticed this?" he muses.

"Right, right. Yes, with Mr. Peppers and the valet guy. And that's it, right?"

That sexy grin of his widens. "You fear I can do more to you?" He pauses, looking me up and down, his breaths quickening. "That I can hear your thoughts?"

I swallow past the boulder in my throat. "What? Why would you ask that? Crazy. But you can't because no one can do that, right?" God, why am I babbling? He has to guess about now that it's exactly what I was worried about and knows why my face is on fire now.

He closes the distance between us, never taking his gaze from my lips. Reaching across, his large hand cradles the side of my head, a thumb brushing across my cheek.

My breath hitches at his touch, like it has since the first time I met him. And us being this close isn't helping my raging heartbeat or focus.

Eyes of shattering blue meet mine as a tremble of fear and arousal ripples through me. It's wrong of me, but my thoughts burst out of control as my pulse roars to life. All I can picture is me biting his lip, licking them, climbing this mountain of a man. To have him reach for that throbbing pulse between my thighs.

"I can't read minds," he says, blazing right through my fantasy. "But my brother Luther has that ability."

I exhale loudly with relief and lock that piece of information in the vault in my mind for later, trying to shove back the lust that's heating me as if I were standing in front of a fire. "Okay, gonna freshen up. Don't steal my bed." I make my way quickly into the bathroom and shut the door behind me. I release a long exhale, finally able to breathe with ease.

What is wrong with me? I'm out of control around him.

Frantically, I search the room for anything I can use for a weapon. Something to knock him out. Then I'll leave, because what will he do to me when I can't open the damn portal he keeps talking about? I don't even know what happened back in the elevator.

I splash cold water over my face and across the back

of my neck. Looking back at me from the mirror that's chipped at the corners is a girl with bloodshot eyes and red cheeks. I honestly can't remember the last time I looked so tired and hyped up on adrenaline at the same time. When I think of Deimos, my stomach flutters like I'm back in high school. Yet he annoys the hell out of me.

Gripping the counter with both hands, I look closer at myself. "What are you?" I don't know how long I stare, expecting my brain to finally crack open and spill the answers, but they never come. So I pop open the button of my jeans and go to the toilet.

I have the plan already in my mind. Pretend to sleep, and a couple of hours after he's in deep REM sleep, I slide out, grab the keys, and I'm gone.

Once finished, I heave my jeans back up my thighs, and there begins my battle with my jeans. Hopping up and down, tugging them up and over my butt. Why did I wear these again? Right, because these bad boys defy the law of physics as to how they even fit me. But they do, and they give me the best toned looking legs and curvy ass. Sure, they're two sizes too small, but it works. I suck in my gut, holding my breath, and force the button closer to the hole, getting it halfway in.

Bang. Bang. Bang.

I flinch from the knocking at the door, and my jeans spring open.

Gah! "What?"

"Food's here."

"Okay, thanks." Not that I can fit anything into my stomach while wearing these pants. Ten minutes later of jiggling, I'm zipped up. Okay, no going to the toilet the rest of the night.

Out in the room, Deimos is sitting at the round table, with so much food in front of him, I'm convinced he can feed everyone in this motel. How much power does Deimos have over people?

"Wow, you're hungry."

He's taking a slice of a pepperoni pizza into his mouth and waves me over, then points to the seat across from him. The waft of food calls me, and I'm sitting at the table with a slice in my hand before I know it.

"If you and your brother have an ability, and I'm a fae, what is mine?"

"Only you will know yours. It's something you're born with."

"Well, that's a bit hard since I had no clue what I was until today."

"You knew two years ago," he corrects me as he keeps eating. How can someone be so sexy, even as they stuff their face? Yet, I just want to shove his face into the food for being so arrogant.

"Right." I take another bite of pizza and eye the small bowl of mac and cheese before I claim it as my own. He reaches for it at the same time, his hand on mine. Those tingles come back, the ones that engulf me each time he touches me.

I snatch the bowl from his grasp. "Mine," I say. No one comes between me and mac and cheese. It's my staple, my go-to dish, my everything when I need comfort food. And probably why I don't fit easily in these jeans.

With a shrug, he pulls back his arm and keeps eating while watching me spoon the baked noodles into my mouth. His mouth opens slightly when I part mine.

I swear, seeing him drool over me eating has my body reacting so fast. His gaze isn't on the bowl in my hand, but on my lips.

"Would you like a taste?" What the fuck am I doing? Flirting with him? My head isn't screwed on right.

He reaches over and takes my mac and cheese without hesitation. "Hmm, this is so good." It's done in seconds.

"Yep, it was good." My stomach growls for more while my chest clenches at the thought that it was the food he drooled over and nothing more. "Anyway, tell me more about your realm, more about what's going on there."

"There are two realms," he begins. "Shadow Court and Ash Court. Dire enemies for as long as I remember. A curse was unleashed on our world, and now everything is in chaos. The Seelie fae, those from my kingdom, are being hunted."

"Curse? Like those Bloodcursed?"

"No, this is different." He lowers his head and keeps eating, having fallen quiet.

"How is it different?" I ask.

"This isn't the time to talk about such things." He shuts me down with those few words, and the air thickens between us. I don't understand what's going on, or why he's reacting this way. But I get up, having had enough of the food.

"I'm going to lie down."

"Good idea."

A twinge of fear unfurls in my chest. He's hiding so much from me, and it scares me, since there is so much that still doesn't make sense. I pull off my heels, surprised I haven't snapped these stilettoes in all my running around. Nickie will murder me if I do. I rip off the top blanket from the bed and toss it to the ground. Still clothed, I crawl under the bedsheet and shuffle to lie on my side in the middle of the bed. Now I wait.

The bed bows under me at my back.

My eyes snap open to darkness, and Deimos is climbing into bed with me.

I must have fallen asleep. I wriggle to turn around to claim more of the bed and push him out.

A large hand loops around my waist and hauls me toward him so fast that I don't have a chance to react.

My back crashes against his chest, and all my thoughts fade at having him pressed up against me so close that I can feel every inch of him. Even the soft bulge nestled against my ass. I squirm to get away, but only manage to rub myself against him, as his grip isn't letting up.

"You enjoying yourself?" he purrs.

I feel a faint twitch from the growing hardness pressing against my ass. "Oh, that better not be what I think it is."

"You keep rubbing yourself against me, and it'll be a much bigger problem for you."

I grit my teeth and push away from him, but in truth, I'm burning up. I'd never felt such intensity for a man before. Shivers travel over my skin. My dating record is non-existent to compare this to, though if I'd had some serious boyfriend material, I somehow doubt they'd compare to Deimos.

"You're not going anywhere," he whispers in my ear, and his leg clamps over the top of mine. Which is so wrong because, like a flick of a flame, my desire surges like a volcano and it's unstoppable.

"Hope you're comfortable because I'm not."

"This is the most comfortable I've been in years." His sarcastic breath tickles my ear.

The pleasure building in me is blazing over me.

"Liar," I say, lying still on my side, knowing moving is futile against this mountain of a man. I can't move.

Can't think. Only listen to my heart pounding in my ears while my nipples tighten.

"Do you know what they do those who call a prince a liar?"

His deep voice grazes over my nerve endings, and a shudder travels down my spine. Not from fear, but from the proximity of him against me. From the slight twitch of his fingers as his palm splays out over my stomach.

"They kill them," I mutter, focusing on his touch, on how I'm certain he's slowly inching his hand up my stomach.

He doesn't respond, but breathes heavily, and I laugh. "Did I steal your thunder?" I ask.

"There are far worse things than death, Guendolyn."

Those words affect me—they haunt me—because his tone tells me he's experienced such punishment firsthand. "Who would threaten a prince?" I say, glancing back over my shoulder at him. The shadows steal his expression, except for those green eyes that seem to glint in the night.

"The king," he confesses.

His father? I want to ask more questions, but I turn back around and lie there. He has an asshole father... I can only guess mine is similar, since he gave me up. Still, to hear the hurt in his voice, to know he struggled, touches me. I can relate so fucking hard.

"I ought to tie you up," he mumbles so close to me, his breath is on my neck.

"Yeah, bet you'd like that." I squirm against him.

"I might," he teases, his hand adjusting to hold me against him. In a swift move, he rolls me up and onto him.

I'm frozen, lying on my back on top of him. All I can picture is him losing control and claiming me. Taking what he desires. My body aches, and I'm shuddering with lust. I picture him ripping off my clothes and dipping down between my thighs. My pelvis curls upward from the thought alone. Each rapid breath sears my lungs. My heart is beating so fast.

My core clenches, and I'm slick with desire from the anticipation when he suddenly rolls me back down on my side. His arm is now tucked under my neck. "That's better."

I'm as still as the night, and my cheeks are on fire from expecting something...else? I feel like a fool. I want to disappear. Thank the universe he can't see my blushing face.

"If you say so." I try to pretend my pulse isn't out of control, that I feel nothing for him.

His skin is hot against my cheek, and that doesn't help me in the slightest. He feels ridiculously amazing.

He falls silent, and it isn't long before his breaths deepen with the sound of him falling asleep. Well, it kinda hurts that here I am all revved up from his touch, and he just crashes.

I lie here and bide my time and wait. In my mind, I'm already picturing how fast I'll drive out of here. I need to be as far from Deimos as possible before something terrible happens... like throwing myself at him.

CHAPTER 26

GUEN

"*I prefer girls with more, not less.*"

A shiver shakes me, and I push my fists against Deimos' chest, but he stands there, trapping me, unmoving. His fingers slide into my hair, twining the strands.

"Maybe you should have put your hair up tonight. Would have looked prettier."

"Is that all you do, insult people? Well, it's not working on me, so move out of my way." I clench my jaw. He thinks it's okay to speak to me that way?

His hand grasps my hair, and I wince. "You're adorable when you're angry. I think we'll have a lot of fun together. Don't you agree, my kitten?"

"I'm not yours, and I am damn sure I am not staying in this insane palace with you and your brothers." Despite my words, my body hums from his closeness. My body betrays

me when it comes to this jerk, my lips still tingle from his earlier kiss.

His breath washes on my face, and as much as I want to say it reeks, I love the way he smells. Woodsy, earthy, sexy. "I hate you."

He grins. Seemingly, my words turn him on. "You're not Luther's, either, and where will you go? It's no easy feat moving between realms without magic. You're stuck in our Wandering Realm now."

"I'll find a way back." I jut my jaw out.

He presses his mouth to my ear. "So human of you."

I stiffen. "What's that supposed to mean?"

His green eyes flash to mine, desire deepening within them. His lips meet mine too fast for me to react, and he nips my lower lip, his teeth nicking flesh.

"Ouch." I shove my hands into his chest, but he doesn't move, just stands there hard as a boulder, licking the trickle of blood on his mouth.

I touch my lips and my fingers come back bloody. "What did you do?"

Fingers slip over my shoulder, his touch drowning me, clouding my thoughts, leaving me leaning into him while trying to recover any control of my wavering emotions.

He presses his face to my neck, inhaling, tasting. I shudder under him, the softness leaving me shivering with a new kind of arousal. I should stop him, should drive him away, but I can't. Something brushes over my mind, feather-soft, before it pulls away.

Teeth are on my neck, a sharp prick fast and electrifying.

Mist blurs my mind. Everything erases except Deimos and me. Focusing on steadying my breathing does nothing to calm my thundering heart. Arousal trembles down my spine, invisible fingers sliding over my back and lower still.

A shadow tears through the room, ripping me out of my lulled state.

"What the fuck are you doing?" Luther growls.

Deimos breaks from me. His laughter is hypnotic. He wipes his bloody mouth with the back of his hand, his eyes devouring me, calling to me like nothing I've ever felt.

"She's exquisite, brother. So much more than we could have anticipated. You were right to collect her for us."

"She isn't yours to touch or mark. Fuck, Deimos!" Luther hisses.

I wake with a sudden jolt, my eyes springing open. Sweat collects over my nape as I push myself up in bed. Reality and dreams blur in and out. I sit there, the vision tilting my world upside down because I remember that moment in the kingdom. It comes back to me crisp and clear. It's only a pocket of time, and what comes before and after remains clouded by shadows.

I fist the bed sheet draped over my lap, starting to

recall more of Deimos from when we first met. His cruel words. His devious flirting. And that ass *bit* me.

The space next to me on the bed is empty. I frown in confusion and swing my attention to the open bathroom door.

As if on cue, the devil steps into view, wearing only black pants that hang low on his hips. With him standing there almost naked, my resolve to escape dissolves into a puddle in his presence. That isn't fair.

The way he looks isn't fair. Not those strong lines of muscles, his biceps, the ripped abs that have me staring far too long. My body hums, and I seem to have forgotten what I was thinking moments earlier. I can't tear my gaze from his strong, hard form, from the sprinkling of light hair trailing below his navel and vanishing beneath his pants.

"How did you sleep?" He leans a shoulder in the doorway, and I'm starting to breathe harder.

"All right," I squeak before clearing my throat, cursing myself for falling asleep when I had plans to get up and leave. I can't seem to control myself around him apparently—well, not when he looks like perfection. And after last night's vision, I'm not so quick to escape Deimos. If we've met before, then what secrets is he withholding from me? Why can't I remember my memories? He knows so much more than he's letting on, and I intend to find out.

My throat dries as he strolls into the room, a

twisted smile curling into a smirk. He's studying me and can see exactly the effect he has on me because I suck at poker. My emotions are scribbled all over my face, and like a damn fool, I'm drooling over him.

I shake those thoughts away. "I had a dream last night," I begin.

"You can tell me about your fantasy dream later." He dismisses me with a wave of his hand.

"*Excuse me?* It was not a *fantasy* dream. It was a dream featuring you being a jerk."

He ignores the comment. He seems distracted and says, "We need to leave. Put your shoes on."

I drag my gaze from him and climb out of bed before finding my stilettos and staring at them. How I'd love flats right now. My feet throb with pain just looking at these shoes. I place them on the bed for now, and my stomach rumbles with hunger. Then I make my way to the bathroom.

A shuddering shriek comes from somewhere outside, piercing and skin-crawling. I flinch, and my head jerks back at Deimos. He's at the window, pushing the curtains aside and peering outside, where the rising sun streaks the sky in reds and oranges.

"What is it?" Is it one of those things?

"Get ready quick," he commands, his words deepening with fear. "I'll be back fast."

"No, don't leave," I cry out, but he's already pulling the door locked behind him.

Fear drums in my chest, quickly turning into a storm. I've always tried to be strong, to be cautious, but to do whatever the fuck it takes to get through life. My foster mom always said I had a strong sense of self-preservation, and I agree. But the feeling of being hunted is a blade in my gut that keeps twisting and twisting. And at this moment, I feel powerless.

I rush into the bathroom, and by the time I'm finished and zipping up my jeans with shaky fingers, my panic is full-blown. I press my back to the wall near the bed and stare at the window. I try to slow my breaths, to not make a single sound.

Deimos hasn't come back. There's no sign of the car keys… Of course, they'd be in his pocket. So I can't steal his car. What the hell am I supposed to do?

I'm breathing fast, picturing Deimos lying some-where dying, while those stalkers are coming for me.

The faint creak of the balcony comes from outside. My equilibrium is jarred at the sound, and I stumble on my feet. I won't fall apart with fear. I won't.

Scanning the room for a weapon, the only cutlery I find with the leftovers from last night is a disposable plastic fork. I grab it anyway and lightly push aside the curtains to look out the window. All I see is the free-way. Not a car in sight. What am I meant to do? Sit here and wait for those creeps to find me? If anything, I can let Mr. Peppers know in reception something is going on, and to call the cops. After my dream, I know

I've seen Deimos before; I remember us having that conversation. And he saved me from those creeps, so I want to believe he's telling me the truth.

A quick look at those stilettos. I can't bear to wear them just yet and endure their excruciating torture.

Barefooted, I creep to the door, and my hand is shaking furiously as I grab the handle. In slow motion, I pull it open and my gaze darts left and right.

All clear.

Cowering in the doorway, I struggle between staying and going. Deimos said to wait, but he's been gone for too long. Maybe I'll find him outside somewhere.

Clutching the fork in my hand, I slink left and make my way outside. *Please don't let me bump into those stalkers, please.* The silence is almost deafening.

At the front of the motel, there's not a soul in sight. The reception door swings open and shut in the breeze. I rush inside, but there's no one there.

"Hello?" I whisper.

No one responds or emerges through the closed back door. I approach and hold my breath as I push down on the handle, figuring I'll plead ignorance if Mr. Peppers gets mad. Except it's locked, and I exhale heavily. My nerves are on edge and sweat beads down my neck. I give a light knock and grit my teeth, waiting while staring out the door. *Come on, come on.*

Any hope I held on to earlier is snuffed in seconds. I

scan the reception desk for a phone, but there's nothing. No computer, either. A glint draws my attention to a silver letter opener. I dump the fork and snatch the dull blade off the desktop.

On the balls of my feet, I push back outside, and unease crawls through my gut. Trees flanking the motel sway in the wind, and a bird crows somewhere in the distance. The morning sky has turned orange, staining the heavens.

I lift my gaze to the freeway along the front of the motel. No car has passed since I came out here. There are no houses out here, nothing but this lonely motel and trees in every direction.

I hate the apocalyptic feel to this place, how Deimos just *vanished*, and where the hell is Mr. Peppers? Danger ripples over my skin, and I have to find Deimos and get out of here with him.

Before I can think it through, I'm following the driveway to the rear of the building.

The Lamborghini is still here, so there's that, I guess. He hasn't taken off without me.

I wish I knew what the fuck was going on.

There's a strange energy in the air today, and I turn to head back to the room, when a thunderous scream bellows. The sound invades my thoughts from the woods behind the motel.

I freeze, the gravel cold on my bare feet. Leaves rustle, and shadows dance from the forest in front of me. My heart drums quickly. All I can think of is of Deimos in danger.

Fury and terror surge to the surface, sending a line of ice down my spine. I pull away but stop and look down at the silver weapon clutched in my hand, at the white of my knuckles. But Deimos might need my help.

I suck in a shaky breath and push one leg in front of the other, then another until I reach the edge of the woodland. All I want is to turn and run back to the room, but then what? Wait and when Deimos doesn't return, go back out to search for him again? I might be too late to help him then… I'm not sure how me with a letter opener can make a difference, but I have to try.

Farther in the woods, the earth is sharper under my feet, and I cringe with pain from every step.

Up ahead, movement stirs. Definitely a person, maybe two or three. My heart stutters, and terror cuts through me like a blade. Their voices murmur somewhere ahead, angry voices, and I squint for a better look, refusing to move.

Is Deimos with them? I swallow hard and take a step forward. *Please don't let me be making the worst decision of my life.*

With careful steps to avoid making a sound, I move closer, my ears pricking.

Tucking myself behind a huge gnarled-looking tree, my spine presses into the trunk. My breaths are racing. Why did I think this was a good idea? I should have banged on Mr. Pepper's door, or broken it down, found a phone, and called the cops.

In the span of a breath, a guttural snarl, one flooded with engorged pain, roars through the woods. A whimper presses on my throat, but I swallow it back.

I glance out from my hiding spot.

The two goddamn stalkers are there, and my heart slams against my ribcage at the realization that they followed me all the way out here.

They're tracking you down by your scent. Deimos' words swirl in my mind. He was telling the truth.

Deimos stumbles on his feet in front of them, cuts grazing his arms and chest. Fury lashes over his face. Blood seeps into his clothes, while another wound bleeds from under an eye.

Incisions lace his neck, crimson dripping down into his jacket. He's a complete mess, losing so much blood. He's going to get killed.

I'm trembling at seeing him this way, my heart shuddering at his state.

He isn't backing down but stands firm, hands fisted, eyes narrowing. He's going to fight to the end, but he sees his death. It's right there in his haunted gaze.

Both Bloodcursed lunge at him, their feet pounding the ground in their rush, kicking up detritus.

Deimos is thrown off his feet, his head hitting the ground with a sickening thud. I cringe as he grunts in pain. The monsters throw themselves on top of him, laying punch after punch into his face and chest. They're going to murder him, and tremors are racking my body.

Muscles tight, I lurch forward, my grip tightening on the letter opener.

The stalker with almost black eyes snarls, his head tilted back.

From my angle, his extending fangs are in full view.

I want to yell, to tell them to fuck off, anything but approach them.

Except anger rises to the surface within me, bubbles like an explosion about to detonate. I'm running toward them before I can think this through. Letter opener raised in my fist, I'm on him in seconds.

He turns toward me as I attack. Dark eyes with a glint of red blink in my direction. The momentum has me spearing the weapon toward him. His dark eyes widen, and he starts to retreat, but he's too slow.

Silver glints in the sunlight as I plunge the weapon into his back. Ripping into shirt and flesh, the dull blade drives right into his back like butter.

He roars, arching backward. Black wisps float from his wound. His back is reacting to the silver, seeming to smoke. I scramble backward, but he howls and stumbles about, grasping for the letter holder shoved deep into his flesh. His arms swing wildly, and one clips me in the head with a backhand.

I'm thrown off my feet and hit the ground hard, my vision wavering.

There's a shuffle as Deimos shoves off the forest floor, a scuffle breaking out as the other stalker jolts in my direction.

I try to push myself upright, but the creep is too fast and throws himself against me. We hit the ground, me beneath him.

Fangs.

That's all I see.

Long, pointy incisors dripping with saliva. He hisses in my face.

I throw my fists into his jaw, scratch and tug on his hair, but he doesn't stop.

The beast's mouth gapes wide, his strong fingers pressing my chin up, exposing my neck.

I scream and thrash against him. I can't breathe.

"You should have died long ago, bitch."

Death. That's what I picture coming for me. I hate how pathetic I sound, how tears are already blurring my vision, how all I can think about at this moment is my foster family and Nickie, and how much they'll cry at my burial. Stupid, painful thoughts crowd me.

His hand dips between us, and he's tugging at my jeans.

I hate him, loathe this piece of shit. I mean so little to him that he'd rape and kill me at the same time.

I rake my nails down the side of his face.

His lips jerk to my neck, teeth scraping my skin.

I'm paralyzed.

In a fraction of a second, he flies off me and hits a tree before collapsing to the ground like a sack.

Deimos stands in front of me, bloody and my fucking hero. "Don't move." He growls and snatches a thick branch off the ground, its end naturally pointy.

He lunges at the stalker and seizes him by the throat. With his other hand, he thrusts the stake into his gut ferociously and pins him to the tree. Releasing the monster's neck, he grabs hold of the branch and drives it deeper still. I can't even imagine the kind of strength he needs for that.

Arms quivering, he steps back.

The beast is crying out with pain, blood pouring from his wound. It's gruesome and cruel, and the creature is still squirming, but they were going to kill us both.

Deimos hunts down the black eyed creep who's staggering farther away, still trying to remove the silver embedded in his back. It isn't long before Deimos has both monsters staked to different trees. Blood spills over the leaves like bright red paint. It doesn't look real.

But I can't look away, wanting these stalkers to suffer for what they almost took from us. Our lives.

I'm shaking so hard, and stars are still dancing in my vision. Rage still mingles with terror.

They almost killed us.

Deimos storms over to me, takes me by the elbow, and marches us out of the woods in long strides. My bare feet are screaming with pain each time I step on something sharp.

I fight against him, and I know he's pissed. He drags me all the way to the Lamborghini, then hauls me against him. Chest to chest.

Out of instinct, my hand juts up between us and splays across his chest. He's on fire, my hand searing from our connection.

I shake so hard, my hands curling into balls. "They could have killed you."

"I told you to stay in the room," he reprimands me.

"Right. And if I had obeyed your stupid command, you'd be dead. Then what?"

"You coming out here could have gotten you killed," he roars, his cheeks flushing with anger. Fingers squeeze my arms tight as he holds me so close, so damn hard. "I want to spank your ass for pulling that shit out there."

We stare each other down, and that burning fire in my chest explodes. All I see are those full lips, the look in his eyes drowning in need. "Let me go!" I yell.

Instead, he angles closer, and my body responds instantly. Our mouths clash, and our kiss is primal and chaotic. Teeth and lips and hands everywhere. I rake through his hair, fisting it, wrenching him closer. I bite down on his lip, and sweet, metallic blood lingers on my tongue. My hands seize his collar, and I'm hauling him against me. I've been dreaming of kissing him since seeing him in the bar, and now this is actually happening.

I may hate him so much, but I want him even more.

Strong hands grasp my hips, and he has me in his arms and off my feet so fast, it takes me off guard. I clasp my legs around his hips, and he pins me to the side of the car, kissing me with the hunger of a wolf.

The bulge in his pants is rock-hard, and he's working it between my thighs, grinding into me. Liquid fire melts me from the friction, and I am lost to the feel of him.

He groans deeply as his hand is on my breast, his fingers pinching a nipple.

I gasp at his touch, and I'm soaking wet instantly.

I'm drowning under him, unsure of who I am right then, but I clearly feel like a woman ready to die if she can't have him. I forget all about the stalkers, fae, and my lost memories.

"I want you," I breathe into his mouth, and I hear the growl in his chest, the animalistic desire that slams into me too.

He claws at my shirt, dragging it off my shoulder as he finds my lips again. I'm breathing frantically. "You want me to fill you?"

I nod, my breaths coming so fast now, I can't trust my voice.

His tongue plunges into my mouth as his hand slides under my shirt.

I still with the touch.

He rips the fabric of my bra, and his fingers clasp on to my pebbled nipple, squeezing it. A moan spills from my lips as he tugs at my flesh while grinding into me.

God, I'm going to explode.

He pushes and pushes me, devouring me.

"You're mine," he commands.

With those words, I burn alight. I lose all control, and I'm shuddering against him. Nearby, there's a groan of warping metal, but I'm too lost to work out what that is. I release a whimpering moan and convulse with euphoria pulsing in my body. The orgasm comes so fast, so damn harsh, that the world blinks in and out. The climax tears through my body, my core clenching.

Deimos bites down into my shoulder, breaking the skin.

I cry out with painful pleasure.

The parking lot around us suddenly ripples and is stolen away from around us, the Lamborghini with its doors buckled startles me because that was the sound I heard. It then vanishes in a flash.

Darkness smothers us, closing in in a snap.

A vicious wind slaps against us as a howl in the distance rends the air.

We blast apart, breathless, and we both stumble in dimly lit woodland. But when I turn to look behind me, I rock on my feet with shock.

Gone is the motel and daylight.

An enormous castle wall sits behind us. Fading night smothers the land, and overhead, two full moons descend from the heavens.

I want to run, to flee, and it takes all my willpower to not scream.

Confusion pummels into me, a feeling of dread crashing over me. "What did you do?" My voice shakes.

"This is all you, my kitten."

"What the hell?!" I wrap my arms around myself, trembling. All I can do is stare with wide eyes at the stone castle towering over us. A goddamn castle with arched windows up above, turrets, and crenellations. No doors anywhere.

"Where are we?" I mutter, but in the back of my mind, the words *Wandering Realm* stream over my thoughts.

I know where I am from the snippets of memory I have, from what Deimos has told me... and goosebumps sprout over my flesh.

Knowing and believing are two very different things, though. But I can't deny what my eyes are seeing right now.

"Fuck," Deimos growls, his human guise gone. He's standing here beside me in all his fae glory. Long, white hair beating in the wind against his back, his striking green eyes narrowing as a sneer develops on his face. "Of all places, you have to bring us here."

I stiffen. "Is this your realm?"

The dense woodland nearby shudders in the wind, and I jump in my skin, half-expecting something to leap out at us. My blonde hair tumbles over my shoulders and in my face from the blustering air. My heart is racing so fast, and my brain is trying to catch up but failing miserably.

My skin prickles and tingles as a surge of heat thrums through me in undulating waves. The sensation comes and goes, feeling like static, the hairs on my arms standing on end.

Cold air whooshes past and does little to cool me down.

The realm from my dreams, the palace where the princes are from… This is where we are. And still, the hole in my memories stretches into a black abyss.

"We need to leave now." He snatches my hand, and we're running. "We're in the fucking Ash Court." A snarl rumbles in his chest—he's furious—and he grumbles things I don't hear under his breath.

He pounds the ground with each step, and I'm practically flying behind him because of how fast he's hauling me. His grip pinches my arm so hard, I wince.

"You're hurting me." I pull against him, but he's dragging me behind him until we're under the shadow of an enormous oak. Its shiny, bronze leaves glint in the moonlight.

We stop, and I'm gasping for air.

"Listen to me," he whispers in a rushed voice. "This is the Ash Court, home of the Unseelie fae. They find us on their land, they'll kill us in the most painful way possible. Do you want to die today?"

His dark words leave me shaking, and I see the fear in his wide eyes, his dilated pupils taking in our surroundings constantly. And all I can think of is what the Bloodcursed had said to me back in the elevator: *The King of Ash Court has called for you.*

I'm breathing hard, and my words won't come, so I shake my head. To hear the fear in Deimos' voice doesn't make me more inclined to meet this king.

"Good. Then we run as fast as we can, and no matter what happens, you don't stop. If I fall behind, you don't stop. If I die, you don't stop. You run until you reach the fence and you climb over it. Then head north. Do you hear me?" His hands are on my arms, fingers curling tight into flesh. He's terrified. I haven't seen him like this before, not even when facing those two stalkers.

"You're scaring me." Sweat is pouring down my back now, and for the life of me, I have no clue which way is north.

"You should be scared. The Unseelie are ruthless

and malicious—they are the darkest of the fae. We are their enemy."

There are two realms. Shadow Court and Ash Court. Dire enemies for as long as I can remember.

I don't even know these fae, but he classifies them as my enemy. "Aren't you all just fae?" The words dribble from my lips as tension flares over me.

"There are two sides to one coin." He glances over his shoulder.

Terror drags through my chest like barbed wire. I don't know this place, but someone wants to kill me.

"I'm not afraid." I lie terribly, but I want to convince him so he doesn't see me as helpless.

Breaths are coming fast, and I keep staring at the castle behind us. At the shadow the lofty castle casts. I suck back the tears, hating the fact that I'm so scared, that I can't control my emotions. I don't want Deimos to see me crying and freaking out. Even if my pulse is raging like a wild river in my veins.

"Let's go," he orders.

I barely flinch at his command, but on the inside, I'm shuddering.

He starts to move out, his hand tight over mine, fear flooding his gaze.

We're running across a field, my bare feet hitting the grass and soft soil. The more distance we put between us and the castle, the heavier the woodland grows.

I promised myself I'd try to be normal and stay in the real world. I'd not lose control of my emotions again.

Then came Deimos, and today sucks beyond words. Not even foster care, where other kids beat me, stole my stuff, and cut my hair while I slept, scared me this much. In my chest, my heart is rupturing, and it has everything to do with that grating feeling in my chest. The one that tells me this isn't in my imagination but real.

That I am a fae.

That this is where I belong.

Déjà vu hits me like I've been here before.

I have no clue what's really going on, but I'm running for my life. I still don't know why me coming back here will in any way save two realms at war. That has nothing to do with me.

Shadows shift around us, but I don't look. I can't, not without letting fear steal the sliver of control I'm grasping on to.

Adrenaline floods my veins, and each breath runs ragged through my lungs.

Deimos kept talking about a portal, and I never understood. I don't know how, but we came through it while I experienced the best kiss of my life. Go figure.

In the distance, mountains rise around us, the peaks white with snow.

"This way." Deimos swings me into a sharp left toward the woods.

I look quickly behind me to the castle, to the shadows sweeping over the land like figures following us. A flickering light illuminates from one of the arched windows.

I burst into the woods in a heartbeat, my bare feet tripping over dead branches and foliage. My soles are screaming with agony from the sharp things I keep stepping on, but Deimos won't let me stop. He's moving so fast, I might be flying soon behind him.

We rush out of the woods and into a small clearing. Feet away stands a fifteen-foot stone wall that spreads out from either side.

"Stand on my shoulders." Deimos already crouches low. "Hurry."

I'm breathing so hard now, and I have no time to overthink this. A cold wind hits my back as I quickly climb up, my hands flat on the icy stone wall for balance.

Deimos shifts, standing up slowly, his hands tight on my ankles.

I stumble for balance, lurching sideways. My stomach hits the back of my throat, but I dig my fingers into the grooves of the stones and hold myself in place.

My hands reach up for the top of the wall, fingers gripping the small edge protruding out. My heart is galloping at a thousand miles an hour. I cling to the wall like a monkey, sweat bathing me despite the cold.

"Quickly, climb over and jump."

I push myself up, but my arms tremble. I don't have the strength to pull myself up from this angle. "I can't," I breathe.

Next thing I know, Deimos grasps my ankles hard and shoves me upward.

The food in my gut swirls, and I'm grappling to push myself up. I swing a leg over and stare down on the other side. Dried, brown grass that leads down a slope to a river down below. Beyond that lies a ragged, shaggy forest that gives me the shivers. The land on this side doesn't have glinting leaves or perfect lawn, and instead, resembles a haunted woodland.

"Jump over," Deimos reprimands.

"What about you?" I look over at his side, but he's already scaling up the wall with perfect ease. I hold on to the top for dear life and stare out over the treetops to the castle. It gleams almost golden beneath the dual moons' hue. It's spectacular, and that earlier buzz over my skin intensifies.

Deimos snatches the back of my shirt and drags me up on my feet like I'm a feral cat he found on the street. Pressing me up against him, he jumps down with me in tow.

I want to scream, but I swallow back the panic.

We hit the ground hard, and I fall to my knees, a grunting sound spilling past my lips.

"Let's move." He grabs my arm, and then he's whisking me down the hill.

I want to stop and catch my breath, to ease the ache in my thighs, to stop my racing heart before it explodes in my chest.

We finally pause, and I slump against a tree while pain seizes my body. I can barely feel my legs except for the throbbing pulse, the sting of strained muscles. Breathing steadily is impossible. "Where are we going?"

"Shh," he throws my way, his brow furrowing. "Not a sound."

So many questions pound through my mind, like why the two courts hate each other. But more than anything, I wish I had my phone to Google fae and understand exactly what *Seelie* and *Unseelie* mean. There's a reason behind every dispute, every war. Throw in power and all chaos will break out, so do these fae battle because of politics, for power over the land?

Deimos is as silent as the night, not heaving for breath like me, as he surveys the dark woods around us. He's been protecting me from the beginning, and even now, I trust him to do the same. Though what worries me is where we're going, and what that will mean for me. Instinct tells me I'm not going home anytime soon.

Deimos jerks toward me instantly, his face blanching. Dread hits me square in the chest... I know that look. It means something terrible is going to happen.

I begin to pull back, but he's grabbing my arm and shoving me behind the tree.

Air swooshes against my back, tossing hair over my face.

And in an instant, Deimos is ripped away from me, gone from sight.

I stumble from the motion, and I'm clamping a hand over my mouth to keep from screaming.

Sweat prickles my nape. I spin on my heels, my back jammed up against the tree. I have no idea what to expect, but the terror throbbing in my veins is spreading.

I can't see Deimos.

And holding it together is impossible.

A scream rushes out past my lips.

The darkness shifts, and a shadow lunges at me.

My knees buckle out from under me as my life flashes before my eyes.

A figure rushes at me from within the shadowy woods, and I freeze in terror.

Adrenaline beats inside me, fueling my instinct.

I need to move, to fucking escape.

I swivel around on my heels and run. As quick as they can, my feet pound the forest floor. Air swooshes in and out of my lungs frantically. Branches swipe at my hair and face, but I don't stop. I don't care.

Panic grips me, numbing my brain. It's the stalkers. They tracked me down.

A large hand snatches the back of my top and wrenches me backward.

I'm screaming as my back hits the ground.

A man is staring down at me, offering me his hand. Dark hair peppered with silver is cut short and parted down the side. He has a white, short beard, and there's a softness in his eyes that confuses me.

I roll in the opposite direction and scramble to my feet, backing away.

"Who are you?" I snap. "Are you one of them? A Bloodcursed?"

The man with a healed scar running down the side of his face laughs at me, and I instantly hate him. He's wearing a black leather doublet, laced up at the front to his throat. A thick belt circles his waist where a blade sits in its sheath on either side of his hips. There's a menacing look to him... a warrior who has me swallowing hard.

"You're not from around here, are you?" he asks, his voice raspy, his gaze dipping to my chest and lower, then to my bare feet. My toes curl, grass and dirt squished between them.

He steps closer to where the moonlight slices across his face, revealing an older man, maybe in his fifties or sixties. Pointy ears catch my attention. They aren't super long... but they're fae ears. Deimos' words come to me about some family lines having long ears.

I blink hard.

"Master of Game, Gabel Wulfe." He reaches for me. "Come. We need to get out of the woods."

"Don't touch me," I snap, flinching away from the man, breathing heavily. "Where's Deimos?" The dark woods reveal nothing, and all I feel are the waves of fear rolling down my body.

A shadow stirs to my right, in the direction opposite of where I came from.

The bushes shake ferociously, and I'm struggling to breathe.

Gabel doesn't bat an eye, and I squirm under his stare. "What court are you from, lovely lady?"

Leaves and branches from the shrubs are swooshing about, and my heart is about to burst out of my chest. "Deimos, that better be you!"

A groan from the darkness trembles on the wind.

My mind drowns in images of a beast about to attack us. I recoil when someone explodes out of the shadows so fast, they're a blur. They lunge at Gabel. Both of them crash and hit the ground with expelled breaths. All growls and fists, they roll about in the dark.

I suck in ragged and harsh breaths, shaking all over. I reach down and grab the first thing my hand finds. A rock. The need to run presses on my mind, but my feet aren't moving.

In the tangle of limbs and snarls, white hair catches in the moon's hue.

"Deimos?" I bellow, my voice suddenly rising. My hand constricts around the stone.

Gabel is laughing hoarsely as he shoves Deimos off him with such ease. Deimos grumbles and climbs to his feet. Without a glance my way, he stalks over to the old man and drags him to his feet by an arm.

"You know each other?" I blurt out, barely restraining myself from tossing the rock at them for scaring the hell out of me.

I want nothing more than to tell everyone to go screw themselves. I'm tired of jumping at every sound, of being so afraid. I've forgotten how to react like a normal person.

Deimos turns to me as he brushes off dirt and leaves from his clothes. "Huh? Did you say something?" He has a tiny twig and more dead foliage tangled in his hair.

I pinch the bridge of my nose, ready to scream at him.

As if sensing my frustration, he says, "Gabel is an old family friend. He taught me good ambush moves when I was younger, like that stunt he just pulled. Plus, he used to take me out to hunt game a few times when he wasn't hunting with the king."

"Son, I don't think everyone at Shadow Court would agree I was a family friend." He claps a hand to Deimos' back.

I drop the rock from my grasp. My gaze moves from one man to another until they both turn to me. No matter how hard I stare at Gabel, I don't recognize him.

"Gabel, this is Gue-Gainy. An acquaintance of

Luther's. She's not from these parts, so expect strange questions." He laughs, and I grit my teeth. He is the worst at making up names. Looking down at the rock by my feet, the earlier idea pulses through my head.

Fine, I don't mind if Deimos doesn't want this man to know where I'm from, but don't make me out to be an idiot.

"A pleasure to meet you." Gabel stretches out his hand toward me, and I accept it reluctantly. He draws my knuckles to his mouth for a small peck before releasing me. I didn't expect that. I didn't expect many of the things I've experienced these past few days. But a kiss from a stranger surprises me.

"Any acquaintance of the princes of Shadow Court is a friend of mine," he admits, though there is tightness around his eyes, frustration flashing over his face.

"While night is still upon us, we need to leave this place," he says.

There's something unsettling about the way he talks about the night. The cold wind sends a chill up my spine, and I'm ready to move quickly out of here.

Gabel turns around, surveying the woods, and the sword strapped to him catches my attention. It sits in a leather sheath sitting diagonally across his back.

Deimos is quiet, and I wonder if he's really a friend of Gabel.

"Are you out game hunting?" Deimos finally asks Gabel as he steps closer to me in an almost protective manner. I'm still seething over the fact that he scared me, but I can feel the heat radiating from his body and am glad to have him near me.

Deimos cuts me a quick glance with a look in his eyes that confirms my fears. An ominous feeling prickles along my skin. I don't know if I should be afraid of the woods or this armed stranger.

Gabel is combing a hand through his hair, still messed up from their earlier battle, weariness drawing at his features. He glances over his shoulder. "I have personal matters to take care of with your father, the king," he whispers.

"He's not my father." Deimos spits the words. "I hated when you said that years ago, and I detest it even more now."

"Being married to your mother makes him your father in the eyes of the court."

Deimos lowers his head momentarily, mumbling darkly to himself before addressing Gabel.

"Are you here under orders of Queen Sarey? Or are you changing allegiances from Ash Court and coming back to ours?" The hatred in Deimos' voice startles me, and I may not know what's going on, but what I do know tells me there are two opposing kingdoms, and the words *Ash Court* trigger alarm bells in my head.

Those from my kingdom are being hunted.

"Son, you know why I had to leave Shadow Court all those years ago."

"We would have protected you." Deimos' voice climbs, his body leaning forward, like the past with Gabel is a wound still not healed. The wind picks up, tossing his white hair like a banner over his shoulders.

"Prince Deimos, you think me a fool? Do you honestly think that you and your brothers could have saved me from your mother's wrath? She convinced King Tibout to slaughter so many loyal to the previous queen. I had no choice but to leave."

"Why Ash Court of all places? There are two other courts farther east."

Gabel doesn't respond right away, but darkness gathers under his eyes. "Survival." He keeps his chin high, and deep inside, I feel he's telling the truth. "I hoped to do more good from within the enemy's walls."

A distant wolf's howl distracts me, and I bite my lower lip, feeling vulnerable standing out here. I pray there aren't monstrous wolves out here. Werewolves? *They aren't real, right?*

"Is that the reason for your trip to my court?" Deimos asks, his posture stiff, and he somehow looks different from the man whom I first met at the bar. Back then, he carried incredible sexiness that called to me. Now... he still affects me like no other, but there's also an air of authority about him.

Gabel gives a sharp nod, but offers no insight into the message he's delivering. "We must leave this place. We're too close to Ash Court."

"We're headed in the same direction. Join us," Deimos adds, and his hand is already on my elbow. His invite isn't a friendly one—I can hear it in his voice—but one filled with hope that he might pry some of the information out of the man who defected to the enemy's court.

"Stay close," Deimos whispers, and he draws me into a quick walk. The soil is cold and hard on my bare feet. What I wouldn't give for sneakers right now.

There's no pause, and with Gabel taking the lead, we're moving with speed. Deimos holds me against him, making the walk easier as he takes a lot of my weight.

"When do we go back home to my world?" I whisper.

He hushes me and shakes his head before lifting his gaze to Gabel ahead of us and back at me.

Sure, later when Gabel isn't around. It's always later, and by then I might be eaten by wolves out here.

I don't remember how long we've been traveling, but I'm out of breath and my feet are killing me. I'm also pretty sure I've stepped on every sharp object in this forest.

Groaning, I draw Deimos' attention. "Is something wrong?" he asks.

"I'm tired."

He lifts his head. "Gabel, let's take a break. Food would be good."

The man nods and veers left, where the land slopes downward. At the base, we come across a ragged stone mountain, and we follow a path. I don't remember where we are, but the hardness of the ground is excruciating. I'm about to wrench free from Deimos, when Gabel waves us closer. He vanishes into a cave.

Yes, thank you!

Inside, the air smells musty, and I can't see a thing.

Gabel rushes in and out of the cave, bringing sticks with him. Within moments, there's a frantic scrape of wood. It isn't long before a flicker of fire flashes from the middle of the cavern. Gabel is kneeling in front of a pile of sticks piled up right into the shape of a teepee.

Deimos gathers large rocks from around the cave and creates a circle around the wood.

I stand there, completely clueless about how to start a campfire without matches. The only camping trip I've ever been on was with school, but everything was set up for us.

My eyes flicker over to Deimos, who leaves the cave and comes back with more wood piled into his arms.

"I'll let you finish," Gabel instructs. "I'm going hunting for food."

"Thanks," Deimos says, like there wasn't a bucket-load of tension earlier between them.

I don't feel comfortable in the slightest with Gabel conveniently heading out to hunt. I press my tongue to my teeth, praying that Deimos knows what he's doing.

Deimos

I sit next to Guendolyn, stretching out my long legs toward the fire. The crackle and snap fills the silence. She watches the cave's entrance like a hawk.

"You are safe," I say.

"What if Gabel returns to Ash Court and brings back an army? Aren't you worried?" She swivels on the ground and stretches out her bent legs.

My attention falls to her bare feet, the dirt covering them, the rawness of her soles. Something hurts deep in my chest at the fact that I didn't notice she's been barefoot until now.

"First, the court is too far for him to go there and return before we leave this cave. Second, why didn't you tell me you aren't wearing shoes?" I reach forward, grab both her ankles, and swivel her around by her legs to face me. Placing her feet in my lap, I hold on to her as she fights me to pull away.

"What does it matter? I'll be fine." She pushes against my arms, and I eye her sharply.

"It's the least I can do after making you suffer."

She's shaking her head and huffs. I adore how cute she looks when she's angry at me, her nose scrunching, her breaths loud, her lips pinching to the side of her mouth.

"Fine, but just be careful with your big hands."

I smile to myself at her intended insult and turn my attention to her small feet. A large leaf is stuck to the base of one foot, and I peel it off, followed by every loose piece of debris attached to her. With both hands, I rub my thumbs in small circles over her soles. She has scratches all over them. She's lucky they aren't cut up and bloody.

Out of the corner of my eye, I catch the pleased smirk she tries to hide by looking away.

There's only silence between us, the fire keeping us warm, and all I can think about is the strange attraction I feel for her. How wrong it is knowing Luther adores her. How I selfishly don't want to return her to my brother's arms.

"Why am I here?" she asks, breaking me from my thoughts. "I know you said something about helping the realms and a curse, but why me?"

I brush more of the grit off the tips of her toes, scrubbing with a thumb where the dirt stains her skin.

"Because you were taken from here as a baby and left on Earth with human parents."

She stiffens, her eyes widening, and whispers fall from her sweet lips. "My parents aren't human, are they?"

I meet her gaze and keep massaging in the tender spot in the arch of her foot. "No."

"So you know who they are?" Her voice is hopeful, and she's staring at me with that look that breaks me because I have to lie. I don't want to, but telling her the truth puts her in harm's way. It's better for now that she doesn't know.

I shake my head and decide to change the topic, as I can tell she'll keep asking questions. "My brothers and I believe you have a power that can end a lot of blood-shed in our court."

She blinks, studying me, and I can see the wheels behind her eyes spinning. "Is that why my mother aban-doned me? Because of my power?" Her brow furrows, and she looks at me with panic in her eyes. "I don't even know what my power is, but it must be horrible for her to dump me in another world and never come to find me again." The heartbreak in her voice is gut-wrenching.

I tighten my hold on her feet in my lap. "Nothing about you is horrible." I fight the truth wanting to come out, words I can't tell her without hurting her worse. At least not yet, not until she's safe and understands how all of our survival depends on her. This is not the kind of information I intend to scare her with tonight.

She sits with her hands wrapped around her middle, her brow furrowed, her eyes half-hooded.

There's an innocence to her she tries to hide, and no matter how hard she fights her destiny, she can't push away what is meant to be. Not when so many other lives are at stake. Like the rest of us, she didn't pick this life, but as my grandmother once said to me, *"Living with fear is a life wasted, so do everything like it's your last day alive. Live."*

I lower my gaze and run my fingertips over the length of Guendolyn's toes and back up to her ankles. Her skin shivers under my touch, her breath quickening, and I swallow hard. Her reaction to me has me twisted in knots. I can't seem to get her kiss out of my head. Her intoxicating desire is like a storm. It sweeps in and tears anything in its path apart. In this case, me.

Everything about her calls to me. I want her all to myself ridiculously bad, but there are dozens of reasons I can't get involved with a woman like her. A dozen reasons that don't align with her destiny. This is the moment I should vow to never kiss her again, to never think about her in any way but being a savior to our kingdom.

The words don't come, and tearing my gaze away from this girl is impossible. I want her beneath me, ruddy cheeks, crying out my name, splayed open. For me to show her the darkest sins that will have her begging for more.

I always thought it fickle to see Luther pine over Guendolyn since losing her two years ago, but now I understand. Not that I'm in love... hell, that's not for me. I've seen what broken marriages do to families, and I don't want any of that. Shattered hearts, endless tears, rejection... That knife is still embedded in my chest.

My real father comes from House Larmathier, one of the oldest families in the Wandering Realm. He went out hunting one day and never returned. He's a gutless weasel, living in a court in the east, married to a princess half his age. Mother tried to have him assassinated—as one does—but the assassin ended up dead. I know Mother will never give up until he's buried. I've given up caring.

"Is it common for fae children to be abandoned on Earth?" she asks as she looks at me with desperation in her eyes, wanting me to tell her this is commonplace, that she's not alone.

I don't want to lie to her, though.

"It's an old practice from the ancient traditions that isn't seen too much these days. Fae would replace human babies with their own as a way to infiltrate the Earth Realm, to uncover what magic that world held. But once they discovered it didn't offer much in the way of enchantment, they stopped doing it."

"What happened to those children?"

I swallow hard but answer her question. "A guard would bring them home, where they were interrogated on everything they discovered. Not many survived. Those were barbaric times that have been outlawed. My stepfather has made going into your realm illegal and punishable by death."

Her head tilts up. "But you risked coming for me?"

"Because we need your help. And he doesn't know I went there—and he won't until we are certain you're safe."

Her breaths quicken, and I see the shiver in her trembling body. "That's why you didn't want Gabel knowing who I am," she whispers as she takes a quick look to the cave's opening.

"If anyone finds out who you are, they'll hurt you to gain power in this world."

"But you got to me first. Took me before anyone else could." Her blue eyes darken, and her voice fills with venom.

"No, that's not—"

She looks away just as Gabel returns, holding two rabbits he already skinned and gutted.

Guendolyn quickly draws her feet from my lap and tucks them under her. I want to pull her aside, tell her she's wrong to think we're the enemy. I want to rip away the pain etching her face. She looks away and wipes at her eyes. Watching her is a punch to my gut.

"I brought food," Gabel says as he sets about skewering the meat.

I toe my boots off and remove my socks, before laying them near the fire to warm up. "Gainy, I'd offer you my shoes, but you'll trip in them. Take my socks at least."

She stares at me, still mad, but doesn't touch the socks, so I leave them there for now. I know she'll take them.

With my boots back on, I take one of the skewered rabbits and hold it over the flame as it starts cooking.

No one talks, and I let my mind wander anywhere but here. To the river behind our castle that no one else visits. Where I can swim for hours and be left alone to sleep under the sun, to hunt, to escape the chaos of the kingdom. That was before everything went to hell after the curse spread. Now, the Bloodcursed are rampant around Shadow Court, breaching the walls to get inside. One bite and the virus takes the victim. We're under attack, and those easy times feel like a world away.

"Back in the woods," Gabel begins, turning the almost cooked rabbit, "I swore you were going to tell me this lovely lady was Guendolyn." Gabel laughs, and I join him, chuckling louder.

"I heard she's long dead," I offer, hearing the sudden hitch in Guendolyn's breathing. "Gainy here is just a girl Luther met at a tavern east of our border and has been obsessed with. A common barmaid, but if she makes my brother happy for a night or two, who I am to question his carnal needs?"

Guendolyn starts choking, and I reach over to pat her back hard. She whacks my hand away, and her stare can peel the skin right off my body. She's on her feet. "I'm going outside for fresh air," she growls.

"Just outside the cave where I can see you," I command.

She glares down at me, and I pray she doesn't say something stupid. I meet her gaze, imploring her to keep her anger in check.

Gabel turns to grab more wood for the fire just as Guendolyn kicks me right in the ribs. I groan from the sharp pain, gritting my jaw. *Damn.*

I watch her march out, and all I can stare at is that tight ass and think how much I want to spank it. She stands just outside. I see only part of her from where I'm sitting, and it takes everything I have to not follow her out there. She glances over her shoulder at me and flips me the middle finger. Wonder what that means?

Fuck, she drives me insane with desire.

Suddenly, she storms back in, snatches my socks from near the fire, and saunters back out with her head high.

"Feisty," Gabel says. "She must be from very far east, as she wears strange clothes and doesn't show respect to princes and nobles alike."

"You know Luther. He likes his girls wild and fiery." I reach over for more cooked meat, and my side flares with pain from her kick. I rip into the charred rabbit.

The small issue of her not remembering her past is something we'll work with once we get her safely to our kingdom.

I get up and go outside to where she's standing with her back to the rock, hands folded over her chest. "Come have something to eat," I say to her. "We have a long way to travel."

We stride through the dark woods, Gabel on my right and Deimos on my left. Night cloaks the forest in every direction, with only the two moons overhead lighting the way.

Deimos' socks slide over my feet, but they offer a layer of protection from the forest floor, so I suck it up and keep tugging them up my legs.

It's hard to decide if I want to kiss him or punch him most of the time. He's hiding so much from me, and I can't help but feel as though I'm walking into a trap. They want me to somehow help with their realm problems, but I have no clue how to begin, or if they even have the right person. What will happen to me if I can't perform whatever miracle they're expecting?

I keep catching Gabel stealing glances my way, and fear burrows deep in my gut. The kind that tells me he didn't buy Deimos' lies. But I don't know who to trust. These two fae don't trust each other. So where does that leave me?

"Gainy, what village are you from again?" he asks, and there it is, the web unraveling at my feet. I hold back a grimace, my mind scrambling for what to say.

"Wavertorn," Deimos responds on my behalf.

"It's a wonderful place," I add quickly. "My family and friends are there. I grew up right by the water."

"Water? Isn't Waverton located near the desert?"

My throat dries like the desert, and a flash of confusion washes over his face. "Near the oasis, of course." I need to stop pretending like I know anything about this world. Under his gaze, I'm squirming, so I change tactics.

"What exactly is a Game Keeper?"

Gabel's face cracks into a smile, and he lets out a heavy laugh. "I guess this must all be very new to you, having come from such a small town." His words scare me... He knows I'm not from Waverton. I can hear it in his voice.

But I keep it cool. Breathe normally while my head is screaming to stop talking.

"My role in the kingdom is to take the king or queen out on hunts for game."

"Is that all? Sounds like a fun job." Sweat trickles down my back, and I glance over to Deimos for assistance, but he offers nothing.

"It may seem that way on the outside, but there's so much more to the role." He leans closer. "When we hunt, it's usually just me and the king with only a few guards traveling for long periods of time. I use that time to everyone's advantage."

My eyes widen. "You have him all to yourself, to find out things, to whisper in his ear."

He nods with a curt smile. This man is dangerous, because I suspect he's holding so much knowledge and influence. That's why Deimos told me to be cautious, to hide my real identity.

"That's a matter of perspective," Deimos adds. "What one man imparts to the king or queen can be very intentionally skewed in his favor."

"Absolutely," Gabel responds. "But I have always been a man of honor, if you recall from when you first arrived at Shadow Court with your brothers. It was me who influenced the king to give you three your own palace, away from the court drama, away from the hatred your mother, the new queen, brought to the kingdom. Royalty should be servants of the people, not focusing on petty court politics. You three are the future of Shadow Court."

"And you were the one who convinced the king to make us work the land, ploughing soil. I remember hating you so much for that." His features contort toward Gabel, still not over the incident apparently.

"Aww, come on, Deimos, you know the benefit of

royalty working with the land, not owning it. It was something the previous queen had believed in strongly. Something you admitted you saw the benefit in when you were younger."

"Working on farms sounds like a good idea." I add my two cents, though no one seems to be paying attention. Both of them are caught in their own mini battle of words. At least it takes the attention off me.

Deimos grumbles under his breath before responding. "Every action has a consequence. Wasn't it an ambush of villagers who attacked and killed the previous queen as she worked in the field? Angry, hungry fae, who didn't have enough food for their families so the queen could sell our crops to another kingdom at triple gold crowns?"

Gabel's lips draw down. "She did it to pay off the debt of this kingdom, so you're right. Everything comes with balance. What happened to her was devastating. But you want to know the truth," Gabel says, turning to me.

I jerk my chin at him and nod.

"I consider myself a fae searching for the truth and bringing it to the common folk. They have a right to know what is happening in their kingdom. Always be alert, because nothing is what it seems in any court."

"You tell the truth, even to the detriment of the court, right, Gabel? When—" Deimos pauses as soon as a guttural roar sounds from the woods ahead of us.

I ease back, not wanting to find out what made that sound. "Maybe we should choose another path."

Deimos grabs my arm and hauls me to his side, clutching me tightly. I feel the fear rippling over his body, and that scares me more.

My muscles tense with the urge to run, except I have nowhere to go.

"They're coming from two sides." Gabel twists around to look behind us at the trees and bushes. He draws the sword from the sheath on his back with such grace, I can't stop staring. Nothing compares to the reddish gold of the metal; it looks as if it's made of gold and blood. It has a rounded tip and resembles a long, thin leaf more than the swords I've seen in movies.

"Deimos," Gabel calls as he hands him the sword, then pulls out the two blades from his belt. Silver glints in the moonlight, the tips seriously sharp.

I want something to defend myself too.

My gaze is swinging back and forth at the shadows everywhere, and I can't distinguish shapes from the night. Glancing at my feet, I find there are rocks and twigs all over the place. I quickly grab a thicker branch.

Deimos watches me, and he nods approvingly, but he's scared. It's in his eyes, in the tightening brackets around his mouth. "Whatever you do, don't let them bite you. Stay behind me as much as you can, understand? And remember what I said before about going north should anything happen."

I nod, unable to find my voice. My heart is beating so hard, I can't concentrate. I nibble at my lip, my hand squeezing the life out of the stick.

Wielding his sword, Deimos steps forward. I hate to admit it in this moment, but this fae is so attractive, especially while holding a sword. The muscles in his arms flex, his chest sticks out, and I'm lost in the sight. That whole protective vibe radiates off him. I'm melting on the inside. It annoys me that he affects me so much, yet I don't look away.

The snap of a twig comes from somewhere in the woods around us.

I freeze, lifting my weapon.

Two figures burst out of the woods with such speed, I stumble backward. Their skin is pale and blotchy, blood dripping from their mouths. Clothes hang off lithe frames. Their ribcages are so pronounced, I want to gag. It pains me to see how scrawny and starved they look.

Deimos lunges toward them in a heartbeat, moving so gracefully and swiftly, I'm left stunned.

Holding the sword with two hands, Deimos slashes it through the air ferociously. The weapon cuts right through the first creature's neck, the head sliced right off. Blood gushes out from the wound as the body drops to its knees and flops forward with a thump.

I scream, unable to hold it back. I can't take my eyes off the head rolling away into the treeline.

Bile hits the back of my throat.

More Bloodcursed pour out of the woods.

I forget everything but fear. Gabel moves with speed, hacking his blades across the beasts coming for him. He throws himself into a roll and leaps onto the creature's back before slitting its throat. The skin where his blade touches the Bloodcursed sizzles on contact. Just as the letter holder did when it broke through the skin of the stalker back home.

These monsters drop to the ground, the burning flesh eating away over their bodies.

Sickness surges through me.

I can't do this. The stick is trembling in my hand, while Deimos spins away from an attack, his sword swinging wide, and catches two of the attackers across the chest. They stumble backward but don't fall, and come at him again.

One of them bypasses him and scrambles in my direction with savagery in his eyes. Instinct takes me over while my brain remains mush. I don't want to die here. So I swing the branch at his head, sending him into a sideway stumble. Then I whack the end of the stick at his chest as he unleashes a savage screech. Lips peel back to stained teeth and breath that could call death itself from Hell.

As if on cue, Deimos whips around, his blade slicing through the Bloodcursed's neck.

"Ouch." I cringe and look away, but bump into someone behind me.

My heart is pumping hard, and I swing around, branch high in my hand.

"It's just me, lovely lady," Gabel says, gasping for air.

I take a breather and stay close to him. Trees around us are rustling in the breeze, and the only sound is that of Deimos groaning as he fights.

Deimos is all power and brawn. He dodges an attack and kicks the assailant away before swinging his sword and chopping off its head. Then with a spin, he regroups with us.

"That wasn't too bad," he brags, his chest huffing and puffing. Blood splatters are across his cheek, and he wipes it with the back of his hand, making it a smudgy mess. He turns to me and cups the side of my face. "Did any of them bite you?"

I drag in a quivering breath and shake my head.

His thumb grazes under my eye, and a hopeful look crosses his gaze. I imagine him leaning in close, tracing his lips across mine. That single thought has my nipples hard. But he breaks away and juts his chin toward Gable. "Time to get out of here fast."

The land is scattered with half a dozen bodies, most missing their heads. I take mental notes that decapitation and silver works against these monsters.

"A handful are easy to kill," Gabel murmurs. "What worries me is how many others are near."

Deimos grabs my hand, his palm swallowing mine, and the three of us are running through the woods. I can't think straight and am barely keeping it together, praying we find somewhere to lie low. I gasp for air. All I can picture in my mind are the heads rolling.

But just as I think we're far away from the attack area, that screeching sound I'm beginning to loathe closes in around us.

I shudder and inch closer to Deimos.

A raging river of Bloodcursed breaks its banks. So many are racing toward us from the woods ahead.

My knees wobble under me.

Twenty, maybe thirty.

All I can see is my death. Slaughtered and bitten, I'll roam this world forever as one of those creatures. I curl my fists, ready to fight, and lift my stick.

Electricity pricks down my arms suddenly. It crawls over me like an army of ants swarming across my body.

Crack.

Crack.

CRACK!

The sound booms and fills the night. Beneath my feet, the ground trembles as though it's coming to life.

I flinch with fear, my adrenaline skyrocketing.

Trees rip back and forth, even though the winds have stilled.

Roots shudder across the ground, breaking free from the confines of the compact dirt.

They grow and stretch before my eyes. Slithering like vipers, they strike the Bloodcursed, curling around limbs, around throats, dragging them backward and into the ground itself.

Claws scratch at the soil, their screams ringing the air with terror.

I'm shaking, startled at what I'm seeing.

Their hollering is terrifying.

The few Bloodcursed who escape the tangled woods scramble toward us with gaping mouths, fangs exposed. Their greedy fingers are stretched out for us. They snarl like rabid dogs.

I recoil, my heart thumping hard against my ribcage. I never signed up for this. I'm just a normal girl… Well, *normal* is subjective and overrated, but before those stalkers arrived in my life, my life wasn't in danger. I blame them for everything. Except in the back of my mind, I know the real danger is the person who ordered them to come after me.

Gabel lunges forward and cuts his way through the masses. His grunting and their screeches pierce my ears. My pulse is jumping with all kinds of emotions. Fear mainly—that overpowers everything else.

I look up at Deimos, close to nudging him to go help him. I absolutely want us to survive the night.

Except his eyes are glowing white, and he's mumbling silent words. The air from his outstretched hand ripples outward like a sonic blast. It travels out toward the woods, to the spot where the Bloodcursed emerged.

Where the tree roots have come to life.

He's doing it. He's making them attack. I have no real idea how, but he's a fae. They have magic, just like he could convince people to do things with his voice alone.

The ground trembles beneath my feet. It's hard to tell if that's from the stampede of Bloodcursed or moving trees.

With Gable fighting frantically, I rush to help him with a fury that borders on insanity.

Swinging my branch, I go wild and whack a Bloodcursed latching on to Gable's arm. I don't stop and slam the stick into the thing's head until Gabel slips free. With a swift turn, he plunges the blade into the side of the creature's neck. Blood splatters, and I stumble out of its reach and watch the creature stumble to the ground, gurgling his last breaths.

The ground is shaking furiously now, a roar belching up from under our feet.

Bloodcursed are wailing, the roots attacking as many as they can. The hairs on my arms stand on end from the magic.

It's chaos.

Panic rattles in my veins, and I gasp for air. Everything is happening too fast, and I don't understand half of it.

The ground at once jolts with ferocity. A gaping hole cracks open, stretching to the length of several small cars. It groans with the might of tearing the world apart.

Soil under my feet softens, and it starts sliding under me in seconds, pulling closer to the fissure's edge.

I scramble backward, leaving behind the socks sucked off my feet. Ten feet away, Gabel slips to the ground with a thud, and he's sliding fast to the deathly edge.

"Gabel!" I throw myself at him and grasp his arm with two hands.

He squirms and groans, his legs dangling off the edge. Pure terror lashes over his face as he thrashes for escape.

Bloodcursed are tumbling in all around us, and Gabel's weight is too strong for me. He's pulling me with him.

The fingers on Gabel's free hand dig into the ground for purchase, but my feet are now caught in the quicksand. I'm slipping forward, lurching backward.

"Deimos!" I bellow just as a horde of more Blood-cursed rush onto the scene. Growls fall from the monsters, lips curling as they expose sharp fangs.

Whatever these vampire things are, I want them as far away from me as possible.

The trees are turbulent and unrestrained, their branches and roots striking and whipping the creatures.

The hairs on my nape rise, and I'm pulling at Gabel with all my strength, with everything I have.

"Deimos!" I'm yelling, but it's not his shadow that falls over me. He stands in my peripheral vision, casting his power to hold back the swarm of monsters trying to kill us.

All I can think is that this is the end. This is *my* end.

Strong hands snap around my waist in that instant and rip me away from the chasm.

"Gabel!" I shout as I fight against the creature dragging me away from him. He's sliding fast now, and my stomach plunges.

Another figure rushes forward and yanks Gabel to safety by the back of his doublet. Relief washes over me to have these strangers jump in and help.

I fall to my feet and stumble free from my captor before turning around to find a tall man in a cloak, his hood concealing his face.

"Who are you?" I ask. They're too tall, too broad to be the stalkers from home.

But when a heart-shattering scream cracks the air behind me, I jerk around just as two Bloodcursed crash-tackle Gabel, ripping him out of the other man's arms.

Gabel's feet skid over the rich soil. He's crying out, and I lunge for him, but the momentum tears him down into the chasm with the Bloodcursed, swallowed by the ground in seconds.

"No!" My scream echoes in the night.

*D*eimos is on his knees, his shoulders curled forward, his head low. He heaves for each breath, and I'm terrified for him. The power he used brought trees to life!

I'm numb all over.

I hurry over to Deimos. He's still fighting for each inhale, his body shuddering. He's so pale, and his lips have bled to white. That magic he used has worn him out. When he opens his eyes, I expect to find them glowing white, but instead, I stare into spectacular green eyes. Bloodshot as though he's been drinking all night, but still stunning. I crouch down next to him.

"Are you okay? What you did out there was insane and amazing. Guess as a fae, anything's possible, right?" My words just pour out of me like the emotions that overwhelm my mind. But talking helps me not think about them, or panic that I just saw someone die. "I'm so sorry about your friend Gabel."

He doesn't say anything.

"Who are those two guys? Should we be trying to escape?"

"They're with us," he murmurs, his voice low and distant.

I want to ask so much more, but I don't. Instead, I sit with him for the longest time.

"I will ensure his heroic battle will be remembered, and that his family is looked after. Are you hurt?" he croaks as he raises his hand to my cheek. I lean against his touch, the warmth electric. I want to cry, that's how I feel after everything that's happened so fast.

"I'm not sure I'm made out for this life-and-death lifestyle." I try to laugh, but it comes out as a clumsy snort, and I don't even care how embarrassing I sound.

"Once we get out of this, I promise to teach you how to fight."

The idea sounds perfect. In truth, this world is my picture of Hell, so if survival means learning to master a weapon as I'd seen Deimos do, then I'm ready. "Deal. I want to wield a sword as well as you."

His smile brings one to my face.

He draws in a long breath and lowers his hand. The tips of his fingers look like they've been plunged into ink. I stiffen and quickly take his hand into mine, studying them.

"What is this?" I run my index finger over the blackness. It feels rough, like a peach's skin.

"Bits of my soul, burned away each time I use magic."

My mouth gapes open, and I lean back, eyeing him warily. "Is that meant to be a joke? Because it's not funny."

Except he's not laughing. There's only the twitch at the corners of his lips. Why does everything in this realm have to be deadly and come with gigantic problems? Deimos was right. *Every action has a consequence.*

"You're going to die?" I gasp.

"Eventually, we all do, but my time might come quicker. I lose years of life with each use of Arcana magic." He must notice my confused expression because he explains more. "Don't worry for me. It's the magic I harness from nature around me. Elemental magic, the oldest of its kind for fae. A power I gained from my father. I've accepted my fate long ago."

My fingers curl around his hand, and I hold on, his warmth seeping up my arm. I want to ask him how many times he's used his magic, how many years he's lost already. But I can't bring myself to do it. I'm too terrified of finding out the truth.

When I stare at him, I notice the sharpness of his cheekbones, the hardness of his jaw, the soft angles of his nose. His breathing has calmed, and he looks at me with those vivid green eyes. He wants to say something. His lips part, but the words never come. His gaze lifts over my shoulder.

Behind me, the two cloaked men are staring in our direction, and I'm not sure what to expect.

"So you definitely know them, right?" I ask Deimos.

They stroll around the gaping hole in the ground, stepping over the bodies and coming toward us. Their swords drip in blood. I'm convinced if they were after me, even Deimos couldn't stop them. I inch closer to him.

They're both large in stature, broad-shouldered and powerful.

Deimos climbs to his feet. "We're safe," he says, even if his voice is stiff, and I'm not sure what to make of it. He takes my hand and helps me up.

My muscles twitch with exhaustion. I look over at the chasm. We lost Gabel, and my chest clenches. I barely knew him, but he fought alongside us, he believed in helping others. I'll never know his true intentions, but he didn't deserve to die. Not like that.

Deimos walks up to the men, and he hugs each one with hard claps on their backs. Their mumbles confirm he knows them very well. One of the strangers hands his blood-stained sword to Deimos, then motions toward me. Deimos and the other man wipe their blood-stained swords on the clothes of the dead. Then they step closer to the gaping crack in the ground and stare down. Are they looking for any sign of Gabel?

The wind comes out of nowhere as I stand, the air swirling around my legs, throwing my hair over my shoulders. There's something about these strangers that holds me captive. The man coming toward me is striding with purpose and so much power.

His cloak billows in the air behind him. It tears open at the front, showing me a glimpse of a military-style jacket, silver buttons and a high collar underneath. Black pants stretch over strong legs.

His hands reach up, and he pushes the hood off his head. My heart beats faster... he's incredible. Stunning. Mesmerizing. Hair dark as midnight tumbles to his shoulders, piercing eyes the color of flames. They flicker as if alight, crowned by the darkest eyebrows.

Rugged jaw, sharp cheekbones, and lips full with an upward curve, reminding me so much of Deimos'.

My breath catches in my lungs. My brain is stuttering, and I bite on the corner of my mouth.

"Luther?"

The way his gorgeous mouth pulls into a grin confirms I'm right. I've seen him in my dreams, his name having never left my thoughts. The strange thing is that I don't recall much about him or our time together or the emotions I know should be there, yet the ache in my chest at seeing him deepens and is close to knocking all the air out of my lungs.

He chuckles and closes the distance between us.

Standing right in front of me, he looks down at me, intensity burning in his eyes.

"Do you remember me, little wolf?" he asks.

My body shudders at hearing that deep baritone voice, and I release a harsh chuckle that comes out awkward.

He looks at me with a crocked grin.

But I'm drowning in his scent of freshly cut timber, perspiration, and something like dark cinnamon. It engulfs me and leaves me trembling with a need I don't understand. Fire rages across my chest. There's something about him that sets me alight with desire, something that responds to his presence with a savageness I've only felt with Deimos.

What I feel for Luther is so different. It comes from deep inside me, from a place I didn't know existed until now.

Winds roar around us, my hair lashing across my head.

Luther. The name sweeps over my mind like it has so many times.

"Yes," I breathe, my gaze dropping to his full lips before climbing back to his gaze. "I know you."

He laughs with a sound that breaks me, surprising me by how much it turns me on to just hear that gorgeous sound. "That's a good start."

"But there's more, and I just can't..." I squint, trying to concentrate. My chest tightens, feeling like I should recognize my own yearning ache, but it's buried in my mind and unreachable.

"It's okay," he says. "Part of the curse included wiping your memory. The main thing is you're home."

I feel so many emotions. Excited, confused, unsettled. "This isn't my home, Luther."

That's where you're wrong. I just need to help you remember things.

His voice streams over my mind, insistence clipping his words. I'm blinking hard at him. He's spoken to me in my mind before. Yet my heart is pounding in my chest.

He pauses as if searching for something to say. Staring at me like he knows more about me than I do.

Don't worry, little wolf. I'll show you everything in due course. And I can only read your mind if you let me. He smirks devilishly.

Everything has happened so fast. Stalkers attacking me. Deimos rescuing me. Me arriving in this world. The Bloodcursed. Fae. Gabel. And now Luther reading my mind. It's too much.

The world seems to stand very still.

The tightness around his eyes soften, and despite my crazy emotions, something in my mind tells me to be careful around him.

"Come with me. The woods aren't safe." He takes me by the hand, and we stride toward Deimos.

Confusion blurs my mind, and an ache burrows deep in my chest.

When I look over, Deimos is watching me, his expression hardened.

Foliage pricks the underside of my feet with each step I take, now that I've lost my socks.

"You've met Luther," Deimos mutters, as if he'd prefer to be anywhere but here. "And this is Prince Ahren."

Ahren pushes the hood off his face, and his presence leaves me gasping. Impossibly gorgeous and full of sin. Pale skin. Red lips. Captivating green eyes just like Deimos', except Ahren's are pale and glistening. With his hair, white as the clouds, reaching halfway down his back, he stands regally. His face is longer than his brothers', lips quirking at the edges, and like the other two, he has those chiseled cheekbones.

Ahren is the heir to the throne… a nugget of knowledge that seems to have stayed with me. And he doesn't appear very happy to see me.

A frustrated sigh slips from his lips. "What is she wearing?"

I narrow my eyes at him. "Really? That's what you take out of this whole scenario? Not that we could have died? And I'm standing right here. If you want to say something to me, talk directly."

Right off the bat, I dislike him. And I suspect I didn't like him the first time I met him, either.

"I see you haven't changed and still don't know how to show respect." His voice drips with disdain.

A harsh laugh bursts from my throat, and I love that I can laugh at anything after everything I've been through. "I never asked to be brought here, but apparently, I'm the only one who can save your ass. So maybe it's *me* who should ask for respect." My words are razor-sharp. On the inside, I'm a hot mess, but I refuse to show him that side of me. I keep my chin high, wanting to get a rise out of him.

His nostrils flare when he glances over to his brothers, expecting them to respond.

Deimos stands there without saying a word, and I can't decipher his expression. Gone is the calmness from earlier... Now he's a storm. Dark and wild. He saved me from death, and now he stays away. His hair flutters in the breeze, blood streaking his cheek, a small dimple in his chin I didn't notice before. This image of him sends a blaze to my heart.

Idiot. Thinking I am anything but a savior to these men will get me killed. And I refuse to have my heart broken at the same time. They're princes, and me... I'm merely a cure to their problems.

"She's been through a lot," Luther says, glancing my way with his heart-stopping smile.

Ahren licks his lips like a wolf, his eyes pulling down a fraction. "We move. If she puts us in any danger, we ditch her. I don't care *who* she is."

Luther stiffens, while Deimos shifts, his jaw tightening.

I eye the prick who frustrates the hell out of me. All that whirls in my mind is trying to come up with a plan to get home. Find out as much as I can from these fae about who I am, and get the hell out of this hellhole.

Ahren turns away from me, and it irks me that he treats me like nothing.

"Why do you hate me?" I blurt out, hating that I sound desperate.

He pauses and glances over his shoulder at me, his brow a furrow of lines. After looking me head to toe, I expect him to respond. No matter what he says, I'd rather know than wonder why he detests me.

Just one crack of an arrogant, I'm-going-to-make-you-pay smile and he walks off. "We leave now."

Lifting my chin, I watch him walk away with Deimos at his side. *Rude bastard.*

Here I am stuck with three brothers. Three princes who might just kill me with insanity.

Deimos is keeping his distance, suddenly pretending I don't exist.

Luther is a mystery I haven't worked out yet, but he radiates danger, and it scares me how easily he slips into my mind.

And Ahren, staring at me like he's conjuring up the best way to kill me.

Well, this is going to be fun.

I'm too frustrated, too worked up, and to be honest... too damn disappointed. There's no one to blame but myself for expecting a curse to be anything but a fucking blade to my heart. But I'll take it over never seeing Guendolyn again.

She's my weakness, always has been since I first discovered her.

For years, I spoke to her by thought alone; with me, she shared her fears, her aspirations, her broken life. I never meant to fall for her... far from it. But she crawled under my skin, and now I fight the urge to continue from where we'd ended.

Where she fell for me, looked at me like only I existed. That's gone, and I bristle at the thought. We're strangers once again, and I'm left with empty memories.

When I look at her rushing alongside me in the forest draped in night, her breaths racing, I want to kiss her. To put my hands on every inch of her body, to strip her, to sink deep into her. But most of all, I want her to remember who I am.

I'm the prince who found a lost girl, a girl who thought herself shattered, a girl who needed finding. And I was that man who found her. *I* am that man.

The mage's spell I bought so long ago was meant to track down my fated mate… all fae have one, and I was tired of waiting to find mine. Turns out my mate happened to be a cursed fae, the girl who'd destroy us all. But she's also the only one who can save us all… at a price. Of course it comes at a fucking price.

She stumbles over a tree root in the night. I grasp her hand to keep her from falling.

"Thanks." She offers me a soft smile, one I remember well. But I just nod, and we keep racing ahead.

Long, blonde hair so pale, it might be almost white glimmers in the moonlight. She hasn't changed much since I last saw her. Milky white skin. Still on the thin side, but that's made up for by her full breasts. Freckles smatter her petite nose. Everything about her draws me to her, from the strength that comes out in awful circumstances, to the blush on her cheeks, and those rosy, lush lips.

Tasting them floods my mind, as does marking them.

Captivating.

My mate.

Mine.

Wait. I stare at her limping. "You're hurt?" I survey her legs in tight pants for wounds but find her feet bare and coated in dirt. "Where are your shoes?"

"Long story." She frowns, her hair fluttering around her face from the cold breeze whooshing past. "Are we at your castle yet? I'd love to sit down."

"We're only been walking for a short while," Ahren mutters.

"She left her shoes back in the Earth Realm," Deimos tosses over his shoulder, and Ahren pauses, turning toward us.

"What's the holdup?" Ahren growls. He's irritating me tonight.

I have no idea how I didn't end up killing him before now.

He's been bitching for the past few days as we waited for Deimos' return, complaining about the spell I bought to open the portal. How much easier it would have been if all three of us had gotten through. Well, shit happens, and magic is unstable in our world right now.

"She'll leave a trail of blood for the Bloodcursed to

follow soon enough. These grounds will rip her soles to shreds," I say.

Ahren breathes heavily and pinches the bridge of his nose. "Fine. Give her your shoes then."

I lean down to take mine off without hesitation.

"Take mine." Deimos is already bending down to take his off.

"I can't wear those," she says. "I'll trip all over the place. You're like size 100. But thanks." Her blue eyes glisten as she stares out after Deimos, who turns from her. I remember the way he touched her face, how she clung to him while we fought the Bloodcursed. I'd taught him well... care for her with his life, which seems to have gained him her attention.

"I'd rather go barefoot," she says.

Ahren grumbles. "Are all human females this dramatic?"

She glares at him with death in her stare.

I am toeing off my shoes to at least give her my socks to help with her feet. "Let's just get out of this godforsaken forest."

I take Guendolyn's hand and give her my woolly gray socks. She smiles and pulls them onto her tiny feet. And then we're moving again.

She watches the dense woods we pass through. My ears prick to listen for anyone following us.

Ahren takes the lead, a sword on his back. Deimos falls behind us, and we move with haste.

Bloodcursed are active at night, and normally walking the woods is suicide. With the curse on our land, most of the creatures are now surrounding Shadow Court to break in rather than hunting in the woods. And dread of what's waiting for us prickles through me.

Still, the urgency to get Guendolyn out of harm's way smothers me. We need to move faster to reach home, where a mage waits for her to find a way to reverse the curse.

I fight the urgency to pick her up so we can travel faster, my addiction to her growing darker. And that need to keep her safe roars through me.

I sigh and look at the night sky, stars stolen by the storm clouds rolling overhead.

I want to drag her into my arms. The desire ripples through me, but I have control. Semi-control, sure, but I need to wait for her to remember me. Even if it kills me.

Time passes quickly as we move with silence.

"Can we stop? Please." Guendolyn's voice pours over me, awakening something in me, and I halt, as do my brothers.

She's gasping for air. "Just for a bit to catch my breath."

"We need to keep moving," Ahren hisses, staring out toward the dark horizon.

A gust of wind swooshes past us, the trees rustling,

branches groaning. We're sitting targets out here.

Deimos remains behind us. We still have a decent half-day walk ahead of us—at least—but we need to get out of here. "Swindon is not far. We'll go there and get a carriage," I suggest. "Then we'll reach the court faster."

"The outcast town, loyal to no kingdom?" Ahren growls. "The ones likely to kill three princes traipsing through their town?" His tone is venom, but I know my brother. He's being trained for the position of king, trained from the moment we stepped foot into Shadow Court, modeled after our king. Mother's new husband. Doesn't excuse him… I believe a king should be kind and rule with intelligence, not a fist.

Guendolyn's hand in mine quivers, and I glance over. Her face blanches, and I watch her chew on her lower lip nervously.

"We'll disguise ourselves," I offer. "Since when are you averse to concealing your true identity, brother? You used to sneak out of the court every few days to meet—"

"This is different," he growls. "With the curse, everyone is uneasy. We're not welcome here. And you want someone to discover the girl?"

"Guendolyn," she says. "That's my name."

"I know someone at the local tavern who can help us." Deimos' footsteps close in from behind me.

Ahren studies us three with hatred in his eyes… No,

not hatred, but frustration. Like the rest of us, he wants to get out of the woods and to safety.

He impatiently turns from us, his hands on his hips, the same way he does back in the court when we're forced to attend endless boring meetings with the council.

A twig snaps.

I stiffen.

A large shadow leaps out of the woods and slams into Ahren, both of them crashing to the ground.

Instinct pounds into me, and I lunge toward them to save my brother.

Growls ring in the air. It's too dark to make out the beast, but I can smell the wet fur stench.

Fucking Leacnan. Part wolf, part scavengers, part blight on our land. They eat what the Bloodcursed leave behind and attack anything that moves when hungry.

I jump into the chaos of limbs, grabbing a blade at my belt. I snatch a handful of thick, coarse fur and wrench the beast free. Damn thing reaches my waist in height and isn't to be messed with.

The Leacnan snaps back around with speed, its long snout in my face, its razor teeth shaped to needle-like points. It drools everywhere.

I'm going to die from the putrid stench alone.

The beast lunges at me, its mouth gaping. My muscles react too slow, and it hits me. We both slam to the ground. I drive my blade right into its gut and twist.

The crying howl shudders in my ears.

Next thing I know, the beast is flung off my body, and I gasp for air. Deimos shoves the thing aside and draws his sword. He silences the creature's cries in seconds. Thank the gods.

Twisting my head, I find Guendolyn watching us with huge eyes. That innocence, that fear, it does something to me. It turns me on insanely. I want to protect her, keep her safe, have her clinging to me. "You all right?"

Shoving myself up and off the ground, I turn to find Deimos pulling Ahren to his feet.

Guendolyn doesn't move. "Sweet Jesus, he's bleeding." I follow her pointed finger to Ahren. He's stumbling on his feet with a hand pressed to his side. Blood runs in rivets between his fingers and down his pants.

"Hell! It bit you?" I stride closer as Deimos helps keep him upright.

"We need to keep moving. I'll be fine by the time we head home," Ahren insists. My brother wouldn't admit he's in pain with his dying breath.

"Are you insane?" I say. "That was a damn Leacnan. It howled loud enough for others to hear it. Putting distance behind us won't matter. They're coming for us now!"

"Swindon it is," Deimos declares. "We need to run if

we can." He wraps an arm around my brother's back, taking his weight, and then they're running. Ahren limps, but it doesn't slow him.

Panic claws at my heart, and I rush to Guendolyn. *Little wolf, we need to go.*

She beams at me, her curling posture so vulnerable. There's innocence in her eyes, and I inhale her fear.

The forest is a blur. I wrap my arm around her waist, drawing her closer to take some of her weight so we cover the ground faster.

Howls bay around us.

Fuck!

We run and keep going. No stopping, following the downward slope of the hill. These beasts hunt in packs of twenty or thirty animals. We stand no chance of fighting them off.

Faint lights peer out from between the trees farther ahead.

Footfalls pound the ground somewhere behind us. Branches snap.

Guendolyn is huffing, and she keeps looking back, her nails digging into my palm with fear.

The four of us burst out of the forest as a shudder races over my shoulders. I hate being the prey. I do the hunting, not these damn scavengers.

A worn path takes us to a small gated town, its metal doors shut. Walls made of solid bronze stand at least fifteen feet tall.

Deimos is there first, pounding his fist to be heard through the oversized door.

We catch up to my brothers, and I push Guendolyn behind me. I turn toward the woods, to the shifting shadows amid the trees.

Leacnan.

Yellow eyes glint in the moonlight. At least two dozen stare at us from within the darkness.

My fingers fall to the daggers on my hip, each hand wrapped around leather hilts.

"What the fuck do you want?" a grumpy asshole calls out from a tiny window opening in the metal door.

Guendolyn whimpers and presses up closer to my back. In my head, I've got it all planned. If the beasts attack, I'll do my best to hurl her over the wall, and then fight. It's not much of a plan, but it's all I've got right now.

"Hurry the hell up," I snarl as another howl pierces the night.

Deimos is negotiating something with the gate-keeper. Ahren is slumped against the door, his hand clutched to his bloody side, and I pray there's a healer in this town.

Shadows emerge from the woods ahead. Black as midnight, they slink forward. Only their sharp teeth glow in the moon's hue.

My heart's pounding when the loud clank of a lock rings out, and the door opens.

Relief crashes into me as we all dart inside. Guendolyn's by Deimos' side, and I collect Ahren to move fast.

My skins pricks with terror as we charge forward.

The doors shut with a thud behind us, followed by the assault of growls and snarls on the other side. I look back to the entrance rattling on its hinges. How often did this town get attacked by these creatures?

"Fuck, that was too close." I glance over to Deimos, who's raking a hand through his hair like he always does when something bad is about to happen. The ache in my gut hurts. "What did you offer the guard to get us in here?"

He grimaces, and meets my gaze. Dread curls behind his gaze. "You're not going to like it. But this isn't the place to talk about it. Let's get everyone into the tavern so we can deal with Ahren's bite. We need a room."

He takes the lead with the man who let us in, down a small, dusty path with wooden round buildings on either side of us. There's no one around, not at this hour.

"Let me go in first," Deimos tosses over his shoulder as he heads into a tavern.

I turn to Guendolyn and lift her into my arms, one arm under her back, the other under her knees.

She fights me, shoving her hand against my shoulder. "Put me down."

"Quiet, silly girl." Ahren cringes with pain as he grasps his bleeding bite mark. We're standing to the side of the tavern in the shadows. Still, we're easy targets out here.

I cradle Guendolyn to me. She smells beautiful and intoxicating, like the sweetest berries, but beneath that is her heady scent that breaks me.

My heart beats frantically, and all I can concentrate on are her breasts crushed up against my chest.

"Let's go," Deimos orders as he sticks his head out the door and waves us in. Ahren stumbles in, and I follow.

"I can walk," she murmurs, her body tense in my arms, and I grasp her tighter. I adore how she feels so close to me, how she glares at me.

"I'm well aware," I say. "The problem is this is a male's tavern. The only females permitted are hired by the hour. Any females walking into the place are fair game."

"Are you kidding me? So the loophole is you can carry in your own woman?" She's rolling her eyes. "I didn't realize fae were so sexist."

"Why? Females have their own tavern, which we are not allowed inside without an invite."

Her blue eyes are burning with fury. Under her angry gaze, I want us alone so I can force her onto her knees. To remind her of her place by my side. She fights us at every turn, and I miss that about her tremendously. The intensity in her reaction to me excites me.

"And the women carry the men indoors?" she says with sarcasm.

I chuckle. "I'd like to see them try."

She purses her lips and glances toward the Pig's Wheel sign over the tavern door. "Appropriate name."

"Just lower your head." I march into the tavern, secretly terrified of what mess Deimos has landed us in. He's never been a good negotiator. Ever!

CHAPTER 32

GUEN

The dimly lit tavern smells of beer and sex. I hold on to Luther's jacket while in his arms, staring out into the large room. Every eye is on me, and my skin crawls. I'm the woman this fae has claimed and plans to bed, according to all the leering men. Right! I'm blazing with rage about that shit. But it's sucked away, like all my emotions, bleeding me dry since I know I have to play along to survive. Outside the gates, vicious wolves await us, and in here are fae who'll murder the princes. I don't even give thought to what they'll do to me. I refuse to have those notions in my head.

Half a dozen men sit at the circular bar on tall stools. Another handful occupy the scattering of tables around the joint. Animal pelts drape from the wooden walls, and an enormous black fireplace roars to life with a large fire in the far corner. It'd be cozy if it didn't smell like a barnyard in here. Shadows dance across the wall behind the bar. There are shelves of bottles filled with booze of varying colors—greens and oranges and blues.

The enticing note of a flute played by a young man next to a window fills the silence. It's like a bird's call, pure and smooth.

It isn't long before everyone returns to chatting and drinking, having enough of gawking at the newcomers, and the raucous chatter drowns out the music.

Near the bar, Deimos is talking to whom I assume is the owner in whispers. He gives the man something with a slide of his hand. The man glances down, and I catch a glint of gold in his open palm. He's a tall man with a handlebar mustache, his ears pointy and long, similar to his nose. He's wearing simple clothes, brown pants and a button-up shirt, but the greedy smile spreading across his lips shows me he's no different from anyone else. Even in this world, anyone can be bought. With an upward nudge of his chin, he guides us toward a door alongside the bar and opens it to step inside.

Deimos takes Ahren's arm and places it around his shoulders as they follow the bartender. A trail of blood drips in their wake. With that much blood loss, how bad is the bite? Sure, the guy is an arrogant ass, but I don't want him to die—or turn into something

—if he's been bitten. My stomach knots at the thought.

"Will your brother change into a werewolf?" I look up at Luther, whispering the question. I feel stupid asking, but I'm in a world where tree roots attack blood-sucking fae, so anything might be possible.

"He's not shifting into anything. That's not how bites work."

I'm not sure how *anything works* here.

Luther shuffles us sideways through the doorway. He pulls me even closer to him, our chests sandwiched together. It makes me more aware of just how much bigger and more powerful he is than me.

He kicks the door to the hallway shut behind us, closing out the noises from the main tavern and drenching us in darkness. Light spills out only at the end of the hall from a room Deimos and Ahren vanish into, following the bartender.

Luther pauses, looking down at me. Shadows shift under his golden eyes, seeming to flicker like a flame.

My heart hammers, heat pouring over me. When he looks at me like nothing else in the world exists, the familiar ache in my chest surges forward. The one that insists we have a past. But he's secretive and dominating. He hasn't told me anything about our past.

This fae confuses me—they all do. Maybe I'm missing something and just falling for the charm and trickery of these gorgeous men.

He's still for a moment as though he's stopped breathing. Heat from his body engulfs me. "This world is dangerous to someone like you."

I simply stare at him… someone like me?

"You need to be cautious about attracting the wrong kind of attention, especially from fae men, especially in a place like this," he says as he lowers me to my feet.

Fae men like him?

He combs a hand through his dark hair, the muscles on his forearm flexing. I drown beneath his stare, at his rugged appearance. His long dark hair is windblown and messy, the military-style jacket he wears is gaped open at the base of his throat.

His fingers find my waist, and he grips me hard. "I won't let anything hurt you, but you need to stop fighting me."

I tilt my head and stare at those spectacular eyes. "If by not fighting, you mean be a push over, then that's not going to work."

"So what will work? Letting you get hurt to learn your lesson?" His brows furrow together.

"No, that's not what I mean." I swallow down the lump in my throat. "I'm not used to being carried around so other men don't see me as an easy lay."

He blinks at me, and I'm not sure if he's confused or taking in my words. But that fierce determination on his face remains. He's a prince used to getting his way, and I'm a lost girl in this mad realm who has no idea how anything works. Luther's presence rattles me. My heart says he's mine, but my head insists we can never be together. So letting myself believe anything else is stupid. Still, he distracts me with the way his gaze lingers over my body.

"Whether you like it or not, I will always intervene. You don't know this world like I do."

"I can look after myself. I've been doing so for years, and maybe you can tell me what I'm about to do wrong." I snap. "Instead of just taking charge."

His hand grips my arm, and he leans in closer to me. His intoxicating scent leaves me dizzy with bliss. "I'm not saying this to upset you, but to ensure you don't die."

He stays so close, our brows are almost touching, and I'm drowning in the heat of his body. But I hate when all I can focus on is his chest pressing up against mine. I can't stop the thoughts rushing over my mind. Me pinned to the wall, him ripping the fabric off my body before he takes me. My core clenches with need.

I struggle to breath, struggle against him. But I can't let myself go there.

"You said earlier that the curse wiped my memories. Why me? What happened between us?"

He sighs, the corded muscles in his neck flexing. "There is so much I need to tell you once we reach the kingdom."

I stiffen and step back from his reach. "No, I'm not

moving until you tell me something. I'm tired of being kept in the dark. I was dragged here, almost killed. I deserve to know the truth."

Luther swallows hard and seems lost in thought. The corners of his eyes pinch tight.

He's massive, standing tall, and every inch captivating. That chiseled jawline draws my attention to his soft lips. His expression is almost stoic. I want to run my hands through his dark hair, force him to look up and just be honest. But I know us touching will only distract me.

When I meet his gaze, I see he's already staring at me. "You were cursed as a child, Guendolyn."

I blink, staring at him, waiting for more, but that's all he gives me. He watches me, and I have no idea what he's thinking.

He pulls away, but I grab his wrist. "Then what happened? Please, Luther. I have to know."

I reluctantly let go of his arm and study the emotions he fights. Hope flares in my chest that he might finally tell me everything.

"When you returned to the Wandering Realm two years ago, you unleashed the curse that had been lying dormant in you for years." His steps closer, his words low and hushed. "The moment you crossed the threshold into Ash Court on your first visit, the curse activated and you fell into a deep sleep... a spell that wiped your memory. And now the prophecy says the blood of fae, Seelie to be more specific, will spill for eternity."

"I did?"

"Unknowingly, yes." He lowers his head, his voice dark, and places a hand to his chest as if the words pain him. "It's my fault for bringing you here two years ago. But I'll make it right. That's why we brought you back."

"Why was I cursed in the first place?"

The creak of hinges gets me to turn around, my chest clenching from the information I've just learned. A younger woman in a long, blue dress and black apron emerges from a door to our right. She's carrying a bucket of sloshing water, her shoulder strained and sloped from the weight.

Luther pulls away from me.

"Let's join my brothers. We'll discuss this later, in a place where walls don't have ears." He brushes past me and marches up to the younger woman to aid her. He says something, and she giggles, clearly captivated by his charm. She pushes aside the hair fallen over her face and bats her eyes at him.

I'm sucking in sharp breaths. I ignore that tiny tingle in my chest as Luther carries the bucket into the room, and she trails after him. I'm angry at how my body trembles from his absence.

The shadows in the hallway seem to close in around me, and for the first time in the last few days, I'm partially alone. Running anywhere isn't an option. I'm stuck with these fae. Stuck to returning to their Shadow Court. Stuck until I remember who I am exactly and how to return home. Add to that a need to understand this curse and why Luther would bring me here if he knew I was toxic?

Just thinking like that leaves me with a bad feeling in my gut. Why would anyone make me carry such a curse and then hide me on Earth?

I've always dreamed of discovering the truth of who my real parents are, and why they got rid of me. I know those answers lie here. The sliver of information Luther shared confirms it for me.

The princes know so much more than they're telling me yet. My life is anything but a fairytale.

Coldness from the stone floor seeps into my soaks and sends a chill up my legs. The whispered voices from the room reaches me.

Deimos sticks his head out of the room and looks at me. No words, just a quirked eyebrow.

I sigh and march toward the room, filled with frustration. I glance into another room along the hallway where the woman with the bucket had come from, and candle light reveals another door. The wind nudges it open from the outside and curls inside. It wraps around me with its icy claws. My skin crawls from how cold it's grown outside. I hurry down the hallway.

Inside, a glowing fireplace crackles, throwing light across the bare, white walls. The smell of stuffiness and dust fill my senses as I step inside the large, wooden room.

Ahren lies on one of the two beds on his back, groaning. His jacket and white top lies on the floor near the bed. He's bare-chested, his hands clenching the bedsheets. My stomach hurts at seeing the excruciating pain wash over his face.

All I can do is stare at him, at the perfect angles of his body, the light drizzle of light hair over his muscular chest, his strong jawline, the muscles on his biceps. I shouldn't be going there, but my gaze roams over all of him.

Luther is next to him, aiding the woman in cleaning the bloody mess on Ahren's side. There's so much blood, and I'm fighting the urge to turn away from the open wound. The dark red blood, the torn flesh.

"Clean these." Luther hands me a blood-stained rag.

I stare down at the water swirling with blood in the bucket. Biting down on my tongue, I plunge my hand inside with the rag and squeeze the blood out of it with both hands. Soaking and rinsing until it comes out semi-clean, I wring it and hand it back to Luther.

"He needs the wound sanitized," I say, gaining myself strange looks from everyone. "Alcohol," I explain. "To avoid the wound getting infected."

The bartender nods. "Of course. Boy, you come with me." He gestures to Deimos.

They both hurry out of the room, and when I look back, Ahren raises his gaze to me.

Vulnerability. That's all I see in his eyes. His lips twist with a snarl, then his eyes clamp shut. His body convulses. I wince at his pain. Maybe I'm a fool, but I don't want to see him hurt this way.

Thundering footfalls enter the room, and I look over to Deimos, who rushes in, carrying a clear bottle by its neck. The pale blue contents inside swish around like a wild sea during a storm.

"Good timing," Luther murmurs, meeting Deimos' gaze.

The maid wipes her rag over the bite mark with four distinct puncture wounds.

Deimos goes to his brother and lifts his head off the pillow. "Drink. You'll need this."

Ahren gulps down several mouthfuls before he spills the drink. Alcohol runs down the sides of his mouth and over his chin. He pushes the bottle away and growls. "Just get it fucking over with."

The young maid sweeps the damp cloth across his wound once more. Deimos lowers the bottle and tips the blue liquid over the injury. It splashes and runs into the torn gashes before running over his side and onto the bed.

Ahren hisses, then howls, his body thrashing.

My stomach roils at the sight of his flesh sizzling around the injury.

I turn away for a moment, my chest clenching, unable to look at the agony. My eyes tear up, and I can't cope. I glance around at the worn room, at the sun-tinged curtains, the scratched dresser. There's an adjoining small room that might be some kind of medieval bathroom with only two wooden pails in sight. I study the long, coppery rug running the length of the room, the wooden floorboards—focusing on anything but the screams.

Someone nudges my arm, and I flinch.

I glance back around to face Luther. "You need to hold the bandage down and apply pressure. You think you can do that?"

I'm nodding and already sidling up against him. "Of course." I breathe so hard and place a palm over the layered bandages on Ahren's side. The heat leeches through the white fabric easily and skitters up my arm.

The corded muscles in Ahren's neck twitch, his eyes still shut, pain straining his face.

I press my hand against the bite, holding the bandages in place, and sit on the edge of the bed.

Deimos is helping the young woman pack up, thanking her, and he carries the bucket of dirty water out for her. Luther goes with them, closing the door shut behind them.

My heart is beating. It's just us two, and I look over at Ahren.

Sweat beads his brow, and I look around to find a

damp cloth left near his feet. With my free hand, I grab it and wipe it across his forehead. There's something almost normal about him lying here. Almost human. Except he's the heir to the throne of Shadow Court, the information that has always stayed with me about him. Will he make a good king?

"Guendolyn," he whispers, his voice barely audible.

"It's all right," I say. "You're safe."

His eyes slide open to reveal the palest green irises, like a faded green leaf. They're half glazed over. I expect him to wrinkle his nose or glare at me, but he doesn't. He just stares, like he's seeing someone else.

"Did you know you're destined to be the death of us all?" he says softly.

His words leave me gasping. I'm trying to decipher his insult.

"What do you mean?"

His face scrunches up with pain, and I wait a few moments for his breaths to slow as he glances at me again. "Luther was never meant to bring you to our realm. You aren't supposed to be here."

I don't know what to say, and feel the weight of the world on my shoulders.

"You need to make this right," he murmurs with his eyes shut tightly.

But I'm getting tired of these games. "Then tell me what's going on so I can make the right decision."

Annoyance roars through me. "Tell me what I need to know." My voice climbs.

He grimaces with pain.

His hand moves down to mine and eases the pressure I'm placing against his wound.

Breathing easier, a curl pulls at his lips.

"Wow, did you just smile?" I say. "Pretty sure the world is going to come to an end now."

"Your sharp tongue will get you in trouble." He opens his eyes.

"Is that what you want? To see me punished for coming to your world?" I position myself near the bed to face him better, my hip against the mattress, my hand still on his bandages.

He shrugs and winces with pain.

"You deserved that," I say, not regretting one word. He's the eldest of the princes, the fae poised to become king one day, but right now, he's pissing me off.

"It's not to insult you that I tell you these things, but for you to be prepared for what you have unleashed." He pauses for a moment, his jaw tight as he battles the agony ripping through him.

"If someone cursed me, be angry at them, not me." Fury races through my mind.

"One day, I intend to kill the fae who spelled you."

I still, taken back by his admittance, and shoot him an incredulous look. "Who was it?" I say through an adrenaline rush. "Do you know why they cursed me?"

His breaths grow shallow, and a shadow slithers in his eyes. "To kill you." He glances at me. "You are from the Unseelie Court, Guendolyn. If you return there, they'll kill you on sight."

Unseelie Court… Deimos' words come to me.

"The Unseelie are ruthless and malicious. They are the darkest of the fae. We are their enemy!"

Am I these princes' enemy?

I glance at Ahren while my mind is spinning out of control. "So that means the Unseelie fae cursed me! Why would they, when the curse affects everyone in the realm, including them?"

"There are four kingdoms in the Wandering Realm, each aligned with different gods, elements, and magic." He goes quiet and still for a moment, then he clears his throat. "The curse was made only to affect Shadow Court, to eradicate us. And for the past two years, we've been at war with an endless ocean of Blood-cursed attacking our kingdom, destroying nearby towns, and leaving everyone running for their lives." He swallows hard, his face growing paler.

"I don't know how to remove this curse, you know that? If I knew, I'd remove it instantly."

"You need help from our mages to undo this catastrophe, so you need to trust us."

The words come blurting out before I can tame them. "I *don't* trust you."

The hurt is clear on his face, but let's be real… Did

he really expect anything else? I don't know him, and I've been dragged into this world.

"I don't *know* you," I murmur.

"So what will it take to gain your trust?"

My back straightens at his comment. "Show me how to go home."

"I promise to aid you in your return home. Unharmed." He studies me with narrowing eyes. "Once we remove our curse."

"How long will that take?" I ask with clipped words.

"As long as is needed."

A battle rises within me, and fury burns me from head to toe. He has no intention of rushing to help me. It's only his court he cares about, and me... I'm the key to dealing with his problems, then I'll be disposed of. Maybe killed. I am their enemy, according to Deimos. All Unseelie are.

"I hate you," I mutter. "I thought you said you wanted me to trust you."

"You can't hate someone you don't know. Not yet anyway, but once we reach home, I will show you so much more. I can work with stubbornness." That smirk spreads his lips again, and I want to punch him right in the wound. Even with the bandages over it. Yeah, it makes me a bitch, but I'm fuming at his arrogance.

"Ouch." He tries to shift in bed, his nose wrinkling. "It's burning."

"What are you talking about?" I almost forget about his wound.

He shoves my hand away from his injury. "Your hand is burning me through the bandages."

"What?" I say, trying to replace the bandages. But he's squirming on the bed, trying to slide away from me.

"Your hand feels like it's on fire."

"That's your wound fighting infection. Don't be such a baby. Be still."

Heat flares across my palm, growing hotter by the second.

Ahren howls with agony and jerks away from me on the bed.

The bandages fall to the mattress.

His bite mark is completely healed—no broken skin, just the stain of blood.

I blink hard at the burning hot handprint on his flesh. *My* handprint.

He looks down at his side and back up at me. There's fury in his sharp eyes. "What did you do?"

I have no idea, but I can't keep the grin from stretching my lips.

CHAPTER 33

LUTHER

"*The problem with love is that it makes you weak.*" The king's words drum through my mind. I used to loathe when he'd say that to me, because the bastard married *my* mother. I still hate the asshole king, but I see some truth in his words. Falling for someone steals your focus; it gives your enemies an easy target. It's how his first wife died while pregnant with their firstborn.

The only reason he wed my mother was because of her House Larmathier lineage, as she's a prominent member of one of the oldest and wealthiest families. After the death of his first wife, the king needed money and a wife quickly… before his sister stepped in and took the rulership from him.

Our kingdoms are absolute monarchies. The king

and queen hold the power, but there are some restrictions to their authority, such as the fact that they must be married to an appropriate bride or groom of an acceptable heritage, or they'll lose the throne. The king or queen cannot rule alone. And when it comes to the heir to their throne, it's always the firstborn—the oldest. So with the current king having no children of his own from his first wife, Ahren is set to take the throne when the king and queen are no longer fit to serve. Add to that the king had a devastating fall from his horse many years ago, leaving him incapable of bearing any more children. So, he resigned himself to adopting us three as his own and for Ahren to take the throne one day.

Of course it becomes tricky, because not only does Ahren as the heir ascend to the throne, but he must marry immediately to claim that position.

I look down the hallway to the closed room, where Ahren and Guendolyn wait. My little wolf brings chaotic confusion to my life. Seelie and Unseelie fae are forbidden from being together. My chest clenches, and my nerve endings crackle with the apprehension of what is coming. The wreck is about to drag me down to the pits of Seven Hells, and I can't seem to move out of the way of the charging destruction.

The door across the hallway opens, and I push off the wall. Deimos emerges.

I say to him, "We should talk."

He bristles and regards me from behind hooded eyes. "What about?"

"The trip into the Earth Realm—since we haven't had a chance to properly talk."

"You've been sitting out here all this time while I helped them collect more water from the well to ask me about her? Fuck, you're so transparent, brother."

"You misunderstand me," I lie through my teeth, but I'm tired of him giving me shit over Guendolyn. "Earth isn't an easy place to navigate. And you took too long to return."

He runs a hand over his face. "Well, firstly, I wasn't meant to go there alone, or deal with that stubborn girl alone, or have two bloodthirsty Bloodcursed on our asses I had to deal with on my own. But *you're welcome* for the fact that I brought her back to you. I went through hell," Deimos growls.

"Don't be such a wuss."

He stiffens at my response. There's a darkness in his eyes, an unrelenting anger.

At this rate, the two of us will end up in a brawl over pure stubbornness. I reach over and place my hand on his shoulder, squeezing lightly on the thin, human shirt he wears. "Lighten up. Since when are you so serious and can't take a joke?"

He shakes me off him and rakes a hand through his

hair. It takes him a few moments, and he glances back at me with a grin. There he is, the brother I grew up with and went through so much shit together.

"Thank you for bringing her safely here."

He half-smiles, but his brow is furrowed.

"What's going on with you?" I ask.

For a moment, Deimos stands frozen, his eyes locking on the wall behind me. "I might have fucked up."

Deimos never admits to a mistake—ever! Those words sit on my chest like a mountain. "What did you do?"

His lips thin with obvious pain. His gaze shifts to mine. "I need a stiff drink." He turns for the door leading to the tavern, but I lash out and grab his arm.

"Talk to me now. What happened?" My mind is racing with scenarios... something to do with Guendolyn and him together.

His hesitation is killing me, and my fingers grip him harder. My muscles are tense as hell.

"I may have offered this backwater town, Swindon, our kingdom's allegiance." He rips free from my hold and trudges up and down the hall.

"Why the fuck would you do that? Didn't you use your persuasive voice?"

"I you think I didn't fucking try. It doesn't always work when I'm stressed."

I march after him and snatch his elbow before dragging him into the tavern. "I need that damn drink now."

I shove open the door from the hallway and into the tavern. Half the drunks have left the place, so it's a lot quieter. There's a soft melody in the air performed by a single flute.

"Two glasses of Noxious," I toss over my shoulder at the bartender as I drag Deimos to the farthest corner of the room, where we can be alone and near the fire to shake away these chills.

"Sit," I order my younger brother. "So then, that's how you got us past those gates. Offered him our allegiance?" My knees are bouncing under the table. "Couldn't you offer him something else, like your first-born?" Clearly, my sarcasm isn't working, but this shit could get him killed. King Tibout may be our stepfather, but he'll take any excuse to eradicate us. "If the king finds out, he'll either kill you or imprison you for life. No one is allowed to decide whom we assign allegiance to."

"You think I don't know that?" he barks just as the bartender delivers two glasses brimming with a coppery-colored drink. Noxious is made from a poisonous plant and fermented for weeks until it's safe to consume. The stuff comes with a slight tingle, and is known for fast intoxication if you drink too much. But it's fucking strong, and I need that shit now.

Once the bartender leaves us, Deimos swigs downs

half his drink. His nose scrunches and he shudders, then he drinks the rest. "We were at the gate. The Leacnan were almost on us. You were yelling. Guendolyn was whimpering. And Ahren looked ready to die. And that bastard asked for our allegiance at a time I couldn't say *no*."

Deimos swallows hard and waves at the bartender, then points to his empty glass to order another round of drinks. "I tore the sigil pin of our court from Ahren's coat outside the gate. I gave it to the man as confirmation to let us in."

"You know what this means?" My breaths came sharp and fast, my jaw clenched tight.

"Hell, yes. They can call for our commitment to aid them anytime they need it, but they in turn don't need to hold any allegiance to us. Gods, I'm so fucked."

"This was exactly how House Gailet went down, you know. Forced to hold up such a pact, and they were ambushed and killed. And now, we're obligated to protect these townsfolk who'd stab us in the back the moment they get a chance." Unease settles under my ribcage with that feeling of being cornered. This affects all of us, and it irks me that we ended up in this shitty situation.

I glance around the room of drunks. Most are probably mercenaries.

"You're not making me feel any better!"

I'm nodding as I finish my drink, swirling bitter and

sweet citrus aftertaste lingering at the back of my throat. Our second round of drinks arrive.

"So what do we do?" Deimos asks, his face panic-stricken. "After I helped the maid with the water bucket, I went to speak with the guard just now about taking the pin back and offering a large sum of gold in exchange. He laughed in my face and said he's already given the pin to the Lord of Swindon. I would have killed him right there if he still had the pin. Fucking swine."

"Shit! All right. First, we don't breathe a word of this to Ahren." I lean closer and scan the room to ensure he hasn't snuck up on us. "You know how he is when he gets stressed. Acts like a prick and can't keep his mouth shut. Second, what else does this horrible deal get us? A carriage back home?"

"I'll get on that," he says, reaching for another glass of Noxious.

"And third, we're going to have to come up with a plan to deal with the king when this lord turns up on our doorstep."

"This is going to go bad—I can feel it." Deimos finishes his drink in one long gulp. He's going to feel this in the morning if he doesn't stop.

"The king doesn't know that you brought Guendolyn back two years ago and she unleashed the curse. He sure as hell doesn't know we went back to bring her back again now. This is just us. If we want to survive, no one can find out."

My head is already swaying and maybe drinking these so quickly on an empty stomach wasn't such a great idea.

"We stick together. Get Guendolyn home safe, then we speak with my mage to help fix her connection to the curse," I say. "We pray the lord in this town doesn't come knocking at our court anytime soon."

Deimos is on his feet, and I get up to join him, the room tilting slightly. We both head across the room, and I feel like I'm floating. The rush to my head is fast. "That drink is stronger than I remember," I say.

"Ahren is going to be so pissed to see us stumbling about."

"Hush." I shove my hand over his mouth, feeling so drunk now, I can barely stand on my own feet.

He shoves my hand away and laughs. It's contagious, and I'm howling in laughter. We're in so much shit, and I can't stop chuckling.

I glance over to the bartender, who watches us. I dig my hand into my pocket and pull out five gold crowns which more than covers our drinks. I hand them over, and he stares at them with huge eyes. In truth, this town owes us so much more than a room for one night and a handful of drinks for our kingdom's allegiance, but I won't make this man pay for the decisions others make.

Side by side, Deimos and I are leaning close and staggering down the hallway. I thump open the door abruptly with a palm.

Guendolyn and Ahren are facing off from across the bed. They both jerk to stare at us. Deimos bangs the door shut and turns around before faceplanting to the ground. Two seconds later, he's snoring like a bear.

"What the fuck?" Ahren growls.

But my attention falls to the pulsing red handprint on my brother's side. "Hey, your bite mark is gone." I hiccup, and my laughter bursts past my lips as my head spins.

"Apparently, Guendolyn is a healer," Ahren snarls. "Have you two been drinking?"

I glance over at her, and my heart beats so hard, that's all I can hear. "You're so beautiful." I'm drawn to her, like always since we first met. Stepping over my brother is a mistake. The toe of my boot catches on him, and I fall forward too. My head hits the floorboards, and all I can think about is Guendolyn. Guendolyn and sleep.

Guen

"What just happened?" I murmur as I stare down at the two princes lying on the floor, fast asleep.

"Damn idiots went and got drunk."

"That fast?" They were only gone fifteen minutes, if that.

"They can't hold their liquor," Ahren snarls, stomping across the room and locking the door.

I watch the fluid movement of the muscles flexing across his back, the strength of his shoulders, the tightness of those black pants over his ass. When he walks, it's more like prowling, his body radiating power. And I can't help but shiver in at his primal presence.

The closer I stare at him, the more I notice the healed whip marks crisscrossing his back. I cringe, and my heart squeezes. Someone hurt him that much?

He turns toward me, and I drop my gaze to his brothers. I chew on my cheek, unable to unsee the wounds.

When I glance back up, Ahren is studying my handprint, trying to rub it off with his thumb.

"Is that going to scar?" I ask as I crouch near Luther and push the hair off his face. He's fast asleep and will probably feel like shit tomorrow. Serves him right for drinking while leaving me alone here with his grumpy brother.

"It should vanish once my wound completely heals.

Your print is like a magic bandage. Though I've seen some healing marks remain for years."

"A girl's handprint on your body might be hard to explain on your wedding night if that remains." I half-laugh to myself at the image.

"She would know it's a healing mark," he answers stiffly, my sarcasm completely wasted on him.

"That was a joke," I say as I stand, but he's looking at me, confused. I'm too tired to explain my lame jest. "So what do we do now?"

"Get some sleep, and in the morning we head home." He walks over to his bed with a slight limp, telling me he's still in pain.

"What about them?" I point to his brothers.

"They're sleeping. They can stay there for all I care. That's what they get for getting drunk."

"You're harsh." I move to the other bed and grab one of the two pillows, then snatch one from Ahren's bed and head toward the princes on the floor.

"A soft heart will get you killed in the Wandering Realm," he explains as I lift Deimos' head and stuff a pillow under it. I do the same with Luther before I return to my bed. It's located parallel to Ahren's, and I'd rather it were in a different room. He's shaking his blood-stained sheets before climbing in on the clean side. My handprint on his side seems to have paled slightly.

"Guess you need to have a heart in the first place," I

retort as I take Luther's woolly socks off my feet before getting under the sheets of my bed fully clothed. How I'd love to peel off these tight jeans, but that isn't happening anytime soon while in the company of these three fae.

"One day I will be king, and to show such disrespect can get you strung up by your ankles in the field of death."

"I don't care if you're a god. You're still an arrogant jerk." I groan. He annoys me to no end, and after everything that happened today, I'm ready to sleep and forget it all.

I turn my back to Ahren as he blows out the candle on the bedside table between us. He grumbles, and his bed groans as he shuffles about, trying to get comfortable. I've never done anything to hurt this fae. I even freaking healed him… god knows how I did that, but I don't understand how antagonistic he is toward me.

Once he settles, only the flicker of the low fire in the hearth remains, throwing shadows over the wall. There's something soothing about the sound of a crackling fire. Well, except for the light snores from the two princes sleeping on the ground.

"Guendolyn," Ahren says, his voice soft and seemingly calm.

"Yeah?"

"Thank you."

I don't expect such words from Mr. *I Live in an Ivory*

Tower and Will Kill You Anytime I Feel Insulted. "You're welcome," I breathe, peering up at the ceiling covered in swirling shadows. I assume he's thanking me for healing him. And with that, all I can think about are the marks on his back. Is that why he's such a prickly ass?

"How did you get those wounds on your back?" I ask.

He doesn't respond right away, and I assume he won't. It isn't my place to pry, but curiosity always gets the better of me.

He heaves a breath, and the bed creaks under him as he shuffles around to face me. "My real father would use a whip on me as a child whenever I disobeyed him." His voice is very matter-of-fact, like he's practiced for so long to disassociate any emotions from the beatings he got.

I surrender to the pity that scoops out my insides, and now I can't help but feel horrible for snapping at him. I roll onto my side and face him. Shadows dance over his strong face.

"He sounds like a fucking dickhead," I say.

"That fae had a dark side, and when he looked at you with evil in his eyes, you knew what was coming. But when he started paying attention to my younger brothers, I stepped in and attacked him. He broke my ribs and arm, and it took me weeks to mend, even with a healer's help. Nothing Mother did stopped him."

"So sorry you had to go through that." I don't know

what to say to someone who's experienced such abuse. It hurts to hear his story, and it reminds me how lucky I was with my foster mother, who loved me from the moment I moved in with her family.

"It was long ago and a reminder of the kind of king I will not become one day. Anyway, good night, Guendolyn."

Only the brother's soft snores filled the void between us.

"Just one more question, please," I say. "Why do you dislike me?"

"I don't dislike you," he responds quickly, his tone snappy. "Quite the opposite. I just worry about my brothers." He doesn't say anything else and rolls onto his back before he shuts his eyes.

Quite the opposite… Does that mean he likes me? But he thinks I'll hurt his brothers.

The thought swirls on my mind.

I don't know what to make of that, so I pull the bedsheet to my chin and shut my eyes. Sleep rushes forward quicker than I expect.

The tops of the trees seem to glint against the moonlight. Standing up here on the platform amid the trees, it feels like I can touch the stars

"Look at me." Luther's voice is raspy and fierce.

I turn and train my gaze on his heart-stopping countenance.

Arousal curls behind his intense eyes, and I clench my thighs with the building heat. I adore that look on his face, the idea that I hold such control over him.

Electricity sizzles over my flesh.

He leans closer, burying his face in my hair, inhaling me. "Mine," he mutters.

He closes his lips to mine, and lust floods me. A desperate ache blazes through me, my brain firing off sparks. I open my mouth and moan as he slides his tongue inside, battling with mine.

I rake my hands into his long hair, tugging it.

His grip tightens, and I let out a gasp of excitement.

I run my hands down his strong shoulders, over the hard planes of his chest and stomach. My fingers slide under his shirt, finding fiery skin. He hisses a breath at my touch, drawing me tighter against him, kissing me with savagery. It scares me how much I let myself go, how much I desire him.

I want him. Need him. Plain and simple, I have to have this gorgeous man.

His kisses drift over my cheek, across my brow, and to my ear. "There are so many secrets I plan to share with you, my little wolf. Secrets that will make you the most powerful fae in the Wandering Realm."

I freeze and look up at him. Gone is the deadly edge of arousal he brought me to. "What are you talking about?"

His hands snake down my back, curving over my ass. His

gaze narrows on me. "Why do you think everyone in the realm knows you?"

"Maybe because—"

A piercing hoot sounds from somewhere down in the woods. I flinch in response, and my heart shudders.

Luther jerks away from me and glances down over the railing. His face pales two shades when he looks back up at me. "We need to go. Now!"

CHAPTER 34

GUEN

The smell of eggs cooking rouses me from sleep, but my mind still floats on the dream of Luther. A perfectly arousing dream that has me longing for his lips and touch, but at the back of my mind, I feel the urgency from the dream too. The need to run from something bad. I sigh at not remembering what that was… It's another piece of the puzzle that is my memory. I recall the moment, but not what came before or after. Just the emotions of how much I longed for him. If that is even just a sliver of what we had together, I'm starting to understand his reaction last night over me not remembering him.

My stomach rumbles loudly with hunger, and I hear the clink of cutlery against plates as I push myself upright. I lift my head, my eyes opening to find the three princes around the small table in the room, having breakfast and drinking what smells like coffee.

"You better not be eating my portion," I croak. My mouth feels like I've swallowed a porcupine.

"Morning," Luther says. "There's plenty for you."

Deimos shuffles over and squeezes the fourth chair between him and Luther.

Like a zombie, I lurch toward the smell of food and flop down on the chair. I grab a slice of bread and smear it with butter and marmalade. It takes like heaven on my tongue, and I soften in my chair as I devour it. The last thing I ate was a bit of rabbit and I wasn't a fan.

Luther is filling my plate with eggs and slices of fried meat.

I glance from one prince to the next, each one dressed up in the same clothes as yesterday, but their faces are fresh, their hair perfect, while I feel like a monster who's just dragged herself out of a swamp.

"Why didn't you all wake me up if you were up so early?" I ask.

I pat down my wayward blonde strands from what I assume is horrible bed hair.

"You looked so cute sleeping," Ahren says before drinking coffee from an earth-colored ceramic mug like he hadn't just publicly called me *cute*. All I can think is back to our conversation from last night, his worry that I'll somehow hurt his brothers. I want to laugh because I am the furthest thing from a girl who plays guys. I don't have guys fawning over me—all this attention is new to me.

Halfway through the food on my plate, I look over to Deimos. "How was the floor?" I mock, grinning at Luther.

"Best sleep I've had in years," Deimos retorts, that sly smirk curling his lips as he stands to leave the table. He walks over to the dresser and picks up a pile of clothes and shoes. "I managed to find you something clean to wear. Hopefully, they will fit."

I swallow the food in my mouth and swivel on my seat. "Wow. Thank you. Where did you get them from?"

"The guard to this town owes me," he says quietly.

I'm on my feet at once. "Where's the bathroom?"

Ahren and Deimos stare at me, confused. "The what?" Ahren asks.

"The privy," Luther answers, and I've never heard the toilet called that before.

"We'll leave you here to change, then I'll show you the privy…bathroom once you're ready." Deimos is already crossing the room, and his brothers follow him. Without waiting for me to respond, they're out in the hallway and close the door, leaving me alone.

I drag my jeans off with a bit of work from my clammy body. It feels refreshing to have my legs free. I peel off my shirt and grab the dress from Deimos. It's the color of garnet stone. I drag it down and over my head, threading my arms into the short sleeves. The fabric is on the thicker side, like a plush velvet, and it cascades down to my ankles in soft waves. Around the black corset, I tug at the laces to tie it up without constricting my lungs. I look down at myself, at the square neckline sitting low over my chest. My breasts are pushed up significantly in this outfit. I tuck down the corners of my black bra peeking out, then reach for the black boots and step into them. Perfect fit. Deimos did well.

Tucking my clothes on my bed, they are filthy and the hems of my jeans torn. I move to the door and open it to find the princes suddenly fall silent from their conversation.

Three sets of eyes on me.

"Damn," Luther says. "You look gorgeous."

Ahren and Deimos don't say anything, but I'm not blind to the appreciation on their faces. It leaves me bushing. I'm not normally a dress-wearing kind of girl so their admiration gives me a huge confidence boost.

"Let's go," Deimos says.

With my head low, I pass the two princes and follow Deimos to the far end of the hallway.

I look back over my shoulder to see Ahren step into the room and Luther staring out after me. It's too dark to see his expression from his angle, but my butterflies are swarming in my gut.

Deimos stops in front of a door and guides me through another corridor to a door that opens up to the outside.

A freezing breeze washes over my face, and I hug myself. The sun is out, the sky is blue, but it's icy cold. Still, somehow, today feels like a new start. Farther away, horses are bound amid towering dark-bark trees.

Deimos doesn't wait for me but is marching ahead along a path in the woods to a wooden outhouse. I sigh loudly, my skin already creeping at the whole notion of going in there.

"Hey, wait up," I call out as I hurry up keep up with the prince. "What's going on?" I ask him. "Why are you so standoffish?"

He looks at me. His lips quirk as if surprised by my question, but I'm not blind to his behavior. Instead, he opens the door to the outhouse and says, "Hurry up. We need to leave soon. I've put a fresh bucket of water in there for you."

I stare up at him, words bubbling in my mind, but the impatience in his gaze tells me he's not going to tell me anything. So I march inside, then draw the door shut behind me.

Light drenches the room from a tiny window high up on the wall. A small bench to my right has a bucket of water, and I peer inside. It looks crystal clear but I'm not touching it.

"Guendolyn," Deimos calls from outside, his voice

rushing. "I'll be back in two quick moments. I've spotted the lord of this town. I have to speak to him. I won't be long."

"Okay, sure." Whatever.

His footsteps fade.

Against the back wall is an enclosed bench with an oval lid over what I suspect is the toilet hole. Nearby is a small pile of thinly trimmed leaves. Wow, I can't believe I'm about to do this. I swallow hard and hurry and get this over with. To my surprise, it doesn't stink that bad, and I take my time. Turns out the leaves weren't too different to toilet paper and just as malleable. By the time I finish and wash my hands, I head outside and breathe easy. The cool breeze swirling over my skin and around my legs is incredible.

Glancing around, I see no sign of Deimos. Figuring he's still talking to the lord of this town, I head back down the worn path amid the scattering of pine trees. The air smells fresh today, while the temperature has dropped to freezing.

The crackle of dried leaves comes from my right, and I look over, expecting Deimos. Instead, it's a brute of a man in black breeches with buttons running down the side of his pants. His white shirt has ruffled long sleeves, and that scraggly beard and wild golden wiry hair tells me looking after his appearance isn't a priority.

"Are you lost?" he asks, his gaze leering over my body, pausing on my chest.

I frown and turn away. "No, I'm not lost." I march forward, but he grabs my wrist and wrenches me back. His grip pinches so hard, it hurts. I swing around with my fist and slam it into his fat head.

He doesn't shift or even react, just smiles, revealing missing teeth. The ones that are still there are stained yellow.

A shiver slithers up my spine.

"Ew, get off me." I kick him in the shin.

"Ow, you fucking cunt." He hauls me against him, one hand grabbing my breast.

I drive my fist into his chest and scream, my pulse on fire over the fact that this dick thinks it's all right to hurt me.

A large hand snaps around the man's wrist, another to his throat, and wrenches him away from me.

I'm left stumbling from the momentum.

"The lady said *no*," Deimos snarls and shoves a fist into the man's face, sending him reeling back. The prince's muscles clench as he marches after the pig of a man.

"I-I d-didn't know she was with you," he stammers.

Deimos doesn't pause and pummels fist after fist into the asshole. The prince moves fast and snatches his wrist, then snaps the forearm over his knee.

Ouch. I cringe, gobsmacked at what I've just seen.

Cries of pain pierce the air, stealing the earlier feeling of a gorgeous morning. But I can't look away. I want that man to suffer for what he intended to do to me.

The man falls to his knees, cradling his arm bent the wrong way.

I rub my sore wrist, my heart beating loudly in my ears.

Deimos is rubbing the blood on his hands down his pants and marches back to me with determination.

And all I can think about is how much I adore him for what he just did, how incredibly handsome he looks being all protective. Something inside me warms up at the thought. And that's when I realize why it bugs me so much that he's ignoring me. I'm falling for him too damn fast.

Luther

"We need to leave," Ahren orders, standing from the table. "We have a fair distance to cover before we reach home."

I don't want to think about what's waiting for us, so I nod. We step out into the hallway and make our way toward the bar. The place is barren, except for the bartender, who's washing glasses in the sink.

"Luther, go get the other two. I'll find the horses Deimos arranged for us and pay for our stay."

I'm ready to leave this town, though part of me toys with the idea of paying the lord here a visit… Would it make a difference? What Deimos offered the man is equivalent to finding a dragon's treasure. He's just gained immunity from our attack and protection from anyone. But in truth, how can I blame Deimos? I would have done the same thing in his position. Life-or-death situation, right? I just doubt our king will be so quick to agree. But we'll have to tell Ahren once we arrive home. He has to know, no matter how pissed he'll be.

The rules state that an allegiance offered by any immediate royal family members must be honored. Hence why the king forbade any of us bestowing such gifts.

Outside, the wind is crisp and cold. A few people are about town, including a farmer walking two cows down the middle of the town. Three of his boys, around ten or eleven years old, are dragging a stack of hay behind them by a rope. The children are tiny and thin, their ears pointy and eyes huge when they glance over at me. I dig my hand into my pocket and take out three gold crowns, then approach them.

"Something for your hard work. Put it in your

pocket and don't look at it until you arrive home." I place one in each of their tiny, dirty hands.

I turn away from them just as Deimos' voice rings out from around the building, so I walk in that direction.

A small child cheers with excitement in the background, and I smile to myself.

I step around the corner of the tavern to see my brother and Guendolyn.

"Did he hurt you?" Deimos growls, grasping Guendolyn by the arms.

I pause and watch, my pulse suddenly racing. I shouldn't be seeing this moment, but I can't get myself to move. Farther to the left is a sniffling man on his knees, crying like a baby. That bastard must have laid a hand on Guendolyn, and my rage roars. I'm going to rip his spine out.

She's shaking her head at Deimos.

My brother drags her into his arms, a hand on the rear of her head, another on her back.

The inferno in my chest is burning. She's melting against his chest, and to see her affection toward him has my lungs closing up. I can't breathe.

"Good," he says. "Or I would have gutted that son of a bitch. Maybe I still will for daring to touch you." He holds her tight, and she embraces him. Those small arms wrap around his body.

She looks up at him the way she used to look at

me… I recoil back around the corner and press my spine against the wooden building. A blaze lashes across my chest. My hands clench when they shouldn't, because I share everything with my brothers. The problem is that I've lost what I had, and that coils tight in my chest.

I shove off the wall just as Ahren emerges from the tavern.

"Have you found them?" he asks, then his eyes widen as he glances over my shoulder. Footsteps close in, and I don't have to look back to know it's them. If I look at Deimos now, I'll end up slamming him up against the wall. I shouldn't be jealous, but it bleeds through me like poison. I just need time to think this through.

The first time Guendolyn arrived in Wandering Realm, I caught Deimos biting her. The bastard marked her. I knew then he'd been drawn to her, despite his denial. And I should have known the taste of her blood would affect him too. As it did me.

"There you are," Ahren says. "Deimos, they insist on giving us just one horse, something to do with whatever you negotiated with them."

"Fucking bastards," he snarls, and marches past me and back into the tavern, with Ahren on his heels.

"Horses," Guendolyn says. "I'm not sure how I feel about that. I've only ridden them once in school. I thought we were getting a carriage?"

My breaths are racing. *Calm down.*

"You alright, Luther?" she asks as she steps in front of me, that gorgeous face staring up at me. Blue eyes more spectacular than the sky search my face for a reaction, for anything. That deep scarlet dress follows the curves of her tiny waist, drawing attention to the tops of her gorgeous breasts. She looks every bit fae in that gown with her long, blonde hair dancing in the wind, her pale skin, and those mesmerizing eyes.

"I'm fine." Venom drips from my words, and I hate that I struggle to control my emotions around her. That she makes me feel vulnerable.

She blinks, taking a moment to process my words. "You seem upset." With the inflection in her voice, it seems as though she's surprised.

I swallow past the thickness in my throat, wanting to roar.

She narrows her eyes at me, and I'm reduced to her giving me pity.

Except, Guendolyn is the key to our survival, to all of the fae in Shadow Court, so letting emotions test my limit will turn everything into a mess. As infuriating as the situation is, as tempting as my little wolf is, I need to get my head straight. Focus on our mission. And stop letting my cock make my decisions. I refuse to let her see how deeply she impacts me, how much I desire her, how I will never give her up until she remembers us.

"Nothing to worry about," I say, and the scuffing of shoes on the dirty path draws attention from a few passersby along the road running down the middle of the town.

Flames lick at my heart. Like Mother says, I'm weak because I think with my heart, not my head. That is my weakness, that is who I've become.

"Okay, but if there was something, you'd tell me?"

I nod and smile, my gaze falling to her ruby lips. She looks innocent in every way, but I know what lays inside her is anything but innocent.

Images of Guendolyn in my arms, naked and calling my name, plague me. Her breaths pick up, the swell of her breasts rises and falls quicker. My cock twitches at the sight. I raise my gaze once again to those full lips. How I'd love to nibble on them as I fuck her and bring her to the edge of climax, before slowing and building her up again and again.

"We're ready," Ahren states, ripping me from my beautiful vision.

Guendolyn doesn't stop staring at me… I feel her eyes on me. What is she thinking? That I'm hiding a secret from her?

"Horses are waiting for us at the front gates." Deimos takes the lead, and we cross the town in no time. I ignore the stares from the locals following our every move.

Outside the town, the guard with a shaved head and

round face from last night is smirking at us. My hands twitch with the urge to rip that smile off his face. He took advantage of us during a moment of weakness. Instead of helping us, he filled his pockets.

"Guendolyn rides with me," Ahren announces as he moves to stand near the biggest of the three horses. His is a monstrous black stallion digging at the dirt with his front hoof.

Everyone is staring at Ahren, his decision out of place for him, but I'd rather she goes with him right now.

Guendolyn is hugging herself, her teeth chattering. The weather has turned fast, and winter isn't far. I wouldn't be surprised if it started snowing in a day or two.

While they saddle up, I swing back to the guard and snatch the fabric of his shirt, tightening it at his throat. "Listen here, you fucking idiot." I sneer in his face. "Be very careful about coming to claim your stolen allegiance. I will not forget how you only helped us once you were paid a heavy price."

I shove him backward, and he stumbles. His eyes narrow with hate. I expect him to respond, to say something, but he just stares at me with fury in his eyes. Grasping the reins of my chestnut horse, I lift my foot to the stirrup and swing up and onto her back.

Deimos takes the lead. Guendolyn sits on a double saddle behind Ahren, her arms looped around his waist, clearly terrified. And me… I will trail behind. A nudge of my heels into the horse, and we are on the move.

What I need is to forget everything and focus on what is waiting for us once we reach home. That is going to be the most dangerous part of our journey. Yet all I can picture is Guendolyn in my arms.

CHAPTER 35

GUEN

The ride through the forest is quiet, leaving me lost in my thoughts and growing uncertainty. I hold on to Ahren's waist, fisting his jacket so I don't slide off the enormous horse. No matter how much I try not to bump my breasts against his back from each jostle, I fail miserably. So fuck it. I give up and just attach myself to him. There's something extremely intimate about sitting behind someone while riding a horse. Legs straddling their backside, being plastered to their back. Yep, I'm starting to wonder if the reason he insisted I ride with him is because he wants me all to himself. He did say last night he didn't hate me.

The clopping of hooves beating the ground keeps us company, along with occasional snorting and tail swishing. A chill settles in my bones, and my teeth gnash as I jolt and jerk on the horse's back. Ahren's body is warm, so I hold on to keep the cold at bay.

The forest blurs around us, greens and bronzes and purples, the trees so colorful, they're mesmerizing. It reminds me of the park near home during fall. Would Nickie be freaking out right now? Have the cops put out a missing persons search for me? There's zero I can do about that when the priority is surviving here first, then finding a way home.

I glance back to Luther, who rides farther behind us. Even from this distance, I see him brooding. It's hard enough remembering my own memories, let alone dealing with the prince's drama.

"How much longer to go?" I call out to Ahren. It's past noon, and we've been traveling since early morning.

Ahren's hand reaches back and finds my thigh as he glances over his shoulder. A sizzle of warmth races up my leg and into the pit of my gut. My heart is immediately racing. All it would take is for him to stop and drag me over his lap, then I'd be at his mercy. It's ridiculous how quickly my body lights up to these three fae. Those thoughts confuse me. He's been a jerk since I met him, yet having his hand on me like this stirs something inside me.

"Not long." His hand lingers on my thigh, and suddenly, I'm struggling to breathe. All I think about is his touch, the way his thumb curls in on the inside of my knee. Yesterday, we were ready to kill each other, and today… today, he's sending out mixed messages that toy with my emotions.

Except we aren't from the same world, and I don't see how anything can work between me or any of the princes for the simple fact that they *are* princes. Me… I'm a woman who doesn't even know what she wants out of life, or who her real parents are. Well, according to the princes, they're in this realm… in Ash Court. Oh, and I'd be killed on sight if I went there. My head is still reeling and hasn't pieced all that together yet.

We soon crest a hill, and I tighten my grip on Ahren, his hand drawing away from my leg. We come to a stop on the peak of the hill. All of us stare out across to the huge castle sitting on another mountain. My mouth drops open.

It's magnificent, standing tall and proud atop the mountain. It's a picturesque fairy tale view, and I desperately wish I had my phone with me. Which I would, if Deimos hadn't destroyed it.

Steadfast stone walls glint in the sunlight. Turrets, cone shapes project into the sky above the towers, flags fluttering in the breeze. Trees greedily crowd around the castle.

"Wow!"

"Looks impressive, doesn't it?" Ahren says with pride in his voice. "Now look lower into the valley, into the woods leading up to our home."

My gaze sweeps from the spectacular wonderland, and it takes a few moments to make sense of the valley below. There's so much movement down there, as if a river has broken its banks, but when I squint for a better look, I see them and gasp.

Hundreds upon hundreds of people are shoving and fighting and clambering over one another to reach the castle. The trees shake viciously all around the mountain; glimpses of bodies climbing between the branches reveals the swarm.

My mouth goes dry. "They're all Bloodcursed, aren't they? Oh shit, with that many, how are we going to get past them?"

"Let's get moving." Ahren nudges his horse to canter along the apex of the hill we're traveling. "Our kingdom is protected by mages who have erected a magic shield. We've been facing this onslaught for the past two years."

"You've been living with those things on your doorsteps for that long?" The curse… I remember them explaining to me the blight I apparently unleashed, and this is the impact?

"The Bloodcursed are hexed. They throw themselves to their deaths every day to enter our kingdom," Luther explains. "We have villages filled with fae living in the kingdom, families and children and animals, and then the castle. There are so many lives at risk of being killed if the Bloodcursed breach the magic."

Panic is clawing up my spine and over my head. I can't even fathom what it would be like to live with that on your doorstep for two years.

We travel swiftly without a word. My heart is drumming, and I hold on to Ahren tighter. Our travels take a while as we seem to be going around the mountain.

When we finally come to a stop, I'm scanning the woods, half-expecting the creatures to burst out of the shadows.

"Let me help you down," Luther says to me, and I turn my head to find him standing near our horse. Worry pinches his face, and that only scares me further.

"Yes, please."

He reaches up with strong hands around my waist and drags me off the horse, which is probably the worst way in the world to dismount from a horse. Especially in a skirt. Somehow, I managed not to flash the world but end up stumbling into Luther. My chest presses against him as I try to catch my balance. His hands steady me, and I'm embarrassed at how clumsy I am.

"I've got you." His hands don't leave my hips, and he looks at me like he might kiss me.

My heart is pounding so loud, all the princes have to hear it.

Ahren clears his throat, and I quickly pull out of Luther's arms. "Thank you," I say.

"Of course." He then turns away from me abruptly and proceeds to pull the saddle and straps off his horse, as does Deimos. Ahren climbs down from his steed and pulls out the sword from a scabbard attached to the animal's side. Then he unleashes the horse.

"What's going on?" I ask, staring at the forest around us, feeling like it's closing in on me.

"We're on foot from here, and these horses have earned their freedom," Deimos explains, his voice taut. Everyone is tense, and I'm trembling. How have they been living like this for two years, too terrified to leave or return to their home?

The fae shoo their horses away, guiding them in the direction opposite of the castle. And something warm stirs inside me that even during such horrifying times, these princes care about those horses.

Something light falls onto my nose, feather soft and cold. Then another and more. I glance all around me and stick my hand out.

"It's snowing!" I gasp, not expecting such a change of weather.

"Winter is running early," Luther says, staring up at the billowing clouds overhead. White snowflakes land on his face, and I can't stop looking at how handsome he is. How much I want to remember if we had kissed when we met two years ago. How he tasted. God, did we have sex? The thought ought to shock me, but instead, my core quivers with anticipation.

"Luther, you're with Guendolyn. Deimos, you and I take the lead," Ahren orders as he draws out a knife from his belt. His abrupt voice draws me back to reality.

Luther settles in closer beside me and slips a dagger into my hand. The leather on the hilt is soft and comfortable to hold. "Don't hesitate to use that. Hopefully, you won't need it."

"I hope so." I remember Deimos' offer to help me learn to wield a sword, and maybe it's something I'm going to insist on if I'm going to be stuck here.

Ahren and Deimos are whispering quietly about the best direction to take, pointing to different parts of the woods.

"Do you think we'll be alright?" I ask Luther in a low voice.

He steps closer and towers over me.

I swallow hard, staring into his spectacular eyes, the color of golden flames. "If I die today," I say, "please let my family know so they don't keep worrying about me being missing somewhere."

His hand takes mine, our fingers interlacing. "The only way you will die is if all three of us are killed first. And if that happens, gods help Shadow Court."

"Okay." My voice squeaks. Talk about scaring the hell out of me, but whatever.

He leans closer, and his breath brushes my ear. "How can I let you die when I still haven't collected my kiss?"

A heady feeling overcomes me as I study his sexy expression. His exhale is like a feather on my neck.

"I haven't agreed to such a thing," I tease.

"It's the protocol when meeting a new prince," he counters, still so close, all I can smell is that sexy cedarwood, musky scent that drives me wild.

"Well, I'm afraid I'm going to have to decline the offer."

"There you go again, opposing a prince." The faintest smirk touches his mouth, and now all I can picture are his lips on mine. Hell, I will more than enjoy it, as I remember the way Deimos kissed me. Intoxicating. And with that intoxication comes a scorching heat that refuses to leave me. I clench my thighs at the lingering pleasure.

Luther straightens himself and places a hand on my back, putting pressure on it to nudge me forward.

The more time I spend with the princes, the more I realize I'm losing control around them.

"It's time," Ahren announces.

I look over to him, his long lashes obscuring his eyes as he looks down at the weapon he tightens in his grip.

Deimos has already started marching ahead, so we follow.

The path darkens the farther we travel into the woods, the slope ascending with each step. In this forest, there are hundreds of Bloodcursed. That's all I need to remember to keep my head screwed on. Sweat rolls down my back from fear alone, and I'm walking faster now. Luther remains at my back.

Ahren's white hair flutters over his shoulders like a cape, the long sword strapped diagonally across his back. I remember the way he and Luther swooped in without hesitation to fight the Bloodcursed in the woods last night. They're strong, but their inability to stop and think things through might make them dangerous. Still, if I have to trust anyone in this damned world, it will be them.

My breaths are rasping from the steepness of the slope; my thighs sting not only from this climb, but from the horse ride. Everything hurts.

When we reach the edge of the woods, we pause. I lean against a tree to catch my breath. I need to begin going to the gym. I'm huffing while the three princes haven't broken a sweat. The snow is now falling quicker and heavier, tainting everything in the forest with its white touch.

They peer out to a small clearing ahead of us, where a blanket of white gives the place a fairy tale look. Except it's deceiving... monsters live out here. Eyes will find us, then those freaks will attack. I try to ignore my panic, but it's gathering speed like an avalanche.

Across the field lies more forest, but behind the trees, a towering rugged stone wall merges into the mountain.

"Are you ready?" Ahren asks me.

"Not really."

"You have no choice," he answers, which of course I know. "Behind those trees lies an enchanted tunnel. We just need to reach that, and once we're in, we're safe."

"You make it sound easy, though I feel a *but* coming on." I wipe the sweat from my brow with the back of my hand.

He looks at me with that confused expression, and I just shake my head. "We run for our lives, then we enter the magical tunnel."

"Yes, and you must watch out for the fairies that live on those trees."

I still, a chill settling into my bones. "And there's the *but*," I mumble to myself. "Okay, so how do we deal with the fairies?"

"Don't stop," Luther says. "But don't hurt one, as that angers them all."

"Got it. Escape from the bloodthirsty creatures, be nice to the nasty fairies, and stay alive." I'm being sarcastic, yet all three are nodding.

Ahren lifts his knife. "As a precaution, we should do

a blood bond so you can open the tunnel, just in case we don't make it."

I glance out past him. It doesn't look that far. "Pretty sure we can run that quickly."

Ahren slashes the meaty part of his palm with a short slice. Blood bubbles across his hand.

"Whoa, we're doing this now?" I back away, but I bump into Luther, who steadies me with his hands on my hips.

"It won't hurt you," Luther says, while Deimos looks away, his expression darkening. "He's simply offering to transfer some of his magic so you can open the tunnel."

"Will I change?"

Deimos growls. "We're wasting time."

"Let me do it for you," Luther says.

The pressure is coiling tight inside me, and I like the idea of being able to rush into the tunnel in case I'm trapped. But I hate the idea of a blood bond when I have no clue what it means or what impact it will have on me.

"Quickly," Ahren rushes me.

Luther takes my hand and turns it palm side up. In his other hand, he grips a dagger.

I look away, cringing before the tip even touches me. "Just hurry up."

The slice comes fast and sharp, followed by a deep bite. "Done."

I look back around just as Ahren takes my hand into his, both our wounds pressed together, blood merging.

"Blood for blood, I transfer the magic of Tathrey to you for the length of one day."

"Tathrey? What—?" An electric charge jolts through me, and I rock backward, but Ahren holds me locked to him. Power sizzles over my flesh like hundreds of ants swarming over my skin. The sensation vanishes as quickly as it arrives.

"Done." Ahren draws his hand back.

I glance down at my bloody hand, noting the cut was barely a nick. Yet it thumps like it has its own heartbeat. I shake my hand and can't help but feel that something more than just this Tathrey power has passed into me.

Terror clings on to me but I can't keep cowering in fear. I am done with hiding and being weak. I am now left with no option but to stand and fight.

"Let's go," Deimos mutters as he gestures toward the clearing with his chin. Luther pushes me to stand in front, and in a heartbeat, we're running.

My stomach lurches to my throat. My feet pound the ground. Fifty yards to cross.

Shadows fall over us, blotting out the sky.

I make the mistake of looking up.

Bloodcursed are falling down toward us. They're

throwing themselves off the cliff's edge all the way around. Some from dizzying heights.

Fear drags through me like barbed wire.

I sprint faster as the creatures hit the ground around us with a thud. The splattering sound sickens me. Bones crack, but still, they climb back up, arms dangling by their sides, necks twisted and broken. They still fucking climb to their feet.

One hits the snow covered grass right in front of me. I trip over the body and tumble forward, head over heels. I scramble to my feet, shaking frantically. When I turn, I find the princes slicing the Bloodcursed, who don't seem to die easily.

The ground shudders under my feet as though a stampede approaches.

"Run! Go to the tunnel!" Deimos yells.

I spin around just as an ocean of Bloodcursed emerge from the trees either side of us, running like ravenous demons toward us. All I see are those hellish dark eyes and gaping mouths.

I sprint like I never have before. Like a madwoman.

Death. It's all I see.

I don't look back. I can't.

Terror is latched around my chest, and I'm traveling on adrenaline. I don't feel my body, but my head is shouting at me to never stop.

Growls and screeches ring through the air.

Get to the tunnel.

I can't stop myself and look back. Deimos is the closest to me, battling three monsters coming my way. The others are under siege. And swarms more are almost upon us.

"Run!" I yell to them. They can't kill them all.

"Go!" Deimos growls while swinging his blade across a Bloodcursed's throat.

I pivot on my heels and dart toward the trees. In seconds, I burst through them. Branches lash out, tearing at my face and arms, pulling my hair.

I don't stop as I tear through the woods.

Heavy footfalls fall behind me, and I glance back quick.

Three Bloodcursed are charging after me. I'm shaking, and I want to cry. My knuckles are white around the blade I was given. But I can't fight three of them. I just can't.

Something swooshes right over my head, yanking a hair strand. But I'm barely feeling it when I'm sprinting for my life.

Another swoosh, but I keep going.

The woods are thicker, darker here, the snow only trickling in through the gaps in the canopy, and I can't see any mountains or tunnel. God, please don't let me have steered in the wrong direction.

There's more buzzing over my head and around me. They're the biggest bugs in the world, and I bat them away. But when I catch the iridescent glint of wings, I pay closer attention.

Tiny round faces, big black eyes, and wide mouths. Their bodies are covered in what looks like pale blue and green scales from their necks to their toes. Thin arms and legs remind me of insects. Wings shaped like those of butterflies, translucent in every color.

Fairies.

They are beautiful.

Don't hurt them.

Unless the Bloodcursed behind me does the job first.

I'm pounding the ground, running through the swarm that seems to be growing thicker. They keep fluttering around my arm; I feel tiny nips on my clenched, bleeding fist.

Great, they want blood too. Everything in this world only drinks blood.

I look back and the monsters are closing in.

The cry in my lungs spills past my lips.

Fairies are everywhere, and all I see are rainbows of colors from their fluttering wings. They swarm my arm, taking small nips of my skin, pulling at my fingers to open my fist.

Something crashes into my back.

I scream and fall face-first to the ground, dropping my knife. Not waiting a second more, I scramble to my hands and knees.

Fairies are all over me, fighting and hissing for the blood on my hand. I can't see my arms through the explosion of beating wings. I feel their tiny feet, their tongues licking.

I try to shake them off, but it's impossible.

I scramble away from the charging Bloodcursed, getting to my feet, my screams echoing into the air. The echoes are like tiny screams all around me, which I soon realize are the fairies mimicking me.

The bastard throws himself on top of me. I'm thrown sideways and hit the ground with my back. He's right there, on top of me. I thrash and beat into him with everything I have. Fairies are everywhere, around my arms, between us, in his face.

The other Bloodcursed rush for me, one snatching my wrist. He wrenches me out from that first creature, then drops to his knees.

Lips curl back over fangs sharpened and dripping with saliva. I shove my fist into his face and scramble up to my feet, but the third Bloodcursed lunges. It pins me to a tree, my mouth gaping open.

A fairy with the bluest wings slashes tiny claws over his eye. He flinches, and I rip myself out from under him.

Then I run, fairies coming with me, tugging at my hand, devouring the blood dripping from my wound.

A huge shadow darkens the woods to my left. The mountain. I veer in that direction.

Heavy footfalls shove against the wall, foliage snapping and breaking.

Over my shoulder, the trio charges after me. Behind them, there are more shadows closing in.

My teeth are chattering nonstop, and my whole body is wracking with sobs. Terror consumes every inch of me, but I sprint and keep pushing. I'm not ready to die, not ready. My foot hooks into a tree root, and I stumble forward before landing on my knees.

I swivel back around on my feet, my call for help coming out strained. Fear surges through me like a storm, feeling unstoppable.

The ground quivers, and the branches shake furiously, dropping all their leaves, which drift around us like snow.

A charge of energy jolts through me suddenly, and I stumble into the boughs of a tree.

The fairies around me all rush with me, mimicking my chaotic running.

They ascend around me like a swarm. Sparks of blue lines of light crackle around their wings. I shove myself up from the tree and swipe a branch off the ground to face the Bloodcursed coming for me.

Fairies dip and rise with me, copying me.

The monsters dive at me with their greedy claws and fangs to rip me to shreds. Muscles flexed, I flinch at the oncoming attack.

In a flash, the fairies flock toward the creatures.

Every single one of them attacks to the point where I can't see anything but those fluttering wings. I stagger away from them.

The sight is beautiful. Morbidly beautiful.

Sucking and flesh ripping echo through the woods.

Barely seconds pass when the fairies flutter away, bits of blood and body crumbs falling to the wayside. When they finally disperse, all that remains are bones, three skulls, hair, and a pile of clothes. Some fairies are still feasting, sucking the marrow in the broken bones.

It should sicken me, but it doesn't.

I lift my gaze. Deimos is standing several feet away. Blood splashes his cheek and arms, his clothes a red mess. He looks like he's returned from a massacre. Except his eyes are enormous like orbs, drowning in fear as he stares at the remains. He glances up at me with a look that somehow implies I did this.

Did I?

"Let's go," I call out, finally getting my legs to budge. He sidesteps around the remains before taking my hand. Farther behind him, Luther and Ahren are charging toward us at full-tilt. A mass of attackers race after them. *Fuck!*

Deimos and I are running, abruptly emerging from the trees in front of a stone wall. I was so close.

"Open it." He draws out his sword and rushes back to help his brothers.

I'm shaking so hard. I stare at the entrance wall and

something translucent shimmers over the front entrance. The magical protection.

What am I meant to do? I'm practically hyperventilating, and my world is spinning.

I rush up to the shield. "Open. Let me in. Open fucking sesame." Nothing. I'm rubbing my eyes when a spark from my hand draws my attention to the cut on my palm. Most of the blood is gone and my wound is completely healed over. Tiny sparks are dancing over my fingertips, just as I'd seen them do on the fairies' wings.

"Open it! Use your hands," Luther yells, all three of them charging my way like raging bulls.

I lash out and jam my palms up against the magic. Sparks erupt around my fingers and with a pop, the shimmering vanishes.

Luther runs past, seizing my arm, and drags me into the cave. His brothers are right behind us, and the wall zaps back in place just as fast as it had disappeared.

A horde of Bloodcursed crash into the invisible barrier, thrown back, as if touching a live wire.

I tremble and recoil. "There are so many. What if they break through?"

"They haven't yet," Ahren says. "We need to go."

And we do. With my hand in Luther's, we rush into the dark cave. In the distance, a single light shines, like a beacon of salvation. But I'm not sure I trust anything in this world to not want to kill me.

"Where are we?" I ask. Around us are black stone walls, torches sitting in metal brackets, and statues of lions and bears on either side of the hallway. It adds to the whole gothic, Dracula vibe.

Glass spheres hang from the ceilings on chains, flames flickering inside them.

Ahren takes the lead and pushes open a door to his left. Light streams out, chasing the dark away. I squint at first after having spent the last hour climbing steps to reach the princes' palace. The castle is located even farther up the mountains, and I'm stumbling forward on wobbly legs, still dazed. So I couldn't be happier we're stopping.

My mind still hums with the memories of the Bloodcursed and fairies.

Death had been calling me down in the forest… but destiny had other intentions.

Now I follow the three princes into an elaborate bedroom that drowns in luxury and decadence. The walls have black velvet fabric draped from them. There's a king-sized bed with an upholstered headboard. Midnight silk sheets with puffy pillows look so tempting when I'm barely standing. A dressing table and foot bench are carved ornately, while a candle chandelier drips in crystals and gold. More crystals of every color hang off the ropes tying the curtains to the side of the numerous arched windows with a dim sunlight coming in. Outside, the snow is falling, and if I hadn't just run for my life from monsters, I might have enjoyed the beautiful scenery.

"Holy shit," I murmur. "It looks intense in here."

"A shame you don't like it." Ahren mocks me with his grin. "Because it's *your* room."

My mouth drops open, and I quickly close it, trying to silence my hyped-up heart. "You'll be happy to know I *love* intense." Still, this room is insane. I keep staring at the bed and make my way there. I fall face-first onto it, arms stretched out. I inhale vanilla and rose, and the mattress softens beneath me.

"After today," I say as I roll on my back and stare up at the ceiling dotted with tiny diamond reflections of the light, "I might sleep for a week."

"Some house rules first," Ahren says.

I groan as I push myself to sit up.

Deimos is staring out the window, reminding me of our time in the motel when he looked outside for the Bloodcursed. That feels like a lifetime away. Luther, on the other hand, walks out of the room, and I'm curious to know where he's going.

"You can't leave your room," Ahren starts.

"Wait, what? You did all that heroic shit out there to just keep me locked up here like Rapunzel?"

A confused look flashes over his face again, and I'm guessing it relates to who Rapunzel is. But he keeps going.

"Second, the only people who will know you're here are us three, Luther's mage, and a small handful of our staff. Under no circumstances can the king find out about you."

I arch a brow. "Why?"

"Some very powerful fae want you dead," he growls, and within seconds, the frustration on his face vanishes, as though he hadn't meant to morph back into angry-Ahren.

"Three—"

"How many more rules are there? I'm hungry and exhausted."

Luther returns to the room with a man and a woman following him. The older lady wears a floor-length burgundy dress and white apron, her black hair pulled back into a bun. She keeps her head down, not even looking our way. The thin man with short trimmed hair is in simple black pants and a burgundy button-up shirt. They both seem to be in their mid or late thirties and follow Luther into another room from the bedroom. I try to look inside that room, but I can't see much from my angle, except the corner of a window.

"Three," Ahren continues, "you will share this room with one of us at all times."

I roll my eyes at him and sigh. "So now I have to share my prison with a prince? I thought you said—"

"Lower your voice. These are not matters to debate here. Our priority is to keep you safe."

So many questions whip through my head, but what *is* clear is that I am a secret. And I know it relates to the curse, to me coming from Ash Court, and a dozen other things I still have to learn about. So now he wants me to hide myself from the kingdom.

Ahren crosses the room and sits on the bed next to me. There's compassion in his eyes, and something else... something *darker* when he looks at me. How does he really see me? Only as a solution to their problems? My stomach hurts at that notion. For once, I want to have meaning in life.

"For all of our survival, including yours, we need to be careful. You need to trust us."

"I have questions," I say.

"And we'll answer them. But not before some rest and an enormous feast."

"Fuck, I could eat an entire boar right now," Deimos grumbles from near the window.

Luther emerges from the other room, as do the two helpers, who rush back into the hallway. "They're preparing a bath for you," he says to me.

I straighten and smile. "Sounds perfect." I look over to Ahren, and eye him with a teasing gaze. "Will you three be staying for that too?"

He doesn't flinch or react. "Would you like us to?" Hell, he's completely serious, and I'm blushing instantly.

But I push aside the images of me naked in a tub with him out of my mind. Instead, I tap my chin. "Hmm. Let me think about it." I laugh and fall back onto the bed, loving the idea of being off my feet.

"There's a fourth rule."

Of course there is. I might end up missing the forest quicker than I thought. "Give it to me."

"You'll need to come up with a new name."

I scrunch up my face and sit up on my elbows, staring at him. "Part of no one finding out who I am?"

"Exactly. So think of a name, or I'll come up with one for you."

I arch a brow. "No thanks. I can just imagine what name you'll come up with. Something royal and pompous and embarrassing."

The man and woman who came with Luther earlier now rush back into the room, each carrying two wooden pails of water. "Should we go help them?" I get to my feet just as another man steps into the open doorway to the bedroom. The man stands tall and proud. Short, white hair, a thin, long nose, longer ears, and a scar curling up his neck from under the collar of his military-style jacket. Two rows of golden buttons run from his waist to his shoulders. He looks to be in his forties and glances at me from the corner of his eyes quickly.

"Pardon, Your Royal Highness." He bows his head. "Your father has requested your immediate presence in the throne room."

"Thank you, Mael," Ahren responds, his voice hard. "Tell the king we will be there shortly."

Sighing deeply, the man doesn't move, but his frustration is clear on his face. "Excuse my language, Your Royal Highness. His exact words were, 'Haul Ahren's ass up here now, or your head will roll.'"

"*Fuck*," Ahren roars as he jumps up from the bed. "Okay, Luther, you're with me. He's going to ask where we've been, so come up with something by the time we reach the castle."

Ahren looks to me. "Deimos will take care of you until we return." He turns and marches out of the room. Luther exchanges a worried look with Deimos, who gives a tight shake of his head from whatever unspoken message they exchanged. Then Luther heads out after Ahren.

"Looks like it's just us two," I say.

Deimos hasn't moved from his spot near the window, and I somehow suspect he's not going to make his presence known.

I slide down into the hot water of an oversized crystal tub, made from a large clear stone carved out in the middle to a smooth finish. The round shape can easily fit two or three people inside. I've never seen anything like it and don't want to know how they got this huge crystal up here. Reclining back against the smooth stone and breathing easily, I love how incredible the heat feels against my skin. How my cut and scratched-up feet throb with delight. I glance out the window where the clouds now conceal the sun. The snow falls heavily with the backdrop of the forest and mountains. It's beautiful. Spectacular.

The door leading into the adjoining bedroom suddenly flings open. I lurch forward, splashing water everywhere as I go to cover myself.

"Sorry, my lady, it's just me." The female helper in the burgundy dress walks inside with a tray that she places on the table next to the tub, her head low to avoid looking at me. There's a cup of something steaming and a bowl of fruit. She also hands me a bar of soap from inside her pocket.

"Thank you so much."

"You're welcome." She bows, taking a quick look at me through her lashes, and quickly leaves the room, but she forgets to close the door.

"Can you shut the door please?"

Her footfalls fade, and she's gone. Great. I can see the top part of my bed from here, and there's no sign of Deimos.

"Are you all right in there?" he asks, his footfalls closing in.

"Hope you don't think you're coming in here," I say sternly.

He laughs, the sound delicious and playful, but he never answers me.

Arms clasped over my chest, I wait for him to enter the bathroom, but he never comes. The silence stretches, and I finally recline back into the tub. Lathering my hands with the soap, I run it over my arms and neck and face, then my hair.

"It feels amazing to have a bath," I call out. "Back home, we only had a shower, and it's nice, but this feels like I have my own personal massage spa. If I had a tub like this at home, I'd use it every day."

"Would you like me to come in there and massage you? Will that help?"

"Ha, you're so funny."

He chuckles, and there's something comforting about the sound.

"So, do you think there are fae out there who really want to kill me?" I ask, unable to stop thinking about Ahren's words.

"I want to say *no* so you don't get frightened..." He doesn't say anything else, and I guess I have my answer.

I lie back and submerge myself under the water to my chin, trying to push everything out of my mind.

"What happened in the forest with the fairies?" he asks. "I've never seen them attack one group of people but not others standing nearby. They're predatory, and once they smell blood, they go into a frenzy."

I lift my hand up, water trickling out of my palm. The knife wound from where Ahren and I did our blood bond is completely healed up. I run a finger over the fleshy part—smooth without a scratch. I remember that the blue lines of energy from the fairies' wings were on my hands as well, though I didn't understand what they were at the time.

"They saved me from the Bloodcursed. As I ran, they kept licking the blood on my hand. When I was being attacked, they mimicked my movements, then they went crazy on those creatures. Is that normal behavior?"

No response.

ıat bad?" I say, my voice barely a whisper
chest constricts.

ısed to hunt fairies. They'd attack whole villages
and feast on dozens of fae, leaving little of them. But
I've never seen them behave the way they did in the
woods."

Fear slips into my mind. "Maybe they just didn't
like my blood." My attempt at laughing comes out
strained. Or maybe it's related to the blood bond I had
with Ahren. Did they sense his royal blood? Is that
even a thing?

"Or they liked it a bit too much and were protecting
you for a bigger feast," he suggests.

"Shut up. Stop trying to scare me," I snap, and
grumble under my breath that I let him get to me.

He bursts out laughing, and I hurl out my soap,
hoping to hit the wall to scare him, but instead it flings
through the doorway and slides right under the bed.
Oh, crap.

"I expect you to bend over and go collect that bar of
soap," he mutters.

"And I expect you to jump out of the window, but
none of those things are going to happen now, are
they?"

He chuckles, and I groan under my breath.

So many thoughts refuse to leave me alone, from
what Luther and Ahren have told me, to what I've
experienced. I assumed coming to the kingdom, I'd be

safe. So why am I being kept hidden in this room?

"Hey, Deimos?"

"Yes, Guendolyn?"

"Why do I have to hide from the king?"

His sigh reaches me. "Many know about the girl from our world who was prophesied to unleash a curse that would destroy Shadow Court. And considering the war we've been fighting the past two years, the king has already expressed how he'd like to murder you for bringing this curse to his kingdom."

"But you know that—"

"That someone had cursed you and you were the carrier. But anger can twist people's minds. So we need to keep you safe until we find a way to undo the curse."

I don't know what to say. Someone used me as a pawn, and now I'm mixed up in this mess.

By the time my fingers resemble prunes, I'm out of the bath, dried with a thin towel-like fabric, and slipped on a dress the woman left for me. A pale blue gown with long sleeves. The dress fits loosely until I notice laces in the bodice that wrap around my chest and waist, and I start pulling them tight. The fabric is silky soft and smooth, and falls in waves to my feet. I comb my fingers through my knotted hair and push it off my face as I walk into the bedroom.

Deimos is sitting with his back to the wall right near the door to the bathroom, his arms draped over his knees. He looks up at me with a devious smirk. The door to the hallway from the bedroom is shut.

"How was the bath?" he asks.

"Incredible. That's the way to relax."

He climbs to his feet, standing tall. "Did you know that fae find mates for life?"

"So no dating then?" I study him and the glint in his eyes. "Where did that question come from?"

He runs a hand over his gorgeous mouth, pulling at those full lips I can't stop staring at. "Just thinking about when I first saw you in your realm, and how humans attempt to find their life partners."

"To be honest, I don't know if people really have a true life partner." Explains why the divorce rates are through the roof. "Does anyone anywhere really know if we do?"

He takes my hand and places my palm over his heart. "Fae feel it in here. It's electric and instantaneous and punches you in the chest."

My heart starts racing. All I feel right now are strong muscles. "So it's not based on family status and money?"

"Some marry for those things. Others for companionship. And the lucky ones find their fated mates."

"Have you found yours yet?" I feel stupid asking, because I sound like I'm prompting him to pick me, and I want to retract my comment. I look away, but he steps closer and tilts my head up by my chin.

"I'm looking at her right now," he responds with a glorious smile. This gorgeous man who makes my breath stop can't be serious.

"You don't need to say that."

But he's leaning in already, and his mouth touches mine. My body reacts immediately, softening against his, arousal surging through me in the span of a single breath.

His thumb brushes across my jawline and down to my neck. He kisses me softly, our tongues sliding together, exploring each other. Deimos fills me with desire and an explosion of need. Everything about him is heaven.

And the pulsing thump between my thighs reveals the thought that I have any sort of control to be a lie.

Our kiss grows impatient. I'm drowning under him, and I slide my hands to the back of his neck, lifting myself to my toes to reach him. Just like during our last kiss, my heart is roaring in my chest, and the arousal is liquid heat between my legs. He has this way of captivating me. Is that what being his mate means?

I break from him to catch my breath, our foreheads touching. His touch is cool against me as I'm burning up.

"I've been waiting to kiss you again for days," he murmurs. "You don't understand how special you are, how beautiful."

"Maybe we shouldn't do this," I whisper, still holding on to the front of his shirt.

"Why not?"

"How can I be your mate? That doesn't make sense. I'm nobody, and you're a prince. You live here, and I'll end up going home to Earth."

"Finding your mate isn't about logic. It's primal and raw and instinctual. I want to show you that you are mine. That you will beg for me, and I'll give you everything."

I try to speak, but his hand is on the back of my neck and draws me closer. Our mouths clash, and I'm falling for him. I couldn't stop myself if I tried. But that's the problem. I don't want to try. His hands pull the fabric away from my shoulders, his mouth finding the soft skin.

He's so built, his chiseled muscles rippling under my touch.

Moans spill from my lips.

Kissing me again, he walks me back with urgency until my heels hit the wall. He smells divine, intoxicating. His hands tug up on my dress and with his hands on my thighs, he hauls me up to be eye level with him. I wrap my legs around his waist. I love this side of him. The dominance. The hunger.

I'm turned on as hell. Every inch of me hums with pleasure, and the inferno between my legs is so wet. I adore the Deimos who is straight to the point when it comes to taking what he wants. I've craved him from the first time I laid eyes on him.

His body presses into me, the bulge in his pants grinding at the apex between my thighs.

A moan wells in the back of my throat when his hand lowers. The backs of his knuckles skim the tight peak of my breast, and I arch in response. His hand dips farther between us and slips under my skirt, his fingers quickly finding my clit. I gasp. He flicks my nub over and over.

"Please, Deimos," I beg, my heart pounding in my chest. I've only been with one other man before, and he didn't compare in the slightest.

"I've been waiting so long to touch you like this. To taste you. To fuck you. So are you ready to fall?"

I can barely think straight as his fingers slide over my heat. One pushes into me, and my moans morph to cries. I buck against him, my body burning up. His tongue plunges into my mouth as he fingers me.

He dips his head to my neck, nuzzling me. "You smell incredible."

I groan, aching for more. So much more.

Something shifts in the atmosphere around us. My skin pricks, but all I can feel is the power from Deimos, his intoxication fogging my brain. I brace myself, holding on to his shoulders, crying out with pleasure.

Fire slams into me, the kind that rips right through me. It explodes within me, and I scream from the building intensity. The force causes me to shudder, and I tremble in his arms.

Scorching hot energy flares, and suddenly, electricity is flooding the room, thickening as I inhale it.

Deimos lets out an animalistic growl and buries his face into my neck, his teeth dragging across my skin. His fingers rub over my pussy so fast, I can't see straight.

The wall feels like it's trembling behind me. I must be imagining it because I'm drowning in waves of ecstasy, erasing everything else.

Deimos is all that matters. He pushes two fingers into me, stretching me, and I scream with pleasure, letting myself go. An orgasm shudders through me.

And in that exact moment, the whole room shakes violently. Energy radiates from my chest, and bursts out. Spilling down my arms, pulsing through me.

Blue shards of electricity shoot out from my hands and criss-cross through the room.

Was I hallucinating?

Ahren

The sight of the throne is imposing, but it doesn't compare to who sits in it. A ruthless king without sympathy. Speaking out of place can get you killed here. The great hall is long. Marble and gold statues of maidens in flowing gowns and wings line each wall. Columns flank the passage running down the middle. No matter where you stand, the point of focus of the room is the same—the throne.

Black as the night, it sits high up on a platform thirteen steps high as a good omen. The chair is large with a high back, jagged across the top with bear claws at the ends of the armrests. Behind the throne stands an enormous round window, light pouring inside. From our angle, all we see are clouds. Dragons once roamed the Wandering Realm, and the window was created for the beasts to fly in view in the background as guards to the king.

Now, the king, my stepfather, sits in the chair, the one next to him empty. Where is Mother?

Luther marches alongside me, his strong shoulders straight and confident. He knows... never show weakness in the court. We've always faced Father together. I bring the voice of reason, he brings the knowledge, and Deimos is the dreamer and fighter. He loathes court drama and always says the wrong thing. So it's better he's not involved.

"My king," I say, fisting a hand to my heart two

times as I lower myself to one knee. Luther does the same.

"Get the fuck up. It's just us," he roars.

As I stand, I lift my gaze to see the king trudging down the steps, his bulky form taking up a good width of the stairs. The golden crown sits on his head, his wild hair seemingly tangled in it like it has become a part of him. He's dressed in a black coat buttoned to his chest. He's trimmed his long, white beard, and his hair is cut short like Mother has always asked of him. Seems she finally has him listening to her.

"I've been hearing rumors," he bellows, stepping closer to us, disdain in his gaze. "Rumors that my three sons have left the kingdom without my permission."

I swallow hard but don't flinch.

"Rumors are like a bad wine, Father. They always leave you disappointed," I say. "If you have need of us, come directly to our palace."

He huffs and scratches his neck as he always does when he considers traveling the hundreds of steps between the castle and our palace. He never does, which I'm grateful for.

Luther says, "We heard of breaches down with the villages in the kingdom, so we personally went to inspect them and assure our people they're safe."

"Inside and *outside* the kingdom?" he snaps back.

"Both," Luther answers.

The king's eyes narrow with a disgruntled look.

Feeding him a partial truth covers our asses should anyone have seen us reenter the kingdom. *Thank you, Luther.*

"Is this true, Ahren?" He pauses in front of me, those dark eyes rounding, our words taking him by surprise.

"Yes."

He studies us with doubt and disbelief. "Seeing as how you're still breathing, I assume you addressed any breaches?" He half-snorts a laugh derisively.

"Just a little magic, no harm done," I say. "And the families feel safer."

Shadow Court is filled with traitors. I've learned this from the moment we entered this kingdom. So beyond my brothers and a few close staff, I trust very few. Including my mother. I love her dearly, but she's like the sun. Glorious and all providing, but they both burn you should you get too close.

"Is Mother not at court today?" I ask, just as a crackling energy shivers up my arms, lifting the hairs across my nape.

The air thickens, and I stiffen. Magic, I feel it in the air, stinging my nostrils with each inhale

The king stiffens. He feels it too.

"Ahren!" Luther cries out just as a spark of blue electricity dances right in front of the throne.

"Guards!" the king yells. "Breach!"

Shadows unfold out of nothing before our eyes, and

they spread outward. The mass grows into an oval shape, blackness peering back at us from inside.

My heart is beating too fast, and I reach for the blades at my hips, stepping in front of the king.

In seconds, an ear-piercing bell shatters the silence.

Footfalls hit the marble behind me as the guards approach, except my gaze is locked on the shimmering shadow. Luther is by my side, sword in hand.

The dancing blue lightning quivers around the black hole, holding it open.

Magic.

Out of the black lunges a thin figure, head tilting back and unleashing a terrifying screech. Then another creature emerges and half a dozen more.

My palm pricks, and I glance down to the healing cut on my palm from my blood bond with Guendolyn. A pale blue spark jumps over the closed wound… identical to the one around the portal.

Panicked thoughts tumble over my mind. "Fuck!" I have no such magic… this is Guendolyn's. Gasping for air, I look up at the portal and the same power dancing around its edges.

"Bloodcursed have breached the castle," the king yells.

More creatures pour out of the passage like a river, and death flashes in my eyes.

Death for all of us.

481

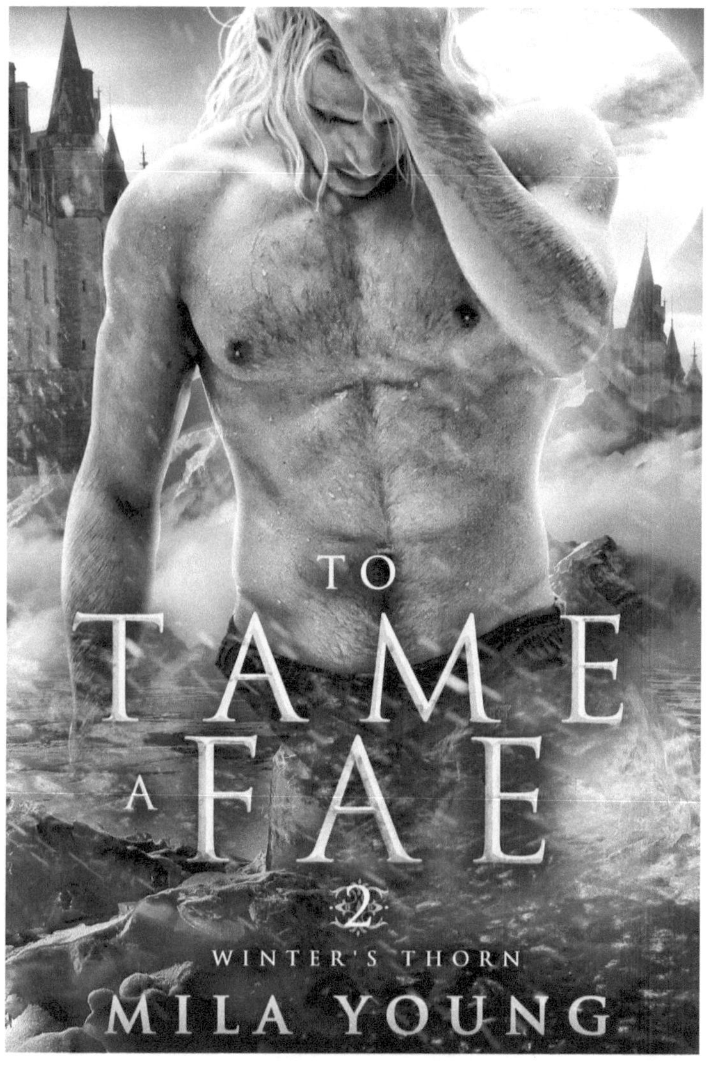
TO
TAME
A FAE
2
WINTER'S THORN
MILA YOUNG

APOLLO
IS MINE
Harem of the Gods
Book One
MILA YOUNG

INTERNATIONAL BESTSELLING AUTHOR
MILA YOUNG
SHADOWLANDS SECTOR
ZOMBIE YEAR 2099

Mila Young XOX

www.ingramcontent.com/pod-product-compliance
Lightning Source LLC
Chambersburg PA
CBHW060722190726
48285CB00001B/36